. . . for identical twin sisters as different as fire and ice.

"High-quality, homegrown storytelling has long been Michaels's stock-in-trade."
—*Publishers Weekly*

Other Books by Fern Michaels

Late Bloomer
No Place Like Home
The Delta Ladies
Wild Honey

Published by POCKET BOOKS

FERN MICHAELS

TRADING PLACES

POCKET STAR BOOKS

New York   London   Toronto   Sydney   Singapore

An *Original* Publication of POCKET BOOKS

 A Pocket Star Book published by
POCKET BOOKS, a division of Simon & Schuster Inc.
1230 Avenue of the Americas, New York, NY 10020

Copyright © 2003 by First Draft, Inc.

ISBN:0-7434-5794-3

First Pocket Books printing June 2003

10 9 8 7 6 5 4 3 2 1

For information regarding special discounts for bulk purchases,
please contact Simon & Schuster Special Sales at 1-800-456-6798
or business@simonandschuster.com

Printed in the U.S.A.

TRADING
PLACES

Prologue

*H*is hand reached for hers inside the dark car. She'd almost forgotten how soft his touch could be. She decided it was okay for him to be doing this, and returned the pressure he was exerting. She wasn't sure if the tremor she felt was coming from him or herself. In the back of the unmarked four-by-four, behind the grate that was open in the cargo hold, the K-9 whined softly.

"It doesn't *feel* right," Tom Madsen whispered. He jerked his head in the direction of the K-9. "Gustav is picking up on it, too." He turned to check the dog's bulletproof vest one last time.

Agnes Jade, Aggie to her friends, nodded. "Are you thinking this is a setup?" she whispered.

"That's exactly what I'm thinking."

"Pippy," Aggie continued in a whisper, referring to her snitch, "has never steered us wrong before."

"There's a first time for everything. Pip goes for the bucks. It's not *smelling* right either."

"We're sitting in a dark alley, Tom. Derelicts urinate in alleys. There's rotting garbage everywhere, plus the sewer gas and a hundred other smells. Five more minutes and we're out of here. Agreed?" She could feel him nod.

Tom was saved from a reply when he felt the K-9's paw on his shoulder. Someone had just entered the alley on foot. Alone or with company? He didn't know.

Aggie heard it, too. "How many?" she whispered.

"It's too dark to see. I'm thinking three, maybe two." The K-9's paw pressed hard on Tom's shoulder. He was ready to go.

"Wait till they get past the car." They both knew the drill, so did the K-9.

Tom half turned and placed two fingers against Aggie's cheek.

"Easy, baby, easy," Aggie said softly but still loud enough for the K-9 to hear. Gun in hand, safety off, the automatic door opener in her other hand so Gustav could hit the ground running the second Tom gave the order to *go*. Tom was her eyes and in charge of the headlights. In the past they'd worked together like silk and satin. Right now it felt more like burlap and fine linen. She wasn't worried at all. They had a job to do, and they'd do it together, just the way they always did.

A chill ran up Tom Madsen's back as he leaped from the car, shouting, "Freeze! Police!" At the same moment, he fumbled blindly to turn on the high beams to illuminate the area, and still hold the car door in front of him as a shield.

It all happened just the way it was supposed to happen. The element of surprise, the headlights trapping the two dark figures in their glare. "Atlanta PD," Tom shouted. His voice carried down the long alleyway.

He felt the breeze Gustav kicked up on his cheek when he streaked past him.

Aggie inched the door open, doing a tuck and roll, and then slid under the four-by-four to scramble up behind her partner. "Hit the ground and put your hands on your head. I want to see you eating the dirt," Aggie shouted. Tom was right. Something was wrong. Her shoulders itched, but her grip on the weapon in her hand was steady. The light from the headlights was blinding. She'd been expecting normal headlights not the high beams. Tom's first mistake.

Gustav heard it before she did, and streaked out of the light into darkness. "Three o'clock, Tom. We got it," Aggie called out, meaning she and Gustav knew that the perps were only a quarter turn away and would act on it.

Tom whirled around and yanked at the two men's arms, so he could handcuff them. But before he could secure the cuffs, he scrabbled to get to the four-by-four so he could douse the blinding lights, while Aggie covered his six from behind him. The next minute was an eternity as automatic weapons' fire shattered the quiet night. His neck exploded in pain, then both his legs went out from under him. He heard Gustav yelp in pain just as Aggie screamed.

Again and again.

And there was nothing he could do.

Chapter One

*D*etective Agnes Jade was so tense she felt brittle. *If these people don't get out of here, I'm going to shatter into a million pieces*, she thought. She did her best to tune out the conversation. She thought she heard someone say something about awarding her a medal at some ceremony. That would be the day.

Aggie looked up to see the officer from Internal Affairs she'd been dealing with staring at her. *Go ahead, stare, you bastard, see if I care.* For six months he'd hounded her until she thought she was going to lose what little mind she had left. And now he was forced to hear one of her colleagues say not only was she reinstated on the force, all charges dropped, but they were going to give her a damn medal in the bargain. She wished she cared enough to interpret his expression. She didn't.

She could see her gun and badge on the desk waiting to be claimed. No one was saying where she'd be assigned, which probably meant a desk job. *Well, you can all just kiss my butt.* For one wild moment she thought she'd voiced the thought aloud. She hadn't.

"Ninety days' leave with full pay, Officer Jade," the police commissioner said.

Aggie nodded as the police photographer did his best to position her, the mayor, and the commissioner, and still get both of her walking canes in the picture. The canes were for effect. She really didn't need them anymore. Well, hardly ever. They wanted her to smile and say something. Her tired brain struggled for the words. She wanted to talk about Tom. Maybe she should pick up the gun and badge. Would that satisfy the photographer? Like she cared. They were waiting for something important to pass her lips. *You want important, you bastards. I'll give you important.*

Aggie looked directly into the camera. "Where's my dog?"

Taken by surprise, the little group of dignitaries stared at her. It was the mayor who responded first. "The K-9 is at the pound, and he's being taken care of. We tried to put him back to work when he recovered, but he refused to cooperate. He wouldn't obey his handler. You can pick him up anytime you're ready, Detective Jade."

Aggie digested the information. Gustav uncooperative. Never. He was safe and sound, and that was all she cared about. She had to smile now and say what they wanted so she could get out of there.

At best it was a sickly smile. The words were just words. She was glad to be reinstated, glad her six-month medical ordeal was over, and glad that she'd been given a clean bill of health. She didn't care to answer questions about Detective Madsen at this time. She had plenty to say about him, but that could come later.

Outside the mayor's office her friend Alex Rossiter waited for her. He tapped his horn lightly. Once, a long time ago, she'd had a serious crush on Alex. The only problem was, Alex had been engaged to a model who looked good on his arm. Unfortunately for her, Alex's relationship ended *after* she became involved with Tom Madsen. She'd been there for Alex because that's what friends were for, something Tom never understood. Alex had been there for her, too, during those horrendous weeks when they didn't know if she would live or die.

She knew he was there even when she'd slip into her black hole. He'd squeeze her hand and say, "C'mon, Aggie, fight. We have things to do and places to go."

It had been his mantra for six long months. When she finally climbed all the way out of her black hole, he'd switched up to a new mantra in the therapy room which was "Show me what you're made of. You can do it!" He was better than any of the physical therapists. He'd been so bossy, so sure of himself and his capabilities, he'd managed, somehow, to schedule her therapy when his last class was over. Dr. Alex Rossiter was the head of the engineering department at Georgia Tech.

Aggie looked at him now as he stepped out of the car in the dark, gray morning. He was wearing jeans that fit him like a glove, Nikes, and an old tee shirt that said he was a member of some fraternity. He was tall, lean, and muscular, with a shock of dark brown hair that was so unruly he tended to wear a baseball cap to smash his hair against his head. The one he was wearing today said, Atlanta Braves. He had remarkable pearl gray eyes and a magnificent smile.

She wondered how she looked to him. She'd lost a lot of weight these last six months. When they'd weighed her before discharging her from the hospital, the nurse had wagged her finger, and said, "Eat a gallon of ice cream every day." Of course it was a joke. Her hair just hung about her face. She needed a good haircut, some conditioning treatments, and maybe a hair color touch-up. She'd seen gray hairs yesterday. She'd been tempted to pull them out but knew two more would sprout in their place. In the end, it was just easier to look away from the mirror. It was better not to think about the sack dress she was wearing.

He hugged her. It felt good. "I want to pick up Gus. Will you take me to the pound?"

Alex held the door for her, made sure she was comfortable and belted in before he tossed her two canes into the backseat of the Pathfinder. He nodded.

Settled behind the wheel, he looked over at Aggie. "I swear to God, Aggie, I did everything but turn myself inside out to get Gus. The department said he was police property and wouldn't release him. I went every single day to see him. I know, I know, you bought and paid for him yourself, but they wouldn't let me into your house to get his papers.

That damn crime scene yellow tape is still across your door. I don't get it, your house wasn't a crime scene. As late as yesterday afternoon, I tried to get them to remove the tape so I could send my cleaning lady there to spruce up the place. No dice. You work for a bunch of assholes, Aggie."

It was true. She leaned her head back. "Cleaning up the place will give me something to do. I'm okay. I can do stuff like that now."

"Maybe tomorrow but not today. Don't argue. We're taking Gus to my place and I am going to cook you a big spaghetti dinner and I'm making a steak for Gus. I bought him some new toys and a bunch of dog treats. He really likes me."

"I bet he does," Aggie said. "I hope he remembers me. Six months is a long time for him not to see me. I thought he would feel I abandoned him."

Alex threw back his head and laughed.

Alex's laugh was one of the things she liked best about him. It was always genuine, and his eyes crinkled up at the corners.

"I don't think you have a thing to worry about. That first day, after he was on the mend, and they let me visit him, I took him an old sweatshirt of yours that you left at my place one time when we went running together. I tried to get it away from him to wash it, but he wasn't parting with it."

"No kidding! Thanks, Alex."

"What are friends for?" He reached across the console to pat her shoulder. "It really is going to be all right, Aggie. Okay, we're here. He knows you're here. Listen."

Aggie closed her eyes and listened. She could pick his bark out from a thousand different dogs. She laughed then, her face lighting with joy. She would have hopped out of the truck and run through the gates, but she was a bit slow these days. She had to take it easy for a little while. Shattered femurs, shoulders, and gut wounds healed, but she was still fragile. Kevlar vests didn't protect those parts of the anatomy.

And then she saw Gus in his cage. She started to cry. The big dog whined and tried to scale the cage, only to slip and fall down. She opened the latch and dropped to her knees. The shepherd lathered her with kisses, his big paws on her shoulders. Then he was in her lap and hugging her with his big paws.

Alex watched in awe. In his life he'd never seen such devotion. He smiled. She was whispering something to the dog, and he appeared to be listening, as if he understood the familiar words. He strained to hear what Aggie was saying.

"He is your friend, your partner, your defender, your dog.

"You're his life, his love, his leader.

"He will be yours, faithful and true, to the last beat of his heart.

"You owe it to him to be worthy of such devotion.

"God, I missed you, Gus. From now on, you are not leaving my side. Ever." The dog burrowed deeper into her lap, happy at last.

Cicero's words. Alex knuckled his eyes. "If you hold him any tighter, you're going to squeeze the life out of him, Aggie." His voice was so husky, sounded so gruff, he had a hard time believing it was his own.

Aggie loosened her fierce hold on the big dog. "Are you sure he's all healed and has no problems?"

"The surgeon told me he's good to go. He's as healed as you are, Aggie. I think now, that you're both together, it's going to be even better. It's a good thing you bought him that bulletproof vest. His legs are healed, his tail is two inches shorter, but he's as healthy as ever."

"How much do I owe you for the operation, Alex?"

"We can talk about that later. Right now I just want to get my favorite person and my favorite dog home. Let's go."

"Come on, boy, we're going *home*." Home was a small three-bedroom house on Peachtree that she'd bought eight years earlier. It had a front porch and a fenced-in yard. In the spring and summer she filled the porch and the yard with flowers. At Christmastime she always bought two Christmas trees, a balled tree that could be planted in the spring, which she decorated on the front porch, and a second one for her living room. It was a cozy house, small and comfortable. She'd furnished it slowly, buying a piece at a time, agonizing for weeks until she was certain it was just the right piece, and always paying cash because she hated seeing bills arrive in her mailbox.

Aggie gave the dog a quick hug. "Actually, we're going home tomorrow. Today we're going with Alex to his house. Okay, let's go."

Tears continued to drip down Aggie's face as she watched the big shepherd sprint to the far end of his cage to return with her tattered sweatshirt. "Do you want that other stuff in the corner?" The dog looked at her as if to say, why would I want that junk? His cropped tail swished importantly as he waited for her to fasten his leash. He hugged her legs as they made their way out to Alex's Pathfinder.

"I'm going to sit in the back with him, Alex."

Alex listened, a smile on his face, to the soft murmurings coming from the backseat as he drove to Buckhead, where he lived in a big old house with wonderful shade trees and woodburning fireplaces. He'd gutted and refurbished the house summers and holidays when he was off from school. He'd done a lot but still had the second floor to go. It was the kind of house that begged for a bunch of kids and a couple of dogs. He had two goldfish named Yin and Yang, though. Until he could get the kids and dogs, not to mention a wife, Yin and Yang would have to do.

He took his eyes off the crowded highway long enough to risk a glance in the rearview mirror. Aggie was sound asleep against Gus's broad back. The dog's eyes were closed, too. He returned to his thoughts. There for a while he thought he was ready to trip down the aisle because he'd been convinced he'd met his soul mate. Stacey had said she was willing to sign the prenup he insisted on. What she objected to was his friendship with Aggie. And she hated Gus, which meant he wasn't going to have a bunch of dogs running around his house. He'd cooled it right then and there because there was no way in hell he was going to give up his friendship with Aggie or Gus.

He'd thought his heart was broken, but Aggie convinced him it was just bruised. Citing the vet who tended to Gus, she'd said, "As long as you can eat and poop, you'll be all right." She was right, of course, because he had survived. Stacey, the last he'd heard, was engaged to some disc jockey.

Alex risked another look at his passenger. His heart fluttered at how wasted she looked. They'd been friends for longer than he could remember, even before it was fashionable to say you had *friends* of the opposite sex. Even after all these years he still couldn't get over the fact that his friend packed a gun, wore a badge, and was an expert in martial arts and knew everything there was to know about automatic weapons. It was still a mystery to him how she'd managed to have a relationship with Tom Madsen with all she packed into a twenty-four-hour period.

He'd never liked Tom Madsen. He'd tolerated him for Aggie's sake just the way she had tolerated Stacey Olin. He wondered now the way he'd wondered hundreds of times during the past six months why he and Aggie had never hooked up as a couple. Once, he'd thought she had a crush on him. She'd pooh-poohed that idea right out of his head. He'd lusted after her, that was for sure, but she'd chopped him off at the knees from the git-go, saying she'd invested too much time and energy into making their friendship work to have him foul it up. If he'd had a tail, it would have been between his legs when he'd scurried away after that remark.

It was a wonderful friendship. One he cherished and treasured.

Alex slowed the Pathfinder and drove up the long driveway that led to his house. Gus reared up and looked out the window. A paw slapped down on his shoulder. Smart dog. He knew they weren't *home*.

"It's just for today and tonight, Gus. Up and at 'em, Aggie! We are at my abode."

"Really. So soon? I can't believe I fell asleep. I can't wait to sleep in a real bed with nice sheets. You have some nice sheets, don't you, Alex? Do you have some with flowers on them?"

"Nah. I'm a guy. I have striped ones—360-thread count. My sister gave them to me. Will they do? They're kind of soft, you know, *slithery*."

"Slithery, huh? Stripes will do just fine. Do you mind if I give Gus a bath in your tub? I want to wash away all that smell. I don't want any reminders of the pound. I'd like to borrow some of your clothes. I know I'll swim in them, but that's okay. Did I thank you for everything, Alex?"

"About five hundred times. C'mon, I'm going to cook for you. You're going to eat it, too. I even bought you a bottle of super-duper vitamins this morning. While the sauce is cooking, I'm going to your place and rip off that damn crime scene tape and meet my cleaning lady there. Tomorrow when you go home, it will be like you never left."

She nodded. "I always liked this house. It's an Alex house. I never met a guy who has as much junk as you do. You have to stop storing stuff for other people or else charge them rent. Sometimes you are so dumb, Alex. I wish you'd quit being such a soft touch. People take advantage of you." She waved her arms to point out three mountain bikes, assorted cartons and boxes, picture frames, and other things she called junk.

"You want me to be hard as nails like you, is that what you're saying?"

Aggie stopped in her tracks and looked up at him. "Is that how you think of me, Alex?" she asked softly.

"Sometimes. Most of the time. A lot of the time. Yeah."

"Hard as nails goes with the job. I do know how to . . . *purr*."

He was standing on a slippery slope, and he knew it. "That's great. You know where the bathroom is. Do your thing, and I'll start the sauce. It has to cook all day. Stir it every so often. I'll bring something for lunch when I get back from your place."

"Okay. Thanks for signing me out and bringing me here. I'll make it up to you somehow."

Alex got a vicious pleasure out of ripping away the yellow crime scene tape. He wadded it into a ball before he tossed it on the front porch. He took a moment to look around. The porch looked drab and ugly, like no one ever walked or sat on it. He knew Aggie loved the porch. She'd fix it up as soon as she got back. Spring flowers were out now. The next time he came here it would probably look like a rainbow.

The key fit easily into the lock. Before he turned the knob he looked down at his watch. Sophia, his twice-a-week cleaning lady, was due any minute. He walked into the dim interior, did a double take, then backed out to the porch. This was the right house. He'd been here hundreds of times. He liked it because it was small, cozy, and comfortable, the way Aggie could be when she wasn't packing heat and her billy club.

He sucked in his breath, reentered the house, where he fumbled for the light switch. Seeing the front room or as Aggie called it, the parlor, in the dim light was one thing but seeing it flooded with light was something else.

He cursed then, using every obscenity he'd ever learned. The room, and probably the rest of the house, was a shambles. The furniture, the comfortable two-seater chair that Aggie liked to curl up in with Gus was nothing but a frame, the contents of the cushions spilled everywhere. The couch was in worse shape. The lamps were smashed, the pictures ripped and tattered. Even the rug in the middle of the floor was slashed and half-rolled-up.

Shambles was too kind a word.

"Who did this?" Sophia asked, coming up behind him and scaring the daylights out of him.

Alex whirled around. "I don't know. I just got here. I'm no cop, but even I can figure out someone was looking for something. That's as far as I've gotten. I'm sure the rest of the house is just like this. Look, I can't let Aggie come back here until we get this fixed. I'm going to leave you my cell phone. Call the trash people and have them come here now to cart off this stuff. Pay them whatever it takes." He stuffed some bills in her hand. "This is a lot for you to handle, Sophia, so call a couple of your nieces and have them come to help you. I'll pay you all double. Just get it all cleaned up. I'm going out to buy some new furniture. Take this credit card and go to the Lenox mall and buy some new sheets with flowers on them. Make sure they're soft."

The cleaning lady nodded. "You better check the bedroom to see if the mattress has been cut up before you go shopping, Mr. Alex."

Alex sprinted up the steps. "Son of a bitch!" The bedroom and the guest room were just as bad as the living room and dining room. A murderous look on his face, he careened down the steps and out to the kitchen. Every dish appeared to be broken. Flour, sugar, coffee, and pasta crunched under his feet. The oven door was hanging on one hinge. The refrigerator door hung open, everything in the freezer smelled rotten. He looked at the back door to the house, which opened into the kitchen, and saw the dead bolts in place.

As he bolted from the house, he called over his shoulder. "Send one of your nieces to the store to replenish the refrigerator. Buy some staples to get her through a few days. And, for God's sake, don't forget the dog food and hamburger meat for Gus."

Two hours later, he had the promise of the furniture salesman that delivery would be made by six o'clock. While the furniture wasn't the same as what Aggie had had, it was brand new, comfortable, and soft. It was the best he could do.

There was no way he was going to mention this to Aggie today. Tomorrow would be soon enough.

He was almost to his own house when he realized the front door to Aggie's house had been locked. The kitchen door had a dead bolt at the top and one at the bottom, and were keyless. The bolts were for night-time use. Whoever had entered the house had a key. Tom Madsen would have had a key. Tom Madsen was dead. Who got his personal effects? Or were they still at the police station?

Aggie looked down at her empty plate. "I don't re-member the last time I ate that much. I think it's your kitchen, Alex. I like all your green plants and this big bow window. I might get up early in the morning and sit here with the sun coming through. Do not even think about trying to shove that ice cream into me. Maybe later if I can stay up long enough to even want it. You make better spaghetti than I do." She hitched up the oversize tee shirt that was sliding off her shoulders.

Alex leaned back in his captain's chair. "Do you have a game plan, Aggie? Or are you going to go home and vegetate?" His conscience pricked him. *Tell her now.*

"I might veg out for a few days. I've done nothing but think these past two months. The four months prior to that I was in too much pain even to think."

Alex made his voice carefully neutral. "Do you want to talk about it, Aggie? Two heads are better than one. I've been known to come up with a good idea now and then. I think what I want to know right now is are you going to go back to work at the end of the ninety days? You don't have to. You majored in criminal justice. The FBI would love someone like you." *This might be the time to tell her about the condition of her house.*

"I'm . . . working on something in my mind. It could be dangerous, and it could be risky. I don't have to take the whole ninety days. As long as I show up for the shrink appointments, I'll be in compliance with the department's rules. I can do it over the phone, too. If I wanted to, I could go back to work next week. I don't want to. I'm going to go to the farm and raise organic carrots. Gus will have a great time running around in all the open areas. He needs lots of exercise now." At her friend's look of disbelief, she grimaced. "What's wrong with raising organic carrots? Nothing, that's what.

"Don't you get it, Alex? They won't be able to find me. You and Lizzie are the only ones who know about the farm. Hell, they don't even know about Lizzie's being my sister much less my twin. I didn't *exactly lie* on my application, I just didn't include that information. I didn't want anyone to know my sister was a professional gambler. Among other things I'd rather not talk about. I was born and raised right here in Atlanta. The farm came to me and Lizzie from an uncle on my mother's side of the family. It belonged to his wife, but they never had children. Lizzie and I were next in line to inherit. I never even told Tom. Before you can ask, I guess I didn't trust him enough to tell him. Our relationship was over months before the . . . the accident. I call it an accident because I don't know what else to call it."

Alex fiddled with his napkin. *Organic carrots.* "Why didn't you tell me?"

Aggie ran her fingers through her hair. She looked away. "Because I didn't want to hear you say, I told you so. Two days . . . before . . . I put in for a transfer. If Tom knew, he didn't let on. He really thought we would get back together at some point."

Alex looked down at the old brick he'd laid for his kitchen floor. He looked for flaws but couldn't see any. Maybe he should have been a mason. He really didn't mean to ask, but the words tumbled out. "What went wrong?"

Aggie licked at her dry lips. "That blue wall. I didn't like some of the guys Tom hung out with. He told me he thought three of them, Dutch Davis, Joe Sandors, and Will Fargo, the property clerk, were helping themselves to some of the confiscated drugs and selling them. He said they didn't know he was on to them. That was the reason for the stakeout that night. The Big Three, as he called them, were going to peddle several kilos of cocaine to two buyers in that alley. A whole kilo would have been missed, so Fargo stole little bits at a time. Then when they had enough for a big score, they'd sell them. We're talking big bucks here. I'm not sure in my own mind that Tom wasn't in on it. I think Tom thought I was on to him and that was why I broke it off. He never said that. It's just my opinion.

"I can't get it straight in my mind. Either it was a setup to take me out, or he was on the up and up and they took him out. I guess I was supposed to die, too. And, of course, Gus. I want to know what happened, but I'm realistic enough to know I might never find out."

Alex thought he probably should change the subject to organic carrots rather than the condition of her

house. The only thing was, he knew squat about carrots other than they were on the sweet side and
crunchy as well as good for the eyes. He knew even
less about breaking and entering and cop stuff. He
opted for another alternative altogether.

"Where does your sister enter into this?"

"I don't know. I thought . . . maybe I dreamed it,
but I was going to call her and ask her to take my
place while I . . ."

"Raise organic carrots."

"Yeah. See, even you got it. Keep it simple, I always say." She yawned, then apologized.

"You said your sister was *squirrelly*, a flaky kind of
gal. I tend to think your department would frown on
such shenanigans, and isn't it against the law to im-
personate a police officer? That's what she would be
doing, you know."

Aggie yawned again. "Everything you said is true.
Look, I didn't say I was going to go ahead with it. I
said I was thinking about it. I could pull it off. Lizzie
looks just like me. Maybe not right this minute, but
in a couple of weeks, after I put some weight back
on, no one will be able to tell the difference.

"One time, when we were seniors in high school,
Lizzie was juggling three or four different boyfriends
and she got things a little mixed up. She liked these
two guys and somehow or other made a date with
each of them for the same night. She asked me to
stand in for her on one of them that particular night.
Then she said I had to date the other guy so we could
decide which one to pick. Do you believe that? I did
it because I always did what Lizzie wanted for some

reason. Even back then she liked living on the edge. Anyway, I picked guy number two because he didn't have arms like an octopus. Two weeks later she was on to some other guy and neither one of those guys had a clue they were going out with me.

"We used to fool our mother, too. You'd think a mother would know her own kids. Ours didn't. For a long time she made us wear bracelets with our names on them, but as we got older, she just gave up. It was fun, I do have to say that. Today, there isn't anyone who can tell us apart. Unless they look at Lizzie's butt. She has a tattoo there. They'll probably assign me to a different precinct, where no one knows the old me.

"In her . . . ah . . . line of work, Lizzie had to learn about firearms. She's a crack shot. She's almost as good as me in the martial arts arena. Again, in her line of work, those skills are necessities. Plus, she can bullshit her way out of any situation. The end will justify the means, Alex."

Alex tipped his chair backward and stared up at the ceiling. "Let me make sure I have this straight now. You and your *squirrelly* sister are going to trade places in the hopes that she can ferret out what went down that night. While she's doing that, you are going to be at the farm you think no one knows about, raising organic carrots."

"I might try onions and peas, too. Yeah, that's right. I don't ever have to work again unless I want to. That takes a lot of the pressure off me. Lizzie and I inherited five hundred thousand dollars when our uncle died and left us the farm because with our parents gone, we were the only surviving relatives. We split it. It was his insurance money. Lizzie is a multi-millionaire these days. She wanted to take my share and gamble with it, but I was afraid, so I only gave her seventy-five thousand. Guess what I have today in my bank account?"

"A hundred and fifty?"

"Think *BIG*, Alex."

"Double that?"

"Really *BIG*, Alex. Lizzie is a high roller."

"A million dollars!"

"Times five."

Alex's eyes popped wide. "No kidding!"

Aggie's head bobbed up and down. "It's a good thing I'm smart, considering my present circumstances. I'm sure the department already ran a check on my finances. It's all in Lizzie's name in Vegas and the Caymans. And she pays the taxes on the earnings."

"I guess that means you trust her."

"Of course I trust her. She's my twin. We're close. Besides, she knows I'd kill her if she ever touched a penny of it. She knows how to do that offshore thing, too. I could probably start up a truck farm of some sort with my organic vegetables."

Alex groaned at her confidence. "Do you know anything about raising vegetables?"

"Not one little thing. When I get home, I'm going on the Net. How hard can it be? You dig a hole, put a seed in it, cover it up, and wait for it to sprout. You water and then you harvest. Voilà, organic whatever."

Alex didn't have the heart to tell her there had to be more to gardening than that. *Then again, what do I know? I'm just a stupid engineer.* "I'm going with you, Aggie. I just decided. I wouldn't miss the first batch of carrots for anything."

"Really! You don't have any conferences or summer classes scheduled?"

"Nope. I was going to putter around upstairs installing new woodwork and new door frames. I can do that over Christmas break. I think we're going to need a plan, though."

"You're real good with plans, Alex. Why don't you do that while I take Gus out for his walk. Then, if you don't mind, I'm going to bed. I know you cooked, and I should be doing the cleaning up, but I'll do both next time. Okay?"

"Well, sure." *Now, tell her now. Get it over with.* He knew he wasn't going to tell her because if he did, she wouldn't sleep all night long. She'd also demand to be taken to her house, something he wanted to avoid as long as possible. Morning would be time enough.

He was a whirling dervish as he cleared the table, stacked the dishwasher, and scrubbed out the spaghetti pot because it was too big for the dishwasher. The leftovers would do for lunch for a few days. He was sitting at the table, his feet propped on a chair, smoking his pipe and swigging on a Corona, when Aggie returned.

"You're going to make someone a good wife." Aggie grinned.

"When and if I get married, I'm hanging up my

apron and my culinary skills. I only cook because I don't want to starve.

"Aggie, I think you should call your sister from here. *They* might have bugged your phone at home. They do that on television all the time."

"Oh, you're good! I was thinking the same thing on my walk." She looked over at the digital clock on the stove. "Vegas is three hours behind us, so it's only five o'clock there, which means Lizzie should still be home. I wish you could see the penthouse where she lives. It's got wraparound windows, and her view is of the whole city. At night, it boggles your mind. It's really luxurious. It's a comp. That means it's free. All her food is comped, and so is her car. She drives a candy-apple red Mercedes convertible. She even gets a clothing allowance from the man she works for. Of course, if anything goes awry, like she hits a losing streak, it's all gone."

"We're in the wrong business, Aggie. How much does she make a year, do you know?"

"Different amounts. It depends on how high the stakes are. She gets a percentage of her winnings. She travels all over the country for the guy she works for. The advantage of Lizzie's working for someone else is that he covers her losses on the rare occasion that she losses *and* pays her expenses, which are pretty high. Lizzie is a smart cookie who likes the good life and knows how to play the angles.

"Do you know what she *really* wants to do? She just does the gambling thing because she's good at it, and it pays off big-time." Alex shook his head. "She wants to open a dive shop on one of the islands. Her real passion is the water. She loves to snorkel, deep-sea dive, and just swim. Two more years and she can do it and own everything outright. And she won't have to touch her principal. She can be a beach bunny for the rest of her life. She has a degree in marine biology plus a master's. My sister might be a wild card, but she's smart as hell."

"Maybe she can open a produce stand next to her dive shop and sell your carrots." Alex guffawed.

"That wasn't funny. Look, I'm not laughing. Don't ever make fun of my sister again. Hand me the damn phone."

Aggie dialed her sister's private number and waited. "It's Aggie. Listen, sis, I need to talk to you. Yeah, well, I've been kind of busy the last six months. You told me you could take a vacation anytime you wanted. Can you take three months off? You can. Great. Listen, this is what I want you to do. . . ."

Chapter Two

Gus started to howl, a bloodcurdling sound of anger, the moment he raced up the steps to the front porch. Alex watched, his body twitching, as Aggie's shoulders stiffened. She knew something was wrong just the way the big shepherd knew. He heard her indrawn breath, heard her exhale before she fit the key into the lock.

I should have told her. He was gutless. A real *wuss. No, I'm not. I just wanted to spare her*, he answered himself.

The shepherd was in a frenzy as he raced through the house, stopping to sniff, to howl, to growl, then whine. He knew there had been intruders, knew the furniture was new.

Aggie sat down on the double chair and looked up at him. "You did all this, right?" He nodded. "I had a feeling something like this happened. How bad was it?"

"As bad as it gets. My first thought was they were

looking for something. Whatever it was, they must not have found it because they destroyed everything in the house. I must say, you're taking this rather well."

Aggie put her finger to her lips and mouthed the word, *bug*. Her eyes sparked with anger that she was trying to control. He nodded to show he understood. "I told you I was expecting it. I don't know why, I just was. When a house is closed up for six months, something is bound to happen. I really don't understand the crime scene tape, though. Did someone in the neighborhood call in a prowler? Did the police come to investigate and find this? Is that why they put the tape up? The strange thing is, no one told me. Now I have to file an insurance claim. I can't imagine what they were looking for? They didn't take the television or VCR. Maybe they had the wrong house. I don't have any jewelry that's valuable. I have insurance, so I'll be able to pay you back after I file a claim."

"I know my taste in furniture is a little different than yours. But everything is clean and new, and that's the way it should be right now. Later, when you get your cop legs back and are full of your usual spit and vinegar, you can redecorate. You should walk around, Aggie, and see if anything is missing. Paying me back is the least of your problems right now."

"I think I might go back to work, Alex. I don't want to sit around and think. That's not good, even I know that. I'll take the rest of the week off and next week, too. By then, I'll be ready to do what I do best.

I want to go out to the cemetery and put some flowers on Tom's grave. I understand their not telling me he died in the very beginning, but why didn't they tell me his family pulled the plug?"

"I don't know, Aggie." Playing along in case there was a bug in the house, Alex continued, "I'll leave you alone now. If you need me for anything, just call."

"Okay, Alex. Thanks for everything. By the way, do you know where my car is?"

"It was in the impound lot. I had it taken out yesterday. It's being serviced. They promised to deliver it this afternoon. If you want to go somewhere, I can take you."

"The porch looks so bare. I thought I would get some flowers. I love getting the porch ready for spring and summer. If it's not too much trouble, yes, you can take me. I just want to go upstairs for a minute."

Upstairs, Aggie followed Gus as they inspected the bedrooms and the bath. Everything was new. It even smelled new. She felt like crying. Sometimes life just wasn't fair. She dropped to her knees to hug the big dog. "I know you have a new bed, but so do I. We're going to make this work, we really are. We just have to get used to it."

Ten minutes later they were on their way to the garden center, where Aggie bought Gerber daisies, geraniums, impatiens, and tubs of mixed flowers. She also bought packages of carrot seeds and two books on gardening. Alex grinned when he saw the packets of seeds. One of the workers from the center followed them home in his pickup, the cargo area loaded with Aggie's plants.

In the Pathfinder, Alex quizzed her. "Do you know what they were looking for, Aggie? I don't think I told you this, but both your doors were locked when I got there yesterday. The dead bolts were on the kitchen door, and I had to use the key to the front door. I'm thinking someone had or has a key to your house, so I recommend you call a locksmith as soon as you get home to have the locks changed."

"I don't have a clue as to what someone might have been looking for. Maybe my journal. It isn't really a journal. It's an old day planner where I used to jot down things. Tom knew about it. He had a notebook, too. All cops do. He used to razz me and say things like, 'you better not be putting anything in there about me or the guys.' Macho guy stuff that I ignored. And, yes, I will call a locksmith. I made that decision the minute I walked into the house."

Alex took his eyes off the busy road for a moment to look across at her. "Did they find the journal?" He didn't realize he was holding his breath until it escaped his lips in a hissing sound.

"No, because it wasn't in the house. It's in my gym bag in the trunk of my car. If they went through the bag, then yes, they probably found it. I guess I won't know until they bring my car back."

Tom looked worried. "*Exactly* what did you write in that journal, Aggie?"

He looked so nice this morning in his jeans and his dark green Polo shirt. She should look half as good. The minute she saw how Lizzie was wearing her hair, she'd get her own styled the same way. Until then, she was just going to have to look like a ragamuffin in Alex's oversize shirt and sweatpants. Maybe she should have changed into her own clothes before going to the nursery. Too late now. She shrugged.

"You're a million miles away, girl. What are you thinking?"

"I was thinking how nice you look and how *tacky* I look. To answer your earlier question, I wrote down in the journal everything Tom told me, and the date he told me. There were things he said he could prove and other things he said he couldn't prove. Suppositions. I wrote down all his suspicions. And I wrote down his reaction and the things he said when I broke up with him months ago."

Alex cleared his throat. He looked more than a little uneasy. "Would you call that journal a smoking gun? I saw that on TV, too. Those cop shows always have a smoking gun."

"If you were Dutch Davis, Joe Sonders, or Will Fargo, you'd consider it a smoking gun. To anyone else it would be just a bunch of suspicions."

"If they didn't find it, what are you going to do with it?"

"Maybe send it to myself in care of General Delivery. I'll pick it up when I get to the farm. Maybe I'll give it to Lizzie, but I'll make copies first. I'm not sure yet. There may be nothing to this at all, and I'm simply being paranoid."

"You didn't see your house yesterday, Aggie. Whoever ransacked it had a damn key. This isn't a television program where everything is wrapped up in sixty minutes. What if they try again?"

"I'm aware now. I have my gun back, and I also have Gus. I know those guys. They'll lie low for a while before they make another move. Stop acting like a nervous father, Alex."

Alex was so worried he almost hit a dark blue pickup truck blasting music so loud it hurt his eardrums.

A nervous father was the last thing he wanted to appear as. Nor did he want to give the impression he was a nervous *anything*. He knew in his gut the whole thing was going to start to snowball, and he'd be on some farm outside Altoona, Pennsylvania, helping to plant organic carrots. "I hope you're right."

"Do you mind stopping at an ATM? I need to withdraw some money so I can pay for all those flowers. Do you mind loaning me your ATM card? We'll settle up tomorrow. My purse is in the trunk of my car, too. I just hate owing money, especially for all of Gus's medical expenses. I wonder why the department didn't pick those up?"

"Because they thought he was going to die, that's why, and they didn't want to spend the money for emergency vet and surgical services. I threatened to go to the newspapers and television if they didn't let me call in a private vet. They had no choice. This is just a guess on my part, Aggie, but won't Gus be able to pick up those guys' scents if they get close enough?"

"Yes. I plan to keep him away from them. I don't want to traumatize him any more than I have to. You need to find another dog that looks like Gus so when Lizzie and I make the switch, no one will be the wiser. You have a couple of days to do that since Lizzie won't arrive till the weekend. And, Alex . . ."

"What?"

"They're going to be watching you, too, so stay alert. I'm really sorry you got involved in all of this. You can, of course, go home and forget all about us. I'll never hold that against you."

Alex swallowed hard. "Is this going to be a Serpico operation? I saw that movie you know. At least ten times. What if when this is all over, you have to go across the world and hide out like he did?" He could feel his loss already. He told himself he was overreacting. He hoped he was right.

Aggie sighed. "God, I hope not. That guy lived in Europe for a long time, before coming back to live in upstate New York. Look, I'm not saying, and Tom wasn't saying the whole department was into that dirty cop thing, just those three guys. At least that's what I thought he was thinking. I just don't want to believe Tom was in on it with them. I'm going to show you their pictures when we get back to the house so you can be on the lookout. They can only stake us out when they're off duty and on their days off. It's the way it is, Alex. Are you sorry you're involving yourself?"

"No. I need to know everything, though. You have told me everything, haven't you?"

"Everything I know."

Alex parked on a side street while Aggie walked back half a block to the ATM. The pickup truck with the load of flowers parked behind him. He smiled as Aggie sashayed along in his sweats, which hung on her slim frame like a wrinkled old sack. Compared to her, he was sorely lacking in the guts department.

Five minutes later she was back in the car with three hundred dollars in her hand. "I feel rich." She grinned.

Ten minutes later, he dropped her off at her house and proceeded out to the highway. On the way home he made a stop at a high-tech electronics store. He felt nonplussed as he looked at the wide array of gadgets for sale. He also felt ridiculous when he asked for a device that would detect electronic bugs. The young man didn't seem to think his request was ridiculous at all as he pulled out device after device, extolling the virtues of each. "Now, you take this one, it's top-of-the-line and can detect a device that's been planted in your car or under your car. Each time you get into your car, make a sweep. The tracking device can function up to a hundred miles, providing you have a transmitter and a receiver. It costs extra, but it's the one I recommend."

"Okay, I'll take it." He felt like the television character Colombo as he made his way out of the store. All he needed was a baggy trench coat. He didn't need any help in the looking-dumb department. He could manage that on his own.

The following day, Alex drove to Marietta, Georgia, where he purchased a German shepherd named Alice that looked so much like Gus it was downright scary.

Unfortunately, Alice was a female shepherd. He dithered for a whole hour before he made his decision to buy the dog, who loved him on sight. He hoped the three cops in question wouldn't be getting close enough to the dog to inspect her anatomy. Plus, the Big Three, as Aggie called them, weren't K-9 handlers.

In the end he felt pleased with himself when he dropped the dog off at a local vet clinic to get bathed and groomed. They agreed to board her until Saturday, when he would pick her up at noon or as close to noon as possible. The switch would take place when Lizzie arrived in town over the weekend. He mentally patted himself on the shoulder when he exited the vet's office. With a little more practice, he just might turn into an acceptable gumshoe. He winced at the thought. On the other hand, he could excel at helping Aggie raise organic carrots. And to think he went to college to be an engineer and then all those added years of schooling until he got his doctorate. He could probably make more money detecting and growing carrots on the side. The thought was so funny, he laughed until his sides ached.

Now he was going home to heat up his leftover spaghetti.

It was midafternoon when Aggie carried her cheese sandwich out to the front steps. She sat down, Gus at her side. Her front porch was clean now, the windows sparkling, the white wicker chairs gleaming. The flowered cushions were every bit as vibrant as the clay pots of flowers that lined the railing and the steps.

The minute Alex rode off, she'd gone upstairs to change her clothes. When she removed his sweats she held them up to her cheek. Even though she'd been wearing them, they still smelled like Alex. She folded them neatly and placed them on a shelf in her closet.

Now she wore a pair of yellow Capri pants with a matching tee shirt. She wished she'd chosen a shirt with three-quarter sleeves. Her arms were thin and bony. The whole of her was thin and bony. Her hair, which hadn't been cut or styled in six months, was tied back in a ponytail. Keds, because they were lighter, instead of clunky running shoes, adorned her feet. She was exhausted from cleaning the windows and scrubbing the porch, not to mention watering all the plants. She probably needed a nap, but she couldn't take one until her car was delivered.

She finished the sandwich before she attacked the pint of ice cream she'd carried out on a tray. She ate it all and licked the spoon while Gus chewed contentedly on a rawhide bone.

Her car arrived fifteen minutes later. She signed her name, handed over a ten-dollar tip, and accepted the receipt as well as the key. She waited until the driver and the backup car left before she walked down the steps and over to the driveway. She opened the door to examine the Honda. Her bright red windbreaker was lying on the backseat, along with a police procedural manual. An oversize tartan plaid umbrella leaned against the door. A library book about murder and mayhem in the White House was on the floor. It had to be at least eight months overdue. It had been overdue before the night of the stakeout. She'd meant to return it that day but had gotten sidetracked. Next to the library book was her shoulder bag. She reached for it and hung it over her shoulder.

Aggie closed and locked the doors after she popped the trunk. Because she was a tidy person, the trunk of her car looked the same way. Her tennis racket in its protective cover was still there. Her golf clubs were pushed farther back but looked intact. A square Rubbermaid container held dog treats and rawhide bones. There were three unopened bottles of Evian water for Gus, and his water bowl. Her gym bag, which matched her umbrella, was zipped shut. On the off chance that someone might be watching her, she lifted out the gym bag and set it on the ground. She checked to make sure the trunk was locked before she walked back to the house. She was on the porch itself when Gus whirled around, the hair on his neck standing on end. Across the road at the curb, a cruiser slid to a stop. *"Seitz."* All the K-9 commands were in German. Gus obeyed the order, his whole body trembling. His hair was still on end, his ears flat against his head.

The enemy, AKA, Dutch Davis.

The detective rolled down his window and leaned out. "You okay, Aggie? Do you need anything?"

She was trembling, too. "No. I'm fine."

"Okay. You're on our cruise list. Keep your doors locked. Those flowers look real nice. Call in if you need anything."

"Okay." She waved one of her bony arms before she reached down to scratch Gus behind the ears. "Easy boy, this isn't the right time."

Inside, with the door locked, Aggie collapsed on the oversize chair. The big dog was as agitated as she was. It was a good half hour before either one of them was calm enough to get up and walk around.

Aggie bit down on her bottom lip as she eyed the tartan gym bag and her purse. Dutch must have seen both items sitting on the front porch. Bastard.

Was the day planner she used as a journal still in the bag or wasn't it? Yes or no?

She unzipped the bag with one quick motion. The sound was so loud, Gus growled. The bag was stuffed to the top. Her New Balance running shoes, her sweats, her water bottle, two towels, makeup bag, headband, wristband, ankle and wrist weights, six granola bars, a pack of Dentyne chewing gum and . . . the day planner wrapped in the leg of an extra pair of sweatpants. She was so light-headed with relief she had to sit down.

Aggie sucked in her breath when she reached for her purse. Everything appeared to be intact. She rifled through her wallet. Two credit cards, seventy-four dollars, a few paid receipts, a dry-cleaning ticket, a candy bar, checkbook, pen, small notebook, a cigarette lighter, her keys, lipstick, small atomizer of perfume, and a package of Kleenex.

She was so dizzy with relief, she closed her eyes and was instantly asleep.

The K-9 hopped onto the sofa that sat under the window, then onto the back, where he stared out the window. When the cruiser crawled by an hour later, his body stiffened, but he didn't move.

• • •

Aggie sat in the kitchen savoring the day's first cup of coffee. With the long nap she'd taken the previous afternoon, her night's sleep had been anything but restful. Gus had prowled the house all night long. That had to mean one of the Big Three was keeping an eye on her. Let them.

Uncertain where to hide the journal for safekeeping until it was time for her to leave for the farm, she'd finally decided on the fireplace, where Alex's cleaning lady had laid firewood in case of a chilly spring night. She'd moved the logs and the kindling until she had enough room to burrow the black book underneath. She fretted about the hiding place all night long. Maybe that's why she hadn't slept well. She should have just left it where it was.

She had to carry on today as if nothing was bothering her. She had her car, so she could go out and about. A trip to the grocery store was a must. So was a trip to the cemetery. She needed to buy some new clothes, but she could do that on the Internet or by calling any of the 800 numbers from different catalogs. She also had to go to the bank so she could pay Alex all the money she owed him. She wondered what he was doing right now? Like her, Alex was an early-morning person. Maybe she should call him. She was about to pick up the phone when a shadow crossed the kitchen window. Gus was on his feet a second later. The knock was Alex's rat-a-tat-tat! Aggie got up to open the door.

"I brought six jelly donuts, one for me, five for you. Eat up!"

"This is nice, isn't it, Alex? Neither of us has anything to do. We can take our time and just fritter away the whole day if we want to." She bit into one of the sugary donuts.

"I'm a good fritterer. Is there such a word? So, what's on the agenda?" He mouthed the words, "Did you find it?" Aggie nodded as she reached for a second donut. She smiled at the look of relief on her friend's face.

"I was just sitting here thinking I need to go to the grocery store, and I want to go out to the cemetery. I don't know why I feel like I have to do that. I should probably call Tom's parents, too. I did meet them several times, and they're nice people. I don't know if Tom told them we broke it off or not. These donuts are good. Three's my limit, though. Go ahead, eat the other two."

"Just what I need, a sugar high." Alex chomped down on a donut, the sugar scattering over his navy blue shirt. "I'm ready if you are. Should we take the Pathfinder, or do you want to drive your car? If you're going grocery shopping, I suggest we take mine. There's more room for Gus."

Aggie was agreeable. "Okay. Let me get a sweater. While I'm doing that, I want a total of how much money I owe you. I'll write you a check. I want to stop at my bank anyway, and you can deposit it at the same time. If you don't know, guess. Like I said, I hate owing money even if it is to you. By the way, how do you like the front porch?"

"I like it a lot. Let's sit out there when we get home and have a couple of beers."

"Okay."

Alex calculated the amount of money in his head, knowing if he was off it was only by a few bucks. He handed a slip from the sticky pad by the phone to Aggie when she returned with her sweater.

Aggie looked at the amount and reached for her purse. She scribbled off a check and handed it to him. She let out a loud sigh of relief. "Thanks again for doing all that for me, Alex." He shrugged as he pocketed the check.

They really didn't talk about anything until they were walking up and down the aisles in the busy supermarket. Alex showed her the gizmo he'd purchased at the electronics store. "Good choice. Did you sweep your car this morning?"

"You bet. I didn't find anything. I was afraid someone would see me, so I didn't do yours. We'll do the house when we get back."

She told him about Dutch Davis and Gus's reaction to the detective the day before. "The drive-by was to let me know they're watching me. It's bothering me that they didn't find the day planner. I'm glad they didn't, but how did they miss it?"

"If you want a guess, I'd say it was because of the guard dogs at the impound lot. Maybe they couldn't get to it. Maybe they did get to it and didn't find it. You did say you wrapped it in your sweatpants. They would have been in a hurry. You also have to log in and out and give a reason for going to the lot. Think about it. What reason would they have other than to snoop?"

Aggie shrugged as she poked, then shook, a melon. "It's safe for the moment. I hid it in the fireplace under the logs. Okay, I'm done. I think I have everything."

Everything turned into $286.14 plus eighteen grocery bags.

As fast as Alex slid the grocery bags into the cargo hold, Gus pawed them, looking for a treat. Aggie laughed as she opened a bag of cherry-flavored licorice. She handed him one of the long sticks. "He likes root beer, too. I think he likes the fizz going up his nose. Root beer is a *special* treat. Let's take the groceries home. While you put everything away, I'll sweep the house for bugs. I know how to do it. Then we can go to the cemetery. Is that okay with you?"

"Sure."

They were almost to Peachtree when Alex said, "There's a light blue Taurus behind us. Don't look now. I noticed it earlier, too."

Aggie grimaced. "It's not the unmarked Taurus you have to worry about. It's the unmarked dark vehicle two cars behind it. We're supposed to spot the Taurus. Ignore it."

It must be a cop thing. Alex did as he was told. He ignored the light blue Taurus as he turned on his directional and headed for Peachtree.

An hour later, Aggie took Alex by the hand and led him into the living room, where she pointed to a vase of glass flowers. She held up one finger. She motioned for him to follow her to the second floor, where she showed him the second bug underneath a picture frame that held a picture of Gus in his protective armor and wearing his badge. He watched as she pulled out two pieces of crinkly, noisy cellophane from the pocket of her Capri pants. She wrapped the bug and placed it back where she found it. Whoever was listening in on her private life would only hear static. They would think one of two things, either the bug was malfunctioning or that she had found it and done exactly what she'd just done. At this point, she really didn't care what they thought. She smiled. Alex's thumb shot in the air.

Downstairs, she did the same thing to the glass flowers.

"I think we're ready to head out again, Alex." She whistled for Gus, who came on the run. "Maybe we should take my car since we're just going to the cemetery. It hasn't been driven for a while. Do you mind checking the tires and the windshield wiper fluid? The pollen is really heavy right now. I might need some gas, too." She palmed the electronic device to Alex as she held the door open for Gus.

"You could probably use *one* quart of oil, Aggie. The windshield wiper fluid is okay."

"I'm almost on empty. I guess we're going to have to go in your car after all. Darn. Come on, Gus, we have to relocate. Don't forget to stop at Della's Florist Shop so I can pick up some flowers. I'll drive over to the gas station later and fill it up."

Alex climbed behind the wheel, turned the key in the ignition, and gunned the engine. "It's right under the driver's side door."

"Damn. Those guys have been really busy. My thinking is this: They probably kept on with their little side business while I was incapacitated. Now that I'm home, they don't know what I know. That means they have to be really careful. When a buyer wants his stuff, he wants it when he wants it or he goes someplace else. That tells me their sideline is in a holding pattern, and they want to get back into business. They have to sit tight until they figure out how much I know."

"Are you sure it's okay to bring your sister into all of this?"

"I think so. We'll know for sure tomorrow when she arrives. If she says no, then we let it all drop. The one thing I know for certain is, I'm in no physical shape to take them on at this point in time. I've got one big gun I can still fire."

"And that would be . . . what? Or, should I say, whom?"

"It's whom. Nathan Hawk. He's a reporter with the *Atlanta Journal-Constitution*. Nice guy. Doesn't go off half-cocked. Stays with the facts. Plus, he's a hell of an investigative reporter. I worked with him a few times. Like I said, he's a nice guy. He actually has ethics, and he protects his sources. That's a real plus in my book. I think he would be just perfect for Lizzie. The cops are really wary of him. He's got snitches and sources all over the place, and he pays well. If he dogs Lizzie, the cops will stay away from her. I'm thinking that's the way it's going to go down."

"In my experience, Aggie, I've found that if you give a person two choices, the stupid one and the smart one, invariably they choose the stupid one. That's just another way of saying you can't count on anybody doing the right thing."

"I know that. I'm hopeful, Alex. What else can I say?"

Alex shrugged. "The cemetery is about a quarter of a mile down the road. Are you sure you want to go there?"

"No, I don't want to go there, but I'm going anyway. I owe that much to Tom. Damn, we were so busy talking, we forgot the flowers."

"I don't think he'll mind, Aggie."

"I mind, Alex. That means I'm slipping. Good cops don't slip because they could get killed. You need eyes in the back of your head, you need a photographic memory, and you need the guts of a fool. Right now I'm sorely lacking in all three categories."

"Stop being so hard on yourself, Aggie. You've had a rough time of it these past six months. It's all going to come back. Give it time."

Aggie's voice sounded so sad, Alex shivered.

"Time has a way of becoming your enemy. Especially in the world I live in. I feel terrible that I didn't get the flowers."

"It's not the end of the world, Aggie. You can bring flowers the next time."

Aggie looked across at Alex. "It is the end of the world for Tom. I don't want to come back here again."

He said he understood, but he didn't. Women didn't think like men. He got out of the car, ran around to the passenger side, and held the door for Aggie. Gus bounded over the seat, then out the door, landing neatly on the ground.

Together, they walked toward the site map outside the memorial office.

Twenty minutes later, they found the simple stone. Tears blurred Aggie's vision when she saw Tom's name chiseled in the granite stone. He was too young to die, too young to be gunned down because he was a good person and objected to his friends' wrongdoing.

Guilt washed over her. Guilt that she was alive and Tom was dead. She reached down to pat Gus's head. He whimpered softly. She wondered if he knew who was buried here. Gus had liked Tom. Not as much as Gus liked Alex, but he did like him.

Aggie mumbled a prayer she remembered from childhood, her eyes downcast, tears rolling down her cheeks.

"I feel terrible, Alex. Why do I feel guilty? Why do I feel like I let Tom down?"

"You didn't let him down, Aggie. It's natural that you feel a little guilty. You're alive, and he's not. This is the end of the road for everyone. For Tom it was way too early. Life goes on because that's the way life is. Come on, it's time to head for home. Anytime you want to come back here, I'll bring you. I want your promise, though, that you won't come here alone."

Aggie wiped at her eyes with the back of her hand. "All right, Alex."

Chapter Three

*E*lizabeth Corinthia Jade, AKA Lizzie Jade, and also known at one time as Sugar Pye during her short-lived stripping career, sauntered off the plane, the eyes of every man in first class on her swinging derriere, her incredibly long legs, stiletto heels, and a tight spandex dress that left absolutely nothing to anyone's imagination. Her long blond wig with the jagged bangs bounced and swished as she made her way from the plane to the Atlanta concourse.

Lizzie Jade loved it when people looked and stared at her. But it was strictly a hands-off policy as far as she was concerned. You could look but you could not even *think* about touching her person. Aggie said she was an exhibitionist, which was probably true to a certain degree. She loved fancy, daring clothes and considered herself a trendsetter among her peers. She was rich, she was talented, she was beautiful, and she was educated with a degree in marine biology plus a master's. She was also a cardsharp, a disco dancer, a stripper, a runway model, an actress, a private divorce dick who worked only on the female's side, and a gas station attendant. Now she was going to be a cop. A pistol-packing cop. Detective, actually. She wondered what it was she would be detecting. Aggie had been rather mysterious on the phone. Maybe she was going to have to go undercover to ferret out some deep, dark secret that would blow the city of Atlanta wide open. She had her outfit all picked out in her mind for the photo op when she blew the case wide open by the time she rode the B Train to the baggage area. She'd probably get some kind of commendation or maybe a gold badge. Solid gold, of course. Lizzie Jade would never wear anything gold-plated.

Never.

Lizzie Jade loved Lizzie Jade.

Lizzie turned around to see more admiring glances as she hailed a porter. She smiled at one and all, her scarlet lips glistening. A scarlet-tipped nail that matched her lipstick pointed to three crocodile suitcases—two large and one medium-sized.

She looked around for a limo driver holding a card that was supposed to say, Patricia Newfeld. She made eye contact and smiled. She wiggled her fingers to show she was *the* Patricia Newfeld he was to pick up and drive to the Ritz-Carlton in Buckhead.

A twenty-dollar tip brought a smile to the porter's face as he stowed her bags in the trunk of the limousine.

The twenty-five-minute ride to the Ritz-Carlton was made in silence. She'd closed her eyes the minute she'd settled herself inside the limo. Closed eyes meant no conversation. She didn't open her eyes again until the driver said, "We're here, miss."

The game plan was for her to register as Patricia Newfeld, pay cash in advance, then go to her suite of rooms and wait for Aggie. She could handle that with no problem. She held out a fifty-dollar bill to the driver, whose eyes popped wide. Among other things, Lizzie Jade was a big tipper.

Lizzie followed the three pieces of crocodile luggage to the check-in counter, where she announced herself, plunked down twenty crisp hundred-dollar bills, signed in, accepted her keys, and made her way to the elevator. She wanted to look around to see if she could spot Aggie, but she didn't. She knew how to follow instructions.

Her bags arrived, by way of the service elevator on the twenty-seventh floor, at the same time she did. Money changed hands again before she felt comfortable enough to lock the door. She unlocked it ten minutes later to admit her sister and a tall, muscular-looking man.

Lizzie ignored the man, focusing on her twin sister. "Aggie? Oh, my God, what happened to you? Are you all right? You're sick, aren't you? You have some incurable disease and your days are numbered and that's why you called me. Is it contagious?"

"Shut up, Lizzie. I'm not sick, and I don't have an incurable disease."

"That's a relief. I'd hug you, but you look like you'll snap in two. What's wrong with you? Don't tell me you went on some stupid diet and this is the result. I don't want to hear that, Aggie."

"This is Alex Rossiter, a friend of mine."

"Yeah, hi," Lizzie said as she led her sister over to the king-size bed and plopped her down. She herself dropped to her knees, the spandex dress hiking halfway up her rear end. Alex grinned at the view, hoping to get a glimpse of the tattoo Aggie had told him about.

"Tell me everything." She yanked at the blond wig and tossed it across the room. She finger-combed her short, silky, brown hair until she was satisfied that it felt right. "Everything means everything, Aggie."

Aggie was like a runaway train as she spit out the happenings of the last six months. When she wound down, she heaved a great sigh.

Lizzie was outraged as well as almost speechless. "And you're just now letting me know all this. What if you had died, Aggie? How would I ever have known?" Fat tears rolled down her cheeks, smearing her mascara as she hugged her fragile-looking twin.

"Alex would have told you. I never listed you on my application as next of kin or kin of any kind. No one knows about you."

"Why? I tell my friends my sister is a cop. Are you ashamed of me?"

"Embarrassed is more like it. You lead an exceptionally colorful life, Lizzie."

"I do, don't I? *Organic carrots.* For God's sake, why?"

"Why do you want to open a dive shop? I like organic carrots. They're good for your eyesight. They're really good if you add brown sugar and make it kind of syrupy. That's what you got out of everything I just said?"

"I heard everything you said. I committed it to memory. It was the organic carrots that threw me. I have to wear a shoulder holster? And your clothes. When was the last time you updated that skimpy wardrobe of yours? What am I supposed to do with those?" she said, pointing to the three suitcases. "I don't know about the dog. I never had a dog. What if it doesn't like me? They *poop*. All right, all right. I'll make the dog love me. Does *it* talk?" she asked, jerking her head in Alex's direction.

"Yes, *he* talks. So, do you think you can handle it?"

"Of course I can handle it. There's nothing I can't handle except maybe your clothes. I'm assuming you are going to get a haircut like mine. How am I supposed to cover up my fifteen extra pounds?"

"By going on a starvation diet for a week while I eat everything under the sun. By the end of the week we should be in sync. I'll put on weight, and you'll take off weight. It's simple."

"I could go to jail for impersonating a police officer."

"Only if you get caught. It's up to you to see that you *don't* get caught. This is your chance to prove what you've always said, that you're smarter than I am. Right now I have limitations, and I'm not so stupid that I don't know what they are. My partner was killed. I was almost killed. My dog almost died. As much as I hate to admit it, I can't cut it. I have this gut feeling that time is of the essence. I don't know why. Know this, though: If you go to jail, so do I, and I do not want to spend even one day in jail. Do you understand that, Lizzie? I have to leave now. I don't like leaving Gus alone too long after all he's been through. I want you to read through everything in this envelope I'm leaving for you. Alex cut out all the articles pertaining to that night. There are pictures of the Big Three in there, so study them carefully. I'll be back tomorrow, and we'll talk it all to death. I'll take you through a day in the life of a cop. Listen, Lizzie, all the bull aside, this could be dangerous for you. So many things can go wrong. Maybe this isn't such a good idea after all. I'll be so worried about you."

"Stop it, Aggie. It's a good plan. I wish you had called me earlier. I would have been here in a heartbeat. You know that, don't you? I can do it. I know I can. You can go off to plant your organic carrots knowing you left your case in capable hands. Do I really embarrass you?"

"Nah. I just said that to get a rise out of you. Hell, I admire your . . . illustrious career. You even made me a millionaire in the bargain. Remember to wear that wig when you go out and about. You can hang out at the two malls across the street during the day to pass time if you get bored. You're gonna love Phipps Mall."

"Aggie, are you *really* all right?"

"I'm really all right, Lizzie. Right now, I'm not all right enough to do what I'm asking you to do. Even I know I need the downtime. Like I said, my partner was killed. That's hard to take. The shrink is going to dwell on that, especially since we had a personal relationship for a while. I haven't told him I'd already called it off before Tom got killed. Some instinct told me not to tell. I still have some bad moments. Oh, I forgot to tell you that you have to check in with that shrink twice a month. It's a piece of cake. We'll go over that tomorrow, too. Thanks for coming, Lizzie." Aggie threw her arms around her sister and hugged her fiercely.

"For you, anything. Any good-looking guys around here? Besides him," Lizzie said, pointing to Alex. Alex's chest puffed out at the compliment.

Aggie could feel herself start to bristle. "I'm going to pave the way for you to meet Nathan Hawk. You two deserve each other."

"Oooh, I like the way that sounds."

"I'll see you tomorrow."

"Bye."

In the hallway waiting for the elevator, Aggie looked up at Alex, and said, "Wipe that sappy look off your face. She'd chew you up and spit you out inside of five minutes. I saw you looking at her butt."

"I was hoping to get a glimpse of her tattoo." He did his best to wipe the grin off his face. She sounded jealous. Maybe she even cared about him. Other than in a friendly way. He rather thought that was a good thing.

"It's a damn purple-and-yellow butterfly," she snapped. "I'll draw you a picture of it when we get home."

"Testy, aren't we?" Alex asked with a smile.

She was on her knees in the garden planting a bed of bright pink impatiens. Gus was lying in the shade under an oak tree. The old oak dripping with moss was the main reason she'd bought the house years ago. It sat in the middle of the yard like a giant umbrella and shaded the back end of the house during the brutally hot Atlanta summers. She'd envisioned herself sitting under it with a glass of lemonade. It had never happened.

She half turned when she sensed Gus getting to his feet. His growl was low and deep. Scary-sounding to anyone but her. He was looking at her, waiting for a command. She shook her head, her hand motioning for him to stay. Trowel in hand, she walked over to the fence in time to see Will Fargo, the evidence clerk, walking around to the back of the house. From where she was standing, she could see that the double padlock on the stockade gate was in the locked position.

"Aggie! It's me, Will. The department asked me to bring this by. Dutch said he rode by the other day and saw that you were putting flowers on your porch. You're on a twenty-four-hour cruise patrol. We took up a collection. Everyone signed the card."

"That was nice of you . . . them." She reached up to take a large basket of mixed flowers that could be planted in the ground. "I don't even know where the key is to unlock the gate," she lied.

"No problem. I have to get back to the station. How're you doing, Aggie?"

"Good, Will. I think I'll go back to work week after next. I'm going to call the chief later today. They offered me ninety days, but I don't need it. I can handle a desk job now."

He looked just like a ferret, all sharp angles and points. He was tall, pencil-skinny. Bony with sparse hair over an exceptionally high and wide forehead.

His jaw jutted down to a point that somehow seemed to meet the middle of his sharp-ended nose. His teeth were of the canine variety, narrow and pointy at the ends. The clothes hanging on his skinny frame were like the ones hanging on her own body. Maybe that's what happened to a person when he spent ten hours a day in a windowless room guarding other people's property. Will usually worked nights and slept the better part of the day. His sallow complexion was a testament to his rarely seeing the sun. He looked startled at her news.

"Do you think that's wise, Aggie?"

"Wise or not, I'm not going to sit around for ninety days twiddling my thumbs. I want to find out what happened to Tom. He was on to something. He was a good cop. And a good partner. I'm having a real hard time accepting the fact that the force can't find the guys who did this. Cop killers are . . . You should have found them by now." Her voice was so vehement, it surprised her.

"Yeah. The whole department is in a funk. No clues, no nothing. We've been on it twenty-four/seven. It's a real mind bender. You were the only one there. You and that dog!"

"You're right, Will. We weren't supposed to live either, but we did. Miracle of miracles. I'll work on it myself on my own time. Tom was my partner. I owe him that."

"Did you see or hear something, Aggie? What do you think you could possibly find out that the whole department couldn't find?"

Aggie shrugged. "You know how it is when

you're shot up that bad. You aren't sure what's real and what isn't. I'll . . . ah . . . *ferret* it out. I have Gus to help me." She almost laughed out loud at Will's expression. "Gus was all over the place that night before they shot him down. He's *never* going to forget how those guys smelled."

Aggie watched as a small brown wren settled itself on the fence. He appeared to be listening to their conversation.

"I don't know what you think you can do that the whole department couldn't do," Fargo grumbled.

"They weren't there. I was. Internal Affairs cleared me. I'm still a tad upset that I had to go through all that. You know, the suspicions, the veiled accusations. Even when you die in the line of duty you have to put up with that garbage, and that's what it was, garbage. You guys should have been out there busting your humps to find the people who killed Tom and wounded me and Gus. It's been six months, Will, and you have squat."

"I can see you're the old Aggie. Dutch said you were like the Lone Ranger, Buck Rogers, and Tom Mix all rolled into one."

Aggie's face wore a fierce scowl. "Is that what old Dutch said?"

"Aggie, if you plan on going back to work, you might as well know now. You're going to hear it sooner or later anyway. Once you get off desk duty, none of the guys want to partner with you."

Aggie wondered if what Will said was true or if he made it up on the spur of the moment to hurt her. "That doesn't surprise me. Guess what, I don't need a partner. I have Gus. You can go back and tell them for me that I'd rather pick poop with the chickens than work with any of them ever again. When your own can't find cop killers, there's something *dirty* somewhere. I'll figure it out. You can take that to the bank."

The brown wren moved farther down the fence and was joined by two other birds who looked just like him. Now, all three appeared to be listening to the conversation, which was starting to sound ugly.

"Aggie, what the hell are you saying?" He didn't bother to wait for a response. "Are you saying the department is dirty?" His sallow complexion had turned as white as some of the flowers in the basket Aggie was holding.

Aggie turned away. "IAD cleared me. How many guys in the department do you think could get a clean bill of health the way I did? Well, Will, how many? You know what, on second thought, take these damn flowers. I don't want anything from any of you." Before Fargo could react, she lifted the basket over the fence and jammed it into his hands. "You can go now, Will."

Gus squirmed, but he didn't move as Will Fargo walked away, shaking his head. "I know, you want to chase his skinny butt all the way down the street. Not yet, big guy. Come on, time for a break. How about some root beer. You deserve it for sitting tight." The K-9's reaction to Will and Dutch's drive-bys was all the corroboration she needed that the two of them were somewhere in the alley that night.

The shepherd followed her up the steps to her

small back porch. He waited patiently while Aggie opened two cans of root beer. She poured his into a bowl and swigged at her own.

She needed a cigarette. Neither she nor Alex was a smoker, but on occasion they did smoke. Alex had left some on the kitchen counter the other day. She remembered seeing them. She walked back into the house, found them, and carried them out to the back porch. She lit up. Gus finished his root beer and walked away. He didn't like cigarette smoke. That was the main reason she didn't smoke.

Aggie puffed on her cigarette and swigged at the root beer as her mind raced. Will Fargo was probably already on the phone to his buddies Dutch and Joe. Maybe she was going about this all wrong. Maybe she should be concentrating on Tom Madsen instead of Dutch, Joe, and Will. She could hop in the car right now and go to visit Tom's parents. *Yes, that's exactly what I'm going to do. Right now.* "C'mon, Gus, we're going visiting."

Four blocks south of Peachtree, she spotted the tail. She smiled. She drove steadily in stop-and-go traffic before she turned into a side street, made a left, two rights, and finally slowed down on Exeter. The senior Madsens lived in a yellow house with brown trim. They had a swing on the front porch and a statue of the Virgin Mary in their flower garden. There were two cars in the driveway, so that meant both Virginia and Gray Madsen were home. Mr. Madsen had retired last year. She'd attended the retirement party with Tom. She'd even had a good time as she recalled.

Gus at her side, she walked up the driveway to the kitchen door and rang the bell. She could see the neatly-kept kitchen through the screen door.

Virginia Madsen covered her heart with her hands when she saw Aggie. Even through the screen, Aggie could see her eyes flood with tears. "I have Gus with me, Mrs. Madsen. We can talk out here if you don't want him in the house."

"Nonsense. Tom loved that dog. Oh, honey, Gray and I were just sick over what happened to you and your dog. After . . . after the funeral, we wanted to visit with you, but the department said it wasn't a good idea. When I read in the paper the other day that you were being discharged, I said to Gray, you watch, the minute she's settled in, she'll come to see us. Can I get you a soft drink or some coffee? Does the dog need anything?"

"A soda pop would be nice. Gus is fine, don't worry about him. It's so hot, and it isn't even summer yet. I wanted to tell you how sorry I am about Tom. I went out to the cemetery yesterday. It was so hard."

"I know, dear. Gray and I go on Sunday afternoons."

Virginia Madsen was a soccer ball of a woman. Even her face was plump. Aggie loved her gray top-knot and wire-rimmed granny glasses. She exuded motherhood. She was wearing a loose lavender-flowered dress and house slippers.

"Mrs. Madsen, did you hound the department about Tom? I can't understand why they haven't found the people who shot him. You know what happens when a cop is killed. They never give up. But it appears to me they have given up. It's been six months and they still don't have any leads."

Virginia dabbed at the corners of her eyes. "We went down to the station every day, sometimes twice. It was always the same response, 'we're doing everything we can.' "

"I don't believe that," Aggie said quietly.

"Well, guess what, Aggie, Gray and I don't believe it either. I told Gray as soon as you got back you'd find out who killed our son. Tom loved you so much. Two weeks before . . . before . . . he started coming by almost every day. Gray said something was on his mind, and he was trying to figure out a way to tell us. He never did. I know my boy, and he was troubled. I was hoping you'd know what it was all about."

If Tom was troubled, it could mean a variety of things. Maybe he'd wanted to tell them that he and Aggie had broken up. Maybe he knew she'd put in for a transfer and wanted to talk to his parents about that. The third possibility was that he wanted to confide in his parents about what he either knew or suspected was going on in the department.

"I wish I knew, Mrs. Madsen. That night is a little vague in my mind. I remember Tom's saying it didn't smell right. I remember that clear as a bell. I tried to help him, I really did, but then I got hit. I've come to the only conclusion possible—we were set up. Do you have Tom's things?"

"Yes. Gray made them turn everything over to him that very night. Everything is in a box in my closet. Well, almost everything. We had a break-in shortly after Tom . . . passed on. Gray and I went to a senior citizens' meeting, and that's when it happened. In broad daylight. I have to say the police were here within minutes when we called them. The only things they took were my pearls and Gray's watch and twenty-seven dollars Gray had left on the dresser. They even opened the box of Tom's things and rummaged through it the way they rummaged through the box of papers I keep on the top shelf.

"I can show you Tom's things if you like. I can look at them and touch them now. I couldn't in the beginning. Would you like something of Tom's?"

She didn't, but she said, "Yes, perhaps his key chain. I gave it to him for his birthday last year." Virginia nodded as she led the way down a short hall and up the steps to the second floor. She headed straight for her bedroom closet, where she opened a box that said STAPLES on the side.

Aggie almost fainted when she peered inside. She imagined she could smell Tom's aftershave. When Virginia said, "Tom's things," Aggie had assumed it was things like his keys, his wallet, his watch and whatever was in his locker at the station. She didn't expect to see his bloody clothes. She backed away, her face white with shock.

"Oh, my dear, I'm so sorry." Virginia quickly jammed the lid back on the box and led Aggie back to the stairs, her plump arms around her shoulders. "Sit down, dear, and put your head between your knees. I'm so sorry, I didn't think. I had the same reaction when Gray showed me . . . Tom's things. There was just so much blood. I can't bear to throw the box away, and yet I feel ghoulish keeping it."

"Did I hear you right before, Mrs. Madsen, when you said almost everything was in the box? Do you have something of Tom's that you took out of the box?"

"Yes, his little notebook."

Aggie's heart kicked up a beat as she looked around the tidy little kitchen. It was homey and cozy, with a green fern hanging over the sink and little clay pots of herbs on the windowsill. Cheerful strawberry-patterned wallpaper adorned the walls. Small rugs by the sink and stove were the same color as the strawberries. Even the salt and pepper shakers were ceramic strawberries. Virginia Madsen must like strawberries.

She watched as Virginia walked over to the counter, where there was a stack of cookbooks propped up against the side of the refrigerator that jutted out past the counter. She waddled back to the table with a four-inch-thick Betty Crocker cookbook. She smiled when she turned it over and flipped open the back of it. Aggie looked down at a bulging pocket that held recipes and a little notebook. "I knew you would want this when you came here. I hope you can make more sense of it than Gray and I could. It's gibberish to us."

"I'll take it home and study it and compare it to my own. Somebody ransacked my house while I was away. My house is bugged, too. Just so you know, Mrs. Madsen. Your son . . . Tom . . . Tom was a good cop."

"He said you were the best. He told his dad he'd rather partner with you than any guy on the force. Nothing would have made Gray and me happier than to have you for our daughter-in-law."

Tears blurred Aggie's vision. Tom hadn't confided that part of his life to them. They didn't know she'd severed the relationship. She saw no reason to tell them now. She didn't want to cast one iota of suspicion on their dead son. Whichever way it played out, the Madsens as well as she would have to live with it.

Aggie finished her soda as they made small talk. "Gray is going to be upset that he missed you. A friend took him golfing today. I like it when he isn't under my feet all day. Retirement isn't all they say it is." She sighed. "I wish our daughter didn't live so far away. Gray's pension and social security only allow for one trip to Washington state a year. I miss the grandchildren. When Tom was alive he'd stop by once or twice a week, and if he was off on Sundays, he'd always come to dinner. For Christmas last year, he gave us two airline tickets to Seattle. Gray and I couldn't have asked for a better son."

"Are you lonely, Mrs. Madsen?"

"Yes and no. I read a lot. We go for walks. We garden. Gray and I joined a senior citizens' group. They're a bunch of *stiffs*, I'm sorry to say. They are so sedentary. Bingo isn't my idea of a night out. I guess I shouldn't say things like that. All the ladies in my group want to do is have bake sales so they can eat it all, gain weight, and become even more sedentary."

Aggie stood up. "I'll be back. I'm not sure when,

Mrs. Madsen. If anyone comes by, some of the men from the department, and they ask you about me, don't tell them anything. Whatever you do, don't tell them about the notebook."

"We won't say a word. Call me if you need anything. Gray and I are always here. I made a Boston cream pie this morning. Would you like to take some home?"

"No thanks. I don't really have a sweet tooth." Aggie hugged the little woman, said good-bye, and herded Gus out to the Honda. It was going to be interesting to see if she had a tail on the way back. Having Tom's notebook gave her a small amount of courage.

Mindful of the bug that was on the bottom of the driver's side door, Aggie punched in Alex's phone number on her stationary car phone. "Hi, it's me. I was wondering if you'd like to come over for supper. I'm on my way home now and should be there in thirty minutes or so. I went to see Mr. and Mrs. Madsen, but Mr. Madsen wasn't home. Virginia and I had a nice chat. She misses Tom terribly. He was her only son. She told me he used to go home on Sundays for dinner if he was off. Listen to this. She told me someone broke into her house and stole her pearls, her husband's watch, and some money. Why do people do things like that to older people? They're barely squeaking by on Mr. Madsen's pension and his social security.

"So, do you want to come for dinner or not? You are not supposed to ask what I'm cooking. Think of it as a surprise. Six o'clock is fine. See ya.

"How does chicken parm sound, Gus? I'll make you some without the sauce. Tomato sauce is not good for dogs. I might even whip up a dessert now that I don't have to count calories."

Gus plopped both his paws on her shoulder and nuzzled her neck. "I'm going to take that as approval of my menu. I think I'm being followed. Damn, I am. It's the same car that followed me when we started out. Someone must think I'm important enough to watch. Wonder why?" Gus tweaked her ear. She laughed.

Chapter Four

—

Lizzie Jade, AKA every name in the book, paced the spacious suite of rooms. She alternated between excitement and dread. This was the day she was moving out of the Ritz-Carlton and into Aggie's house. Her agile brain sifted and collated all the facts and directions Aggie had jammed down her throat. Always a quick study, she didn't think she would have any trouble posing as her sister. She hoped this gig would be short-lived.

Atlanta was boring. Just how much could one person shop? She already had everything under the sun. She was also ticked off that nothing on this gig was comped. She'd been spending her own money left and right. It had been years since she'd done that. If it wasn't free, she didn't want any part of it. Whatever *it* was.

These last ten days she'd been living like a normal person, going to bed at ten o'clock and getting up at seven to watch the early-morning television shows, as opposed to going to bed around four in the morning and sleeping till late afternoon. She'd had no idea who Katie Couric was until nine days ago. On top of that, she'd lost nine pounds.

Lizzie plopped down on the love seat. Life certainly was strange. In a million years she never would have thought she'd be sitting in a suite of rooms at the Ritz-Carlton in Atlanta while she waited to turn into a cop. She felt like Cinderella in reverse.

Her eyes started to burn when she thought of Aggie and how close she'd come to dying. They were twins. Why hadn't she felt something, anything, during that time of crisis? Normally they were tuned to one another. Had she become so self-centered, so into herself, that she'd lost that special connection to Aggie? Was it time to stop and smell the roses? Obviously the answer was yes.

Aggie was looking better with each passing day, but Lizzie could tell that Aggie still didn't have her old stamina and vitality back. She blinked back the tears that filled her eyes. "Don't you worry, Aggie, I'm going to kick ass and take names later. I'm going to make this come out right for you," she mumbled.

Lizzie looked down at the papers scattered over the coffee table and floor. Her methodical mind had put everything into chronological order as she memorized each and every thing Aggie had said was important. Barring any unforeseen complications along the way, she felt confident she could pull off the switch with no one the wiser. She'd gone so far as to set up an escape hatch known as Plan B, more for Aggie's sake than her own, if the situation got really hot and dangerous. She didn't want to think about Plan B. At least not right now.

She would not be sorry to leave this place. As nice as it was, it was still a hotel suite. She liked her own things, didn't like living out of a suitcase. The bottom line was she missed Vegas and her exciting life. She sighed with relief when her cell phone rang. Her greeting was guarded, her voice low. She literally squealed when she heard her friend Noreen's voice. They jabbered the way friends do about everything and anything. "Girl, if you can take some time off, come stay with me for a while. Bring the girls along. It'll be one big slumber party. Not till next week, though. You will! Great! No, no, I'm fine. I have to help out my sister. Yeah, the cop. She got wounded, and I didn't even know it. That's the way it is. We aren't going to be partying, Noreen, just hanging out. Great, call me when you know what time your flight gets in."

Lizzie dusted her hands dramatically. This was one little secret Aggie didn't need to know about. Plus, the girls just might come in handy. All four were showgirls at the Mirage. Big-busted, long-legged, and beautiful. Things were looking up.

She started to pace again as she waited for Aggie, but this time there was more gusto to her movements. Her cell phone rang again. She grimaced when she heard the voice on the other end of the phone. This was going to be sticky. "Hello, Mr. Papadopolus." Usually, she called him Papa or Pap. "I'm sorry you've been looking for me, Pap. I'm in Atlanta. My sister managed to get herself shot up in a stakeout. She's a cop. She needs me right now. Yes, that's what I always say, family comes first. How long will I be here? As long as she needs me. She got shot up pretty bad." She listened, a frown building between her brows. She bit down on her lower lip at what she was hearing. "I'd go for it, Pap, but this is cop territory. Gambling is not legal here as you well know. No, I can't fly back. My sister is depending on me. Here! You want to set up a game *here!* I need to think about that, Pap. Really think about that. How much? You're kidding, right? You're not. How soon is soon? I'm not even going to have time to spit in the next two weeks. The third week is iffy, but it might be doable. Tell me how much again. Hmmmm. I'll get back to you."

Lizzie's heart was beating so fast she had to sit down. Every cell in her body told her she could pull off a high-stakes poker game. Every corpuscle backed it up. If she 'fessed up and told Aggie, Aggie the cop would nix it. She was just *pretending* to be Aggie the cop, she reminded herself. *Think Plan B, Lizzie. Think Plan B.*

Her heart was beating normally, and the color was back in her face when Aggie arrived thirty minutes later. "You're looking good this morning, Lizzie. You must have slept well."

"I've never had so much sleep in my life. And I've lost weight. I know every damn show there is on television. I bet you don't even know *Hardball* comes on at five o'clock in the morning. It's a rerun from the day before. I bet you don't even know there's a cable network news war going on either. That O'Reilly guy on the Fox network is a piece of work. He scares me because I think like he does. I could do what he does with more panache. I think I'm going to look into that when I get back to Vegas."

Aggie had no idea what she was talking about. "Are you ready?"

"Honey, I've been ready from the minute I got here. Please don't make me go through the whole thing again. I have it down pat. Trust me. Thank God this is the last time I have to wear this stupid wig. I'll meet you at the vet's, where we will change clothes and the wig. I will pick up my new companion, Alice, who you said would love me on sight. At that moment, I become you and you become me.

"Remember that time you wanted me to switch up with you when Dad said he smelled cigarette smoke on your clothes because you were smoking behind the garage with Putts Peters and Louie Molino? You said I was the better fibber, so you sent me in to do battle for you. I didn't even have to lie. Well, technically it was a lie. As I recall, you took a shower, washed your hair and brushed your teeth about twenty times in the span of an hour. Ah, the good old days. No reason to think it won't work for us again. Switching identities I mean.

"I go straight to your house, settle in, and report to work Monday morning. In the meantime you are off on a lark wearing the blond wig to raise organic carrots while I corral the bad guys. See, I remembered everything."

"You screw this up, and I'll kill you, Lizzie."

"Just for that, I'm not going to tell you about a guy I know who will buy all your damn organic carrots.

Sooner or later you're going to realize it's not *what* you know, it's *who* you know." Lizzie sniffed. She donned the blond wig.

"Are you sure that friend you've been hanging around with is going to pick up my luggage and keep it till this is over? I have some pricey, high-end stuff in those bags. Just remember, sister dear, you're on the hook for the contents."

"I'm sure. Did you check out?"

"I did it on the TV. They even brought up my change. They'll hold my bags till four o'clock. What time is the friend coming to pick them up?"

"Any minute now. Move your tail, Lizzie, and let's get this show on the road."

"Wait a minute, Aggie. Let's cut the bull, okay. I'm a big girl, and I can take care of myself. I'm as good a shot as you are. I got my brown belt six months before you did. I'm used to walking around with eyes in the back of my head. You'll make me really happy if you tell me you're going to concentrate on those organic carrots and stop worrying about me. I really do know someone who will buy them from you when it's time to dig them up.

"I have my laptop, you have yours. Both are new, so no one can tap into them. Yet. Mail from me to you goes to General Delivery. Both of us are dealing strictly in cash from here on in although I don't understand why, and at this point it doesn't really matter to me. You're the cop. Oh, yes, we check in using our cell phones, too." Lizzie paused and looked her twin directly in the eye. "And remember everything I told you about Plan B!"

Aggie nodded solemnly.

"Okay, let's do it!" Lizzie held up her hand, palm outward toward Aggie, who gave it a resounding slap. "I know you can do it, Lizzie. I wouldn't have asked you otherwise. I'm allowed to worry a little. We're sisters, remember."

Lizzie Jade settled herself on the double chair in Aggie's living room, her new roommate Alice beside her. The dog looked at her adoringly before she lowered her head to lick at her hand lightly. Lizzie scratched her behind the ears the way Aggie told her to. The dog wiggled closer. She felt warm and comfortable.

Woman and dog. Woman's best friend. Things could be worse.

Lizzie worked the remote control and finally settled down to watch Hannity and Colmes on the Fox network. She'd heard all the news they were rehashing earlier, but other than watching a stupid sitcom there wasn't much else on the tube that interested her. Her thoughts started to drift to the phone call she'd received at the hotel from Anthony Papadopolus. She might be able to pull it off with a little help from her friends. It wasn't as if Aggie got a lot of company who stopped by uninvited. She could close the shutters, have the players arrive separately. A pretend party wasn't out of the question in case the neighbors got nosy or colleagues got curious. She was, after all, a party girl. She frowned. *She* was a party girl. Aggie was a stick in the mud, and no way could she be considered a party girl. She frowned. She needed to rethink her plan.

Alice's head jerked upright when Aggie's phone rang. Lizzie sucked in her breath as she stretched out her arm to reach for Aggie's cordless phone sitting next to the double chair. She chirped a greeting, wondering who she was talking to.

"I wouldn't go to work on Monday if I were you, cutie-pie. Things have a way of happening to nosy bitches like you." Lizzie blinked when the dial tone buzzed in her ear.

"Oooh, you're scaring me, you creep." Lizzie replaced the phone and went back to watching television. More to have something to do than anything else, she started to channel surf. Sensing her distress, Alice bellied onto her lap.

Lizzie stared bug-eyed at the shopper's channel when she saw a line of fiber-optic Christmas trees being hawked. Christmas in May? It must be a sale from December's leftovers. The phone was in her hand as she was about to order one of the twinkling trees for Aggie when she remembered she wasn't supposed to use a credit card. The phone rang. Her greeting was as cautious as before. The voice was different but the message was the same. "Watch your back, lady, things happen when you're least expecting it." The connection was broken before she could say a word other than hello.

Lizzie was off the chair in a heartbeat. Hanging on a hook by the back door were a spare dog leash and a whistle. Aggie must have used the whistle to call Gus into the house. She removed it and hung it around her neck. Minutes later, she was back on the double chair with Alice. She was just in time to see a big, red

SOLD OUT sign flash across the screen. All the fiber-optic trees were gone at half price. They were now selling socket wrench sets, obviously another left-over, and marked down 70 percent. She was all agog as the phone rang again. She brought the whistle up to her mouth and clenched it between her teeth. The moment she picked up the phone, she let loose with one, shrill, long blast. "How do you like that, you bastard," she muttered.

"It's okay, Alice, we're taking the phone off the hook, and we're going to bed."

Lizzie woke on Monday morning to a dismal, gray day. A steady drizzle was falling outside as she disengaged all three locks on the back door and ushered Alice outside. The dog did her business and beelined for the house. While the coffee dripped, Lizzie fed the shepherd. She'd bonded with the Gus look-alike in the short time she'd had her and was now reluctant to leave her behind on her first day of work. Aggie had assured her the dog would sleep while she was at work and take care of herself. Just to be on the safe side, Lizzie spread papers down by the back door. She planned on coming home for lunch, but she knew if things went awry, she might not make it.

Her first day as a cop.

Lizzie carried her coffee to the second floor, where she showered and dressed. She hated the feel of the shoulder holster. She hated guns period.

She spooked herself when she looked into the long mirror hanging on the back of the bathroom door. She felt smug knowing she was going to fool Aggie's colleagues. Fifteen minutes later, just as she was about to go out the front door, the phone rang. She reached for the whistle but thought better of it. She made her voice light and cheerful.

"Aggie?"

"Yes."

"It's Nathan Hawk. I know you're on your way out. How about lunch today?"

"Well, hello there, Nathan. I have to come home for lunch today to let Gus out. I can make us both a sandwich if you want. Okay, how does twelve-thirty sound? Good, I'll see you then."

Nice voice. Virile-sounding. Aggie said he was tall and good-looking. She said he worked out faithfully and ran five to ten miles every morning. And, she'd gone on to say he had a different girlfriend for every day of the week. Nathan had integrity and never wrote anything he couldn't back up with two or three reliable sources. Nathan didn't fit into any gray areas. It was either black or white where he was concerned. And then her final assessment of Nathan Hawk. The guy's sharp, so don't try pulling anything over on him. Well, there was sharp, and then there was *sharp*. She herself was no slouch in the sharp department. Lizzie wondered if Hawk's professional attitude carried into his personal life as well.

Lizzie spent another few minutes tussling with Alice before she grabbed an umbrella and left the house. Yesterday she'd taken a dry run to see how much time she needed to allot herself for the drive to work in the morning. Eighteen minutes with light traffic. Twenty-seven minutes with normal Monday morning traffic.

Today she wore a light gray pantsuit whose label said Talbots. Talbots, for God's sake. The jacket was loose enough to cover the gun and holster and to cover the extra pounds on her frame. The hairstyle that she'd gotten before leaving Vegas, the one that Aggie now sported, was sleek and trim. All she had to do was run her fingers through it and voilà, casual to the nth degree. Even though Aggie wasn't big on daytime makeup, Lizzie had applied it skillfully this morning. She looked the picture of vibrant good health. Actually, she looked like a force to be reckoned with.

Lizzie parked the car, slid out, and opened her umbrella. Her fellow officers were everywhere. She didn't know if she was supposed to know them or not. She nodded to some, waved, smiled, and kept up her steady pace to get inside, out of the rain.

Inside, she removed her raincoat, shook it out, and walked down the hall. She heard halfhearted—at least to her ears they sounded halfhearted—welcome back greetings. She nodded and smiled as she found her way to the chief's office. She knocked politely and was told to enter.

Her heart thumped inside her chest as she waited for her boss, whom Aggie said she liked, to give her her orders. "How are you this rainy day, Detective Jade?"

"Achy, sir, but they told me my bones would feel the dampness. I imagine I'll be a barometer from here on in."

"How's the dog, Aggie?"

Calling her Aggie meant he was being personal. Aggie said if he called her Detective Jade or just Jade, it meant he was serious and to watch what she said. "Glad to be home, sir. Like me, he's adjusting nicely. I'm thinking of getting him a companion. Chief?"

"Yes."

"Can you tell me why Tom's killers haven't been found? Are we sweeping him under the rug?"

"I don't want to hear any talk like that, Detective Jade. Nobody is sweeping anything anywhere. We have exhausted every single lead that came our way. The case has not been closed. You look a lot better than you did two weeks ago, Jade," the chief said, peering at her over the rim of his reading glasses.

"Thank you, sir. Where do I report in?"

"You sound like you're in a hurry, Jade."

Lizzie looked around the windowless room. It was a tidy room to a point. Desk, three chairs, two huge filing cabinets, the requisite green plant with yellow leaves, a coatrack, and a wastebasket. The chief of detectives looked rumpled and messy, almost like he had slept in his clothes. He was freshly shaven, though.

"It's been six and a half months, sir. I missed this old place." *Liar, liar, pants on fire.*

"Jade, you better not be harboring any thoughts of turning into a one-woman, one-dog vigilante team. You're working the property room. Will Fargo was involved in a head-on collision sometime last night. We don't know if he'll make it or not. If he does, he's going to be out a very long time. Half the force is out with some kind of intestinal bug that lasts at least five days. I don't want you getting any ideas that I'm sticking you there because no one wants to work with you. I heard those rumors, and there's nothing to them. You're one of the best, Jade, and your fellow officers don't have a problem with you."

"Yes, sir." There really was a God. Not that she ever doubted it, but at times she needed a sign, something solid to go by. She could hardly wait to go home to e-mail Aggie and tell her where she'd ended up. Aggie would know what she was supposed to look for.

"You're still standing there, Jade. Get to work. It's good to have you back, Aggie." A big paw of a hand shot out. Lizzie grasped it and gave it a bone-crushing shake.

"It's all those nutrients and vitamins they made me take." She grinned as the chief flexed his fingers.

"Go on, get outta here."

They were trying not to stare at her, but she was aware of everyone's sudden busyness. Why? All Aggie had done was almost get herself and her dog killed. It wasn't her fault that some jerk killed Tom Madsen. Her head held high, she entered the rest room, not because she had to use it but Aggie had told her there was a map of the entire precinct office taped to the wall. Since she had no idea where the property room was, she needed to find it ASAP.

Of course it was in the basement, away from everything. The hallway was dark, the property room well lit, with a locked door and a wire grille over the desk platform. There was just enough room to shove evidence under the grille, where the property clerk logged it in, at which point the officer and the clerk both signed a form in triplicate, one of which was attached to whatever was being impounded.

"Well, hello there, Officer Callahan. I'm Detective Agnes Jade." She held up her shield so he could study it carefully. "Chief Shay assigned me to this duty. I guess you're to report to the chief."

"It's all yours, Detective. I hope you brought a book along to read or at least a newspaper. Did you hear anything about Officer Fargo?"

"Only that he was involved in a bad accident. I don't know if he was on his way to work or on his way home."

"He was on his way in. He had the midnight shift. They called me in on my day off. It's been a quiet night. Days now are something else." He tossed her a ring of keys and left the property room. Aggie immediately locked the door.

It was a room of a thousand smells, none definable.

Her home away from home for eight hours a day.

Lizzie settled herself for the day ahead. She was ready to scream her head off when the noon hour rolled around. She was also so ready to leave the confining room, she tripped over her own feet in her haste to lock up and exit the building. Even a rainy, dismal day was better than that room.

The traffic was light considering the weather, which surprised her. She stopped at the Atlanta Bread Company, which Aggie said had the best sandwiches in all of Atlanta. She picked up two pastramis on rye and a pound of roast beef and liverwurst for Alice. She needed a few minutes to e-mail Aggie before her luncheon guest arrived.

Lizzie smiled when she approached the front door. Alice's bark sounded joyful to her ears. Inside, she dropped to her knees to fondle the big shepherd, who seemed more interested in her than the sandwiches in her bag. This had to be true animal love. She decided she liked the feeling.

In less than eight minutes, Lizzie had the table set, Alice's plate ready, and she'd signed off the computer, her message to Aggie on its way. All she had to do now was wait for her guest.

Alice was at the door the moment the reporter pulled into the driveway. She looked at Lizzie, then at the door, uncertain what she should do. "It's okay, Alice. For now we have to accept him as a friend." The minute the doorbell chimed, she undid the three new locks on the front door. She pulled it open. "Well, hi there, Nathan, nice to see you again. How's it going?" *A hunk.*

He was tall and muscular. What was that wicked gleam in his eye? Whatever it was, she liked it. Sharp, chiseled features. *GQ* good looks. She wondered how Aggie had ever let this guy get away from her? Dark blond hair, no receding hairline. A definite plus in her book. Just the right sun-bronzed tone to his skin. And his pearly whites, ah, they gleamed. Sexy. With a capital *S*. Oh, yeah. Like Aggie said, play it out and see where it goes.

"You're lookin' good, Aggie. I missed you. I tried

to call you at the rehab center, but they wouldn't put my calls through. I'm sorry about your partner. Hey, there, Gus, give me your paw."

Alice looked up at the tall man and backed away to press herself against Lizzie's legs.

"Gus . . . Gus isn't . . . quite the same," Lizzie said lamely.

"I can see that. Looks like he lost some weight. You sure look a lot better than you did on that interview a couple of weeks ago."

"Uh-huh. Gus and I are . . . we're eating and sleeping a lot better. Being home makes a big difference."

Nathan looked around. "Speaking of home, did you redecorate? It looks different. Everything looks *new.*"

Lizzie motioned for Alice to go ahead of her as she led the way into the kitchen. "I had no other choice. While I was away, someone broke in here and destroyed everything." Lizzie saw the reporter's invisible antenna go up. Aggie was right. He was a hottie all right. He looked like he knew it, too. Well, she knew how to handle guys who were full of themselves. *Damn, I'm supposed to be Aggie, and Aggie doesn't care about Nathan Hawk.* She waited for him to sit down before she said, "Coffee or soda pop?"

"Coffee. What were they looking for, Aggie?" Lizzie shrugged. She set the coffee mug in front of him and proceeded to unwrap the sandwiches from the Atlanta Bread Company.

Lizzie set the paper plate with Alice's food on the floor. Alice didn't touch it until Nathan looked away. "I thought you guys would be like white on rice looking for Tom's killers. Six months is a long time not to find cop killers. I expected more from you, Nathan. What happened to those bulldog tendencies of yours?"

Nathan looked across at Lizzie. His slate gray eyes were questioning. "Were you having an affair with Tom Madsen?"

He was sharp. "That's none of your business, Nathan, and don't ask me that again, or I'm going to ask for chapter and verse on all those women you have on the string. How *do* you juggle them?"

Nathan threw his head back and laughed. It was a nice sound. Manly. This was a man comfortable in his own skin. "Very carefully," was his response. Lizzie snorted, a very unladylike sound.

"Will Fargo was involved in an accident last night. He worked the property room. With some virus going around, half the force is out so the chief assigned me to his job."

"And this would be of interest to me . . . because?"

"I thought you were a reporter. Figure it out," Lizzie snapped.

Nathan looked at the kitchen door. "Are those *three* locks new? I noticed there were three on the front door, too."

"Gee, I guess you are a reporter after all. The answer is yes and no. Whoever broke in here had a key. No, Tom Madsen did not have a key. My keys were in my purse in my car in the impound lot. Look, you called me for a reason. What is it you want?"

"When did you acquire this brand-new attitude, Aggie? Not that it isn't becoming." He grinned at the look of surprise on Lizzie's face. "If it's a new you, I like it."

Lizzie looked across the table at the reporter. He was Brooks Brothers from head to toe, right down to the tasseled loafers. He wore his clothes like they were custom-made for his long, lean frame. It was his face, though, finely chiseled, and his alert dark eyes that drew her to him. She knew if she ever got involved with this man, he would be able to mesmerize her with his eyes. "When someone tried to kill me and my dog, that's when. If you have something to say, say it or get the hell out of my house."

"You're a spitfire, too. How come you'd never go out with me, Aggie?"

"Because I'm smarter than you, and you think you're God's gift to women. On top of that you're an obnoxious son of a bitch." Suddenly Lizzie's appetite was gone, and Alice wasn't liking the direction the conversation was taking. She growled, her front paws slapping at the tile on the floor.

"Whoa, Detective Jade. Back up there for a minute. We can argue smarts anytime you want. I think I can hold my own against you. You shouldn't believe all the rumors you hear. You really don't know anything about me other than rumors, and you know what they say about rumors. I do not have a different woman every day of the week. I've had one long-term relationship that hit the skids. I date on occasion. Dinner or a movie. I do not hop in the sack with every woman I take to dinner. It's not my fault women find me attractive. It gets wearying to have women chase you when you aren't interested. I was always interested in you, Aggie."

Lizzie sniffed, pleased with this piece of information. "That's more than I wanted or needed to know. If you aren't going to tell me the reason for this visit, you might as well leave. I have to get back to work."

Nathan looked down at Alice and frowned. "That dog used to like me. I think you were set up, Aggie. I think your partner knew what was going on. I've been working on this steadily but can't pin anything down. It's that damn blue wall you guys deny is out there."

Lizzie's heart took on an extra beat. She snorted. "I *know* we were set up. It didn't go down on schedule. We were just about ready to call it off. I don't remember which one of us said it first. I think it was Tom. He said it didn't *smell* right. I knew I was thinking it at the same time. Maybe I said it, but I really don't remember. Someone broke into the Madsens' house, did you know that?"

"Yeah. I even talked to them. Mrs. Madsen said the only things they took were her pearls and her husband's watch and a few dollars. Neighborhood theft, that kind of thing. It happens."

"Did Mrs. Madsen tell you they went through Tom's box of things, which was in her closet? Did she tell you she hid his personal notebook?"

"No."

"Well, she told me, and she also gave me the notebook. I kept a log myself. I'm going to work on it to match up the entries. Now who's the smart one?"

"So that's what they were looking for? Your work

notes. I more or less wondered about that. Most cops keep a notebook just like reporters do. Aggie, whatever you do, don't share that with anyone in your department. If you're not doing anything this evening, let's get together and work on it. How about dinner?"

"I can't leave Gus by himself after he's been alone all day. If you want to come over this evening and *bring* dinner with you, it's okay. By the way, the house is bugged, but I disabled them. And Will Fargo came by with a basket of flowers that I shoved in his face. Dutch Davis did a drive-by the day after I got home. They want me to think they're looking out for me. They expected me to die that night." She shook her head and stood up. "I have to leave now, or I'll be late. So, are you coming tonight or not?" She held her breath, hoping the response was yes. This guy could definitely grow on her.

"Sure. Chinese at seven okay with you? If we crack this, I get the exclusive, right?"

"Yeah. Seven is good, and Chinese is okay." She gave an inward sigh of relief.

Nathan stood up and shrugged into his raincoat. "You're different, Aggie. I can't quite put my finger on what it is, but I like the new you. I really do."

Aggie shrugged as her stomach tied itself into a knot. "A near-death experience will do that to a person. It's a given that I wouldn't come out of that the same as before it happened. Even Gus changed. You picked up on it yourself. Don't knock yourself out trying to figure it out." Damn, she'd wanted her response to be a little more flippant, a little more blasé. Instead it had come out as angry and defiant.

"No, it's something else. I just can't put my finger on it right now. I will, though. I think I'll go over to the hospital to check on Will Fargo. Take it easy, Aggie."

"Yeah, you, too. If you find out anything, call me."

It was a three-story gray fieldstone farmhouse weathered by years of sun and the elements. You could see it from the road even though the weeds were chest high. The late-afternoon sunshine shimmered on the diamond-shaped windows. A sign hung at the end of what was probably once the main driveway. Alex pointed to it. The lettering was faded from the elements but still decipherable. Spring Willow Farm.

They'd arrived late on Saturday and spent all day Sunday cleaning and dusting the house. They hadn't left the house until this morning to buy supplies.

"This is the middle of nowhere, Aggie. Your neighbors are miles away."

"I know. Lizzie and I came here once right after we inherited it. We wanted to see if we should keep it and pay the taxes or sell it. It's fifty acres. There's even farm equipment in the barn although I don't know if any of it works. We decided to keep it and split the taxes and the insurance bills. They grow a lot of corn and buckwheat around here. I have to get these seeds into the ground.

"I wonder how Lizzie is doing? You don't think anything will happen to her, do you, Alex? This is her first day on the job. I'm hoping she goes home for lunch and e-mails me."

"Your sister looked like a tough cookie to me. I think she can hold her own. If you're going to stew and fret, we might as well go back."

"I'm not going to stew and fret. She's my sister, I have a right to worry about her. She's never been shy about opening her mouth. I'm just worried she's going to say the wrong thing to the wrong person. Damn, I wish I knew where the chief is going to assign her. Lizzie doesn't like to take orders, she likes to *give* them."

Alex looked at the area they'd walked off, which was to be Aggie's truck garden. "Uh-huh. Okay, Detective Jade, let's get on with your new career and get these seeds into the ground."

Aggie beamed her pleasure. "It's nice out here, isn't it, Alex? The air is clean and fresh, the sky is blue. There's no smog. There aren't any cops, just a sheriff."

"I don't think I could live year-round in a place like this, Aggie. I need more life, more sound, more color."

She did, too, but she wasn't going to admit it. Short-term was just fine. She pointed to the Rototiller and tossed him a packet of seeds. She grinned, both her thumbs shooting in the air.

Aggie Jade was on a roll.

Chapter Five

*L*izzie's afternoon was just as boring as her morning until ten minutes before she was to go off duty. She knew who the big detective was the minute he entered the impound room. The pictures Aggie had showed her of the lumbering Dutch Davis didn't do him justice.

When she was a child, her mother had told both her and Aggie there was no such thing as an ugly person. She had lied.

Dutch Davis was one of the ugliest people she'd ever laid eyes on, and she had laid eyes on many such people while living in Las Vegas. His stature alone was cause for alarm. He had to be at least six-foot-five. And he wasn't just fat, he was spongy fat. It was almost impossible to see his mean little eyes in the folds and creases that lined his moonlike face. His nose was broad and flat as if it had been broken one too many times and never healed properly. Lips that were big and rubbery revealed teeth that were pitted and cinnamon-colored. If that wasn't bad enough, half of his left ear was missing. He looked and sounded like a thumping barrel as he trundled down the hallway. The floor quivered under his weight. Lizzie felt a shudder ripple up from her toes.

She schooled her voice to neutrality. "Detective Davis, nice to see you again. How's it going?"

"It's going. How'd you manage to wrangle this cushy deal?" A beefy arm waved to indicate the evidence room.

"Dumb luck, I guess. I heard Will Fargo had an accident last night. Then the chief said half the staff is out with some kind of intestinal bug. I think I'm just filling in until they can find a replacement for Will. I understand he was hurt badly. Have you heard anything?"

Dutch slapped a plastic bag with a knife inside under the grill. His voice when he spoke was a rich-sounding baritone, a direct contrast to his ominous appearance. "I need to log this in, Jade. I heard the same thing about Will but don't know anything else. So, you're the keeper of the keys." He pointed to the vault that took up half the room. It was where the department held confiscated drugs and money.

"During the day I am. I was just going off duty. Sign the form, Dutch, and I'll log in the evidence."

"I thought you'd take the whole ninety days, Jade. Are you some kind of weirdo? Who gives up ninety days with pay to return to work?"

Lizzie looked up from the form she was eye-balling. "People like me, who can't accept the department's investigation into Tom Madsen's murder. It was such a high-profile case. You guys let it get cold. I need someone to explain that to me."

Dutch's mean little eyes got meaner. "Are you saying what I think you're saying, Jade?"

Lizzie fixed her gaze on him. Fifty more pounds and he could have been a sumo wrestler. He was sweating. "Yes."

"You could make some serious enemies saying things like that, Detective Jade. We all busted our asses trying to find out what happened that night. We're still busting our asses on department time and on our own time. Do you think you can do better?"

Lizzie heard her replacement walking down the hall. She felt dizzy with relief when she unlocked the door, turned the keys over to Jim Windsor, and started to exit what everyone called the Fort Knox Cage.

She knew right away that Dutch Davis wasn't going to move out of her way. She moved to the right, he moved to the right. She sidestepped to the left, he moved left. Dutch Davis was one of those cops who didn't believe women had the right to be cops, and all the sensitivity classes in the world weren't going to change his thinking. He was a Neanderthal in more ways than one. Intimidation wasn't something Lizzie subscribed to. "Do you mind moving, Detective Davis? I'm in a bit of a hurry."

He mimicked her, an ugly look on his face. Lizzie sighed. "We can do it the easy way or the hard way, Detective Davis. Which is it?"

"Oooh, oooh, let's do it the hard way, Detective Jade," Davis mocked her.

"This is the last time I'm going to tell you, either you move that fat ass of yours, Davis, or I'll have to move it for you," Lizzie said sweetly. She could feel her heart thumping way too fast inside her chest. Way too fast.

He laughed, an ugly sound that matched the ugly look on his face. The laugh went with his appearance unlike his voice. "You and what army?" Out of the corner of her eye Aggie could see Jim Windsor's hand go to the telephone.

Her voice was still sweet when she said, "Me and no army." He laughed again, the same ugly sound. That meant he wasn't going to move. In the blink of an eye, Lizzie's feet left the ground as she literally pirouetted in midair before her leg slammed straight out into Davis's midsection. Her clenched fists came down on his shoulder with such force, his lunch spewed across the floor. Lizzie stepped over and past the mess. She turned to look at Jim Windsor, whose mouth was hanging open in stunned surprise. She shrugged for his benefit, saying in the same sweet voice, "You heard me asking him to move." She leaned down, grabbed a hank of Dutch's hair, and jerked his head backward. "Get it through your head, I'm the last person you want to go toe to toe with, Dutch."

She dusted her hands dramatically. *And, I'm not even a cop.* Lizzie could feel her heart beating a mile a minute as she signed out and headed for the front door, where she plowed into Nathan Hawk. She mumbled something but kept on going, rain sluicing all around her. She was drenched by the time she got

to her car. She had to get out of there *now*. Decking
Dutch Davis was probably a really stupid mistake.

Nathan opened the passenger-side door on the
run and literally fell into the car as Lizzie pulled
away, her tires screeching on the wet asphalt, one of
his legs dangling outside until Lizzie slowed the car.

"Did somebody steal your hair spray?" he gasped
as he righted himself, buckled the seat belt, and
straightened out his legs.

"Worse than that. I decked Dutch Davis in the evidence room."

Hawk stared at Lizzie in disbelief. "As in he hit
the floor? I know that guy, he must weigh around
three hundred pounds. Jesus."

"He's all blubbery fat, but yeah, as in he hit the
floor. Then I chopped at his shoulder. I might have
broken it. I heard a funny kind of noise, but then it
could have just been him puking all over the floor."

"Remind me never to make you mad. By the way,
where *are* we going?"

Lizzie kept her gaze on the rain-slicked highway.
"I'm going home. You hopped in my car, so I guess
that means you're going home with me. I thought
you were bringing dinner later this evening. Don't
tell me you're one of those guys who arrives early
and stays all night."

"Only when I'm invited. I'm talking about the all-
night part. But to answer your question, my nose
told me there was a story to your bolting out of the
station. I am bringing dinner, but that's later. This is a
good way for us to spend some *quality* time together.
You know, Aggie, I might be able to help you. I've

been on this case since it went down. If we pool our talents, we might get a bead on what happened. Just give me some kind of warning if I'm pissing you off, okay? You sure are different these days. You were never lean and mean like this before. It takes a little getting used to."

Lizzie frowned. Obviously, she was acting in a manner that was raising red flags. Aggie would have a fit if she ever found out. She made a mental note to tone down her rash behavior. "I'd never almost been killed before. My dog was almost killed. My partner *was* killed. I think that might explain any behavioral change you're noticing. Wouldn't you agree?"

"Well, yeah, but it's more than that. It's not like we spent a lot of time together where I could study you. Madsen was always around. You used to smile a lot. I always thought you had a nice smile. I kind of thought that in private life you might be one of those warm, fuzzy people you hear about. I particularly liked that little crooked tooth of yours."

Oh shit. "Some of my teeth got chipped and they capped them while I was in rehab. I think it happened when I hit the concrete. I really don't remember anything other than having a sore tongue from where the broken teeth kept rubbing. Imagine you noticing something like that." *Liar, liar, pants on fire.*

"I'm a reporter, I'm paid to notice stuff like that. It was a little personal, too. I wanted to ask you out a couple of times, but you were involved with Madsen."

Lizzie took her eyes off the road for a split second. "I never knew that, Nathan."

The reporter looked embarrassed. "I didn't exactly shout it from the treetops, Aggie. I did make discreet inquiries, but everyone said you were involved. Would you have gone out with me?"

"Yeah. Tom and I broke up three months before . . . you know, before . . . We were on iffy ground for six months prior to that. I had put in for a transfer because our relationship was starting to throw off my timing where our partnership was concerned. I'm not sure if he knew about the transfer or not. When the transfer came through, and the chief assured me it would, I was just going to say good-bye and move on. It's weird. Sometimes when I allow myself to think about it, I think he knew, and other times, I'm not sure. Can we talk about something else?"

"Well sure," Nathan said affably. "How do you like this lovely spring weather?"

Lizzie risked a quick glance sideways just in time to see a wry grin on the reporter's face. Tongue-in-cheek, she said, "I'm loving it. We need the rain. It's supposed to get cold tonight. Cold enough to make a fire. I love a good fire."

"With popcorn?"

Lizzie tapped her horn lightly at a Saturn that appeared to be stalled. The driver rolled down his window and motioned her to move around his vehicle. She did. "I like popcorn. I don't think I have any, though."

"I like the fluffies. The ones that pop first. Lots of butter and salt. Great roughage."

Lizzie laughed. "Me, too. Guess I won't have to water all the new plants for a few days," she said as she swerved into her driveway. Aggie had told her Nathan lived in a condo. "How do you like condo living? I would have taken you for a backyard barbecue man."

"I'm strictly a takeout man. I can make coffee and boil an egg or maybe make some toast, but that's about it. I don't starve."

Minutes later, Lizzie stretched her neck to look in the backseat. "I forgot and left my umbrella back at the station. We have to run for it. I can put your clothes in the dryer," she said, swerving into her driveway on two wheels.

Nathan clutched the strap overhead, his breath exploding out of his mouth before he stepped out of the car. *Cops*, with their defensive-driving techniques.

Lizzie stifled her laughter. She was sure that when he left his house earlier in the day he'd looked all creased and polished. Now he looked mussed and wrinkled in his khakis and a pale blue button-down shirt.

"It's a warm rain. Did you ever take a walk in a spring rain, Aggie?"

To Lizzie's ears it sounded like the most important question in the world. He appeared to be waiting for her response. She wasn't sure if he was holding his breath or not. "I guess I did when I was a kid, but what comes to mind more than anything was stomping in puddles. As an adult, no, I can't remember ever taking a walk in the rain. Isn't that something lovers do?" She looked up at him, a wicked gleam in her eye. "Was that a trick question, or was that your way of asking me to go for a walk in the rain?"

"I saw some really great puddles farther down the road. Wanna give it a shot?"

"Well, sure, Nathan but let me get . . .Gus first. Were they *big* puddles?" she called over her shoulder."

"Oh yeah."

"Then I'm your girl." Lizzie unlocked the front door and whistled for Alice, who came on the run. She kicked off her shoes and hung her jacket on the doorknob. Alice bounded ahead of her and down the steps, where she skidded to a stop in front of Nathan. She growled deep in her throat.

Nathan backed up a few steps. "What's with that dog, Aggie? He used to like me."

"He's just . . . *schizy* these days. They called him a loose cannon at the station. He has a right to be suspicious of everyone these days. You said something about some *big* puddles."

Nathan reached for her hand. "This is what you have to do. We run really fast so we kind of plop into the puddle and the water shoots up in every direction. You got it?"

Lizzie wondered how she looked with her head soaked and her clothes plastered to her body. Nathan looked *good.* Messy but *good.* "Hey, I was a master jumper in my kid days. Okay, I'm ready!"

Off they went, skimming down the street to a huge puddle at the curb. Lizzie hit it first, the dirty water rocketing upward to soak Nathan's pale blue shirt. Nathan made a bigger splash because he was wearing loafers. Lizzie laughed with glee. So did Nathan. They spun around, stomped the water until the puddle was just a trickle of water.

Alice barked. They ignored her until the barking became more frenzied. Over and above the sound of the pouring rain Lizzie could hear the sound of a car accelerating. It didn't sound right to her ears, and unless she was wrong, it was bearing down on them at an ungodly rate of speed for a quiet neighborhood street. When she looked over her shoulder, horror spread across her face.

"Hit the deck!" she screamed. She knew that Nathan was alongside her as she made a flying dive for a patch of grass at the end of the sidewalk. Nathan was half on top of her, the other half of him on the grass. He was so close she could smell his minty breath. She raised her head to see if the car would make a second run at them. All she could see were two dots of red from the taillights as it careened down the street in the pouring rain.

Alice trembled as she pressed her snout into Lizzie's neck to make sure she was all right.

"That bastard jumped the curb, and don't try telling me he skidded either," Nathan bellowed, the words literally exploding from his mouth.

"Why would I tell you something stupid like that?" Lizzie gasped.

"Did you get a license number?"

"No. It happened too quick, a dark car, older model. That's all I saw."

"They're trying to kill you, aren't they?"

"Yeah. Yeah, they are. Come on, let's go home. Thank God for . . . Gus. If he hadn't barked, that bastard would have run us over."

Lying on the ground, Nathan had a clear view of

Alice's underbelly. "I thought Gus was a boy dog."

Oh shit! "Nope. Gus is short for Augusta. It's that macho guy thing. None of the handlers wanted a female. Not manly, that kind of thing. We told everyone her name was Gustav. Hey, it worked. You're the only outsider who knows, so don't go blabbing, okay?" *Liar, liar, pants on fire.*

"Yeah, sure. I've always heard females are more protective."

"You heard right. Are you okay, Nathan?"

"A little bruised, but I'll be fine. How about you? That looked like a pretty hard dive you took. Aren't your bones still kind of fragile?" He looked worried.

She was limping as she walked along. "I landed mostly on the grass. Skinned knees and elbows, that's about it. Gus is okay, too. I think it's safe to say we both owe this dog our lives."

Nathan nodded. "I'll buy him a big T-bone. It looked like a Honda to me. Do you have a mental image of it? You're more trained for that than I."

Lizzie looked up at him, an expression of weariness on her face. She shook her head. "It was raining too hard. Just a dark-colored car that looked a little old. It could have been a Honda. There are probably a million Hondas in Atlanta, half of them dark in color. Perfect family car, good mileage, low to nonexistent maintenance, dependable. Half the force has one. Home never looked so good," she muttered as she limped her way up the steps to the front porch.

On the porch, she turned around to look at the reporter. "Nathan, you're pretty muddy. If you want, you can take my car to go home for clean clothes.

You can pick up dinner on your way back. I'll drive you to the station later to pick up your car."

"Good idea."

Lizzie tossed him the keys.

Inside Aggie's cozy house, Lizzie slumped against the front door and started to shake. She would have dropped to the floor and cried her misery if Alice hadn't started to shake with cold. She quickly righted herself and ran to the laundry room, where she found a towel and tossed it in the microwave oven to warm it up. She wrapped the big dog in the towel the moment the buzzer sounded. She swore later that Alice sighed with relief. "Down, baby," she said softly. When the shepherd obeyed her and dropped to the throw rug in front of the dryer, she covered her with more towels. Satisfied that her companion was now all right, she stripped off her own clothes. She would have to toss out Aggie's gray suit and buy her another one. "Stay, Alice. I'm going to shower. I'll be right back."

Fifteen minutes later, Lizzie was back downstairs, dressed in a yellow sweat suit and fuzzy, purple slippers. *Where does Aggie get these clothes?* She blinked in surprise when she felt a rush of warm air on her feet. The heat had kicked on. That had to mean the temperature outside was dropping. "Crazy springtime," she muttered to the dog, who was wiggling to get near the vent. Aggie had predicted that she would fall in love with the dog. She shuddered. God, what if she turned into a clone of Aggie and got all domestic. She crossed her fingers that she wouldn't get a desire to plant organic carrots.

Aggie looked at the laptop on the kitchen table. Should she e-mail Aggie and tell her about Dutch, Nathan Hawk, and the attempt on her life? Of course she should. Would Aggie then forget about her organic carrots and return home? Better not to tell her just yet. She moved the laptop to the kitchen counter so that it was out of her line of sight.

Lizzie could feel her stomach muscles start to cramp up. "I'm not scared. I really am not scared," she muttered as she prepared a pot of coffee. *Bull-SHIT!* Her hands were shaking so badly, she spilled coffee grounds all over the counter. Spilling coffee grounds was like cleaning up a broken egg from the floor. It took forever. She decided to ignore the mess, opting to sit down on her hands.

She thought about her colorful life and what she hoped to do in the future. It could all come to an end if she wasn't careful. *Think Plan B.* She almost jumped out of her skin when the phone rang. Should she answer it? She was supposed to be a cop, so she had to answer it. She barked a greeting.

"You ain't gonna be so lucky next time, dee-tech-tive!" Lizzie slammed the phone back into place. Her gaze went to the dripping coffeepot, to the spilled coffee grounds on the counter and the floor, to the three dead bolts, and then to the cookie jar in the shape of a big green frog with red-painted lips that sat on the counter. Aggie loved frogs. At one time, before the ransacking, there had been at least fifty frogs scattered about. The cookie jar was the only one that remained. *Don't think about the phone call*, she told herself. *Go about your business. They're trying to scare you. They're succeeding*. She moaned.

The phone rang again just as Lizzie finished sweeping up the coffee grounds and wiping down the counter. She ran into the living room for the whistle on the coffee table. She stuck it in her mouth, prepared to blow as hard as she could when she heard her friend Noreen's voice. She deflated like a bellows. "Hi," she said, mustering all the cheeriness she could into her voice.

"The airline just called, Lizzie, and canceled our flight tomorrow afternoon. They're putting us on a flight that leaves at the crack of dawn. I hired a car service, so there's no need for you to pick us up. We should be on your doorstep around three or three-thirty tomorrow. We're counting the hours. Girl time!"

"I can't wait either, Noreen. Okay, I'll see you all tomorrow. Hey, guess what. I got a dog!"

"No kidding. Now I'm really excited. I love dogs! Do you want us to bring you anything like Cisco candies or something else? You said you don't get to shop much and I know how you love candy, especially Cisco."

"Nope. Just yourselves. I'll see you tomorrow." Wonder of wonders, her hands weren't shaking anymore.

She felt more like Lizzie Jade when she returned to the kitchen, the whistle secure around her neck. She peeked in at Alice, who was sleeping soundly by the vent, the warm air ruffling the fur on her neck. The

smile stayed with her when she returned to the
kitchen to pour her coffee. Now she could sit and appreciate Aggie's cozy kitchen. Her mind wandered to
Nathan Hawk. What would it be like to sit across
from him eating dinner? He said he had a *thing* for
Aggie. Aggie and *her* background was one thing.
How would he react to *her* own background if he ever
found out she wasn't Aggie? She was two for three as
it was—a gambler in her own right, and she was impersonating a police officer. *Plan B.* All she had to do
was remember that she had Plan B in place.

Lizzie leaned back in the oak chair and propped
her feet on the opposite one. She stared at the fuzzy,
purple slippers, wondering if there was any special
significance to them other than warmth. She herself
liked bright colors. She loved anything that sparkled
and shimmered. Aggie, on the other hand, was conservative in her dress, leaning toward gray, beige,
and black. It must be a cop thing. The yellow sweats
and purple slippers were personal at-home attire.
She'd seen her sister's party-slash-date ensembles,
which consisted mainly of the little basic black dress
that could be jazzed up with a sparkling pin or a
string of pearls, even a brilliant-colored sash. Aggie
was hardly a trendsetter. Aggie would never wear
slingbacks, preferring pumps. Lizzie shook her head
at such a conservative mode of dress.

How attached was Aggie to this little house? She
wished suddenly that she knew more about her sister's life in Atlanta. In the last few years their relationship had been reduced to a few phone calls on
the run every few months. They did try to get to-

gether over the holidays, but it didn't always work. She regretted that now.

That didn't mean she had to live with those regrets. Everything was fixable if you worked at it hard enough. Maybe it was a twin thing that other people didn't understand. Whatever it was, a thought, a sentence, a feeling, one or the other could finish it off. How many times had she called Aggie only to have her sister say, I was just about to call you. On more than one occasion when she hadn't been able to sleep, she'd call Aggie to find her sister wide-awake, too. They would talk about whatever was troubling them, sometimes for hours. And, she always felt better when she hung up. Aggie said she felt the same way.

When they were younger they would always creep into one another's beds after their mother kissed them good night and closed the door. The best part, though, was the sharing. They shared their joys, their sorrows, their highs, and their lows. Always there for one another.

Lizzie struggled to take a full, deep breath. How could she not have known about Aggie's accident? How? Was she so wrapped up in her own crazy life that she'd excluded her sister? No. Yes. Well, that wasn't going to happen ever again. When this was all over, she was going to make sure she got even closer, physically and emotionally, to her twin. When this was over. She felt herself wince at the words.

Lizzie looked around. In her heart of hearts, Aggie was a homebody. It was a shame that she didn't have a nine-to-five job so she could cook, clean, and bake the way she liked to do. Aggie should have a husband and a houseful of kids. Obviously, she had given a lot of thought to the kitchen. To Lizzie's mind, it shrieked Aggie's name. The cabinets were a light-colored knotty pine and matched the wood floor almost perfectly. There were no scratches or black heel marks, so that meant Aggie, on her time off, took care of the floor. She probably spent a lot of time out here at her little built-in desk next to the refrigerator.

She clearly remembered the day Aggie had called and was so elated that she had been able to find tartan-colored curtains, seat cushions, and place mats that matched, saying she had an umbrella and gym bag that were of the same pattern. She'd said, "This is just what my little kitchen needs." She was right. Lizzie wondered how long it had taken her to find them. Probably a long time because Aggie wasn't the type to settle for second best.

Lizzie was pouring her second cup of coffee when the phone rang again. She positioned the whistle and said, hello.

"How you doing, sweet cheeks?"

Lizzie winced. She could identify Anthony Popadopolus's voice in a crowded room of a thousand people. To her, his voice sounded like it was a mixture of gravel and molasses. "I'm the same as I was the last time we talked. I still can't leave here, Anthony. My sister needs me. You have a date for me? Well, yes, I did say at least two weeks, maybe longer. You don't have to remind me about our contract. I would be remiss if I didn't tell you there might be a bug on this phone. My sister's a cop. I think we talked about that. I'll call you later on a cell phone. No, Anthony, I'm not trying to put you off. I'm erring on the side of caution. Well, it's raining here right now. The temperature dropped, too. We might make a fire tonight and either toast some marshmallows or make popcorn. Corny? Sometimes, Anthony, you need to do things like that to get your perspective back. Yes, of course I'll call you."

Lizzie hung up the phone. Damn, now her hands were shaking again. She was sitting on her hands, her coffee growing cold. She looked up when a shadow passed the kitchen window. She sucked in her breath and didn't exhale until she heard Nathan Hawk call her name. Alice was at the door before she could get there. This time she didn't growl, but her tail dropped between her legs, which meant, *beware of me.*

His arms loaded with Chinese takeout, Nathan looked down at Alice, and said, "What a good dog you are." Alice cocked her head to the side, sniffed, and went back to her cocoon in front of the heating vent. "Maybe she's warming up to me. Listen, I forgot to ask you what you wanted, so I pretty much got some of everything. The worst-case scenario is you'll be eating it for a week, in which case you can invite me over and I'll help you eat it. I love leftover Chinese."

Lizzie laughed. *He's flirting with me.* She realized it was a pleasant experience. He looked even better than he did before. He'd changed into creased jeans and a navy blue Nike tee shirt with a matching navy windbreaker.

"Oh, you brought popcorn, marshmallows, and beer. Guess we're going to do that fire after all. Did it get colder?"

"It's a lot colder. I had the radio on on the way over. They said it was going to go down to around forty-eight this evening. To me, that's cold."

"That's cold to me, too. Do you want to eat in the living room? I have some stack tables. I can set us up if you make the fire."

Nathan looked around. "You look like an Easter egg. Where's the wood?"

She looked down at the yellow and purple she was wearing and supposed it was a compliment. "Thank you. You look particularly dashing. There're some birch logs in the woodbox on the back porch. You should bring in a stack. By the way, I had a threatening phone call while you were gone. Unfortunately, the whistle was in the other room, and I couldn't get to it in time."

Nathan stopped in his tracks. "What did they say?"

"They said I wouldn't be so lucky next time. The voice called me, *dee-tech-tive*. Do you know anything about surveillance bugs?"

"A little. Why? I thought you'd disabled the bugs?"

Lizzie nodded. "I put cellophane around them. There's one in my car, too."

"Shouldn't you tell the cops? Your chief? Someone?"

"I'm a cop, remember. I just told someone, you. You aren't going dumb on me, are you, Hawk? Who do you think put those bugs here and in my car? Who do you think ransacked my house?"

"Cops!"

Lizzie clenched her teeth so hard she thought her jaw was going to crack in two. "Who else?"

Nathan opened the back door and went out to the porch. The minute he stepped back inside, Lizzie hit the three dead bolts. She trailed behind him into the living room, Alice on her heels.

"Who's that tall guy you hang out with?"

Lizzie didn't pretend not to understand the question. "Do you mean Dr. Alex Rossiter? He's a friend. We aren't involved if that's what you're asking. Are you seeing anyone special?" She wanted the question to sound crafty, but it just came out as inquisitive. A tit-for-tat kind of thing.

"Surprise! Surprise! I'm not seeing anyone, and I'm not involved with anyone. That means you and I could . . . if we wanted . . . as in . . ."

"Date? I don't see why not. First you have to ask me for a date. I think that's the way it's done." Lizzie started to giggle. *God, when was the last time I giggled? Never, that's when*, she answered herself.

Ten minutes later, Nathan dusted off his hands and took a step backward to better observe his handiwork. "Okay. Now, that's what I call a blaze. I used to be an Eagle Scout," he said proudly.

"Fancy that. I used to be a Girl Scout," Lizzie lied. She motioned to the corner. "You sit on the recliner. This big chair is for me and Gus. He'll never let you sit next to me."

"That might develop into a problem later on if we hit it off."

"You sound like you have some doubts." Lizzie sniffed.

Nathan looked pointedly at the nine millimeter Glock sitting on the table next to Lizzie's chair. "I never dated anyone who packed heat. I'm thinking it could get awkward. Like what if the damn thing went off and shot off my . . . well, what if it went off unexpectedly." His face was red, and he was dithering. The thought pleased Lizzie.

She grinned. "It has a safety. It's only going to go off if I want it to go off. Next to Gus, that piece of hardware is my best friend."

"Uh-huh."

They ate in silence for a few minutes. Lizzie broke the quiet spell when she asked, "Have you ever been to Las Vegas?"

"Once, and once was enough. They don't have clocks in Vegas. I need clocks. No one sleeps in Vegas. They go twenty-four/seven. I need to sleep. The truth is, I work too damn hard for my money to piss it away on a craps table or slot machine. I lost a hundred dollars the time I was there. Gambling is such a waste of time and energy. Have you been?"

"Oh, yes, many times. I like the excitement, the shows, and meeting new people. I always win. I'm partial to poker. My friends call me the double-down queen when I play blackjack. As a matter of fact, several friends of mine are coming to visit tomorrow. They live year-round in Vegas. They're showgirls.

There's another advantage to living in Vegas, and that's no state income tax."

"No kidding."

Lizzie looked at him over the top of her bottle of Beck's. "No kidding."

"Vegas really is an exciting city," Lizzie continued. She wondered why her voice sounded so defensive. Nathan looked like he was wondering the same thing.

"How long are your friends staying, Aggie?"

"I'm not sure. Until they get sick of me, I guess, or until they get bored with the quiet life here in Atlanta. They're used to being up all night and sleeping during the day. They'll have to readjust to normal living, so that's going to take a few days. Do you know any eligible bachelors?"

"A few."

"That's nice. Maybe we can have a party or a barbecue."

"Let's talk about *it*, Aggie."

Lizzie watched as Nathan closed his cartons, gathered up his napkins and empty beer bottle.

"Nathan, that might not be a good idea. You could get hurt. Look what happened today. If you hang out with me, they'll go after you. I know you're a big boy, and you can look out for yourself, but you don't know the mind-set of the men we're dealing with here."

"Tell me about it. Two heads are better than one. You want to talk with the bugs in place? I'm sure the cellophane is working, but you can never be a hundred percent sure of anything in this life."

"Why not? They know I'm on to them. All I have are my own suspicions and Tom's suspicions. I'm not clear in my own head how Tom was involved with all of this. My gut is telling me he wasn't dirty, but my gut is also telling me he knew what was going on and kept quiet. That's the part I'm having trouble with."

"Have you given any thought to going to the chief? You've got me on your side now. When a big newspaper takes on something like this, everyone sits up and takes notice. Now, let's sit here and talk and make a plan." The words were no sooner out of his mouth than Nathan's beeper went off. He checked the number, pulled out his cell phone to make a call.

"Sorry, Aggie, I gotta run. There's been an accident on the interstate with a chemical spill. Duty calls. I have to use your car again. I'll drop it off later." He blew her an airy kiss before he galloped out of the room, Alice nipping at his heels.

Chapter Six

The scent of fresh-brewed coffee permeated police headquarters as Dutch Davis stomped his way to the chief's office. He knew eyes were boring into his back and that the other detectives were mumbling and muttering among themselves. As far as he was concerned, those doing the muttering and mumbling were a bunch of *wusses*.

He felt clumsy and awkward as he lumbered along. His arm in a blue canvas sling made walking a chore, as he was used to swinging his big arms for balance.

Dutch drew in a deep breath before he opened the door to the chief's office. He tried to look affable when he offered up a salute of sorts.

"Close the door, Davis, and park it," Chief Shay barked. The detective inched himself onto the straight-backed chair. He looked at the chief expectantly. If the chief wanted to, he could kick his ass all the way to the Mason-Dixon line. To Dutch, it looked like he was contemplating the move.

"You want to explain that," the chief said, pointing to the soft blue sling on Dutch's arm.

Dutch hadn't expected such a cold hard voice. He struggled to remain affable. "Shoulda zigged when I shoulda zagged. No big deal, Chief."

"That's not the way I heard it, Davis. I will not tolerate any brawling among my officers, especially with my female officers. This is the second time we're having a discussion on brawling. You're going on report, and if it happens again, we won't be talking. Are we clear, Detective Davis?"

"Understood, Chief."

"Good. Now take your sorry ass over to the motor pool and catch up on the paperwork. You don't go back on the street till I make a determination. Physicals are one month from today. You might want to think about eating a lot of lettuce and maybe some carrots until then."

"Yes, sir." Dutch had to grasp the desk to bring himself to his feet. He swiveled and almost fell. His mean little eyes got meaner as he stomped out of the office. He purposely refused to make eye contact with any of the detectives on the floor. It wasn't hard because he was not a popular member of the force.

Dutch was outside, on his way to the motor pool, when Joe Sonders whistled to get his attention. "Hey, Dutch, hold on a minute. Where are you going?" he asked, leading the big detective to the side and out of earshot of other officers who were coming and going. "What did the chief say?"

"He said I should catch up on paperwork at the motor pool. Like I can write. I'll be there till hell freezes over pecking away with two fingers on my left hand," Dutch said, hatred ringing in his voice. "That bitch has to pay for this. A fracture is a fracture, hairline or not. She pays. You hear me, Joe, she pays!"

"Keep it up and everyone else within a five-mile radius will hear you. What you need to do right now is lie low and keep quiet. I just checked at the hospital, and old Will isn't doing so good this morning. A brother from somewhere showed up and wants to pull the plug. They're waiting for another brother from somewhere else before they make a decision. Looks to me like we're going to have to go to a funeral."

"That's what happens when you hit a truck head-on. Here today, gone tomorrow. We need to call a meeting. I can just see that bitch doing an inventory. Will was getting a little too nervous to suit me. I'm beginning to wonder if half the crap old Will was feeding us about the chief being suspicious was true. I think he just wanted to call it quits."

Joe Sonders pulled his sunglasses out of his pocket. He held them up to the light to see if he needed to polish them. Satisfied that they were clean enough, he put them on. He lowered his voice to a hiss. "I think she found the bugs. She went to visit Tom's parents. She's on to us. I told you not to trust Madsen. First he was in, then he was out, then he couldn't make up his damn mind. He knew. Guys tend to share crap like that when they get all gooey at sleepy-time. She knows, Dutch."

"Yeah, well knowing and proving it are two different things. The dog is her Achilles' heel. The professor looks *nerdy* enough to scare. Work on him."

"The professor is gone. School's out. We checked him out last night. He's probably in some third-world country teaching savages how to read and write. That's what guys like him do in the summer. He's a dead issue, Dutch."

Dutch looked at his partner. He was lean and fit, with not an ounce of fat on him. He ran ten miles every morning, lifted weights, and was a vegetarian. His six-foot, 180-pound frame always looked good in his custom suits. He had a different one for every day of the week. His wife got 30 percent off at Nordstrom, where she worked. He had good skin and healthy-looking hair. He looked like a cop's cop. No one on the force liked him either. Jealousy, Dutch decided.

"Then go after Hawk."

"The guy's a reporter, Dutch! Listen, I have to go. I'm partnering with Alan Brady until you're back in harness."

Dutch laughed. "That guy will shoot himself in the foot yet. Have a nice day."

Lizzie made her way down the quiet hall to the nurses' station. She hadn't meant to go to the hospital, but there she was. She waited patiently until the nurse looked up from the chart where she was making entries. Lizzie flashed her sister's badge. "Detective Jade."

The nurse shook her head. "Mr. Fargo's brother is in with him now. You can't question him."

"That's okay. I just wanted . . . to . . . to see him."

"Let me talk to the brother, Detective."

Why was she there? She didn't know.

Minutes later, a short, squat man walked toward her. He held out his hand. "I'm Will's brother, Daniel, Detective."

"I'm sorry about Will. I really didn't know him all that well. I just wanted to stop by and . . . and . . ."

Daniel nodded solemnly. "I understand. I'm waiting for Will's parish priest to arrive. I've been here all night," he said wearily. "There's nothing more that can be done for Will. During the night he tried to tell me something, but I don't know what it was he was trying to say. I don't know why I say this, but it seemed important to him. I don't understand police matters. I sell air-conditioning filters. There's nothing important in that. I could sense my brother's urgency. He knows he's dying. For all I know he was trying to tell me to pull the plug. I can't do that. I know my other brother won't be able to do that either."

"I really am sorry, Mr. Fargo. If . . . if Will rallies, tell him I stopped by." Lizzie handed him one of Aggie's cards.

Daniel Fargo stared at the card, his brow furrowed. "Agnes Jade, Agnes Jade, Agnes Jade," he said over and over. "I'm not sure, Detective, but I think that's what Will was trying to say. I can't be certain, but it sure did sound like your name. I know that only family members are allowed in ICU but at this point, I don't think it matters. Come with me. If Will wanted to see you, we'll know soon enough."

Lizzie followed Daniel to his brother's unit and

stepped inside. She felt faint at the whirring sounds coming from the machines keeping Will alive. He looked even more skeletal than he did in the pictures Aggie had given her. She looked around, memorizing the sight, the sound, the smell, so she could relay it to Aggie later.

"Say something to him, Detective. Get close to his ear and touch his arm. When I did that, he responded to me."

The fine hairs on the back of Lizzie's neck stood on end as she obeyed Daniel's instructions. Will's eyes slid open but couldn't focus. "It's me, Will, Aggie Jade." She leaned closer, hating the smell of death that swirled around the man in the hospital bed. The words were garbled at best, but she was able to make out her name. She turned her head to talk into his ear. "Was it Dutch? Did he set us up, Will? Did you help steal the drugs? I'm trying to understand what you're saying. Try harder, Will. Please. Try to make it right before . . . before . . . try, Will. Please."

He did try. Valiantly, but she was only able to understand the word *yes,* the other words too garbled to understand. Will's left arm flailed the air in his distress. Lizzie watched as he struggled to say the word again. As near as she could tell, it sounded like *cards* or *lard,* maybe even the word *hard.* The brother Daniel shook his head to show he didn't understand it either.

Seconds later, she heard the high-pitched sound and knew Will Fargo had flat-lined. She moved to the side, pulled Daniel toward her, then outside into the corridor, as nurses and doctors barreled into the room.

"I'm so sorry, Mr. Fargo."

Daniel Fargo nodded, his eyes on the door leading to his brother's room. "Did you understand what Will was saying? Was it helpful to you? Whatever it was he was trying to tell you must have been important to him."

Lizzie's mind raced. "Yes. It had to do with police business. I'll say a prayer for your brother. If there's anything I can do, call me."

"I'm glad you came, Detective. It was important to my brother for some reason. I hope he was able to help you. I wish we had been closer. Do you think people always think things like that at a time like this?" he fretted.

"Yes, Mr. Fargo, I do think most people think like that. Take care."

Lizzie rode down in the elevator. She breathed through her mouth, hoping to drive away the smell of death in her nostrils. She ran through the lobby and outside. Halfway to the parking lot she realized it was raining again. She ran faster, her head down. She felt the stiff arm, felt herself whirl around. Her hand was on the butt of her gun in the time it took her heart to beat twice.

"Whoa, there, Aggie. You need to look where you're going. What's your hurry?"

Lizzie raised her head. She hoped her expression didn't show what she was feeling at the sight of Joe Sonders. "It's raining, Joe." She opened the car door and slid in. Joe held the door until she turned on the engine and pressed the power window. When the window was all the way down, he closed the door.

"How's our fellow officer, Aggie?"

"He flat-lined while I was there. His brother is with him. I'm running late. I'll see you later." Joe had no other choice but to move his hands from the window when Lizzie pressed the button that would send the window sailing upward. She peeled out of the lot and didn't look back. *Don't think about Joe Sonders. Don't think about Will Fargo and the sounds you heard in his room. Breathe through your mouth. Make your mind blank. Blank.*

Forty minutes later, Lizzie was striding toward Chief of Detectives Erwin Shay's office. She was twelve and one half minutes late. She rapped on the door and cracked it open at the same time. She poked her head in, and said, "Do you have a minute, Chief?"

"Come on in. What's wrong, Jade?"

"Why do you think something's wrong, Chief?"

"Because you're white as this cup," he said, pointing to his coffee cup.

"Will Fargo died. I was there when . . . he . . . ah . . . there was this . . . noise and then the line went flat on the screen. I was wondering if I can take the afternoon off. I have to see the department shrink on my lunch hour. I have friends flying in this afternoon whom I haven't seen in some time. They want to make sure I'm all right."

The chief nodded. "I got the call about Will a few minutes ago. He's been with the department since he got out of the Academy. He wasn't what you would call a social kind of guy, but he had that evidence locker and the vault running smooth. And, he had a memory like a steel trap. It's not a problem, Detective, if you want to take a few days off to entertain your guests. Whatever that bug was that swept through here has been contained. We're a hundred percent today and for the rest of the week. You okay with the shrink thing?"

"No, I'm not okay with the shrink thing, but I know it's a necessary evil I have to put up with. I hate talking about my private life. I hate the way they pry and poke and turn you inside out." She tried to make her voice nonchalant when she said, "Who are you going to assign my shift to?"

"Jim Evers. He can read and write. He knows how to open a lock. Does it make a difference, Jade?"

She wanted to say yes, it makes a hell of a difference, but she didn't. As long as it wasn't Dutch Davis or one of his cronies, it would be all right. Although Aggie had said she shouldn't trust anyone, not even Chief Shay.

The chief sat down and folded his hands across his barrel chest. "Is there anything you want to talk to me about, Aggie? Anything at all?"

The use of her first name was to show he was on her side, boss as well as friend. Aggie said she liked Erwin Shay because he was fair and didn't put up with any bullshit. That didn't mean she would confide in him. At least not yet. Lizzie shrugged again as she met his gaze. He reminded her of a fat Buddha the way he was sitting and watching her.

"If there is, Chief, I won't be bashful about calling you. Okay, time to get to work. Thanks, Chief."

"Aggie?"

There it was again, that familiarity she was supposed to respond to. "Yes."

"Anytime you want to talk, you know, *really* talk, we can go *off site* and keep it just between us."

"Okay, Chief."

Lizzie looked at the gold lettering on the door. Dr. Sidney Blount. She expected to see the word *psychiatrist*, but it wasn't on the door. Maybe it made patients nervous. Aggie had warned her to be careful and only respond to questions with short answers. She'd gone on to say, Sid might be able to detect the switch in patients. *If it looks like you're getting in over your head, cop an attitude and leave.* With that thought in mind, Lizzie opened the door to a small waiting room that was so ugly she wanted to turn around and leave. Where were the reassuring colors, the fish tank, the new magazines, the comfortable furniture? The room was gunmetal gray from ceiling to floor. Even the four metal chairs with gray plastic seats were gray. The metal table had black legs and a gray top. There was nothing on the table.

Lizzie felt the urge to smash something.

She sat down and crossed her legs. A moment later she heard a voice say, "You can come in, Detective Jade."

Lizzie followed the voice.

He was round from top to bottom. Heavyset men and women tended to be pleasant and happy. Sometimes jolly. At least that's what she'd read in a magazine. Not this man. His eyes said he'd seen it all, heard it all, and don't try conning him. Lizzie nodded and sat down. She waited.

"How are you, Detective?"

"Fine. I went back to work yesterday."

"Do you think that was wise?"

"I'm not the type to sit around and twiddle my thumbs. It's springtime. Yes, it was wise."

"How are the nightmares? The anxiety? Are loud noises still bothering you?"

"I have it all under control."

"Do you still sleep with your gun under your pillow?"

"Absolutely."

"You never did that before. Do you see yourself giving up that security anytime soon?"

Aggie hated this guy. Lizzie decided she hated him, too. "No."

"Why is that?"

"Well, someone tried to kill me yesterday. Actually, he tried to kill me and Nathan Hawk. Hawk is a reporter with the *Journal-Constitution*. The car jumped the curb. If it wasn't for Gus, we'd both be dead. On top of that, I've been getting threatening phone calls."

"Did you report the incidents?"

Lizzie looked around the office. It was as barren as the outer room. It also had a temporary feel to it. Sidney Blount overflowed his gray chair on the sides. "To what end, Dr. Blount? It was an attempted hit-and-run. I can't prove the calls were made. I'll deal with it."

Lizzie looked at the bare walls. "Where are your

degrees, your certificates?" Her voice rang with suspicion.

"In my downtown office. You know I just work here one afternoon a week. Do you think I should carry them with me? You're the only one who has ever asked."

Lizzie felt like patting herself on the back.

"Whatever floats your boat, Doc," Lizzie responded flippantly.

"How are the dog and your social life?"

"That was a mouthful. Which one do you want me to answer first? I guess in the order of importance. Gus is doing well. As I mentioned, he saved my and Nathan's lives yesterday. If he hadn't barked, we wouldn't have dived for cover. He's settling in. My social life is about what it's always been. I have friends coming to visit this afternoon. I've struck up a nice or what appears to be a nice friendship with Nathan. It may develop into something, and it may not."

"What about Dr. Rossiter?"

"What about him?" Lizzie tossed back.

"You know the drill, Detective. I ask the questions, you answer them."

"Stupid me. I forgot. I guess he's fine. He's a friend. He's gone now. He's working on a gardening project I think. Like I said, he's a friend, nothing more."

"What are your feelings about Detective Madsen?"

"The same as they were the last time I was here. I hate it that he died. I hate it that some faceless, nameless person gunned him down and left him to die. I tried to help him, but I couldn't. I'm living with that. No, I do not feel guilty. I am sad, though. Every time I talk to you, you harp and drill me on Tom. Can't we let him rest in peace?"

"You have issues with Tom that you haven't resolved. That's why we can't leave it alone."

"I'm working on that," Lizzie snapped.

"Are you making any headway?"

"No. The answer is inside my head and in my notebook. Tom's mother gave me his notebook. I'm comparing the two to see if I can piece together the puzzle. By the way, Tom's parents' house was broken into. Mrs. Madsen had all of Tom's things in a box in her closet. They rifled through it. They stole her pearls and something else, but I can't remember what it was. She had taken out his notebook and hidden it. She gave it to me when I went to visit her."

"How did you feel when you visited her?"

"Sad. They lost their only son. They're nice people, and I like them."

"What if it turns out that Tom Madsen was a dirty cop?"

Lizzie shrugged. "I don't know. Are we finished?"

"Yes, I think we are. I'll see you in two weeks."

"No. I'll see you in a month. If I need you before then, I'll call you. Coming here is disruptive. I'm doing my best to get on with it. A month," she said firmly.

"All right, Detective, a month."

Lizzie turned to leave the ugly suite of rooms. She didn't bother with the elevator but ran down the steps and outside into the pouring rain.

• • •

Lizzie was sitting on the front porch sipping coffee, her feet propped up on the railing when Nathan Hawk pulled into the driveway. Alice stirred herself, sniffed the air, then dropped her head to let it rest between her paws. "Hi," he bellowed. "I took a chance you might be home. You waiting for your company?"

Not bothering to wait for a response, he leaped over the privet that ran along the driveway. "Will Fargo died this morning."

"I know. I was there. It was awful. I just made some coffee if you want a cup." He shook his head.

"Were you able to talk to him? Why'd you go there? Is it a cop thing?"

"Of course it's a cop thing. I'm a cop. Dutch Davis's partner accosted me in the parking lot. He was on his way to see Will. To answer your other question; it wasn't a question, was it? You said you took a chance I might be here. I had to see the department shrink, and I asked for the afternoon off. I've been sitting here thinking, and yes, I'm waiting for my company. The good news today is I don't have to go back to the shrink for a month.

"You must be here for a reason. What are you willing to contribute?"

"Not much. I spent the entire morning talking to every cop and detective I could corner. I wanted them to know I was no sleeping tiger where the case is concerned. In my own way I let them know if they wanted to slack off or sweep stuff under the rug, that wasn't my style. Most of them know me, and know I don't give up even when the trail is cold. The best I could hope for was that they would start buzzing among themselves. I had the feeling a couple of them—not Dutch or Joe, but the others—were spooked when word filtered down that Will Fargo died. It wasn't anything anyone said because no one said anything. It was more like they grew quiet or their facial features drew inward. Does that make sense? So, when are we going to share and pool our resources?" he asked bluntly.

Lizzie's mind raced. She would spend the entire night talking and drinking wine with the girls. They'd sleep till the better part of the afternoon. "How about breakfast tomorrow morning? I'll meet you at Becker's. Is seven-thirty good for you?"

"Yep. I run at six. Seven-thirty it is."

"Nathan, if I give you something, can I trust you with it? By that I mean you won't try to go off and run with it or try to use it for a byline. If you do, I'll kill you. This is completely off the record, okay."

"Off the record is okay. Of course you can trust me. What is it?"

"Wait here." Lizzie ran into the house and pulled her shoulder bag off the coatrack. She rummaged till she found Tom's notebook, which she had copied and mailed to Aggie, and Aggie's. She hoped she was doing the right thing by giving them to Nathan. Let him decipher Tom's squiggles and Aggie's own neat notes. Maybe he would come up with something she'd missed. She'd pored over the notebook for hours and hadn't come up with a thing.

Nathan stared at the two notebooks. "Are these the proverbial smoking guns?"

"Could be. Just remember that Will Fargo was in charge of the evidence locker and the vault. Today I asked him if Dutch set us up, and he said yes. He was dying, so I don't know if I heard him right. He did try to tell me something else, but I couldn't make out the word. It could have been the word *cards, lard,* or maybe even the word *hard.* It didn't make any sense to me, and his brother who was there didn't understand it either. It was awful. He really struggled to tell me and then . . . and then . . . he flat-lined. It was a terrible sound.

"I was running across the parking lot in the rain and plowed right into Joe Sonders, who was on his way up to see Will. That meeting wasn't very pleasant either. Figure all this out, and we'll talk at breakfast. By the way, I had a nice time last night. Thanks again for bringing dinner. You're good company, Nathan."

Nathan grinned as he jammed the notebooks into his pocket. "I guess that was a compliment, right?"

Lizzie laughed. "It was. Do you think it's ever going to stop raining?"

"On the news this morning, the weatherman said it's going to rain for three more days. I have a canoe, so don't worry."

"Gee, that makes me feel better."

"I know you're waiting for your company, so I'll leave and get on this right away. I'll see you in the morning."

Lizzie was half out of the wicker chair when Nathan leaned over and kissed her full on the mouth. She gave in to the moment and enjoyed every minute of the long kiss.

"You taste like strawberries," Nathan said, his eyes slightly glazed.

"It's the lipstick. You tasted like mint," Lizzie said, her eyes just as glazed.

Lizzie watched in amazement as Nathan leaped over the banister instead of using the steps. He landed with a cursing thump. Alice barked and raced down the steps.

"I was trying to impress you with my agility. I forgot about this bush. I think Gus is starting to like me again."

Lizzie stifled her laughter. "I'm impressed. Gus thinks you're hurt. He's an old softie. I'll see you in the morning, Nathan." She watched as he limped away to his car. The reporter knew how to kiss, that was for sure. She was still tingling.

They blew into the house like a whirlwind, the three of them laughing and giggling like young girls. The hugs, the kisses, the ooohs and aaahs over Aggie's house made Lizzie laugh with joy. Alice joined the fray, running from one to the other to get petted and scratched.

"Alice, this is Noreen Farrell, Candy Lyons, and Honey Buxton. All are famous dancers at the Mirage. Show them what a lady you are and shake hands." The girls dutifully shook the big dog's paw, loving every minute of the solemn byplay.

"As you can see, it's pretty miserable outside. I say we make a fire, order some pizza with the works, and crack open some wine. While I do the fire and the ordering, go on upstairs and shed those fancy duds. You gotta look like me," Lizzie said, pointing to the yellow sweats and purple slippers she'd donned after Nathan left.

"Girl, you are pitiful-looking. But comfortable," Candy said hastily.

"Wash off the makeup and let your face breathe. This is girl time. I have some secrets to share with you." Lizzie stared at her friends. Did they always look so . . . *garish?* In Vegas, with all the artificial lighting, they looked beautiful and stylish. Here in Aggie's little house they looked like high-priced hookers with their heavy makeup, spandex dresses, and spike-heeled shoes. Was she herself perceived the same way? She remembered the way Aggie had flinched when she saw her. It was obvious now that Vegas and Atlanta were at opposite ends of the fashion spectrum.

"Okay," the dancers chirped in unison as they made their way to the second floor and Aggie's guest rooms.

Lizzie sat for a moment after they left. They were her friends, and she adored them. They were kind and generous and would do anything for her. Even if it meant giving her their last dollar. They were show-girls, pure and simple. They all shared the same dream as most of the other showgirls: Find a high roller with money to burn and get married. So far it hadn't happened. More likely than not it would never happen. When their dancing legs and hips gave out, they'd end up taking some menial job to make ends meet if they hadn't managed to amass a nest egg. Nest eggs were something they talked about a lot, but with half their salaries going to fancy clothes and makeup by the pound, it wasn't easy to save for a rainy day. Pension funds and health insurance were something they could only dream about. At best, they had a few years to go before that happened. The thought saddened her.

Her shoulders slumped as she walked through the kitchen to the back porch. She carried in two huge armfuls of wood and dumped it by the fireplace. Within minutes she had a blaze going. Another trip to the kitchen for the wine and the glasses. Her last trip was to call the pizza parlor's number from the magnet on the refrigerator. She ordered two large pies with the works and one plain with extra cheese that would be delivered within the hour. She stuck money from her purse in her pocket to pay for the pies. She settled down on the floor on a pile of brand-new harem pillows. Did Aggie hang out on the floor with the pillows or were they just for show? There was so much about her sister she didn't know. Well, that was all going to change.

And then they were taking their places beside her on the floor, their faces scrubbed shiny and clean. They weren't beautiful, but they were pretty. Any one of them could have passed for Aggie's next-door neighbor. They were dressed now in slippers and lounging robes of varying colors. Their hair was either piled high on their heads or pulled back in ponytails.

Lizzie poured the wine, then held her glass aloft. "Let's drink to good friends." Glasses clinked, the girls smiled and gulped.

"Gather round, girls. I am going to share some secrets with you," Lizzie whispered as she laid her gun in the middle of the circle. "My name is Aggie, and I'm a cop! Now listen up."

Chapter Seven

⌐•

The women stared at Lizzie. As one, their gazes dropped to the deadly-looking gun in the middle of the floor.

"You're joking, right?" Noreen said uneasily.

"You're a professional gambler. You can't be a cop," Candy said.

"What do you mean your name is Aggie? Where'd you get a gun like that?" Honey demanded. "Do you have handcuffs, too?"

Lizzie's voice dropped to a bare whisper. "Listen to me. You all know I have a twin sister who's a cop. Her name is Aggie in case your forgot. I try not to talk about her too much. In my line of work bragging about a cop sister isn't something you do. Telling friends is okay. Aggie never told anyone about me because in her line of work, a professional gambler would come up short and probably throw some kind of suspicion on her.

"Six months ago she was wounded in the line of

duty. Her partner was killed; Aggie almost died. She just got out of rehab last week. Her K-9 dog was wounded, too, and almost died. They never found the guys who did it. Aggie isn't one hundred percent yet. She asked me to come and take over for her. There are no words to tell you what I feel about all this. Every time I think about how someone tried to kill my sister I go berserk. If it's the last thing I ever do in this lifetime, I am going to find out who did it and make sure I get to face them in a court of law. Someone has to pay for what Aggie and Gus went through. I'm in the right frame of mind to make that happen, too.

"How could I say no?

"Aggie gave me a crash course in police procedure and wanted me to take her place so the trail to the killers didn't get any colder than it is. The world usually stops when a cop gets killed. But not this time. Aggie was set up, that's the bottom line.

"In the few days that I've been here, I've had threatening phone calls and someone tried to kill me yesterday. One of the cops in question was hit head-on and died this morning. I don't know if that was a real accident, or if they tried to take him out, too. That's cop lingo. This dog lying here with us is Alice. She's a stand-in for Aggie's dog. By the way, she loves me. And, I met a man. He's a reporter here in Atlanta. Man, can he kiss. Curled my toes, I can tell you that. There's more. Mr. Papadopolus wants me to schedule a . . . game here. I can't get it through his head that this isn't Vegas. It's against the law. High rollers. Big-time. Bushels of money. I could go to jail for a very long time if I'm caught. I don't even want to think about the part where I'm impersonating a police officer. I fooled Aggie's shrink, though. Any questions?"

They all started to talk at once. "Jail. Orange suits. No makeup or hair gel, no pedicures. Greasy, fattening food."

"What do you want us to do?" Noreen asked.

"We need to make a plan," Lizzie said. "I feel better with you all here, but you need to know things could go awry. You could be arrested. For what, I don't know. Bad cops can make things happen to those near and dear to you. Aggie explained all that to me."

"Is your sister okay?" Honey asked.

"Actually, I think she is physically. But not well enough to go back on the street and risk getting hurt again. She's planting organic carrots with the help of a friend. It's a no-brainer, so don't ask. You know, whatever it takes to get past a bad time in your life.

"So are you girls in or out? By the way, that guy I told you I met, he has some friends. I thought we'd throw a little barbecue if it ever stops raining. Nice normal guys for you to play with. What's it gonna be?" Lizzie held her breath as she waited for their response.

"Oh, we're in?"

"Are any of them rich?" Honey asked.

"Probably not. Most nice guys aren't rich. I'm sure they have jobs that pay nice wages. Money isn't everything as I've found out."

"Okay," Honey said agreeably. "Doorbell's ringing. Must be the pizza."

Alice made it to the door before Lizzie. "Who is it?" Lizzie called out.

"Paisan Pizza. Two with the works, one with extra cheese. Forty bucks."

Lizzie opened the door to accept the pizzas. She handed over fifty dollars, closed the door, and shot all three locks into place.

While the girls divvied up the pies, Lizzie fetched paper plates and napkins from the kitchen, along with rawhide chews for Alice, who turned her nose up at them. The girls broke off pieces of crust and handed them to her. Alice's tail wagged in thanks. She settled down and munched contentedly.

Forty miles from Atlanta at a greasy spoon diner off the interstate, six men sat around a scarred, grimy table.

To anyone interested enough to wonder who they were, the men could have passed for a group of guys on a fishing trip. No one gave any of them a second look.

They were drinking beer by the pitcher and indulging in all-you-can-eat deep-fried crawfish. The establishment would lose money on these six with their hearty appetites.

"It's time to call it a day," one of the men said. "I know Will's death was an accident, but as we all know, he wasn't the sharpest tool in the shed. Who knows what's going to come to light now that he's dead. I say we scratch everything and wait till we see if Jade decides to resign. Furthermore, the vibes I'm picking up aren't good. Fear is a terrible thing. Terrible."

The speaker paused while the empty crawfish platter was removed, along with two empty pitchers. Replacements arrived within seconds. The guys were known for their hefty tips. The waitresses hustled when they had their monthly fishing meetings.

Another man adjusted his fishing hat with lures hanging off its brim. He'd never fished in his life. "She's fearless, so get her resigning out of your head. She's already talked to Shay three or four times. Hell, she could be his new best friend, and they could also be telephone pals. Will said Shay was acting different lately. Two plus two equals four." The man finished the beer in his glass, belched, then refilled the glass.

"We are not wimping out here. We have too many loose ends. We still have . . ."

"Dump it!" a fourth voice said. "We cut our losses and come back to play some other day. It's a wise man who knows when to retreat. I'm retreating."

The third voice spoke again. "You retreat when I say you retreat. It's all going to blow over."

The fourth voice spoke again, his tone sharp and angry. "Hawk came visiting. The guy is a bloodhound. His kind never gives up. I saw him hopping into Aggie's car. That means the two of them are in this together. You add that damn dog, and two plus two is still coming up to four."

A fifth voice spoke up. It was older-sounding and nervous. "The guys are right. I'm damn glad I'm retiring. You guys do what you want. Keep my share. Aggie's a good cop, and you all know it. Shay knows it, too, and so does the commissioner. You want to mess with that, go for it, but I'm done. Aggie is never going to give up. Killing was not something I signed on for. The rest of you can do whatever you want to do. Take my advice and give it up. I'm outta here."

The men who remained at the table had mixed emotions showing on their faces. Three of them wanted to follow the fifth man out the door, but Dutch Davis's good arm snaked out at the same time Joe Sonders slammed his fist on the table. "No one is going anywhere."

The fifth man ignored him and kept walking, right through the doorway.

"Look, he's not going to the cops." Davis laughed, an evil sound. "He's going into hiding, but we know where he'll be. We got it made, boys. All those boats and snakes coming into south Florida. Leave him alone. For now."

Lizzie arrived at Becker's a scant five minutes before Nathan Hawk. She settled herself in a cozy corner next to a window that overlooked an outdoor eating area. For smokers, she assumed. With the rain, the tables would be unoccupied today.

Becker's was mainly a buffet-type restaurant with every breakfast food imaginable. Food could be ordered off the menu, but most people chose the buffet because of the mountains of fresh fruit, bacon, and sausage.

Lizzie was perusing the menu when Nathan Hawk appeared in a suit and pristine white shirt. She blinked as her heart kicked up a beat. He smiled. She smiled back.

"You're lookin' good this morning, Nathan."

"I have a meeting with the police commissioner and the mayor. I plan on coming down real hard on them. I have a buddy who works for a rival paper, and he's going to do the same thing. Something fishy is going on where Tom Madsen's death is concerned. We're going to run my piece on the front page tomorrow. Still no leads in the cop killing. Your six months of hell and your dog's as well. I have a few quotes I'm going to use from Tom's parents. I want your permission to add those threatening phone calls and the hit-and-run attempt. It will help, Aggie."

"I didn't report those incidents, Nathan. The chief will chew my tail out. Okay, okay, I can handle it. Go ahead and include it."

"How do you feel about going *live* with the local TV station? I can arrange it so one of the reporters does a follow-up on the print. It will be casual—they catch you on your way somewhere, and it's kind of off the cuff."

"I think I'm supposed to clear stuff like that with the chief," Lizzie mumbled.

"You *think*. Don't you know?"

Oh shit. "I'm a cop, Nathan, not a newshound. Most cops, and I include myself, work overtime trying to stay out of the limelight. I never had to do that before. Tom was my partner, and he usually made comments, if there were any, to the media. I stayed out of it."

"That's weird. Do you want the buffet or order from the menu?"

Lizzie looked around at the line forming at the breakfast bar. "I think I'm going to do the buffet. I don't eat much at breakfast. The bacon looks nice and crunchy and the cantaloupe looks juicy and sweet. Toast and coffee, and that's it for me. How about you?"

"Watch this," Nathan said, getting up to stand in line. Lizzie followed him as he added some of everything to a huge oval plate. "Can you really eat all of that?" she asked in amazement.

"And more." Nathan chuckled. "I'm big on breakfast. Most times I don't get to eat lunch, and dinner is when I have time to pick it up. It could be midnight. May I say you look enticing for such an early hour."

Enticing. No one had ever called her enticing before. She was wearing jeans and a pink tee shirt that strained across her breasts. He must like pink. She knew her face was probably as pink as her shirt. "Thank you." She bit down on a piece of bacon. Something was happening to her where this man was concerned. She looked up to see him smiling at her.

"Aggie Jade, I didn't know you knew how to blush," he teased.

The low-voiced chatter and the clink of china in the restaurant came to a halt at the same moment Nathan's beeper went off. The volume on a small television suddenly squawked to life, mesmerizing the patrons. Lizzie listened in horror as the startled commentator shouted that there had been an explosion at a high-rise hotel in Buckhead. Guests were being evacuated in an orderly manner.

"Gotta run, Aggie. I'll call you. I hate to keep doing this to you, but duty calls. Can you pick up the check?"

"Sure. Go!" Did this mean she should report in to police headquarters? Did they call in all off-duty officers when a disaster like this happened? She paid the check and headed home in case a call came through asking her to report for work. When she stopped for a red light, she yanked her personal cell phone from her purse and dialed Aggie's number in Pennsylvania. While she waited for the call to go through, Lizzie watched the torrents of rain battling with her windshield wipers. A minute later, the mobile operator said the customer she was dialing was unavailable. Aggie must have forgotten to turn on her phone. Or she was still sleeping. Damn.

Alex Rossiter padded his way into the kitchen in the old farmhouse to make coffee. He scratched at his bristly beard and yawned elaborately. He couldn't remember the last time he'd slept till seven o'clock. Forever ago probably.

He'd also turned into a slob since coming to the farm. He looked down at the torn and wrinkled tee shirt and equally wrinkled shorts he'd pulled on. Just in case Aggie was in the kitchen. He'd remedy that when he showered. He scratched at the stubble on his cheeks and chin again before he added water and coffee to the pot. To make breakfast or not to make breakfast.

Aggie's bedroom door had been open, so that had to mean she was somewhere about, which answered his question. He would make breakfast. Aggie had made pancakes yesterday, so it was his turn.

He slapped ten slices of bacon into the frying pan,

knowing how much Aggie loved crisp bacon. Gus loved it, too. Maybe he should whip up an omelet. How hard could that be? You chopped some peppers and onions, added cheese to the eggs, and, voilà, an omelet. Where was she?

Aggie was depressed. *Hell, I'm depressed, too.* If the rain didn't let up soon, he was going to go out of his mind. He hoped the rain was all that was bothering Aggie.

He looked up when he heard the old, wooden screen door open, then slam shut. "They sprouted! Maybe the rain helped. I think that plastic cover with the burlap on top helped. It warmed the ground. They sprouted, Alex. I swear to God, my organic carrots are coming up. Oooh, that bacon smells good, and so does the coffee. I'm starved."

Ah, this is the old Aggie. "They really sprouted, huh? That's great. It's a warm spring rain. The weatherman said the sun might come out today."

"Did he really? That's wonderful."

"Do you know what else I heard on the news? There was an explosion in Atlanta at one of the highrise hotels. Buckhead to be exact."

Aggie washed her hands before she started to set the table. "Was anyone hurt?"

"They didn't say. They said the evacuation of the guests was being handled in an orderly manner, whatever that means. They were rehashing the same thing and showing the same pictures over and over, so I turned it off. Do you want me to put the news back on?"

"No. We're really isolated way out here. All kinds

of things could happen in the world, and we'd never know about it unless we turned on the TV. I guess it was a good idea for my uncle to put in a satellite dish before they became fashionable. I like the idea of not having a phone hooked up. There's something about the ringing of a stationary phone that always sets my teeth on edge. Cell phones don't bother me. Which reminds me, mine is charging. I need to disconnect it."

Alex removed the bacon from the frying pan and placed it on some paper towels to drain off the grease. He used another frying pan for the omelet. Gus barked to show he smelled the bacon and wanted his share. Aggie handed him a piece that he virtually inhaled. He barked for more. She wagged her finger to show he got one piece and that was it. The shepherd walked over to the door, turning around to see if his owner meant what she said. Resigned to the fact that he wasn't going to get any more bacon, at least for the time being, he flopped down on the carpet by the door and stretched out.

Alex turned to eye Aggie. She looked nice today, in coveralls and a yellow shirt rolled up to her elbows. She'd put on a few pounds since coming to the farm. She almost looked like the old Aggie, except for her eyes. He wondered when the old sparkle would return. She brushed at her new haircut, tendrils curling around her ears. She was wearing little gold earrings today. Maybe that meant something. He also thought he caught a whiff of perfume. He hoped those little touches were for him. His culinary efforts would never win friends and influence people. Even Gus sniffed everything he cooked, sometimes actually walking away from it and eating his hard, dry dog food. Sometimes life was a bitch.

"This looks very good, Alex. Let me chop up Gus's food so it cools off faster. You overslept today. What's that all about?"

Alex shrugged. "Don't know. Maybe the sound of the rain. The bed was too warm to get out of. Nothing on my agenda. What time did you get up?"

"Three o'clock. I had a dream that the carrots sprouted. I was always an early bird. Lizzie is a night owl. I spent the time going over and over the notebooks, but I can't find a thing that will help us. I wonder how Lizzie's doing. She didn't send an e-mail last night. I guess that means everything is okay on her end. I need to tell her I came up dry as far as the notebooks go. Maybe she'll have better luck. If the sun comes out, let's go into town."

"Sounds good to me. How's the toast?"

"Good. It would have been better if you had taken the butter out of the fridge so it could soften up." She grinned to mute the criticism.

"I'll make a note of that. Would you look at that!" Alex said, pointing to the kitchen window. "Is that sun I'm seeing?"

"Yes, sir, that's the sun! I just know it's going to be a great day!"

Alex watched Aggie, his shoulders lightening imperceptibly as she carried her plate to the sink and unplugged her cell phone. She was slipping it into her pocket when it rang. She looked up, a startled expression on her face. Gus barked.

"Click the button, Aggie. I'm sure it's Lizzie."

"Spring Willow Farm," Aggie said breathlessly. "Lizzie, is that you? What's wrong?"

"Put the news on, one of those twenty-four-hour news channels. There was an explosion at one of the big hotels. Should I report in, call the chief, what?"

"Are you off today?"

"In a manner of speaking. The chief gave me a couple of days off. Whatever that virus was that hit the department is over and everyone is back at work."

"Yes, check in. You could get traffic duty at the site, school duty, wherever they need you. They should have called you by now."

"I went out to breakfast with Nathan Hawk, and he got a call and had to leave. I'm home now, but no one from the department called. There is a message from Will Fargo's brother. He wants to know where all of Will's records are? He wants me to ask the chief. Will Fargo died yesterday morning, Aggie. I was there when it happened. He tried to talk to me. I asked him if you were set up, and I think he said yes. He tried to tell me something else, but I couldn't understand him. His brother was there, and he couldn't understand him either. It sounded like he was saying, *cards, lard,* or maybe *hard.*"

"I don't know what that means. I'll think about it. Hey, my organic carrots sprouted overnight. What do you think of that?"

"I think you're nuts is what I think. Oh, before I forget, I gave the notebooks to Nathan Hawk. Maybe he will come up with something."

"I sure hope so. I think I'm incapable of analyzing all of that minutely detailed data right now."

"I have to call Will's brother back. What should I say?" Lizzie asked.

I'm sorry about Will. I bet you five bucks he kept all his stuff in the impound locker. Think about it, it makes sense. He'd just log it in under his own name, lock it up. Hell, he might even have told the chief. He was in charge, but there are two extra shifts, and he wouldn't want anyone messing with his stuff. If you're reporting in, ask the chief. I think he's one of the good guys, Lizzie. But, I'm not sure."

"He told me anytime I wanted to talk we could go *off-site*. I wasn't going to tell you this, Aggie, but I've changed my mind. The reason I'm changing my mind is I am not a cop, and I don't know the mind-set. I don't want to screw up. I've had three or four threatening phone calls. I used the whistle after the first couple. The day before yesterday someone in a dark car ran up on the curb, and if Alice hadn't barked, both Nathan and I would have been killed. We dived for the grass at the end of the sidewalk. It was raining real hard, and we couldn't get a definite make on the car or the license plate."

The color drained from Aggie's face. "Oh, my God! I was afraid of something like this. Do you want out, Lizzie? I can come back if you want to go home. No, no, I take that back. I'm going to pack up and leave right now. I never should have involved you in this mess. My God, you could have been killed! This isn't right."

"Aggie, calm down. I'm fine. I'm actually making progress. Nathan is a big help. And before you can ask, he's fine. You were right about him. I trust him and because I trust him, I want you to stay right there with your carrots. Between the two of us, we are going to make this all come out right. Nathan is going to write a story for the front page. That's going to help move things along at the speed of light. So you see, I'm in control. You always trusted me before. This is no different, Aggie. I can handle it. The truth is, I *am* handling it. Don't make me start to worry about you. I want your promise that you will stay at the farm. If you're bored, you can always play house with Alex," Lizzie said, trying for a light tone.

"I don't know about this, Lizzie. You can be a real hothead sometimes. Are you sure, Lizzie? You aren't just saying that to placate me, are you?"

"I'm okay with it all, Aggie. I just don't want to screw up, so stop worrying."

"By the way how did it go with the shrink?"

It went okay. I don't have to go back for a month. I hated him. There sure wasn't anything warm and fuzzy about him at all."

"He's a department shrink. What do you expect? I need to think about all this. I'll call you back this evening, Lizzie. Are you sure you're okay?"

"I'm fine. No, don't call me back tonight. I might have to put in some overtime if they don't contain the accident. I'll call you back. You okay, Aggie? I mean, really okay? How's it going with Alex?"

"I'm okay. I get twinges. We've had a good bit of rain, so my bones are protesting. They told me that would happen. I still get startled with loud noises and it's . . . it's, ah, going just fine. More than fine really. I'm probably going to get fat the way I've been eating. The sun finally came out a few minutes ago. Call me tonight if you can. No one knows about these cell phones. Promise me you'll be careful. I don't want you getting confrontational. Just upset them a little and let them do the rest."

"Will do."

Aggie flipped the cell phone shut. She looked over at Alex. "I'll clean up here, go take your shower. I'll tell you everything Lizzie said on our way into town. I think our little charade is working."

Alex smiled. Was that a sparkle he was seeing in his friend's eyes? If it wasn't, it was close to it. He'd take it. Something was always better than nothing.

Lizzie headed straight for the chief's office the minute she entered the station. She crossed her fingers that she wouldn't have to go on patrol or stand out in the rain.

She rapped on the door. The chief barked something that sounded like "come in." She opened the door and waited.

"Jade, what the hell are you doing here? I gave you time off. We got it all covered."

"I heard about the explosion on the news. I thought . . ."

"Let me do the thinking. Go home. We got it covered."

"All right, but first I need to talk to you about something. I just need a minute, Chief."

"All right but make it quick, Jade."

"Will Fargo's brother called this morning while I was out to breakfast. It seems he can't find any of

Will's papers or records. He wanted me to ask you if he could go through his brother's locker or maybe the room where he worked. Will lived in an apartment complex, and the brother seemed to think he was afraid of break-ins. What should I tell him?"

"Now that you're here already, go check it out. The desk sergeant will give you the master key to the locker. Check out the impound room. If you find anything that has his name on it, sign it out. Call the brother in and let him go through it. The funeral is tomorrow. You know the drill."

"Okay, Chief."

"Go on, get out of here. I have work to do."

Lizzie looked around the squad room. Aside from a civilian secretary, the room was empty. An eerie feeling settled between her shoulder blades as she walked up to the desk sergeant's desk to make her request. He handed over a key. "Make sure you bring it back, Jade. Don't make me come looking for it."

"No problem," Lizzie said, catching the key ring on the first toss.

Will's locker was one of the older ones, which still took keys. Aggie's locker had a padlock with a code. She knew she wasn't going to find anything even before she opened the dark green metal door. She was right. There were two well-thumbed *Playboy* magazines, some vitamins, a shaving kit, a grungy towel, and a pair of rolled-up black socks. A pair of Nike Air sneakers minus the shoelaces sat on the bottom of the locker in a battered gym bag. Lizzie used her hands to feel back into the corners on the floor and the top shelf. There was nothing to be found except a Dentyne chewing gum wrapper. She bundled the things together and put them all in the gym bag. She closed the locker but didn't lock it.

She left the locker room, gingerly holding the belongings of a man who had something to do with Tom Madsen's death and her sister's injuries.

Her next stop was the evidence room, where a young rookie named Christine Delaney was working. Lizzie flashed her badge. The rookie opened the door for her, then carefully locked it.

Would she be looking for a needle in a haystack or would Will's box, assuming it was a box, rear up and hit her between the eyes? She signed in, added the reason for being in the room. The rookie read her explanation carefully before she nodded. "It's all yours, Detective. If you need any help, call me."

Chapter Eight

*I*t was easy to see that Will Fargo had run a tight ship when the evidence room was under his management. Everything was boxed and neatly labeled. In addition, evidence bags, boxes, and folders were dated and in alphabetical order. Lizzie started with the *A*'s and worked her way down the shelves. Will's box was neatly labeled and the first one on the shelf under the letter *F.*

Lizzie called to the rookie. "I want you to observe that I'm removing this box. Make a note that it has red sealing wax on it. Will Fargo, the man who worked this room for a long time, died yesterday. We're going to turn his belongings over to his brother. Take the box up to the desk, then call this number," Lizzie said as she withdrew a slip of paper with a phone number written on it. "Identify yourself, tell Mr. Fargo I told you to call him. Have him meet me in thirty minutes. First, though, I need the combination to the vault, then I want you to watch me take out his things if he was keeping anything in there."

The vault was full of gunmetal gray shelves, all of them full. Again, the evidence was dated, labeled, and in alphabetical order. Drugs, money, and jewelry were the only things kept in the vault according to Aggie. Will Fargo's belongings were on the shelf marked 12 in big bold numbers. Two shelves were assigned for each letter of the alphabet. Three huge cartons in total bore the name Sergeant William Fargo. They were Xerox boxes, the kind paper for the copy machines came in. Again, there was red sealing wax all around each of the lids.

Lizzie stared at the boxes. For a single guy who didn't even own a house, Will Fargo certainly had a lot of personal property he wanted kept safe. Lizzie was unsure what she should do at this point. She posed the question to the rookie, who looked nonplussed. "Call the chief. I don't want to give this stuff up only to find out later I should have checked with someone before doing it. Be sure to call Mr. Fargo, too."

Minutes later, Lizzie winced at the chief's growl when he answered the phone. "They're big boxes, Chief. They have sealing wax all over them. Is it okay to release them?"

"Today it's okay. Yesterday and the day before yesterday it would not have been okay. We ran a check on both the evidence room and the vault the minute word came down that Will passed on. Everything checks out one hundred percent. Will asked me personally for permission, years ago, to keep his property locked up. He didn't live in a real safe neighborhood. He told me it was considered sport for the gangs in the area to break into a cop's apartment. I lost count of the break-ins we've had at that apartment complex. Hundreds over the years would be my guess. You have my permission to release Will's belongings to his brother, Jade."

"All right, Chief."

Lizzie turned to the rookie. "You heard all that, right?"

"Yes, Detective, I did. You're going to need a dolly to wheel that stuff up front. Don't forget the first box we took off the shelf. There's a dolly outside in the hall. I'll get it for you. Hold the door open. Oh, and Mr. Fargo said thirty minutes was fine."

Fifteen minutes later, Will's belongings, including the gym bag, were on the dolly just waiting for Daniel Fargo to arrive and take them away. Lizzie wished she could be with him when he opened the boxes.

When Daniel Fargo arrived ten minutes later, he gaped, his jaw dropping at the sight of the boxes on the dolly. He smacked at his forehead. "It must be Will's butterfly collection. He started it when we were kids because he was sickly and couldn't play with the other kids. He had rheumatic fever. I think his collection was the only thing Will really cared about. I appreciate your help, Detective Jade. I'll say good-bye now. It was nice meeting you. I'm sad that it was under such circumstances."

It was Lizzie's turn to have her jaw drop. "Aren't you staying for the funeral service tomorrow?"

"No. Will was cremated this morning. My brother and I made the decision yesterday. Since both of us live on the other side of the country, we decided this was best. My brother and I are taking his ashes home with us. The service tomorrow is for the department. At least that's what I was told."

"Oh," was all Lizzie could think of to say.

"Thanks again for everything. I'd like to leave my card with you in case you ever have to get in touch for something or other." Lizzie reached for the card and stuck it in her pocket.

"Are you leaving now?"

"Our flight leaves at noon. This stuff is a bit of a problem, but I think we can manage to have the airline box it up since we didn't come with luggage, only our carry-on bags."

Lizzie hated to see him go. She wanted to know *exactly* what was inside the Xerox boxes. Her voice sounded jittery to her own ears when she said, "Aren't you going to open the boxes to check to see that . . . that the butterflies are intact?"

"Good heavens no. Will was so persnickety about things like that. Some, probably most of them, are in glass cases and wrapped in bubble wrap. If I open them now, I'll have to wrap them all back up, then reseal the boxes. I just don't feel right opening them."

Lizzie's voice went from sounding jittery to desperate. "I can give you some sturdy tape. You probably should open them, Mr. Fargo. The chief will pitch a fit if you get them home, then file a claim against us because the cases . . . were broken. How will we know if the airline did do the damage?"

"My goodness, Detective Jade, my brother and I would never do something so silly. We are not the least bit litigious. You have no worry on that score. Listen, would you like me to send you one of the butterflies as a memento when I get home? I think Will would like that. Some of them are very rare."

"That would be very nice, but no, don't send me one. Keep Will's collection intact. I appreciate your asking, though."

"Well, I have to get going. I've got to return the rental car and take one more walk through Will's apartment to make sure we didn't miss anything. His rent is paid through the end of next month. Security deposit and all that. At that time, the Salvation Army will go there with the management company and remove all the furniture. It was nice meeting you, Detective Jade." He held out his hand. Lizzie grasped it. It was a limp-wristed handshake at best. "Bye."

There was nothing Lizzie could do but wave. "Butterfly collection my ass," she mumbled to herself.

On her way out of the building, Lizzie bumped into Chief Shay. "Are you still here, Jade?"

"I'm leaving, Chief. See, I'm opening the door. I am going home. Chief, did you know Will Fargo had a butterfly collection?"

"I thought everyone knew that. It's all he ever talked about. The only vacations the guy ever took were to places that had butterflies. I understand he had some rare ones that to other collectors would fetch a lot of money. He regarded his collection as a security net for his old age in addition to his pension.

He always said when he retired, he was going to roam the world to look at nothing but butterflies. You aren't going to tell me Will's next of kin doesn't want the collection, are you?"

"Oh, no. Will's brother Daniel just left with it. I wanted him to open it to make sure it was intact so they couldn't blame the department later on if something went awry. He is taking it on the plane with him."

The chief shrugged. "Will was pretty fussy with his collection. Every time he got a new one, he showed it to me. I have to say they were beautiful. Most of the butterflies were under glass, then he wrapped them in tissue paper and bubble wrap. A hell of a procedure to go through every time he wanted to look at them if you ask me. Go home now, Jade. I'll see you tomorrow at the service."

"Okay, Chief."

Right at that moment, Lizzie Jade would have given up her favorite diamond earrings to know what was in the Xerox boxes besides butterflies.

Lizzie's friends discreetly withdrew to the backyard when Nathan Hawk showed up a little before six. "I came to pay you for breakfast and to apologize. It was a faulty gas line in the kitchen at the hotel. One of the workers got a burn on his arm, but that's it. Everything is fine. Now, down to business. I'd like a beer if you don't mind."

Lizzie pocketed the breakfast money before she opened the refrigerator. "Don't go getting the idea I'm going to wait on you. Here's your beer. The next time, you get me one. I don't play that Tarzan/Jane game."

Nathan looked uncomfortable with her declaration. "I knew that. You're an independent woman, and I like that. I'm not a male chauvinist, regardless of what you may or may not have heard. I just don't like opening other people's refrigerators.

"Listen, I think I might have stumbled on to something. Do you remember about eighteen months ago there was a big to-do over a drug bust that went sour? It was the top headline in the papers for about ten days before it got pushed to the back pages. A cop named Savitsky took a bullet to his shoulder and another cop got his kneecap shot out."

Oh shit. Lizzie shrugged wondering if she should run upstairs and call Aggie or try to bluff her way through it. "Hmmm," she said. Aggie missed it and so did she. *Damn.*

Nathan took her response to be a yes, and continued. "It seems the department was working on the bust for months. You know, coordinating everything the way you guys do. It was one of those, 'this guy knew this, that guy knew that, and another guy knew something else' situations. Pieces of a puzzle. No one had the whole plan till the night of the bust. That was so nothing could go wrong, no tip-offs, leaks. All the wheels were in motion. Don't you remember, Aggie? The next day they said it would have been one of the biggest drug busts ever in Atlanta, that it was pure China White. Street value in the millions. They were shipping it out in boxes of peaches. When the cops got to the produce warehouse, the only thing they found were peaches."

"And . . . your point is?"

Nathan was staring at her so intently, she felt like a bug under a microscope. "Where did it all go, Aggie?"

Lizzie shrugged again. Her brain raced. "So it was a bad tip."

"That's just it, Aggie, it wasn't a bad tip. It was on the money. They put that guy, the snitch, in the Witness Protection Program. They only do that when it's serious stuff. You know how I know that?"

Lizzie drew in a deep breath, her heart fluttering in her chest. "How?"

"Tom Madsen's notebook, that's how. On that date, he wrote WPP. If you say those initials to any cop, they know exactly what it means, Witness Protection Program. Then he wrote the word, zip. Meaning no drugs on the bust. Two days prior to that, he had some more scribbles with initials. Nothing on those two days matched your notes for those days. In fact, you didn't have *any* entries. You were also off duty the night of the bust, but Madsen was called in at the last minute. Guess who had one of the pieces of the puzzle?"

Lizzie started to wring her hands in agitation. "Please tell me it wasn't Tom?"

"No, it wasn't Tom. Joe Sonders. Except for a few of the other guys who are close to retirement, Joe's the oldest with the most time in. That means he knows everyone. The guy has been around the block quite a few times. He also just got divorced for the third time. I keep track of stuff like that. I think he found out who had the other pieces of the puzzle and made his own deal a little early and they snatched the drugs and stashed them somewhere. Then if you have a really active imagination like I do, you would almost naturally come to the conclusion that it was all stashed in the evidence vault by none other than Will Fargo. It's so damn perfect, it's scary. I don't know why it is that people always tend to ignore the obvious. The department, if you recall, took a lot of heat for the screwup. The police commissioner took it personally."

Lizzie looked across the kitchen at the green frog with the red-painted lips. It seemed to be leering at her. "Too bad you can't prove any of that. Guess what. Will Fargo's brother came to the station this morning to get Will's things. Three big boxes from the vault. His butterfly collection. He signed it out and is now probably back home in Spokane, Seattle, or wherever he lives."

The reporter looked so shocked, Lizzie almost laughed. "Butterfly collection?"

The green frog with the painted lips looked like it was laughing now. "Yes, butterfly collection. The chief knew all about Will's collection. Seems like everyone in the department knew about it but me. The boxes had red sealing wax all over the lids. The chief gave the okay to release the boxes because they'd audited the evidence room and the vault as soon as word came down that Will passed away. Everything checked out one hundred percent. There was no reason *not* to release it, according to the chief."

The stupefied expression stayed on Nathan's face. "Butterfly collection?"

Lizzie sighed. "You said that already. I know what you're thinking because I've been thinking the same thing all day. Those boxes were weighed. The weight was exactly the same today as it was when they were first put in there. That's what I mean by everything checking out. Is it drugs or is it money? I don't know. Paper money is nowhere near as heavy as kilos of cocaine. I'm thinking it's money, and the drugs were hidden somewhere else."

"What makes you think that, Aggie?"

"Cop's intuition. Sometimes my memory gets a little fuzzy. How many kilos were there?" Lizzie rubbed at her temples in an attempt to prove her memory wasn't what it should be.

"It was all speculation, don't you remember? At the paper we just quoted probable street values. You say a hundred kilos and only eighty show up at recovery, people get downright pissy, and all kinds of things go wrong. It always bothered me, and it bothered my boss, too, that the night of the bust, the warehouse was empty. Everything was so synchronized it just smelled from the git-go. The other really weird thing was nothing was being said on the street. The snitches clammed up, no one was talking. There were no shoot-outs or dead bodies at that time. Everything literally shut down. It was like the raid, the bust never happened."

"You're saying this is because . . . because of bad cops?" Lizzie's stomach started to heave. *Think Plan B. Think Plan B.* Nathan's head bobbed up and down.

Lizzie nodded sagely, giving the impression she knew what he was talking about. "I guess we need to try to figure out where *they* stashed it all. Assuming you're correct."

Nathan stared across the table at Lizzie. His gaze was intense and yet smoldering at the same time. Lizzie's body started to tingle as she let her imagination run wild. *What would it be like to . . . ?*

Nathan snapped his fingers. "Earth to Aggie. We need a starting point. If Will Fargo was neat and orderly as well as methodical, I'd say that's where we start. I'll clear it with my boss and go to Spokane. Or is it Seattle where his brother lives? We have to find out. Want to go with me? We can fly up tonight and be back tomorrow afternoon. Aggie, it would be a hell of a bust for you if you manage to solve this and bring down Tom's killers, your very own partner, in the bargain. I get the front page, and we all live happily ever after. You wanna go for it?"

"I have company, Nathan. I can't just go off and leave them like that. Of course I want to go with you. Right now, you need to know and understand something. It will not be happily ever after. The whole department will view me the way they did that cop in New York, Chicago, or wherever he was. First they'll transfer me here and there, and when things heat up, I'll have to go undercover and hide out. Cops do not turn other cops in. Never. No matter what. There *is* a blue wall, no matter how much they protest. There are still prejudices where women on the force are concerned. They deny that also. It's okay, I can handle it. If I'm forced into retirement, I can handle that, too." *Think Plan B.* Plan B—her safety net.

"Attagirl, Aggie. Listen, I'm not going to let anything happen to you. I work for a very powerful newspaper, and I know other reporters around the country who work for even more powerful newspapers. How about this? I call some of my friends to come over and . . . entertain your friends this evening. You say home-cooked meal, they'll be here like white on rice. They're nice guys, Aggie. White-collar professionals on their way up the ladder. All of them are in their late thirties. How about it?"

"I'll run it by the girls. I hate leaving . . . Gus. I guess the girls can look after *him.*"

"Okay, go check with them. I'll call the guys. I'll say eight o'clock, and I'll make the plane reservations. You can pay me back later because I'm going to charge it to the paper. Investigative work, you know. You okay with that?"

"Yeah, I am. I'll . . . ah, check with the girls."

Outside, Lizzie dropped to her haunches and whispered out the deal to the girls, who were sunning themselves on colorful beach towels in the middle of the yard. "You'll have to cook. You're a good cook, Noreen. Someone will have to go to the store. I'll leave money on the table and the keys to my car. Promise me you won't let anything happen to Alice. I hate doing this, girls, but it really is important. I swear, I'll make it up to you. And the guys who will be coming over are yuppies, white-collar, climbing the corporate ladder. What could be sweeter?"

"You sold us," Candy chirped. "Do we go for a

walk after dinner, then watch a video? I'm new to this suburban lifestyle."

"Sounds good to me. Okay, take care of my dog, don't let any strangers in, and don't answer the phone. Unplug it. I should be back sometime late tomorrow afternoon."

"Lizzie, take care of yourself, okay? We're going to worry about you," Noreen said, a frown settling between her well-defined eyebrows.

Lizzie looked at the worried expressions on her friends' faces. "Hey, I'm a big girl. I'm more worried about you with these Southern boys. You take it easy on them, you hear?" The girls laughed. Lizzie felt better when she entered the kitchen through the back door.

"It's done," Nathan said. "The guys will be here at eight. We have a five-thirty flight. That means with all the new airport security, we have time to pack a bag, get a quick bite to eat, and head for the airport. Hartsfield is not a fun place to stand in line, so let's get cracking because I have to stop at my place to pick up my things."

"Yes, *sir*," Lizzie said, snapping off a sloppy salute.

It was raining in Spokane when the plane set down on the runway.

"I feel like I never left home," Lizzie grumbled. "It's late, Nathan. Do you want to find a hotel or go to Daniel Fargo's house first?"

"My gut says we should go to his house first. Since it is so late, let's just take a taxi instead of renting a car. You have the address, right?"

It was raw and damp outside the terminal. Lizzie shivered inside her heavy navy sweater. "Yes, I do. If we can wrap this up tonight, we might be able to take the first flight out in the morning."

Nathan grinned. "Are you afraid of spending quality time with me, Aggie Jade?"

"Of course not. Look, there's a taxi. Grab it, Nathan. I hope it has a working heater in it."

Forty minutes later, Nathan paid the driver, asked for the number of the cab company so he could call for a return pickup, and removed their bags, which he slung over his shoulder.

Lizzie continued to shiver as she looked around the quiet neighborhood. With the exception of two driveway lights, the neighborhood was totally dark. Daniel Fargo's house sat in the middle of the block, seven houses away from the sodium vapor light at the end of the block. The neighborhood had an eerie feel to it.

Daniel's house looked small from the front, possibly a two- or three-bedroom house, kind of like Aggie's house. There was no front porch, but there was a stoop with three steps. Rain continued to pour down and around them. They ran for the stoop.

Nathan set the bags down on the stoop and rang the bell, three quick jabs. They could hear it pealing inside as they waited for a light to come on. The house remained dark and silent. He pressed the bell three more times. Nothing happened.

"Maybe he's a heavy sleeper," Lizzie said, her teeth chattering. "Or, maybe he isn't home. Or . . ."

"Do you know where the other brother lives?"

Lizzie huddled against the pillar holding up the little stoop. "No. I don't even know if either of them is married. Maybe Daniel went to the other brother's house. I don't think so, though. Daniel said he was going home. Ring the bell again."

Nathan rang the bell. When nothing happened, he said, "I'm going to go around to the back and try the door. Sometimes people leave their kitchen doors open. Or, maybe the door leading into the garage is open. My father always used to leave ours open."

"That's breaking and entering," Lizzie gasped.

"I'm not going to *break* into anything. I'm going to turn the handle on the door to see if it's open. If it's open, I'll walk through, and open the front door for you."

Lizzie was too wet and cold to argue. She was also getting crankier by the minute. She yelped in surprise when the door behind her opened and Nathan pulled her inside. "Told you the garage door would be open. I don't think anyone is home. Let your eyes get accustomed to the dark. I don't think we should turn any lights on."

"Let's find the thermostat and turn the heat up first, okay?"

"Look, Aggie, there's his suitcase. You were right, he did come home. I found the thermostat, and I'm turning it up to eighty degrees. Take off your wet clothes and stick them in the dryer. It's in the garage. I saw it when I came through. I'm going to look around. I don't think he was married, Aggie. There aren't any doodads scattered around. I don't see any plants or anything. The kitchen looked pretty bare. I think the guy was either a bachelor or divorced. No kids either because there weren't any bicycles or wagons in the garage."

Lizzie made her way to the garage through the kitchen, where she peeled off her sweater and tee shirt. She pulled out an armful of towels, tossed her stuff in, and turned it on. She wrapped the towels around her.

She looked around. Nathan was right. Three aluminum lawn chairs leaned against the wall. A lawn mower and a ladder were on the opposite wall. A box of blue furnace filters were in front of the ladder. The only other items in the garage were a shovel and a rake in the corner. She made her way into the kitchen. Daniel Fargo appeared to be a tidy man. She could hear Nathan calling Daniel's name as he made his way to the second floor.

Wrapped in the towels from head to toe, she felt like a mummy as she opened cabinets and the refrigerator. Daniel Fargo lived alone. He was a neat, orderly person. Everything in the cabinets and the small pantry was aligned in neat rows. The refrigerator had fresh fruit and vegetables in the bins. The carton of milk, according to the expiration date, hadn't expired yet. A bowl of leftover spaghetti sat on the middle shelf. Cold cuts in Ziploc bags were in the meat drawer. A plate of fried chicken wrapped in plastic wrap was on the bottom shelf. A bottle of wine, six bottles of beer, and three cans of Diet Pepsi were on the door shelf along with various condiments. Obviously Daniel Fargo knew how to cook.

It was warmer now, almost toasty. Lizzie felt herself start to relax. She ran upstairs when she heard Nathan call her name. "What?" she called out breathlessly at the top of the steps.

"I'm in here. Look at this!"

A night-light above the baseboard showed her the way to the room where Daniel waited. He was sitting on the floor. He'd closed the blinds and a small night table lamp gave off enough light for her to see little mounds of red sealing wax all over the floor. "I found it this way. There is one butterfly collection in each of the boxes. Pick one up, Aggie, and see if the box feels as heavy as it did when you removed it from the shelf at headquarters."

Wrapping the towels around her more tightly to keep them in place, Lizzie lifted one of the boxes. She shook her head. "No, they were a lot heavier. I remember wondering at the time what Will could have in the way of paperwork that weighed fifty pounds. I guess I thought each box weighed around fifty pounds. I also remembered thinking I would get a hernia if I picked them up. My rookie helped me. How much do you think one of those glass cases weighs?"

Nathan picked up one of the butterfly cases, moving it around to get a feel for it. "Actually, they aren't glass, they're plastic. Maybe a few ounces, no more. Take a look at these, Aggie. A real good look."

Still clutching the towels, Lizzie bent over the butterfly cases that Nathan lined up on the floor. "They all look the same to me."

"That's because they *are* the same. I'm no expert on stuff like this but my common sense tells me what we're looking at could be ordered from a catalog for $19.95. When I was a kid, I ordered ant farms and bug farms and stuff like that. The ants came in sealed glass, but the bugs came in cases like this. You're the cop, Aggie. What does this mean?"

Lizzie's eyes were wild, and she was starting to sweat. "It means . . . it means . . . Will stashed his real collection someplace else and this was just a red herring. I think the boxes were full of money from his and his cronies' past deals. I might be a cop, but I'm not a mind reader, Nathan. You know what else? I'm going to miss Will Fargo's service tomorrow. Chief Shay is expecting a one hundred percent turnout. God, how could I have been so stupid to forget something like that?"

"They won't hold it against you when the truth comes out, Aggie. You could call him first thing in the morning and say . . ."

Lizzie swiped at the perspiration on her forehead with the hem of one of the towels. "I can't tell him where I am. At least not yet. God, what if the chief sends someone to the house to look for me. I can't even call the girls to tell them to be on the lookout because I told them to unplug the phone. I don't have any of their cell phone numbers with me. This is going to put me in the tall grass, Nathan."

Nathan leaned back against the bed. He'd never seen Aggie Jade this agitated before. She looked vulnerable and beaten. He wanted to reach out to pull her closer to him, but he didn't. What would it be like to kiss her again? His imagination ran wild as he contemplated what would come after the kiss. He cleared his throat, hoping it would drive away his thoughts.

"Say something, Nathan."

His voice was gruff-sounding. "Short term, Aggie. You have to think long term. Think about how it will be when you wrap it up. You'll be a hero. They'll give you a ceremony and a medal. You'll get your picture in the paper. I'll do the write-up personally."

"Dammit, Nathan, I'm not interested in becoming a hero, and I don't need any medals. All I want to do is find out who killed my partner and almost killed me and my dog. That's all I want."

"Okay, okay. Take it easy. Wait right here while I turn the heat down. Don't move, Aggie. I'll bring your clothes up from the dryer and put mine in. Do you want to part with those towels? If not, you're going to have to talk to me when I'm in the buff."

Lizzie thought about it. "Toss my clothes up the steps, and I'll get dressed and throw down the towels."

Nathan laughed. He was still laughing when Lizzie tossed down the towels. He was back within minutes. "You look good in yellow," she quipped. Even in the sparse lamplight, she could see how the yellow towels brought out gold flecks in his brown eyes. Why had she thought he had gray eyes? Maybe it was the dim light, she dithered.

"You should see me *au naturel*," Nathan quipped in return. At her sour look, he asked, "What's our game plan here?"

"I don't think we have a game plan, Nathan. I'll tell you what I *think* happened. I think Daniel arrived home, carried his brother's boxes upstairs to store them, then started to feel bad. I think he opened one of the boxes, saw that it was full of money, was shocked witless, then opened the other two, found the same thing, panicked, and lit out. I bet you five dollars if you hit the redial button on his phone, he made a call to his other brother. They are probably meeting somewhere as we speak, or they're on a plane to God knows where. If they're driving, they ditched their cars, picked up another one, and could be anywhere. When things like this happen, the parties involved start to think like criminals. They're plotting and planning and anticipating. Hey, they could be on their way to Mexico. They could really get lost there. What do you think?"

"It sounds . . . more than believable." One long arm reached up for the phone on the nightstand. Nathan pulled it off and hit the redial button. The phone rang on the other end of the line twenty times before he hung up. He craned his neck to see the numbers on the caller ID. "The area code is 619. That's Chula Vista, California. I know it because I have a cousin who lives there. You can cross the border into Tijuana in fifteen minutes from where he lives. Our guy here is probably meeting the brother there, and from that meeting place, they're lost to us. That leaves us back at square one. What do you want to do now, Detective?"

Lizzie rubbed at her neck. She was starting to feel achy and hoped she wasn't coming down with something. "We can't *prove* there was anything in those boxes except what we're seeing. For all we know, there might have been books or magazines on butter-flies inside. All the suspicions, all the intuition in the world isn't going to change a thing. Cold hard facts backed up with proof are what counts."

"Are you saying the brothers are going to get away with it? Here, let me do that. Sit still. I have magic fingers."

"Ooooh, that feels good. Don't stop. Hmmm. For now they're getting away with it. Right now, like I said, they're full of panic and not thinking clearly. All they see is all that money. They've embarked on a life of fear. They'll be looking over their shoulders for the rest of their lives. Daniel Fargo seemed like a decent man. I'm sure the other brother is the same way. They saw the money, and their world turned upside down. Not that this is any consolation, but half the people in this world would have reacted the same way." She half turned, her face in profile. She felt his lips on her neck, then on her throat. There was no reason to object, so when his lips found hers, she met them eagerly.

"Hmmmm. Oh, yes. Hmmmm."

Chapter Nine

*L*izzie opened one eye and looked around. She felt drugged, as if she'd taken a sleeping pill and still had five hours of sleep to go. She squeezed her eyes shut and stretched out her legs. Naked legs. Legs that felt something next to them. This time, both eyes flew open. She gingerly moved one leg and then the other. Her arm moved just as gingerly. She almost yelped in surprise. She was naked as a jaybird, her partner the same.

"You lookin' for gold or something?" a sleepy voice inquired.

"Or something," Lizzie muttered. "Is this where we ask one another if we'll still be respecting one another?"

"Oh, I respect you all right. In my wildest dreams I never expected . . ."

"What? What did you never expect?" Lizzie asked shrilly.

"That you would be so . . ."

"So what?" Lizzie asked even more shrilly.

"So *uninhibited*. For some reason I had you down as a prude. Well, not exactly a prude but . . . I guess I just wasn't expecting you to be so . . . *boisterous*."

Lizzie reared up, yanking at one of the yellow towels to cover her bosom. "Boisterous? Boisterous! Is that what you said, boisterous?"

"Did I say *agile*, too? Man, you can *move*."

Agile. To her ears it sounded like he was comparing her to a trapeze artist. Lizzie wished the floor would open up and swallow her whole. Unlike Aggie, she *was* agile. She sniffed to show what she thought of his assessment.

If he was a smart man, Nathan would have left it alone. Instead, because he was so happy, he ran with his runaway tongue. "I thought you were going to be full of scars and wounds and stuff. You're *unblemished*."

Oh shit! "You were *looking* at my body?" Pretend anger rang in Lizzie's voice. God, how was she going to get out of this one?

"Well, hell, Aggie, we were . . . you did . . . how could I help but . . . you were looking at me, too, and don't deny it," Nathan blustered.

Aggie had said if all else failed, she was to lie. "Not that it's any of your business, Nathan, but I had plastic surgery because . . . because the scars were so . . . so ugly. The department's insurance paid for it all."

"You should thank that surgeon then because he did a hell of a job. I bet in real daylight on the beach in a bikini you can't tell a thing. I expected you to be a little more on the scrawny side with all the weight they said you lost. You looked real bony at that news conference."

"This would be a real good time for you to shut up, Nathan. I'm having a hard time realizing you and I had sex on some strange man's floor in the middle of the night. Right now I do not care to discuss my scars or lack thereof or my bony frame or my enthusiastic response to . . . to . . ."

"You sure can whoop and holler. I loved it. You got right into it. I do like a willing partner who's *experimental*. At one point, I thought smoke was coming out of my ears."

Experimental. His voice was so delirious-sounding, Lizzie wanted to smack him. It was all coming back to her now. In her life she'd never had such satisfying sex. Her face was suddenly so hot she wondered if she was running a fever. "I'm going to take a shower."

"Let's do it together. Shower I mean. I'll soap your back, and you soap mine."

"You wish. Go downstairs and make some coffee. I don't think Mr. Fargo will mind. He's probably never going to come back here anyway. This whole thing is mind-boggling. If the local police knew we were here doing what we've been doing, they would be entirely justified in arresting us. Prison pallor is a terrible thing," Aggie said, clutching the towels to her body as she stomped her way to the bathroom. Before she slammed the door shut and locked it, she thought she heard Nathan mumble something about still waters running deep. She locked the door, not because she didn't trust Nathan Hawk but because she didn't trust herself.

Downstairs, one of the yellow towels wrapped around his naked middle, Nathan fixed the coffeepot. While it dripped, his mind raced. It was still racing when he got out the milk, the sugar, and the cups. He looked around for Aggie's purse and found it in the living room where she'd dropped it. He carried it into the kitchen where he opened it and pulled out her gun. It looked obscene. It looked heavy, and it looked deadly. He picked it up and almost dropped it, surprised at how heavy it was. He used both hands to steady the gun.

When Aggie entered the kitchen ten minutes later, Nathan was standing with his back to the stove, straight in front of her. She skidded to an abrupt stop. She was about to give Nathan a verbal tongue-lashing when he narrowed his eyes, and said, "Just who the hell are you? Don't even *think* about telling me you're Aggie Jade."

If Lizzie hadn't reached for the doorframe, she would have fainted with shock. She did her best to marshal her thoughts. She needed to be quick and fast. "What are you talking about? I hope you have the safety on that weapon. This isn't funny, Nathan. Never pick up a gun unless you plan on using it. Day one at the Academy."

Nathan's eyes were almost slits now. Both his hands had steadied on the gun he was holding. "Let me worry about the safety. Stay right where you are. No more lies. I'm only going to ask you one more time, who the hell are you?"

Lizzie almost fainted a second time when she heard the safety click back. "You know what, you are crazy! Put the safety back on that gun before you end up killing one of us. I'm Aggie. What's your problem, Nathan?"

"You're my problem, whoever you are. First it was your teeth that were crooked, then they weren't crooked, then your dog who is supposed to be a boy dog but turns out to be a girl dog. A dog who used to like me but hates me now and doesn't answer to the name Gus. You looked emaciated a few weeks ago but, boy, you sure are voluptuous now. I didn't feel any scars anywhere on your body to indicate surgery of any kind. No matter how fine the surgeon was who operated on you, it would still take more than a year for the scars to fade. That's for starters."

"I explained all that. You mean there's more?" Lizzie kept her eyes on the gun the whole time she was talking. She knew she could take him, but didn't want to have the gun go off and some neighbor call the police. The last thing she needed was to be carted off to jail.

"Hell, yes, there's more. Aggie Jade does not have a tattoo on her ass. You know how I know this, Miss whoever the hell you are? Aggie and I had a talk once over lunch when I was trying to pump some information out of her. At the time, some girl walked past our table and she had a tattoo on her shoulder. Aggie said she would never, ever, under any circumstance mar her body with a tattoo. She gave me a ten-minute dissertation on dirty needles and hepatitis C. Then you show up with a nice big butterfly on your ass. C'mon, I'm waiting to hear your next lie. My finger is getting itchy. Butterflies. That guy who died had a thing about butterflies. There are butterflies upstairs. Are you in this with those creeps? Did they ace you out of your share of the money? Did you set me up to come here? I want a damn answer and I want it *now!*" Nathan waved the gun in a wide arc.

He had her, and she knew it. "Put the safety on the gun, and I'll tell you what you want to know. Lay the gun on the counter and walk away from it. Otherwise, shoot me now."

"Like I'm really going to do that. You talk, and you talk now. Don't think you can sweet-talk me because of that wild romp in the sack either." His voice was so virtuous, so offended, Lizzie almost laughed.

Instead, Lizzie clenched her teeth. She was a professional gambler. A damn good one, too. Right now she had to make a decision. "Go to hell, Nathan." She turned and walked into the dining room and then the living room. She was betting her life on the fact that Nathan Hawk wouldn't fire the gun. She prayed with each step she took. When she entered the living room, she sat down on what was probably Daniel Fargo's favorite chair. She waited.

She heard him before she saw him. He looked rather cute with the towel wrapped around his middle. He still held the gun, but the safety was on. Lizzie heaved an inward sigh of relief. He was only a few inches away from her. She thought he looked confused. She looked up at him at the same time her hand snaked out to rip the towel away. Seconds later Nathan Hawk was on the floor with Lizzie's foot on his neck. "How's that for agility, Mr. Hawk? You don't ever want to pull a gun on me, or anyone else, unless you're prepared to shoot. Is that clear?"

"Awk."

"I told you I would tell you what you wanted to know if you put the safety on and put the gun on the counter. I guess where the gun is right now is good enough. You move, and I'll crush your neck. Do you understand what I'm saying?"

"Awk."

"I'm going to take that as a yes. Too bad you can't take notes, Mr. Reporter. I'm Aggie's sister, Lizzie. We're twins. Aggie never wanted anyone to know about me because of my . . . my colorful lifestyle. In my line of work, I didn't actually brag about my sister the cop either. It worked for us.

"I didn't even know Aggie was wounded or that she had almost died until she was back home and called me. I feel really bad about that. When Aggie asked me to take her place, I didn't think twice. I packed up and came right away. Aggie recovered, but even she knew she wasn't ready to return to work. She didn't want to take the ninety days' leave she still had coming to her because she thought the trail leading to Tom Madsen's murderers would grow colder than it already was. Aggie's in Pennsylvania raising organic carrots. We can call her on your cell phone if you like."

Nathan shook his head as though he couldn't believe what he was hearing. "Raising organic carrots?" he mumbled.

Lizzie ignored his comment. "Yes, I'm impersonating a police officer, and yes, I know the penalty for doing that. Aggie and I both thought it was worth the risk. My dog is named Alice. Aggie has Gus with her. We needed a dog that looked like Gus, and Alice was the only one who could pass for him. We didn't think anyone would get down and look at his belly. That was our mistake. As for my tattoo, that's none of your damn business. You shouldn't have been staring at my ass in the first place. What else do you want to know?" She removed her foot and stood back. While Nathan struggled to a sitting position, she picked up the gun. She didn't point it at him.

Alex rubbed at his neck. "I have just one question. Who was I making love to last night?"

Lizzie bent down to pick up the yellow towel. She tossed it to him. "Me. Lizzie Jade. It's not going to happen again, so you can live on your memories. Take your shower so we can get out of here. It's going to be light in a few minutes. I'll call for a taxi to pick us up in fifteen minutes."

It was two-thirty in the afternoon when Lizzie walked into Aggie's house, Nathan Hawk behind her. She looked around at the messy living room and grimaced.

Nathan grinned from ear to ear. "It must have been a hell of a party."

Lizzie threw her hands in the air. "You sent a bunch of party animals to . . . to . . . entertain my friends. My sister said you were trustworthy. Ha!"

Lizzie stomped her way into the kitchen to another mess. She picked up the trash container. "They were your friends, so you do the kitchen, and I'll do the living room. I hate messes like this. How could six people make such a mess?"

"Aggie . . . Lizzie, wait a minute. You haven't said two words to me since we left Spokane. I have a right to be pissed, and you have a right to be pissed. That makes us even. Let's try to get beyond what happened and back on track. I'm not going to blow your cover. We have a better chance of finding out what happened that night if we work together. And, I'm sorry for pointing the gun at you. I mean that, Lizzie. It's just that I felt so confused and angry when I realized you weren't Aggie."

Lizzie sniffed as she plugged in the phone to check the messages. There were six from Chief Shay. She returned his call, her foot tapping with anxiety. "It's Aggie Jade, Chief." She bit down on her lip as she listened to his tirade. "I wanted to go, Chief. I had every intention of going, but I couldn't make myself actually do it. I . . . I went off to . . . to someplace I've never been to . . . to think." It wasn't exactly a lie. She did think about Will's memorial service. "All I can say is I'm sorry. Yes, I'll be in the day after tomorrow. Yes, I will be at Zack's retirement party. A party is different from a memorial service, Chief. I'm fine, Chief. It was just something I had to work out on my own. Thank you."

Lizzie whirled around. "Did you see an urn at Daniel Fargo's house?"

"No. Did you?"

"Maybe it was in his luggage. We didn't check his suitcase. I don't know anything about . . . about cremation. Do they give you the ashes right away or do you have to pick them up later? It's obscene to think they would *mail* them to a person. I'm sure it isn't important to . . . to the investigation. I'm sure he must have taken them with him since we think he was meeting with his brother. Let's think he scattered the ashes somewhere. I hate loose ends." She was dithering and didn't know why.

"Lizzie, it doesn't matter. You *are* like Aggie in some ways. Aggie would have been concerned about Will's ashes, too. After we get this all cleaned up, would you like to go out to get something to eat? If you recall, we didn't eat yesterday. I'm starving. The paper doesn't know I'm back, so no one will be beeping me. I'll buzz on home, shower, and change. I imagine you want to do the same thing. I'll come back and pick you up. C'mon, Lizzie, stop looking so mean and dangerous. You're starting to scare me."

"Okay. But I expect this kitchen to be spotless." It was just too damn hard to stay angry at Nathan. He had such a winsome smile.

"Are you always such a hard-ass?"

Lizzie stopped in her tracks. "Not all the time," she said softly.

"Oh."

Back in the living room, Lizzie, her mind racing, collected beer bottles, coffee cups, and dessert plates. She emptied ashtrays and gathered up paper napkins and carried everything back to the kitchen. Before she went upstairs, she plumped up cushions, sprayed Lysol, and cuddled with Alice, who lathered her with wet kisses.

There was a smile on her face when she made her way to the second floor and the shower. When she was finished, her hair slicked back, and dressed in a khaki safari dress and sandals, she peeked in on her visiting roommates, who were all sleeping soundly, blissful expressions on their faces. Nathan was right, it must have been a hell of a party. She scribbled off a note from a sticky pad and stuck it to the vanity mirror.

The dishwasher was purring, the kitchen neat and tidy. Nathan might not know how to cook, but he did know how to clean up. She felt pleased at the thought. Alice nudged her leg to let her know she needed to be walked. Lizzie fastened the leash and led the shepherd out the front door. They walked around the block twice, and got back to the house just in time to see Nathan pull up in the driveway.

Nathan climbed out of the car, approached them, and said, "Hi there, Alice!"

Alice sniffed his hands, his shoes, and finally decided he had a right to be there.

"I'm ready to go, Nathan. Just let me take Alice into the house. I'll be out in a minute."

Inside, Alice ran up to the second floor while Lizzie searched for her purse. Key in hand, purse on her shoulder, Lizzie was locking the door when the phone rang. She debated a moment too long before reopening the door. By the time she reached the phone, it had stopped ringing. She waited several moments before she punched in the numbers that would release Aggie's voice mail. She stood rooted to the floor when she heard Daniel Fargo's voice.

Lizzie waved to Nathan when he poked his head in the doorway. She mimed Daniel's name and pointed to the phone. She was literally speechless when she hung up the phone. "That was Daniel Fargo. He said he needed to talk to me about something urgent and would call me tonight at eight o'clock my time. I guess my instincts were right. I think he saw all that money, panicked, and ran. I wish he had left a phone number, but he didn't. What do you think, Nathan?" She felt good just looking at him lounging in the doorway. With clothes on, he looked terrific; without clothes on, he looked even better.

"I think you're right. I also think you should call your sister. We can do it in the car on the way to the restaurant. She is, after all, the cop. Maybe we need to go with her instincts. Not that yours and mine aren't good," he added hastily, "but she *is* a cop."

Lizzie nodded as she stepped into Nathan's car. "I think that's a good idea."

Nathan settled himself behind the wheel and turned on the ignition. "You agreed with me?" he asked in stunned surprise. "Does that mean you're over your mad spell?"

Without a doubt, Nathan Hawk was one of the nicest men she'd ever met. She'd been known for shooting herself in the foot, as Aggie put it, when it came to men. It was probably true. As soon as a guy started getting too serious, she broke off the relationship. In her own way, Aggie did the same thing. Lizzie knew she needed to fall back and regroup.

"I wasn't really mad. I felt like I blew it, like I let

Aggie down. On top of that, you and I had that wild make-out session, which, while it was nice, certainly didn't help my frame of mind."

"Nice. You thought it was nice? I thought it was an electrifying experience. I could feel those little hairs in my ears burning."

Electrifying. He was a reporter, and reporters loved adjectives. She laughed. "Okay, electrifying is good." She picked up the cell phone from the console and dialed Aggie's number. Aggie picked up on the fourth ring.

"Aggie, it's me. I have some things to tell you. Sit down and listen, and don't start to scream and yell until I'm finished. If you don't promise, I'm going to hang up. Okay, this is what's been happening . . ."

Fifteen minutes later, just as Nathan swerved into the parking lot of O'Lacy's Pub, Lizzie told her sister, "Now you can scream and yell. Tell me what you want me to do. How are the organic carrots doing? Really, every single seed sprouted? Aggie, that's wonderful. Hey, I forgot to tell you something. I had to tell Nathan the truth. What do you mean, why? Because he figured it out and pulled my gun on me, that's why. What gave it away? The butterfly on my butt. We were having sex, Aggie. He gave me his word he wouldn't blow my cover. I know you can't trust reporters. He says he's different, and we *can* trust him. If he utters one word, I'll kill him and drag his dead body to the quarry. So, what do you want me to do?"

Lizzie leaned back and sighed. "I like it better when you scream and yell, Aggie. I hate it when you get pissy like this. I didn't do anything wrong. I was on top of it all the way. Do I go to Chief Shay? What should I say to Daniel Fargo? Do I tell him to bring the money back? Aggie, for all you know, Will Fargo may have gone to Vegas and won a fortune. Maybe he was a secret gambler. None of us can prove it's drug money at this point. Hell, we don't even know for sure if there was money in the boxes. Maybe he's calling for some other reason. We didn't see the urn with his brother's ashes anywhere. I don't know if that means anything or not. More likely not. Maybe he's calling to ask me to . . . to pick them up and mail them . . . it, whatever, to him. For God's sake, Aggie, I don't know. I'll call you after I hear from him. I'm glad the carrots are coming up, sis."

Lizzie broke the connection and closed the flap of the cell phone. She slipped it back into the console. "You are not on my sister's favorite person list today, Nathan. She said we can't admit we were at Daniel Fargo's house. She said to play dumb and use common sense when he calls. She recommends we dummy up a notebook that looks like the one Tom had and show it to either Dutch Davis or Joe Sonders. And, she says we, that's as in you and I, since I involved you, should let them know we know what was in Will's boxes. It will be okay, she said, to pretend there were records and lists and stuff like that. Incriminating things. Do you think we can do that, Nathan?"

"I don't see why not. We can work out a plan while we eat. I am so starved I could eat grass. If you can sit still long enough for me to walk around, I'll open the door for you."

"Why would you want to do that?" Lizzie asked.

"Because I'm a guy, and you're a girl, and my mother taught me how to treat a lady. Believe it or not, I'm an old-fashioned kind of guy."

"Okay. I'll sit here and wait for you to open the door." In spite of herself, Lizzie felt pleased. She'd never met an old-fashioned guy before or at least one who admitted to being old-fashioned. She'd thought they were an extinct species.

"This place has some really good food. Best ribs in all Atlanta. Their steaks are butter soft. Their baked potatoes are better than Wendy's. They also have this great loaf of garlic bread that comes with a red-hot dipping sauce. There is nothing Irish about this place at all. On St. Patrick's Day they serve green beer, but that's it. For dessert they have this cake called Chocolate Thunder. With a scoop of ice cream. The after-dinner coffee is so good you have to have three cups."

Lizzie laughed. "You like food, don't you?"

Nathan held the door open for Lizzie to enter the restaurant. "I love *good* food. If we get married, will you cook?"

If we get married. She decided to ignore Nathan's comment. "This might come as a shock, Nathan, but I do know how to cook. I just don't have the time. It's easier to eat out. Saves lugging all those groceries home and putting them away. I live in a high-rise on the twenty-fourth floor. Carrying groceries got real old, real quick. I also like to order in."

"Table for two," Nathan said to the hostess. "How about a table in the Rooster Room?" He turned to

Lizzie and grinned. "I really love food. Good food. I'm relieved that you know how to cook." He winked at her.

"The Rooster Room is our most popular room, and I do have a table. Follow me," the perky hostess said as she picked up two menus.

Lizzie's heart fluttered at the roguish wink. She looked around the moment they were seated. "It's nice in here."

"It's my favorite room in the restaurant. I guess the owner likes roosters. He has a duck room, a horse room, and a pigeon room. This one is away from the kitchen and all the noise. Most people want to be closer to the front so they can keep tabs on what's going on. This is a very popular eatery. We're early. That's the only reason we got a table. Usually you have to make a reservation weeks in advance."

When the waitress appeared for their drink order, Aggie ordered white wine and Nathan ordered Coors in a bottle.

"Look at all those roosters," Lizzie said, pointing to the wall.

"They're all the same rooster. His name was O'Lacy. When he passed on, the owner had him stuffed. He's in the lobby."

Lizzie grimaced. "That was probably more than I wanted to know, Nathan."

"They say he died of natural causes. He lived to a ripe old age. Everyone who comes in here gets to hear the story. There's a story for every room.

"So, Lizzie, tell me about your colorful past." His

voice was nonchalant, but the expression in his eyes was intense.

"I really don't think my past is any of your business, Nathan. You don't see me asking about yours, do you?" She was hedging, and they both knew it.

"It's boring as hell, and I'll tell you if you want to know. When someone says they have a colorful past, my imagination runs wild."

Two elderly ladies with blue-white hair walked past their table to take one in the back of the room. They immediately fired up cigarettes and ordered two double Manhattans.

"Go with your imagination, Nathan. I'm sure whatever you conjure up will be more colorful than my real past."

Nathan leaned across the table. "Are you ashamed of your past, is that why you don't want to talk about it?"

"No and no. I simply don't think it's any of your business. I graduated from college and have a degree in marine biology. Then I went on to get my master's. Aggie got her degree in criminal justice. Ah, here's that bread you were talking about." Lizzie stuck her finger in the bowl of hot sauce and licked it. "This *is* hot!" she said, reaching for her water glass.

"I told you it was hot. You have to get used to it. The next time you come here you'll ask them for a container to go. I don't understand why you don't want to talk about your past. If we develop a relationship, we shouldn't have any secrets from one another. Your version of colorful might be different from mine."

"We don't have a relationship, Nathan. We're working together, and we had sex in some strange guy's house. Read my lips. That does not make for a relationship."

"I'd like to develop a relationship, Lizzie. I really would."

Lizzie's heart started fluttering again. "That's going to be kind of hard, Nathan. I'll be going back to Las Vegas when this is all over. It's where I live and where I work." Suddenly, she wished she lived in Atlanta. *Now where did that thought come from.*

The reporter looked stunned. "You mean you're really going to go back there! Why? I know you said you lived and worked there, but you also said you were going to get closer to Aggie. I took that to mean you were considering moving here. Obviously, that was a mistake on my part."

"Why don't we talk about all that some other time, Nathan? Right now my head isn't exactly clear. You have issues, I have issues, and there's a crime waiting to be solved, but I don't even want to think about it until after I eat."

Nathan suddenly looked subdued. Lizzie wished she could wipe the troubled look from his face. She'd grown used to his exuberant nature. There was a tinge of desperation in her voice when she said, "I really like Atlanta. I might fly back and forth on the weekends. You know, to stay in touch with Aggie. And you can fly out to Vegas." She snapped her fingers under Nathan's nose when she realized he hadn't heard a word she said.

Lizzie drained the wine in her glass before she sat

back in her chair and folded her hands. She watched Nathan rip off a chunk of the delectable garlic bread and dip it in the hot sauce. His eyes started to water from the hot chilies. For some reason, she felt like crying. What was happening to her? She finished her wine and held up her glass for a refill. The waitress nodded, looked at Nathan to see if he wanted a second Coors. His head bobbed up and down.

"If we wait to discuss the case, and my past is off-limits, what would you like to talk about, Nathan?"

Nathan stared across the room at a huge picture of O'Lacy the rooster, wearing a cowboy hat and six-gun. His voice was low, soft-pitched when he said, "I woke up once last night and watched you sleeping. I thought to myself I could fall in love with you very easily. Then I realized I was comparing you to Aggie, and I got all confused. I know Aggie. We crossed paths lots of times. I was making love to Aggie, and yet I knew you weren't Aggie. That's the reason I wanted to know about your past. Whatever it was, it doesn't matter.

"And you're right, it's none of my business. We can talk about the weather if you like. I think the sun might come out tomorrow. When we have a spell of bad weather like we've been having, even with that nice afternoon yesterday, the paper always runs stuff from the *Farmer's Almanac*."

Lizzie looked across the table at her dinner companion. More than ever, she felt like crying. She cleared her throat before she took a healthy gulp of wine. "How do you think I felt knowing you thought you were making love to Aggie? It didn't sit very well with me. Then you ragged on me. I think I had a right to be defensive. You want to know about my past, so I'm going to tell you. Past, present, and future so hold on to your seat, Mr. Reporter.

"I was born. I managed to get through grade school, grammar school, high school, and college. It was rough because Aggie and I had to put ourselves through school by working. Our parents died within a year of each other. There was barely enough money to bury them. We had each other for support and comfort.

"I wanted adventure and excitement, Aggie wanted home and hearth. We split up after graduation. I ended up in Vegas. I fell in love with the glitz and glamour, the bells and whistles. I did it all. I worked in a strip club. Yep, I took it all off. I was making five hundred bucks a night. I pumped gas, I drove a truck, I was a disco dancer, runway model, divorce detective, and I'm a cardsharp. I went back to school to get my master's. I was getting by on two to three hours sleep a night. I did it, though, with no help from anyone. I didn't prostitute myself either. Then I met Mr. Papadopolus at a poker game. I won that night. Cleaned them all out. I'm a lucky person. Before I knew it, he hired me. What that means, Nathan, is, I'm a professional gambler. I'm what they call a high roller. Mr. P. pays me a commission. I live in a fabulous penthouse, drive a Mercedes convertible that is candy apple red. I get to shop in the best boutiques, eat in the finest restaurants, and it's all free. Mr. P. comps everything. I've been able to bank all my money. I'm pretty rich. I know I'm only as good as my skill and luck. It could all end, and I'd be out in the street in a heartbeat. I wanted to make sure my future was secure. I'm pretty good with the stock market, too. Like I said, I'm a lucky person.

"Gambling is legal in Vegas. I'm not doing anything wrong, so don't go thinking I am. Do you have any questions?" Lizzie finished the wine in her glass. Her face felt warm, her neck red-hot. She was almost afraid to look across at Nathan, but she did. His eyes looked dark, but there was a smile in them.

"That's a relief. I thought you were going to say you'd been in jail or were an ax murderer or something. I do have a question, though. If your future is secure, why do you keep doing it? Do you love it that much?"

Lizzie thought about the question. "I thought I did. The excitement, the big win, it's heady stuff. It gets in your blood. Could I walk away from it? Of course I could."

"What would you do?" Nathan asked curiously.

"My degree is in marine biology. I love all that stuff, but the pay isn't that great. I love being around water. Vegas is desert. Every chance I get, I head for the ocean.

"One of these days I'm going to buy a dive shop somewhere far away. That's when I'm ready to retire. I might take fishing trips. I like to snorkel, go deep-sea diving. I like to fish. I'm pretty good on water skis. I own a boat I keep docked in California. I won it in a high-stakes poker game. It's not exactly a boat. As long as I'm telling you the truth, you might as well know, it's a yacht. A big one."

Nathan's eyes popped wide. "You own a *yacht?*"

"A big one. Staterooms, the whole ball of wax. I also won a ski chalet in Colorado, and a cigarette boat. I think I might have something like twenty-seven Rolex watches. A cigarette boat is one of those fast jobs that skim the water at a hundred miles an hour. I have six cars. Maybe seven. Of course I have to pay storage on all that stuff. When I move on, I'll have to sell it all."

"Wow!"

Lizzie finished her third glass of wine. "Just tell that waitress to bring the bottle. It's annoying to have to keep ordering by the glass. We need to eat pretty soon. I'm getting light-headed. How about you?"

Nathan held up his third beer bottle. It was almost empty. "I think my eyes are crossing." He held up his hand to signal the waitress. "We're ready to order. Lizzie, what will you have?"

"The filet mignon, the spare ribs, coleslaw, carrots, the baked potato, and a bottle of Luna de Luna. Are the carrots organic?" The waitress shook her head.

"I'll have the same thing, but bring me two beers instead of wine."

Lizzie tore off a chunk of bread and dipped it in the hot sauce that was now cold. Tears rolled down her cheeks, but she kept eating and dipping.

"I'm okay with your past. Did I say that already?"

"Yep. How about my wealth?"

"Yeah, I'm okay with that. I just have my 401k and a lot of insurance. I own my own condo, and my car's paid for. It's mine. I don't have a boat of any kind."

"That's okay, I'll share mine. It costs a fortune just to lift the anchor. I like the cigarette boat best. You can go fast in it, but you can go slow, too."

"I think we might be a little drunk. We've been drinking on empty stomachs. How do you feel about me maybe falling in love with you?" He squinted at her to see her reaction. "Are you maybe falling in love with me, too?"

Lizzie poured more wine into her glass. "You are so sweet, Nathan. What was the question again?"

"I don't remember. We're a pair, aren't we?"

One of the blue-haired ladies in the back said, "He wants to know if you're falling in love with him, too, girlie."

Lizzie leaned back in her seat. "Have you been telling people our business, Nathan?"

"Uh-huh."

"Oh. My answer is . . . my answer is . . . probably."

"We're going to have to call a taxi to take us home. Want to spend the night at my place?"

"Well, sure, Nathan. My house is full of people."

Nathan wagged a playful finger under Lizzie's nose. "See, I knew that. That's why I suggested my place. My place is nice. It doesn't smell or anything. Not like that . . . place last night."

"We need to talk, Nathan."

"About what? I thought we settled everything."

"That's right. Where is our food?"

Nathan shrugged. "Beats me."

Lizzie started to laugh and couldn't stop. She held up her wineglass, and said, "Here's to me and you."

"Bravo!" the two blue-haired ladies chortled.

Chapter Ten

Lizzie swung her legs over the side of the bed before she groaned and dropped her head into her hands. "Oh, God, I have the Queen Mother of all headaches."

Nathan maneuvered his long, lean frame until he was sitting next to her. "I'll fight you for that title. It's been years since I woke up in this condition. I don't even remember getting into bed. We're still dressed."

Surprise rang in his voice. "We slept together in a bed. I wish I could remember what happened."

Lizzie groaned again. "Nothing happened. One of us would remember if something happened. The last time I had a headache like this was the day Aggie and I graduated from college. I never have more than two drinks. I don't like losing control. How did we get home?"

"Remember those two ladies with the blue hair? They drove us home. We promised to invite them to the wedding if we ever get married."

"Oh myyyy God!" Lizzie groaned. "You have coffee, don't you?"

"Yep. That's about all I have. I might have some crackers, but that's pretty much it in the way of food."

Lizzie massaged her temples. "Food is of no interest to me right now. Look, Nathan, the sun is out!"

"You make the coffee, Lizzie, while I shower. Or, I can make the coffee and you shower. I need to call in to the paper. How about you?"

"I'll do the coffee. I have calls to make, too. I guess you know we missed Daniel Fargo's eight o'clock phone call last night. I want to check the messages. I guess I'm just not cop material."

"Don't be so hard on yourself. You were off duty." At the doorway to the bathroom, Daniel turned to face Lizzie, who was struggling to get to her feet. "I used to have a pair of sneakers that smelled like my mouth tastes. I have a spare toothbrush I'll leave on the vanity for you."

Lizzie winced. "Thanks for sharing that, Nathan."

As Lizzie made her way through Nathan's condo, she had the impression that everything was white. Blinding white. She longed for sunglasses. And aspirin. A whole bottleful. Her head felt like a bongo drum someone was beating on. If Aggie could see her now, she'd shake her head in disgust.

A bright red coffeepot stood on the kitchen counter. Next to it was a can of Folger's and a package of brown filters. Lizzie ran water from the tap, filled the pot, and added coffee with a red plastic scoop before she picked up the kitchen phone. She dialed Aggie's voice mail code and waited. "Detective Jade, this is Daniel Fargo again. I need to talk to you desperately. I'll keep calling you till I reach you. I'm sorry I don't have a number I can leave with you. I tried calling you at the station house, but they said you were off duty. I'll keep trying every two hours until I reach you."

There were other messages, too. Lizzie skimmed over them, only clicking on Daniel Fargo's messages. He'd left five other messages. All of them were the same, all of them had the same note of desperation with the possible exception of the last one which was so frantic, the man could barely speak. She hung up the phone, then had an idea.

Lizzie picked up the phone, dialed into the voice mail and changed the message Aggie had left for callers. "This is Detective Agnes Jade. If you need to reach me in an emergency, please call this number, 419-5058, or leave a number where you can be reached."

The minute the coffee stopped dripping, Lizzie poured herself a cup. She didn't bother with cream or sugar.

Nathan entered the kitchen, an aspirin bottle in hand. His hair was still damp from the shower, but he was freshly shaved. He had on khaki slacks and a yellow button-down shirt. Today must be a casual day. He smelled wonderful. She explained about the messages and the phone. "Come and get me if he calls."

Lizzie swallowed four aspirin before she shuffled toward the bathroom and the shower.

Twenty-five minutes later, dressed in the clothes she'd worn the day before and then slept in, Lizzie marched out to the kitchen and headed straight for the coffeepot. The phone rang just as she brought the cup to her lips. Nathan's hand snaked out to pick up the receiver. His greeting was brisk and professional sounding. "Yes, Detective Jade is here. Just a minute and I'll get her." He mouthed the words *it's him* for Lizzie's benefit.

"This is Detective Jade," Lizzie said. She sipped at the coffee as she listened to the agitated voice on the other end of the phone. "Let me be sure I understand you, Mr. Fargo. You're in Atlanta now. Did you change your mind about returning home? Oh, you were home and drove back. Oh, you flew partway and drove the rest of the way and your brother is with you. Is something wrong? Did you come back for Will's ashes?" She rolled her eyes for Nathan's benefit.

"What is it you think I can help you with? You'll tell me when you see me. Well, all right, Mr. Fargo. Where would you like to meet?"

Lizzie looked up to see Nathan pointing to the floor. "Meet him here," he whispered.

"Let me give you an address, Mr. Fargo. I'm staying with a friend for a few days." She rattled off Nathan's address. "Rush hour is over, so it shouldn't take you more than forty minutes to get here. I'll meet you in the lobby and bring you upstairs where we can talk in private. Good. I'll see you then."

Lizzie looked across the kitchen at Nathan. "You heard my end of the conversation. The man is scared out of his wits." She threw her hands up in the air. "I think I should call Aggie. What do you think?"

"I think that might be a very good idea, Lizzie. How's your headache?"

Lizzie grimaced. "About the same as yours. This is a very sterile-looking condo, Nathan. There are no personal touches. Don't you have any plants or junk to put out?"

"No. I'm never here. I don't have time to take care of what I have, let alone plants. You have to water them."

"You could get silk ones. You just blow the dust off with a hair dryer. Some colored cushions would perk this place right up. You don't strike me as a chrome-and-glass kind of guy."

"I bought the condo furnished. I moved in with my clothes and toothbrush. I just sleep here."

Lizzie sat down and wrapped her hands around her coffee mug. "It has a temporary feel to it. Sort of transient, if you know what I mean. Curtains on the windows would add something to your kitchen. You have to have curtains. I think that's a rule or something. Aggie's little house is cozy and warm. She has curtains and drapes everywhere. Welcoming. You want to take off your shoes and curl up when you go to her house."

"What's your place like, Lizzie?" Nathan asked curiously.

"It's kind of like this place but more spacious. It's a penthouse with wraparound windows. The view at night is magnificent. It's not mine, though. I guess you could say it's elegant. It has silk flowers and silk trees. I like the fact that it has a built-in safe. When it's time to go, all I have to do is open the safe, take my stuff, and walk away. It was all done by a professional decorator. It doesn't feel like home. It's just a temporary place to live. A wonderful perk, like the Mercedes."

"So you haven't put down any roots in Vegas. Do you think he has *the stuff* with him?"

"No, no roots. Damn straight he has it with him. That's what's bothering him. I was going to call Aggie, wasn't I?" She reached behind her for the phone and dialed her sister's cell phone number. The mobile operator said the person she was calling was either out of range or the phone was off. Lizzie shrugged. "She's probably outside watering her organic carrots."

"Keep your eye on the clock, Lizzie. I'll make some more coffee. Are you nervous?"

"Yes, Nathan, I'm nervous. I'm not sure what to expect. Let's just say, for the sake of argument, he brings back whatever Will stowed away. We're thinking money. He turns it over to me, and walks away. Then I take possession of . . . whatever it is. What does that make me? A coconspirator?"

"I'm your witness, Lizzie. Listen, we'll make him sign something. I won't let you put yourself on the hook for this."

"Nathan, read my lips. I am not a cop. I am *impersonating* a cop. I can sign papers from now till the end of time, and they won't mean a thing because I am not Aggie Jade. That means all the evidence will get thrown out by a smart lawyer. God, I could just cry right now."

"Don't cry. I have an idea. When my sister was here last year, she left her video camera. How about if we set it up in the living room and tape the guy. I'll put it on top of the TV and put some books around it. That way, everyone is covered, and we have a tape. They do stuff like that in the movies all the time. What do you think?"

Lizzie looked over at the clock on the stove. "Okay, do it. It's better than nothing. Actually, it's kind of clever now that I think about it. Good thinking, Nathan."

Nathan beamed with pleasure. Lizzie smiled. "Listen, while you're doing that, I'll go down to the lobby. They might be early. I just want to get this over with."

Ten minutes later, Lizzie watched as Will Fargo's two brothers entered the high-rise and walked over to the security desk. She intercepted them by waving and smiling. They both looked awful; their clothes looked worse than hers, and they were unshaven, their eyes red and tired-looking. They looked *guilty*.

Daniel reached for her hand and drew her away so they were out of earshot of the security guard sitting at the desk. "We're returning Will's things. Do you have a service elevator or should we just carry the . . . the bags in?"

Bags. Lizzie tried to be nonchalant. She shrugged. "I don't see a problem with your bringing your brother's things up in the tenant elevator. I can hold the door for you. Why are you bringing his things back? You better not be telling me the airline broke the butterfly cases. The chief will pitch a fit. You could just take his stuff back to the station." She was babbling, and she knew it. The brothers weren't even listening because they were twitching with nervousness.

The guard watched curiously as the two brothers made two trips to the trunk of their car to return with dark green lawn bags. For the guard's benefit, Lizzie winked and said, "It's a surprise for my brother's birthday. Don't give it away now." The guard shrugged as he bent forward to answer the phone.

Five minutes later they were riding up the elevator. "What happened to the boxes with the red sealing wax? Did you find more stuff that belonged to your brother? I don't understand any of this," Lizzie grumbled.

"Just you wait. You'll understand as soon as we get inside."

"You certainly are being mysterious." Lizzie held out her hand to Daniel's brother.

"I'm Detective Agnes Jade."

"I'm Donald, the youngest," the brother said, shaking her hand. His hand was wet and clammy. Lizzie wiped her hand on her pant leg.

She held the door of the elevator while the brothers lugged the lawn bags down the hall. Nathan opened the door before she could ring the bell. The brothers, their faces riddled with panic, took a step backward and eyed her with suspicion.

"He's my lover. Why else would I be here? You can talk in front of him, he's not a cop." *And neither am I.* "Nathan, this is Daniel and Donald Fargo. Will's brothers."

"Sit down. Coffee?" Nathan asked, playing the host.

"No thanks," Daniel said. He switched his attention to Lizzie.

"Sit down. Tell me what's wrong? Why did you come back here? I don't think the department can store Will's things. I suppose you could rent a storage locker, but to what end?"

His expression bleak, Daniel dropped to his knees and opened one of the lawn bags. He dumped the contents on the floor. Lizzie gasped. Nathan sat down with a thump, his gaze glued to the pile of money and a key ring.

"Whose . . . whose money is that? Where did you get it?" Lizzie asked, her voice barely a squeak.

Donald, the youngest brother, quickly opened the other bags and dumped their contents on the floor until there was a small mountain of bundled money. "It was in Will's belongings with the butterflies."

"How much is it?" Lizzie whispered.

Daniel wiped at his forehead with the back of his hand. "We tried to count it. It's well over a million, maybe two. We kept getting mixed up when we tried to count it, and then we just said to heck with it. It's a lot, okay? Where did my brother get this kind of money, Detective Jade?"

"I don't know, Daniel. I can tell you what I suspect, but I can't prove it."

"It's drug money. That's the only explanation that makes sense. We were going to keep it at first, but then common sense kicked in. We both read the papers and know how drug people go after you. We don't want to look over our shoulders for the rest of our lives. We don't want to know where Will got all that money. We're giving it back, and that's that. Here it is. We kept enough to pay for Will's cremation, our airline flights, and the rental car. We also had breakfast and two dinners. If anyone wants to kill us for that, then let them. It's all yours."

Lizzie stared at him. "Speaking of old Will, where is he?"

"In the bottom of the bag. He's in a box. He's all yours, too."

"Wait just a minute. He's your brother. You can't . . . you can't just *leave* him here," Lizzie said through clenched teeth.

"No, you wait a minute, Detective. Donald and I are decent people. We don't do drugs, and we don't buy or sell them either. We did get carried away there for a little while, but we're making this right. We want a *receipt*."

Nathan spoke for the first time. "For the money or your brother?"

"Both," Daniel said smartly. "That last bag, the one with Will in it, has some papers that might make sense to you. The keys to his apartment are there, too. We both washed our hands of this . . . this whole thing. If you'll just give us the receipt, we'd like to leave."

Lizzie's eyes were wild. Her head pounded so hard she thought it was going to spin off her neck. "Do you have a receipt, Nathan?"

"No, I'm fresh out of receipts. Can I just write it on a piece of paper?"

The two brothers looked at one another. They nodded. "Just make sure you sign it so your name is legible and you are our witness," Daniel said, jabbing a finger in Nathan's direction. "You sign the word *witness* after your name."

"Okay," Nathan said agreeably. He made his way to the kitchen, where he opened one of his various junk drawers to find a pad of paper. He ripped off a sheet, grabbed a pen, and returned to the living room. He handed both paper and pen to Lizzie.

Lizzie clenched her teeth. She nodded for Daniel to start talking.

"Just say we returned over a million dollars to you with Will's papers. Write down that we aren't criminals. Say we gave you Will, too."

Lizzie stopped writing. If possible, her eyes were even wilder-looking. "Now you see, that's the part I don't like. Your giving me Will. I don't know if you can legally give up a dead relative like this. You're the next of kin. There might be legal complications later on."

"Too bad. Write what we tell you to write. We don't care what you do with Will. He's brought shame on us. Can't you write faster?"

"I'm writing as fast as I can. What if I need to get hold of you? How can I reach you?"

"Don't bother. We don't ever want to see you people again. It's bad enough that we know our brother was a criminal. We don't need any more reminders. Now, let me read what you wrote." Daniel reached for the piece of paper. He read it, then passed it to his brother, who read it, nodded, and handed it back to Lizzie.

"Sign your name. Put your shield number on it and your social security number. You, too," Daniel said, pointing to Nathan. "Put your social security number under your name."

"Why?" Nathan asked curiously.

"Because a person's life revolves around his social security number, that's why. It better be the right one, too," the youngest brother said with a snarl in his voice.

Both Lizzie and Nathan complied. "I have a copy machine in my bedroom. I'd like to make a copy for us, too. I'll be right back." The brothers nodded agreement. When Nathan returned with the copies, Daniel and Donald sighed, one after the other.

Both brothers reread the paper and nodded at the same time. "It's all yours, Detective. You aren't very smart, mister. I saw that video camera the minute we walked into this room. You taped us without our permission. Stay right where you are while my brother takes the tape. See, that's why we wanted this receipt. We can't trust you."

"Listen up, you two. This is not fun and games here. You want to protect yourselves, and so do we. On top of that, you're leaving us your brother. Where's the trust you are so big on?" Lizzie growled. "You guys just dumped a major problem in my lap. I'm not even on duty."

"Good-bye," Daniel said.

When the door closed behind the brothers, Nathan and Lizzie looked at one another. "I don't want that guy's ashes in my apartment. I don't want this money in my apartment either. You better start thinking fast, Lizzie."

Lizzie continued to rub at her temples. "I wish I could think. I need some more aspirin. They said there were papers in one of the bags. I think we should look at those. We can take . . . old Will to the nearest crematorium and pay them to keep him. We can use some of this money to . . . to pay for his upkeep."

Nathan started to pace the room. "They just burn them, they don't showcase them. My paper did an article on crematoriums not too long ago. Seems you can't trust them. Let's not go there right now. You have to take him to some kind of cemetery where they have drawers or vaults to keep them. You know, so you can visit with flowers. That kind of thing."

"I'm not going to be visiting Will Fargo, Nathan. At least not in this lifetime. I shouldn't have to be doing this. That man had something to do with Tom Madsen's death and Aggie and Gus's near deaths. Why should I care what happens to his ashes?"

"Because you are who you are, and it's the right thing to do, that's why, Lizzie. Now, let's look at those papers and count this damn money. Until you know what you want to do with it, let's rent a storage locker and keep it there. How much do you think they kept?"

Aggie laughed, then wished she hadn't. Her head continued to pound. "It's just a guess, but I'd say half a million. They probably took everything after they stopped counting. Enough for them to go far away so they can make new lives for themselves. They're going to be afraid for the rest of their lives, and they don't even know it. A month from now, they'll probably bring the rest back. That's usually the way it goes."

"You are so smart, Lizzie," Nathan said in awe.

Lizzie continued to massage her throbbing temples. "I read a lot," she said by way of explanation. "I have to call the girls. Some hostess I am. They could have packed up and left for home for all the attention I've paid to them. Hand me the phone, Nathan."

Noreen's cheerful voice made Lizzie's eyes water. "Listen, friend, I am so sorry all this is happening. I feel terrible that I've left you all to fend for yourselves. I'll make it up to you. What do you mean I would just be in the way if I was there? You're playing house with *the guys*. Uh-huh. So, what you're saying is you don't want me to come home. Okay. I can stay here with Nathan. If it's not too much trouble, could you throw some stuff in a bag and put it on the front porch? I have to go to a retirement party this evening. Throw in some jeans and shirts, too. I'll whiz by and pick it up at some point today. I'll make sure I don't disturb you and *the guys*. What makes you think I'm mad? No, I just have a . . . a hangover. I guess I'll see you when I see you. You're thinking of extending your visit? Of course I don't mind. Yes, I'll thank Nathan for the introduction. Don't forget to pack up my stuff. How many times did he call? All right, I'll call him. Bye."

Lizzie sighed. "My friends want me to thank you for introducing them to your gentlemen friends, who are now enamored with my friends. They don't want me to go home because I would be in the way. I guess I have to stay here in this sterile atmosphere until they say I can go home. I am welcome, am I not?"

"Stay as long as you like. I told you if those girls cooked for the guys, they'd be eating out of their hands within minutes. Wipe that look off your face. They're great guys. In this town, if you have a job, you are ahead of the game. Let's not worry about them. Let's worry about this mess," Nathan said, pointing to the lawn bags and the piles of money in the middle of the floor.

Lizzie leaned back and closed her eyes. "Nathan, other than the tattoo on my ass, what else gave my identity away?"

Nathan wiggled closer and reached for her hand. "Aggie really thought being a cop would help her wipe out the bad guys. She liked what she did. It was written all over her. You were different. Attitude, I guess. Yeah, attitude. I don't think anyone else will pick up on it, so don't worry about it."

"I'm a born worrier." Lizzie pointed to the stacks of money. "This is a problem. How did they, and there is a *they*, get so much. This must just be Will's share. Stop and think about it, Nathan. One guy couldn't do all this. By this, I mean making it all work for them. There are so many safeguards in place at the department. Then there's Internal Affairs. Those guys are like bloodhounds. I'm thinking a ring of cops. Yeah, that blue wall everyone talks about.

"It happens all the time in Vegas. Some gang spends years trying to figure out how to rip off the casinos. It takes a lot of people, working closely together, to plan something like that. Nine times out of ten, they don't get away with it. There's always a weak link somewhere. We read about it in the papers, after the fact. I'm thinking this is the same kind of thing. They start off small, maybe one or two cops, another cop finds out, they cut him in, which means they have to expand a little, another cop gets nosy, they cut him in, and on and on it goes until it's a *big* operation. Threats and intimidation are pretty powerful in a police department. You need to depend on your partner and the other guys. If they aren't there for you, it's all over. What other choice do they have? At least, I'm thinking that's the way they view it. You never, ever, rat on your fellow officers.

"I'm also thinking Tom Madsen found out, and he didn't want to go along with it. The next thing you know, Tom's dead. Did he tell Aggie? They aren't sure. Better to be safe than sorry, so they try to kill her, too. They have to lie low after something like that. To go at her again could bring in the big guns. Will, now, I can't quite figure that out. Maybe it was a legitimate accident. One they didn't count on. The brothers show up. Where is Will's stash? They've got to be scurrying around. They tried to scare me with threatening phone calls. When that didn't work, they had to do something physical by trying to kill me. How am I doing so far?"

"Your thinking is the same as mine, Lizzie. I think it's the whole damn department." Nathan sighed. "If you could be anywhere else in the world right now, where would you want to be?"

"That's easy—the Costa del Sol. Sunning myself

on some lovely nude beach so I don't get any tan marks. How about you?"

"Either some cottage in the mountains where I could fish all day, and the air is clean and pure, or a shack on the beach where it's always warm and sunny."

"Okay, let's check out the paperwork." Sheets of paper torn from a loose-leaf notebook slid out of the last lawn bag as Lizzie upended it. "It's just pages of numbers and initials. I know it means something. Codes of some sort that Will probably made up and only he understood. Let's take all these papers out to the kitchen. Get some paper and pencils and make some more coffee. You have a laptop, don't you?"

"Yes." Nathan got to his feet, reached out a hand to pull Lizzie to her feet. She swayed forward until she was in his arms. She sighed when her breasts met his chest. He felt warm and strong. She felt safe. It was inevitable that he would kiss her. And when he did she felt the promise of untold wonders.

Lizzie was the first to break away. "None of that right now. We have work to do. Hey, you made my headache go away!"

"At least I'm good for something," Nathan grumbled. Lizzie laughed.

"Tonight is Zack's retirement party. I'm taking you as my guest. If we can figure some of this out, we can throw out some bait tonight. The whole department will be there. The old gold watch presentation."

"I'll be glued to your side, Lizzie."

"That makes me feel really good, Nathan."

• • •

Nathan threw his pencil across the kitchen. "We've been at this three hours and we're no further along than when we started. Like you said, all we have are numbers and initials. Try calling Aggie again. She might have some insight. We're just making ourselves crazy. It's well past lunchtime. How about I go out and pick up a pizza while you call Aggie? My stomach is feeling a lot better. How's yours?"

"Much better. I actually feel hungry. Pizza sounds good to me. Do you have any big suitcases?"

"As a matter of fact, I do. Soft-sided. I think both of them are big enough to handle all that money. I'll get them for you before I leave. Will you be okay here by yourself?"

Lizzie pointed to her purse which contained her gun. "I'll be fine. Lock the door, though."

"Do you think Chief Shay is in on this?"

"I don't know, Nathan. Aggie's not sure either. Bring some ginger ale back with you. My stomach can't handle any more coffee."

Nathan bowed low, his eyes twinkling. "Your wish is my command."

There was a smile on Lizzie's face when she dialed Aggie's cell phone. Her sister clicked on after the third ring. "It's me, Aggie. I need your help. Listen carefully."

Ten minutes later, Aggie said, "Okay, enough is enough. I'm coming home. This is getting out of hand. I thought it was just a few of the guys, Dutch, Joe, and Will. It sounds to me like it's the whole damn department. If there are as many numbers and initials as you say there are, maybe they're doing a shakedown on store owners for protection, that kind of thing. I'm just guessing here, Lizzie. You could go cruising and check out storefronts and match them up to initials. It's a lot of work, but that's basically what police work is, leg work. As to Chief Shay, I don't think he's one of them. Think about it, Lizzie, why would he have assigned you to the evidence room if he was in on it? Then he said he was available off site to talk if you wanted. Still, I can't be sure. I'll pack up and be home by tomorrow."

"What about the organic carrots? No, Aggie. I'm okay with it all. Nathan is here with me, or I should say, I'm here with him. Like I said, we'll throw out the bait tonight at Zack's retirement party. I'll call you in the morning, and if it looks like things are going to blow up, I'll be in touch. Stay where you are for now. Besides, there's no room at your house. Don't ask, Aggie. I'm staying at Nathan's. Well, of course, Nathan is one of the reasons I'm not in a hurry to head back to Vegas.

"Listen to me, Aggie. We talked about Plan B before. Let's firm it up, okay. You understand it will be an instantaneous thing. There won't be time to think or plan or try to change it. You have your backpack ready to go. You go for it. Right that minute. Tell me you agree. I know I can do it but, Aggie, I haven't really walked in your shoes. There won't be any turning back. I want to hear you say the words, Aggie."

"I'm okay with it, Lizzie. You can count on me. What about Nathan?"

"Nathan can't possibly belong to Plan B. Maybe I should ask you about Alex."

"Alex can't possibly belong to Plan B. Don't worry about me. Did you take care of my bank accounts, Lizzie?"

"Yeah, I did, Aggie. I left you six hundred dollars in your checking account. That's it. You have enough cash to see you through, don't you? Cut up all your old credit cards right now if you haven't done it already. How are the organic carrots doing?"

"With all this sun, they're over an inch high. They look beautiful."

"That's great. Aggie, one more thing before we hang up. How do they dispose of all the confiscated drugs they take in on busts?"

"I don't know, Lizzie. I don't know why I say this, but I think they hold them for a long period of time. I probably got that from Tom. I'm almost certain they burn the drugs at some point. It wasn't exactly dinner table conversation or pillow talk, if you know what I mean. Although, now that I think about it, I don't know why Tom would tell me something like that. By the way, I gained six more pounds. All Alex and I do is eat. We really spruced this place up good. I guess we're going to have to sell it one of these days. Too bad. If we ever get married and have kids, it would be a great place for them to spend their summers." Her voice choked up when she said, "Keep me posted, Lizzie, and be careful."

Lizzie's eyes were misty when she hung up the phone. She looked down at the sheet of paper in front of her. She now had a whole page of names that she could match against the initials on Will Fargo's papers. Aggie thought the numbers meant either the days the initials worked or the dates of the busts or possibly payoff dates and maybe even shakedown deals. It was mind-boggling. She decided to leave it all until Nathan returned. Like he said, two heads were better than one.

Lizzie walked into the living room. She dropped to her knees beside the two large empty suitcases and unzipped them. She stared at the bundles of money. It looked just like the bundles of money she'd seen in the casinos. Drug money. Gambling money. They looked exactly the same. Small bills. Big bills. The bundles were so tightly packed they looked like they had been ironed flat. She sucked in her breath as she started to line the bottom of one of the suitcases with the packets of money. Always good with numbers, Lizzie kept a running total in her head until she got to the bundles of thousand-dollar bills. Most people she knew would probably never see a thousand-dollar bill in their lifetime. She saw them all the time in the high-stakes poker games she participated in and also at the casinos.

Drug money. She hated touching it, knowing people were corrupted and died because of what it bought. Suddenly, she wanted to cry. She was wiping her eyes on her sleeve when Nathan walked into the apartment.

Nathan set the pizza and six-pack of ginger ale on the coffee table. "Lizzie, what's wrong?" He sat down next to her before he took her in his arms.

"I don't know. I was sitting here thinking this money looks the same as gambling money. It just looks like plain old money. People do drugs, they pay for them. This is that money. Tom Madsen died. So did Will Fargo. Aggie and Gus almost died. This damn money had something to do with it. There for a minute, it just got to me.

"I talked to Aggie, and she wanted to come back. I talked her out of it. Let me wash my hands before we eat the pizza. I can't believe I'm hungry."

"I'll get the plates and napkins. Did you find out anything new from talking to Aggie?" he called over his shoulder.

"Yes and no. Aggie doesn't know how the drugs in the evidence room are disposed of or who's in charge of disposing of them. She thinks the drugs are burned at some point. She also thinks some of those numbers and initials mean a shakedown of store owners for protection. I'm wondering, Nathan," Lizzie said as she squatted on the floor, "what's really in those bags of confiscated drugs. I'm going to work tomorrow. I'm going to check it out. Who had a perfect opportunity to substitute, say, sugar or flour?"

"Will Fargo, of course. Don't most cops have snitches?"

"Of course. Aggie and Tom had one named Pippy. Aggie told me when I first got here that Pippy was the one who gave Tom the tip the night he got killed. Why?"

"Maybe you should wave some of this money under his nose," Tom said, pointing to the bundles of money on the floor. "How do you get in touch with him?"

"Aggie said she used to put a note on the bulletin

board in a Laundromat, then he'd call her and they'd set up a meeting at some fast-food joint. She said he was a weasel, but he was reliable. She also said Tom hated him."

Nathan tossed the crust to his pizza into the lid of the box. He reached for another slice. "Does Aggie agree with our assessment that it's a big operation?"

Her mouth full, Lizzie pointed to the stacks of money on the floor and in the suitcase. "There's a lot of money here. Multiply this by twenty or thirty cops, maybe more, and it adds up to big-time. But Aggie suspects that the operation was run entirely by Will, Dutch, and Joe. Just little things Tom said in passing. I don't know if that's enough to go on."

"Aggie's a good cop. She has good instincts. She knows how to add two plus two. If she got four, that's good enough for me. It should be good enough for you, too, Lizzie."

Lizzie nodded, her eyes on the piles of money. "If you stop to think about it, Nathan, what good is all this? The guys can't spend it. If they did, it would arouse suspicion. With the exception of Zack, no one is due to retire anytime soon. It makes you wonder if they keep their money in their basements, and every so often, look at it and count it. What good is that? They'll be too old to really enjoy it if they have to wait for retirement."

"Unless they have some kind of plan," Nathan said. "Remember that deal that went sour eighteen months ago that I was telling you about? Where are those drugs if my theory is right? That might be the big score they're all waiting for. If they can trade whatever they confiscated for big cash, that's when they'll bail out. It's a crapshoot, Lizzie."

"You're right. Let's put this money in these suitcases and find a place to hide it temporarily." She tossed two packets of money on the coffee table. "For Pippy, in case we decide we need him. Don't forget, we have to stop by the house so I can pick up my clothes. When we're done here, make sure you wash your hands real good. Handling money can make you really sick. Don't look at me like that, Nathan. It's true. It happens all the time in Vegas. The counters wear gloves. Germs!"

The minute the suitcases were zipped and locked, both Nathan and Lizzie ran to the bathroom, colliding in the doorway. Nathan looked hopeful. "Do we have time for . . . ?"

Lizzie stood on her toes and kissed him lightly on the lips. "Nope. We have the whole night ahead of us, though. You know what they say about wild anticipation." Nathan groaned. Lizzie laughed. And laughed.

Chapter Eleven

*D*etective Aggie Jade held her face up to the sun. It felt warm and comforting. Out of the corner of her eye she could see Alex turning over the dirt by the back porch. Boxes and boxes of scarlet geraniums sat on the steps waiting to be planted. She clenched her hands into tight fists. They felt cold even though the sun was beating down on her.

Aggie dropped to her knees as she unclenched her hands to reach for the bucket at the end of one of the neat rows of carrots. The weeds were growing faster than the organic carrots. Gus prowled the perimeter of the garden. From somewhere off in the distance, she heard a low rumble of sound. She looked up, but the sky was blue, with a fluffy white cloud directly overhead. Not thunder. Alex either hadn't heard the sound or he was ignoring it. Gus was next to her in the time it took her heart to beat twice. She clutched at him. He whimpered.

And then the sound was all around her. She dived

forward, screaming at the same time. Gus was underneath her, shaking. Another heartbeat later, Alex was on his knees beside her. "Easy, Aggie, easy. It was a jet breaking the sound barrier. Are you okay?"

Aggie's face was whiter than the tee shirt she was wearing. Her voice trembled when she said, "It sounded like . . . I thought . . ." She sat up and hugged her knees, Gus crowding next to her. He was shaking as badly as she was.

"Oh, Aggie, jeez, are you all right? What the hell kind of question is that? Of course you aren't all right," Alex said, putting his arms around both her and Gus. He talked soothingly of the plane, the warm sun, the puffy white clouds. "You're safe, Aggie. It was just a bad moment there. You're okay, Gus is okay, and I'm here. I'm not going to let anything happen to you."

"I . . . know . . . it was just the sound. I wasn't expecting it. It was like that night when I half expected something to happen. It was so loud. I guess I'm not over it, no matter how much I say I am. Maybe I'll never be over it. I don't have any business being a cop.

"All I've been doing since Lizzie called is thinking. I need to resign. Lizzie needs to go back to Vegas where she belongs. Let the department handle the investigation. I don't know what I was thinking when I hatched this scheme. Lizzie's going to get hurt or, worse, get killed, and it will be all my fault. God, Alex, why didn't you stop me?" She cried bitterly against Alex's chest.

Alex was so out of his depth, all he could do was

hold the emotionally fragile woman in his arms and croon softly. "It's all going to work out, Aggie." He wondered if what he was saying was true.

"You're such a good friend, Alex. I couldn't have done this on my own. Even I know that. Right now, I have such a bad feeling I don't know what to do about it. Do you think I'm having a nervous breakdown, Alex?"

"No, of course not. You're worried about your sister. That's natural. Look, the weeding and the geraniums can wait till later. Let's go in the house and look at all that stuff Lizzie faxed to you. We can match it up against the pages from Tom's notebook that you copied. Two heads are better than one. Who knows, maybe we'll come up with something we missed the first time."

Aggie was still trembling, but not as badly, as she followed Alex into the old farmhouse, Gus pressing against her leg.

Alex turned on the little radio sitting on the kitchen counter. Soft music filled the kitchen. Dance music, Golden Oldies, according to the announcer. While Aggie gathered up the papers she needed, he made a fresh pot of coffee. Before he settled himself at the table with Aggie, he offered Gus his choice of a Milk-Bone biscuit or a rawhide chew. The dog opted for both before he settled himself at Aggie's feet.

For two hours they made columns and lists and tried to cross-match the numbers and the initials with no luck. "It's probably Will's homemade code, something he figured only he would understand. It could be license plates, house numbers, birth dates, business addresses. Damn, it could be anything. For all I know it could be tied into his butterfly collection. I just don't know, Alex."

"Maybe we're too anxious. Tell you what, let's go into the living room and lie on the floor. I'll give you a back massage, then you can give me one. Maybe if we relax and shift into neutral, something will come to us."

"Now that's an idea. I'm okay, Alex. Obviously loud noises are going to spook me for a while. It's so peaceful here with only the sounds of birds or a rabbit in the brush that when I heard that jet, it brought it all back. Okay, who goes first?"

"I'll do you first. Lie down flat, arms at your sides, face to the side on a little pillow and these old fingers will work some magic. Just don't go to sleep."

"Oooh, that sounds . . . interesting. Why shouldn't I go to sleep?"

"Because I have great things planned for us, and you need to be awake." He leered at her, wiggling his eyebrows at the same time. Aggie giggled. Gus looked up from his rawhide chew and barked. He looked from one to the other, satisfied that all was right with his beloved mistress.

Ten minutes into the massage, Alex flipped Aggie over and straddled her. He bent low, cupping her face in his hands before he kissed her gently on the lips.

"Hmmmm, for some reason, I thought you could do better than that, Alex."

"That was a teaser to see if you . . ."

"No, no, no. No teasers. I want the *real* thing."

"You do, huh?"

"Hmmm."

He kissed her then, both of them moving into uncharted territory.

A long time later, Alex rolled over on his stomach, his chin leaning into the palm of his hand, his eyes glazed. "I just want to know one thing. What was *that?*"

"*That* was me telling you I've wanted to do this for a very long time," Aggie murmured.

"I liked it. We wasted a lot of years, Aggie."

Aggie smiled. "Maybe it wasn't meant to be back then. You know what they say, everything happens for a reason. We're older, wiser, that kind of thing."

Alex flopped over on his back. "I used to fantasize about this moment. In my fantasy, it was never this good. I wonder why that was?"

Aggie rolled over to prop her chin in her hands. "I fantasized about you, too. On nights when I couldn't sleep, I'd think about you, then I could fall asleep."

"That was a compliment, right?"

Aggie moved closer, dropped her elbows and snuggled closer. "The absolute highest compliment I can give. Don't go getting carried away now."

"God forbid! You wanna get married? Your dog loves me."

Aggie squirmed around so she could stare into Alex's eyes to see if he was serious or joking. He looked serious to her. "Well, sure."

"When?"

When? "When we meet up with Lizzie. She's, among other things, a notary public. That means she can marry us. I told you she was a wild card."

"Okay."

"Okay that she's a wild card or okay that she can marry us?"

"Both," Alex said smartly. "I think I always loved you. I know I felt something the first time we met eons ago, and whatever that was, it never went away. I think we were meant to be with one another. Forever and ever, right?"

Forever and ever couldn't possibly work if she and Lizzie had to resort to Plan B. Without missing a beat, Aggie responded. "I know exactly what you mean. Forever is a long time, Alex. Are you sure?"

"Do I need to breathe to stay alive? Of course, I'm sure. How about you?"

Forget Plan B. "I'm sure."

Alex's voice was wistful when he said, "I bet making love in a real bed with you would be wonderful."

Aggie threw her head back and laughed. A sound of genuine happiness. "Don't go there right now. Anticipate this evening. Let's go into town to dinner. We can share a bottle of wine and come home and . . ."

"Yeah, yeah, and what?"

"You'll see. Let your imagination run wild. I'll let mine run wild. When you do that, anything can happen. Time to get dressed. You have geraniums to plant, and I have weeds to pull. Gus here has a rawhide to chew. What could be better?"

Both of them shrugged into their clothes and walked hand in hand out to the kitchen, where they drank glasses of ice-cold lemonade. Life suddenly took on a whole new meaning.

The glass to her lips, Aggie looked over the rim at

Alex. "Do you have good instincts? You know, gut instincts?"

"Sometimes. Why?"

"I always run with my gut instincts. Something is telling me the code to all this stuff wasn't just here or in Will's head. He was a cop. There's a record. I know there is. You know what my gut is telling me?"

Alex sat down and stared up at his newest best friend. "Tell me."

"When people are collectors of anything, they tend to want to know everything about what it is they're collecting. That means researching it, buying books on the subject, talking to people, that kind of thing. I will bet you my retirement fund that Will Fargo has a collection of butterfly books and everything we ever wanted to know about this deal is in there somewhere. What do you think?"

"Honey, I think you might be on to something. Go on, what else?"

"For instance. Butterflies come in all shapes, sizes, and colors. And there are butterflies all over the world. Take Holland for instance. Besides tulips, I bet they have butterflies. Dutch Davis. Dutch. Get it?

"Zack is retiring to Florida. For sure there are butterflies in Florida. Everyone in the department knows that's where Zack is going. It's all he ever talked about. Page numbers on the butterflies might coincide with the guy's addresses or birth dates. You still with me, Alex?"

"Yeah. Pretty clever."

Aggie finished the lemonade in her glass. "Lizzie is going to have to get into Will's apartment. I remember

Lizzie telling me that Will's brother told her the rent was paid through the end of next month. It's not likely he, meaning the brother, told the management people they could rent it out ahead of time. Lizzie also said there was a key ring in the bag of money. Car keys, apartment keys. Could we be that lucky?"

"Sometimes you catch a break. If Lizzie does have the keys, she could walk right in, and nobody could say a thing. It wasn't a crime scene. My God, what if you're right?"

Aggie tucked the mint green tee shirt into her jeans. She looked down at her sneakers, tears springing to her eyes. *Then Plan B will go into effect sooner rather than later.* She blinked away her tears. "If I'm right, and remember, this is just my gut instinct, then it's over. I, or Lizzie, blow the whistle, and the rats scurry for cover.

"Think about this, Alex. Tonight is Zack's retirement party. All the guys will be there. Maybe tonight would be a good time for Nathan to visit Will's apartment. No one will be paying any attention to him. They'll be watching Lizzie. He could slip out, and no one would be the wiser. Those parties get pretty wild and rowdy. What do you think?"

Alex nodded excitedly. "Call Lizzie. If I didn't tell you I love you, I do."

Aggie's eyes misted up again. This time she didn't blink the wetness away. "Really, Alex."

"Really, Aggie. You're supposed to say something."

Aggie's smile rivaled the sun outside. "I love you, too. I really do."

"Wow!"

Gurgling with laughter, and feeling better than she had in months, Aggie said, "Yeah, wow!"

Shortly before six, Nathan stopped his car on the avenue so Lizzie could run into a grocery store for some cream for their morning coffee. While inside, she picked up the cream, a melon, some blueberry muffins, and a scented candle. The candle was for later. Much later.

In the car, she said, "Our last stop is Aggie's house so I can pick up my clothes from the front porch. We'll have just enough time to shower and get changed and head for the restaurant. By the way, is your cell phone on or off?"

Nathan reached inside his pants pocket. "Damn, it was off, Lizzie. Sorry about that. Oh, oh, there's a message. Maybe my boss is firing me." Aggie made a face as he pressed a series of numbers that would identify the caller and the message he or she had left.

"It's for you, Lizzie. It's Aggie."

Lizzie reached for the phone and brought it up to her ear. She listened, her eyes widening at the message her sister had left for her. "I'll be damned," she muttered. "No wonder she's a cop. Listen to this." She rattled off Aggie's message for Nathan's benefit. "What do you think?"

"You know what, Lizzie, it makes sense. A whole lot of sense. I'm an investigative reporter, and I don't think I would ever have come up with that scenario. I'll slip out of the party when it starts to get noisy. Now we have to go back to the storage locker at

Paramater Mall so I can get the keys out of the bag. We have time, don't panic. I promise to get you to the party on time. It's fashionable to be late, you know."

Forty-five minutes later, they were back in Nathan's sterile-looking condo. Lizzie put the cream and melon in the refrigerator and headed for the bathroom. "Takes me longer, so I'll go first, or do you want me to use the other bathroom, the one with the tub?"

"I have a better idea. Let's take a shower together. That way we'll be right on schedule. While you primp and preen, I'll shave and comb my hair. Deal?"

Lizzie held out her hand, palm up. Nathan whacked it. "No tomfoolery now. We don't have time."

Nathan looked at her and nodded agreeably. Too agreeably. The minute she turned her back, Lizzie grinned from ear to ear. She really didn't care if they were late for Zack's party or not. *Some things* were more important.

The fine hairs on the back of Nathan's neck stood on end when he heard Lizzie screaming from the bedroom. He raced from the kitchen, skidding on the tile floor, almost breaking his neck. "What the hell, Lizzie!"

"Look! Look at this! This is what the girls packed for me to wear to the party! This is Las Vegas attire. If I wear this and bend over, everyone will see my tattoo. Oh, God, what am I going to do?"

Nathan looked at the skimpy attire. "Looks kind

of interesting to me. Are you sure you can get into it?"

Lizzie clenched her teeth. "It *stretches*. Furthermore, you do not wear *red* shoes in Atlanta. They'll call me a floozy or a tart. I should go over there right now and shoot those girls one by one. They did this on purpose. A coat. I'll wear a coat. Or a raincoat."

Nathan was enjoying his companion's discomfort. He could hardly wait to see her in the sparkling red dress that matched the shoes she was holding in her hands. "It isn't raining, Lizzie, and it's too warm for a coat."

"Shut up, Nathan. I'm wearing a coat. Oh, God, it's Vegas nighttime makeup! I could just cry. Why are you still standing there, Nathan? See if you can find me a coat."

"Lizzie, my overcoat and my raincoat will be ten sizes too big for you. You have to wear the dress. Now, get cracking and let's go. You'll be the hit of the party. Fully recovered. A new you! Run with it. You can do it."

"Bite me, Nathan!" Lizzie fumed as she stomped her way to the bathroom, where she emerged fifteen minutes later. She felt better when Nathan whistled approvingly.

"You look spectacular, Lizzie. I mean that."

I used to dress like this all the time and never thought a thing about it, Lizzie thought. She heaved a huge sigh. "Okay, let's go."

"Attagirl. Just don't bend over. Are you sure you can walk in those shoes? Are you wearing a brassiere?"

"Yes, I can walk in these shoes. If all else fails, the heels can be used as weapons. Bra. It's bra, not brassiere. And, yes, I'm wearing one."

"What do you call those things on your legs?"

"Fishnets. They're supposed to be sexy. Do not say another word to me or I'll . . . collapse. Are you sure you don't have a coat? How about a sweater?" Her voice sounded so desperate she could hardly believe it was her own.

"Nope. I'm ready if you are."

"All right, I'm ready."

"Ah, Lizzie, if you sit, don't cross your legs. I think it will be better if you stand all night."

"Okay. Don't take all day when you go to Will's apartment. I want to get out of there as quickly as possible. I have to go to work tomorrow. Those guys are going to rag on me all night long."

"Think of it in terms of flattery. I thought women liked it when men drooled over them."

"Are you drooling, Nathan?" Lizzie snapped.

"No. I'm admiring you. Let's just try to get into a party mood and enjoy the evening."

Lizzie marched to the front door, her stiletto heels clicking on the tile floor. If superconservative Aggie ever heard about this, she would shoot her dead on the spot.

She backed up a step when she reached the door in the foyer and looked at herself in the mirror. Actually, if you were going by Vegas standards, she looked *hot*. Her hair was slickly brushed back away from her face and held in place by sparkling combs. Her hair was just long enough to lick the back of her neck. Her makeup, while heavy, was flawless. The slick hairdo showed off the diamonds on her ears. She wore no other jewelry.

She felt like a lamb going to the slaughter.

Terwilliger's, the local watering hole for most of the department, had been rented for the evening. That meant the establishment was not open to the public. It wasn't a sit-down dinner but a buffet. As was the custom, the chief would make a short speech, hand over the gold watch, and that would be the end of the ceremony. Cops had no patience for speeches and long-winded rhetoric. The liquor would flow, the food would be mostly uneaten and taken later to a homeless shelter.

At some point during the evening, the collection the department had taken up for Zack would be presented in a big box. According to Aggie, the usual collection totaled somewhere around two grand. Enough for a nice vacation for the retiring officer and his missus. She herself had plunked down fifty bucks for Zack's retirement.

Nathan parked the car fifteen minutes later. He hated to see Lizzie so subdued. So she looked a little flashy, so what? "It's going to be okay, Lizzie. Just hold on to my arm until you get the lay of the land. I won't leave for Will's apartment until I'm sure you feel comfortable."

Lizzie climbed out of the car, and tugged on the dress that was so skintight it didn't move. "I'm ready."

The moment Nathan opened the door, smoke swirled outward, and both of them clapped their hands over their ears as Elvis Presley belted out something about blue suede shoes. The room swarmed with police, some in uniform, mostly plainclothes detectives and off-duty cops in civilian clothes.

Lizzie pasted a sickly smile on her face and sashayed over to the bar, where she asked for a glass of seltzer. They were all staring at her; she could feel their eyes boring into her back. In her whole life, she'd never been this nervous. She turned around, moved a little closer to Nathan, and smiled up at him. "Gee, Zack got a nice turnout, don't you think?"

"I'm impressed," Nathan said as he handed Lizzie her glass of seltzer water. He reached for his own bottle of Corona and brought it to his lips. "Let's mingle."

Lizzie winced and flinched at the hissing snide comments as they meandered around the room. Nathan was as good as his word, holding her elbow in the palm of his hand, whispering words of encouragement.

Someone bumped into her on purpose. Lizzie half turned to see Dutch Davis, his arm still in the blue canvas sling. "You're lookin' real good, Aggie. Didn't know you owned anything so fancy. Did you dress like this for old Tom?"

"Get your mind out of the gutter, Dutch. My business is not your business. Excuse me, I want to congratulate Zack on his retirement. Imagine retiring to Florida without a care in the world. That he knows of. I'd say he's one of the lucky ones, wouldn't you? You look guilty to me, Dutch," Lizzie said, moving forward when Nathan tugged at her arm.

"Is that what you call throwing out bait?" Nathan muttered under his breath.

"It's not like I have a whole lot of proof on anything. The truth is, I don't have *any* proof. But that man has such mean little eyes."

The jukebox was belting out another Elvis tune. Zack must be a true Elvis fan. Fellow officers, beer bottles in hand, jostled and shoved as they fought their way to the bar or the buffet. Lizzie heard whistles, suffered through the agonizing leers of the men who worked with Aggie. Her sister would never be able to live this outfit down if she returned to work at the department.

"Aggie, nice to see you. You don't look like yourself. You certainly are one of the department's better-kept secrets," Joe Sonders said, sidling up to her. A cigarette hung out of the corner of his mouth, and in his hand was a full bottle of Michelob. Nathan squeezed her elbow, a sign she was to take it easy.

"That's me, secret weapon number one. How are you, Joe?" Her tone of voice clearly said she didn't really care how he was.

Joe ignored the comment. "We missed you at Will's service. The chief was a little disturbed that you were a no-show." Somehow the cigarette in his mouth wiggled from the left to the right side. Smoke spiraled upward. *Neat trick*, Lizzie thought.

When Lizzie didn't respond, Joe repeated his question. "So where were you, Detective?"

Lizzie turned fully around so that she was in his face. She heard Nathan groan. "You know where I was, Joe. I was in Spokane at Will's brother's house.

Seems Will had an attack of conscience there at the end and told his brother some stuff the brother couldn't handle. I'm having a hard time handling it myself. What else do you want to know?"

Sonders threw his hands in the air, the Michelob slopping onto the floor. "Women! Why do you always have to talk in riddles?" His eyes, Lizzie noticed, were just as mean and dangerous-looking as Dutch's.

Lizzie stepped away from him but Sonders reached for her arm and pulled her back. She obliged. "Maybe you should talk to the chief, Aggie."

"Nah. Why upset the chief," Lizzie said as she jerked her head in Nathan's direction. "You get better coverage in a newspaper. And, they protect their sources. When the time is right, that is."

"What the hell does that mean, Jade?"

"What the hell do you think it means, Sonders?" Lizzie said, mimicking his words.

"I don't have a clue, that's why I asked."

"Tsk, tsk," Lizzie said, clucking her tongue. "Excuse me, Joe, I want to congratulate Zack before I leave. Nathan and I rented a movie for this evening. Did you ever see *Serpico*? Hey, you better watch that cigarette or you're going to burn your mouth. See ya, Joe."

Nathan yanked at her arm. "More bait? Why didn't you just draw the guy a picture? For sure you're no cop." He looked so worried, Lizzie felt pleased.

"I'm sick and tired of pussyfooting around, Nathan. I just want to get this whole thing over with so I can get my life back. Look, there's Zack talking to the chief. I'm good for at least thirty minutes with the two of them. This is a good time for you to head to the men's room and out the door. You have the key, right?"

"I hate leaving you here, Lizzie."

"I'll be fine. No one is going to do anything to me in here. Make sure you get everything pertaining to butterflies." She reached up and kissed him on the cheek. Then she gave him her megawatt smile before she shouldered her way to the chief and Zack.

Lizzie turned around to see if anyone was following or paying attention to Nathan. The room was so smoky she could barely see ten feet in front of her. She shrugged. Nathan was a big boy, and, hopefully, he could take care of himself. She moved on to where Chief of Detectives Shay and Zack were, deep in conversation.

Zack noticed her first. Aggie said she'd always liked Zack and his wife Millie. According to Aggie, Zack had had a rough life. Two years ago, his only daughter had died from cystic fibrosis. Earlier, Zack and his wife had lost their only son to lymphoma. Millie, Zack's wife, wasn't well and suffered from Parkinson's disease. Aggie had said Zack was a good cop.

Lizzie touched his arm gently. "Congratulations, Zack! Guess you'll be fishing every day now."

Zack Miller looked genuinely glad to see her. He threw out his burly arms to hug her. "I'm glad Millie can't see that dress, or she'd want one just like it."

Lizzie laughed because she was supposed to laugh. "How is Millie?"

"She has good days and bad days. Lately most of them seem to be bad. Millie never complains. She said she's going to sit and read and do crossword puzzles while I fish."

"Give her my best. Is it true that you're leaving in the morning?"

"Yep. Our stuff was shipped earlier in the week. We're staying at a motel. Our flight leaves at seven. I should be fishing by midafternoon."

Chief Shay tapped Lizzie's arm. "Excuse me, Aggie, one of the guys is trying to get my attention. By the way, you look real nice."

"Thanks, Chief."

"Zack, can we go someplace a little more quiet, like that corner over there next to the kitchen."

"What's wrong, Aggie, are you in some kind of trouble? Can I help?"

Lizzie nodded as she made her way toward the kitchen. "Listen, Zack," she said, leaning close to him so she wouldn't have to shout. "Zack, I know you and Millie have passports because you went to Italy a couple of years ago. Don't go to Florida tomorrow. Go . . . go somewhere else. Someplace they can't extradite you. Argentina, or some damn banana republic. Don't get too comfortable. Move around. Think about Millie. Are you listening to me, Zack? I want you to smile like I just told you a cop joke. In case your friends are watching. Do it, Zack." He obliged.

"Aggie . . . I . . . never . . . it . . . Millie . . . our daughter. The bills . . . I hate those bastards. Honest to God, I do. It was never . . ."

"Don't say anything else, Zack. Travel light. Remember to move around."

"Aggie, why?"

"You're a good cop, Zack, and I adore Millie." Zack looked like he was going to cry. "I just told you another cop joke. Laugh, Zack. They're watching us." Zack obliged a second time. Lizzie leaned over and hugged him. For the benefit of anyone listening or watching, she raised her voice, and said, "Don't you dare send me any fish! Give my best to Millie."

Zack played along. "You got it, Aggie."

That was probably the stupidest thing you've ever done in your whole life, Lizzie Jade. She shouldered her way to the bar, where she asked for a scotch on the rocks. She gulped at it, her eyes darting around the smoky room. A stool opened up at the bar. She almost sat down when she remembered Nathan telling her not to. She turned back to the bar just as she smelled the chief's aftershave. She heaved a sigh of relief when he set his empty Bud bottle on the bar and asked for another one.

The chief rubbed at the bald spot on his head as he locked gazes with Lizzy. "Didn't mean to skip out on you, Aggie. Bring your drink and let's move over there at the other end of the bar where it isn't so crowded." He turned away and looked at the burly Dutch. "You better not be driving tonight, Davis."

"I'm not, Chief. Dumfey is the designated driver tonight. He's drinking Sprite, sir. Real nice party, Chief."

Chief Shay elbowed his way farther down the bar, where he poked a detective second grade to get off the chair. Lizzie had no other choice but to take a seat. She immediately reached for a paper napkin and spread it on her lap. She took the initiative. "How's it going, Chief?"

Shay looked around the rowdy bar. "I wish I was in Zack's shoes tonight. Sometimes the job gets to you. You understand that, don't you, Jade?"

"Yes, I do. I tend to think it's like that in any job. You work all your life just for the day you retire. No one should hate their job."

"Are you saying you aren't looking forward to retirement, Jade?"

"No, I am, but in a different kind of way. I love what I do. All those months in rehab soured me a little. Then those other three months of staring at the walls wasn't for me. That's why I wanted to go back to work. When I retire, I'll have to come up with an all-consuming hobby, like Will Fargo and his butterflies. I would find butterfly collecting boring. I need to interact with people. How about you, Chief?"

"I'm going to play golf seven days a week. I'm not going to join any of those senior groups either. My wife is a club person, I'm not. Will now, he belonged to all these botany clubs. He was consumed with those damn butterflies. Maybe *obsessed* is a better word. I think he has every book ever printed on the subject of butterflies."

"You're right, I'd call that obsessed. You know what they say, Chief, different strokes for different folks."

The chief leaned in closer. "Do you want to talk about it, Aggie?"

There was no use pretending she didn't know what the chief was talking about. He'd called her Aggie, which meant they were talking personally, not professionally. "I do, but not right now, Chief. Can you cut me a little slack?"

The chief nodded as he mopped at his bald head again. "You see all this smoke in the room, Aggie?" She nodded. "It's kind of that way at the precinct right now. Oh, you can't see it, but something's going on. I suspect it involves you in some way. I'm going to figure it out, Jade."

Jade. They were back on a professional footing again. She had to be careful. She fiddled with the napkin in her lap. She nodded.

"If I find out you're out there investigating on your own, or if I find out you're withholding evidence in a murder investigation, I'll slam the book at you. IAD will be on your tail like fleas on a dog. Just so you know, Jade. Speaking of fleas, how's the dog?"

"Gus is fine, Chief. Once in a while he gets spooked the way I do. We're both working on it. I'm thinking of retiring him."

The chief finished his beer and set the empty bottle on the bar. The little talk was now over. Aggie risked a glance at her watch. Hopefully, Nathan was on his way back.

"Where's that reporter you came with, Aggie?"

Lizzie laughed ruefully. "I think he's probably hanging out in the men's room. He said he ate some bad fish last night. At first he wasn't even going to come with me, but he changed his mind. He might be outside. It is smoky in here. I should go look for him."

"Is he your new fella, Aggie?"

New fella. "I'm not sure. I like him a lot. Time will tell. Chief, it was over between Tom and me before . . . before that night."

"I know that, Aggie. Tom and I had a long talk about it. He knew you asked for a transfer. He didn't like it, but he accepted it. Tom was a good cop, one of the best."

"Yes, he was. He was real good to his parents, too. That says a lot about a person in my book."

"My book, too. Remember what I told you. Anytime you feel the need to *talk*, we can go off site."

¹"Okay, Chief."

Aggie fiddled with the napkin in her lap. She debated ordering another drink. Her eyes were starting to water from all the smoke in the air. Maybe she should go outside for some air. She slid off the stool, tugged at the spandex dress, and was about to fight her way through the crowd when she *smelled* Dutch Davis and Joe Sonders.

"Excuse me, Detectives. I was just on my way to the ladies' room."

"You hear that, Joe, Detective Jade is on her way to the ladies' room."

"Yeah, I heard her say that, Dutch."

Lizzie tilted her head to the side and looked up at Dutch Davis. "Didn't you learn your lesson the last time I asked you something nicely?"

"We need to talk about that, Jade. There's two of us now. And a whole lot of others," he said, waving his good arm about.

"Your own little army?" Lizzie clucked her tongue to show what she thought of that statement. "This is the second time I'm asking you to move out of the way so I can go to the ladies' room. I never ask a third time. I hardly ever ask twice, but sometimes I do because I figure the person really didn't hear me the first time." Surely the two of them wouldn't try to pull something nasty with the chief in the room. She looked around and for the first time noticed the officers clustered around the bar. Six deep. The blue wall Aggie always talked about. The chief would never know what happened.

Lizzie stood on one foot, her right arm reaching down to remove first one stiletto heel, then the other. She brought both of them up at exactly the same moment. One gouged Dutch Davis directly below his nose, the other jabbed at Sonders's right eye. Her elbows rammed sideways almost simultaneously. The wall parted as both detectives clutched their faces, cursing ripely.

Lizzie moved forward, muttering something about clumsy men. She leaned over and hissed, "I know *everything*." She almost fainted when she heard her name being called. Nathan.

Roaring like a bull in pain, Dutch Davis was on his feet, charging at her. Zack appeared out of nowhere and stuck his leg out. Davis hit the floor. Hard. "Get the hell out of here, Aggie," Zack hissed.

On her way to the exit, Lizzie passed Chief Shay. "What's going on?" he asked.

Lizzie shrugged. "Some guys are so clumsy. Ask Zack, he was right there when Dutch went down. I'm heading home, Chief. Nice party. See you in the morning."

Outside, Lizzie took a deep breath. "We need to get out of here right now, Nathan. I did . . . I had this little altercation. Run, Nathan."

They ran.

Inside the car with the doors locked, Lizzie gasped. "Did you get the books?"

"Did I ever! Five cartons. I'm glad that guy lived on the first floor. It's all in the trunk."

"I love you, Nathan Hawk," Lizzie gasped as she buckled up. "Hey, I lost my shoes. I bet you five bucks they end up in the evidence room tomorrow."

Nathan laughed. He loved this girl. He really did.

Chapter Twelve

*T*he minute Chief Shay left Zack Miller's retirement party, Joe Sonders hopped onto the bar and let loose with a sharp whistle. The noisy smoky room grew silent. "You, you, you over there, and you, too," Joe said, pointing to his fellow officers. "Let's take this outside where we can talk." To the others who were grumbling about being excluded, mainly the female officers, Joe pointed to the three bartenders by jerking his head in their direction. Party hearty, lads," he said as he hopped down from the bar. The female officers grumbled louder, but no one paid attention to them.

Sonders played the role of the Pied Piper as he led the way out of the bar to the crowded parking lot.

Even though he wasn't one of the officers Joe pointed to, Zack Miller followed the entourage to the parking lot, beer bottle in hand. He pretended to be tipsy for Joe's benefit. The truth was, he'd been nursing the same bottle of beer almost all evening.

God, how I hate these guys, he thought.

"Whatcha doing here, Zack?"

Zack swayed back and forth. "Just want to take some memories with me, Joe. After tonight, I'm probably never going to see you guys again. Makes me sad," he pretended to choke up.

Dutch Davis slid his good arm around Zack's shoulder. "You're going to see plenty of us. We got big plans for you in south Florida. We're gonna make you so rich you'll be able to hire someone to do your fishing. All you'll have to do is watch."

Zack blinked. *Was this guy always so stupid? The answer is yes.* "Sounds good to me," he said, purposely slurring his words.

The group huddled. "She's on to us," Sonders said. "It's just a matter of time before she spills her guts. We have to get to those cars. We waited too long as it is. We shoulda done it at the impound lot. Now it's *out there.*"

"She's got no proof," Davis blustered.

"Don't be stupid, Dutch. All she has to do is rip her car apart. Sooner or later she's going to get wise to Tom's car, too. Will's brother has been talking to her. Do any of you know where Will stashed his stuff? I sure as hell never knew. The brother probably found it and turned it all over to Aggie. Will was a record keeper. That means he wrote everything down someplace even though we told him not to. That's what Aggie has. I'd stake my life on it. We did a shakedown on that ratty apartment where he lived. There wasn't even a phone bill to be found. Aside from the normal apartment stuff, the only other thing in it was all those damn butterfly books. That means he stashed his stuff someplace else or the brother took it all. I sent Karl Locke to Spokane this morning to pay a visit to the brother. He got back to me right before the party. The brother had already split. That's more proof, Dutch."

Zack swayed to the right, then caught himself before he could topple over. "Whatcha gonna do, Joe? You kill her, the whole thing is gonna fall apart, and I won't be here to help you."

"Don't worry about it, Zack. You just worry about sobering up so you can get on that plane in the morning. I say we go after her brand-new boyfriend. She'll play ball with us. She'll clam up, I can almost guarantee it if she thinks he's in our sights."

"Yeah, well, what if you're wrong?" Zack persisted. "If you guys get hung up on this, they're going to come after me and drag me away from my fishing pier. You need to be fool . . . fool . . . proof," Zack said triumphantly. He slurped from his beer bottle. "You guys want me to stay on and help?" *Please God, make him say no.*

"Nah. You gotta take care of Millie," Joe said. "You should be heading out, Zack. The party's over. We'll be seeing you."

"You sure, Joe?"

"I'm sure, Zack. You got your gold watch and the money?"

Zack tapped his jacket pocket. "Right here."

They all clapped him on the back and shook hands. There was nothing for Zack to do but head for his car. He knew they were watching him as he got in, started up the engine, turned on the lights, and left the parking lot. He drove around the corner, parked, got out, and ran back as fast as he could to the parking lot. He wove his way among the cars until he was within listening distance of his coworkers.

"I'm telling you, it's safe. Half is in Tom's car, the other half in Aggie's. There's no way we can get to her car at her house with that damn dog. We have to wait till she parks it at the station or in a supermarket lot. There's a bunch of people staying at her house. That's out for now. Madsen's car, complete with all the bullet holes, is in his old man's garage. Beats the hell out of me why they would want to keep that, but they did. It's not going to be a problem to get to it. I say we do it before it gets light out."

"What's that mean, Dutch? Man, you are one drunk dude," Sanders snarled. I told you to go easy on the sauce tonight. Are you saying you want us to take it out of the cars before it gets light, or are you saying you want to leave it and get her busted for possession? Which is it? I thought that was supposed to be our big score. The score we were going to unload in Miami with Zack's help. Then we were going to split for parts unknown."

Dutch leaned against the cab of his Dodge pickup. "Yeah, that *was* the plan. Now I want to fry her ass. There will be other scores. We need to get her out of the way. If she's arrested, it solves our problem."

"You're letting this get personal, Dutch. You aren't the only one who has a say in this. We all do. I say we call a meeting first thing tomorrow morning when everyone is sober. Majority rules. Time now is our enemy. In case you were too drunk to observe the chief tonight, I wasn't. He knows something is going on. He's been talking to Aggie a lot lately. Now that she has that reporter on her string, things are going to move real fast. I say we take the stuff and hit the road. I'm okay with leaving a couple of kilos in Tom's and Aggie's cars, but that's it. You can send in an anonymous tip when we're safe and sound and away from here. Now, let's go home and get some sleep. Spread the word, and we'll meet up at six o'clock in the squad room."

"Who made you the boss of this outfit?" Dutch growled.

"You did when you got too drunk to think," Sonders said. "Talk to me about giving the job back to you when you sober up." Without another word, he stalked off toward his car. One by one, his fellow officers followed suit until only Dutch Davis remained.

Zack watched from his hiding place as Dutch lashed out with his foot to kick the tires of his pickup. He listened to the venom he spouted until he got sick to his stomach. *I have to warn Aggie somehow. But how? The reporter? He can get a message to Aggie. I'll have to use a pay phone, though. Maybe the one at the motel where I'm staying. Yeah, yeah, that's what I'll do. No, the guys know the name of the motel. Another pay phone, maybe one near where the reporter lives or by the paper he works for. Yeah, that sounds better.*

Zack waited until he felt safe enough to leave his hiding spot and head for his car.

• • •

Their arms loaded with boxes of books on butterflies, Aggie and Nathan made their way to the elevator in Nathan's high-rise. "Did you look through the books?"

"No. I was too antsy, I just wanted to get out of there. The place gave me the heebie-jeebies. You said you were going to tell me how you lost your shoes. This might be a good time, Lizzie."

Lizzie took a deep breath. "I got in a little over my head there at the bar. I saw the way the guys crowded in so the chief couldn't see what was going on. They had something planned. I could see it in that disgusting Dutch's face. I took off those spike heels I was wearing and jammed the heels into Dutch's and Joe's faces. Then I elbowed them both in the gut and got out of there. That's when you showed up.

"Do you know what I think, Nathan? I think the whole squad is a ticking bomb. They don't know which way to go right now. They are going to do something, though. That's a given. It would be nice if you made us some coffee while I get out of these clothes."

Nathan stared at her, worried, yet in awe of her bravery. "You need to stop being so fearless. There's not a single one of those guys or women that I would trust. I wish you'd stop inciting those creeps, and stay out of harm's way. Do you need any help?"

Lizzie laughed. "You need to have a little more faith in me, Nathan. Not right now, but later I'm certain I'll require your help. Two sugars and a dollop of cream."

"For you, anything. What's a dollop?" he called over his shoulder.

"A quick squirt. I like to taste the coffee."

Fifteen minutes later, they had Will Fargo's butterfly books divided equally. They had coffee, their previous lists that had so far made no sense, pads, and pencils perched in their laps ready to start to work. "If my sister is wrong about this, I'm going to be really upset," Lizzie muttered.

"My reporter's nose tells me she's right. Okay, here's the master list Aggie gave us of every cop in the precinct. Next to the name is the address, and we hope it's current, along with social security number, badge number, birth date, and the usual physical characteristics. I had the paper run a check on their license plates, and by the way, that's a no-no, and that's all we have to go on or match up."

"If you stop and think about it, it's a lot. The only reason Aggie had all this stuff on those discs you printed out is because she updated the files for the police commissioner. It was some kind of special project the chief assigned her to last winter. She wasn't allowed to do it at home, so she did it over a two-day weekend in the office. A weekend, she said, with double time. She said she was supposed to return the discs, but she made a copy. Her reasoning was rather simple. She said you just never know when you're going to need stuff like this. It's a no-no, too. Good thing, huh?"

"Damn good thing. Are we saying they weren't doing a shakedown of store owners for protection?"

"I don't know. I tend to think not. Too many

voices. Store owners tend to band together and talk. My gut says no. Aggie thought it might be a possibility. We won't rule it out, though. For now, we'll just ignore it. Let's get started."

It was an hour later when Lizzie let out a whoop. "God, how I love that sister of mine! Look at this! I know who this guy is. He's the warrant officer, and his name is Leonard Pipe. See this butterfly. Look what someone wrote on the page. Someone . . . Will, of course. Look at the numbers under the actual picture of the butterfly. It matches up with the last four numbers of Pipe's social security number. The butterfly is called Pipevine Swallowtail. It's iridescent blue or blue-green in color. According to our file here, Pipe has blue-green eyes. The Pipevine Swallowtails are common in Georgia in late summer. Pipe lives here in Atlanta, and was transferred to the precinct in August of '98. He lives at 713 Linn Avenue. The Pipevine Swallowtail has a seven-to-thirteen-centimeter wingspan. The botanical name for the Pipevine Swallowtail, according to this page, is *Battus philenor* (Linnaeus). Put it all together and it spells Leonard Pipe to me. Talk about clever. I think we can assume the numbers in the margin on this page are the *dates* of Pipe's payouts as well as Will's own payments, and the numbers at the bottom of the page are the amounts of money Pipe *received*. My God, it must have taken him *forever* to do all this bookkeeping." Lizzie whistled to show how impressed she was by Will Fargo's records.

Nathan's eyes almost popped out of his head at what he was seeing. "No, not forever. If he knew everything there was to know about butterflies, it was easy. It was probably a simple matter to Fargo. Maybe a few hours to document each one of his fellow officers. It would be a simple matter, minutes really, to update the records. I have to admit, this is something I never would have stumbled on. Your sister is an absolute genius!" Zack said generously. Lizzie smiled. An intimate smile that brought a sparkle to Nathan's eyes.

"Let's get back to work."

Forty-five minutes later, Lizzie let loose with another whoop of joy. "Wow! Look at this! There's a vice cop on Aggie's list named Cassius Bluewood. He was born and raised in Columbia, South Carolina. This butterfly is named, Cassius Blue. Or *Lepotes cassius*. It has a 3.5-centimeter wingspan. The Cassius Blue is a South Carolina butterfly. Says the caterpillar host is lima beans. They have plenty of lima beans in the South. They're like a staple in the diet. Aggie told me that once, and she loves lima beans and corn bread. You can also find this butterfly in Texas and Florida. Bluewood lived in Texas for three years before he moved to Florida, where he worked for two years. He finally moved here to Atlanta five years ago. See, it all fits. It's all here, Nathan.

"Here's one that literally jumped off the page. It's a female cop, and Aggie partnered with her before she was transferred to a different unit due to a disability of some kind. Her name is Holly Azure, and she's Spanish. Holly is a nickname. Her real name is Hollyfina. This butterfly is named, Atlantic Holly Azure. Holly has gray hair. This particular butterfly, according to what I'm reading, has wings of pale gray with dark gray markings. It's official name is *Celastrina idealla*. Holly's birthday is 3–9–45. This butterfly has a wingspan of 3.9 centimeters. The really large males can have a wingspan as large as four to five centimeters. Are we on a roll or what?" Lizzie's voice was so excited, Nathan laughed out loud.

Lizzie looked across the coffee table to make eye contact with her host. She smiled. "I think, Nathan, in your own way, you half figured it out yourself. That night at Daniel Fargo's house when you pulled that gun on me, you said something about butterflies, and the one on my rump made you think I was in on it. By the way, it's a pink-and-yellow Monarch." Nathan shrugged, uncomfortable with the reminder that he'd pulled a gun on Lizzie. Or was it the butterfly on her rear end that was making him uncomfortable? He brightened almost immediately as he remembered the delicate pink-and-yellow butterfly on Lizzie's rump.

They went back to work.

By midnight, they had what Lizzie said were four perfect matches and six pending.

"It's your proof, Lizzie." Nathan was so exuberant, Lizzie burst out laughing.

They looked at each other when Nathan's phone rang. He reached behind him to grapple with the phone. He barked a greeting, hoping it wasn't the paper sending him on a case somewhere.

"Mr. Hawk, can I leave a message for you to give to Detective Jade?" the voice queried without offering a greeting of any kind or identifying himself.

"Detective Jade is right here. You can give the message to her yourself. Just a minute, I'll get her." Nathan shrugged as he held up a finger to mean she should wait to speak till he got to the kitchen, where he could pick up the extension and listen to the conversation. He dragged the extension cord to the doorway so Lizzie could see he had the phone in his hand that held down the button. He nodded.

Lizzie picked up the phone. "This is Detective Jade."

"Aggie, it's Zack Miller. I only have a few seconds so listen up. I want to give you a heads up. I want you to do something as soon as we hang up. I want you to get your car and take it someplace where no one can find it. Do it right *now*. As soon as you do that, go to Tom Madsen's parents' house and take his car and do the same thing. Are you listening to me, Aggie? Do you understand what I'm telling you?"

"Yes. Do you want to tell me why?"

"No. You're smart, Aggie, you'll figure it out. I have Millie in the car, and we're leaving now. We're square now. You're a good cop, Aggie. One of the best I ever worked with. If Millie knew, she'd thank you, too. Have a great life."

Lizzie blinked as she looked down at the phone in her hand.

"That was Zack Miller. He said I was to take my car and Tom's, too, and put them someplace safe. He didn't elaborate. I guess we better do what he says. Aggie said she knew it was too good to be true that her car was untouched. Where's a safe place? I don't know that much about Atlanta. Nathan, do you know a safe place where we can hide two cars?"

"As a matter of fact, I do. Artie Bennigan, a friend of mine, gave me a key to his house because he's forever losing his keys. It's in my desk drawer at the office. Actually, he gets the keys made by the dozen, and I'm the keeper of the keys. I give it to him when he locks himself out, which is at least twice a week, then he never gives the keys back because he either loses or misplaces them. Anyway, he has a two-car garage. We can slide his Beemer out and leave it in the driveway and put yours and Tom's cars inside."

"Nathan, you are the marvel in marvelous." Lizzie inched closer to give him a hearty lip-smacking kiss. She wanted the kiss to go on forever but knew there would be time later. Now, they had to take care of business. Nathan groaned when she said, "Up and at 'em, big guy. We have work to do. I hate waking up the Madsens at this hour, but we gotta do it. We'll do Tom's car first, then mine, okay? I'll call on the way to alert the Madsens. We don't want a whole bunch of lights going on all of a sudden to alert the neighborhood."

"One of these days I have to get some sleep, Lizzie. I'm going on adrenaline."

"Okay, we'll sleep tomorrow night. No, we can't. I have to get back to the girls. We'll figure something out, Nathan, I promise."

Nathan was on his feet looking down at her. He reached for her hand. "I'm falling in love with you. I want you to know that." Lizzie bit down on her lower lip. She wanted to say, *I'm falling in love with you, too,* but she didn't. Plan B didn't allow for falling in love. Instead, she smiled and hugged him, hating the way his eyes clouded over, as though he knew what she was thinking.

The night seemed exceptionally quiet. Almost as quiet as Lizzie and Nathan tooling along the side streets on their way to the Madsen house.

Lizzie stared out at the quiet night. She rolled the window down so she could smell the warm evening air. She loved springtime. "Should I try the number again, Nathan? It's well after midnight. Where could they be? Do you think they're sound sleepers? I always thought as you got older you slept less and were light sleepers. I know I read that somewhere."

Nathan turned to look at his companion. "Is it possible they're out of town?"

"Mrs. Madsen said they didn't get to visit their daughter too often. I think the daughter lives in Seattle. That's how I got confused with Daniel Fargo. I'm dithering here, Nathan. Help me out."

"I don't know too much about elderly people, Lizzie. My parents are always in the house by ten because my dad likes to watch the late-evening news. He has a bowl of cornflakes, gets into his pajamas, and watches the news. It's a ritual. It's one of those absolute musts that he be home by ten. He makes my mother nuts with his routines. Maybe the Madsens are like that.

"It's hard to see the street signs. I think it's one block over. Will you be able to recognize the house if we can't read the house numbers?" Nathan asked.

Lizzie peered out into the darkness. "I think so. Drive slow. Their mailbox is at the end of the driveway. It's white with flowers painted on it. It matches their trash can. The flowers I mean. The trash can is white, too. I remember thinking Mrs. Madsen must have painted it herself. Okay, there it is. There's a car in the driveway. If they went away, they didn't go by car. Since it's a one-car garage, do you suppose Tom's car is really inside?"

Nathan turned off his headlights and drove up the driveway and parked behind the Madsens' car.

"You try the back door, and I'll go around front. Just keep your finger on the bell until a light goes on."

Lizzie did as instructed. She finally removed her index finger from the bell when Nathan appeared. She shook her head. "Maybe they went to see their daughter. What do you think we should do?"

"Let's try the garage. It's detached, so that means there's a door on the side. Maybe they're like Daniel Fargo and don't keep it locked. Sometimes keys can be a pain in the neck. Now if you were a *real* cop, you could jimmy the lock with one of those picks you see cops use in the movies. Do you have a hairpin or something?"

"No, I don't have a hairpin or something. It's locked." Disgust rang in Lizzie's voice.

"If this is a senior citizen housing development, we need to get out of here. Cops patrol senior neighborhoods. My dad told me that. Seniors are nocturnal. My mom and dad prowl around all night long. My mother loves looking out the window to see if anything is going on. Someone might see us, report us to the cops. One or possibly more of the neighbors are probably looking out for the house. You know, keeping an eye on it, bringing in the mail and newspaper. My dad does it for Charlie Wilson when he goes on his golfing trips. How's it going to look if cops show up here?"

Lizzie felt like her heart was leapfrogging inside her chest. Common sense told her they should leave. She remembered the anxiety in Zack's voice. The anxiety and the sense of urgency. Then she thought about her sister Aggie and her career. "Not good, Nathan. Let's look around for an outside key. If we can't find one, we'll break one of the panes of glass. Mrs. Madsen loves Aggie. She won't sign a complaint. She'll understand if the cops call her after they talk to the neighbors. I know as sure as I'm standing here, one of these neighbors knows where they are and also knows the daughter's phone number. This looks like one of those nice neighborhoods where people all look out for one another. Start looking, Nathan. Just don't make any noise."

Nathan returned minutes later. "I came up dry. Maybe the Madsens don't believe in leaving keys outside, especially after they were burglarized. It's understandable. If you break that pane of glass, Aggie, you are going to make some serious noise. We can come back in the morning as soon as it gets light out. Seniors get up before dawn breaks. I don't know why that is. My dad couldn't wait to retire so he could sleep in. He gets up at quarter to five. My mother gets up at five. Oh, she's awake, she just stays in bed so my dad will make the coffee. She said she did it for fifty years, and it's his turn now."

Nathan was babbling, and it worried Lizzie. She wondered if she would ever get to meet the elder Hawks. Probably not. She grimaced in the darkness. Sometimes, things just didn't work out no matter how hard you tried. Nathan was probably right, and they should leave.

"All right, let's go. We can go get my car and take it to your friend's house. I'll put it in neutral, and you can push me down the driveway. That way we won't alert the dog or the girls. Are you okay with that, Nathan?"

"Lizzie, I am not okay with any of this. Think about it. What the hell are we doing anyway. I know you didn't ask for my opinion, but I'm going to give it to you anyway. I say we take the butterfly books to Chief Shay, you tell him what you suspect, and let the department and the commissioner and mayor do the rest. Aren't you supposed to go to work tomorrow?"

"Oh, God, I forgot about that. That means we have to break the glass and do it now. There's no way I can do this in the morning. If you tap the glass, it should fall inward and cushion the sound. Or, you can take off your shirt, and I'll hold it under the window to catch the glass if you're worrying it will fall outward. We have to do it now, Nathan. I'll look around for a stone or a brick. Don't worry, I'll be quiet."

Lizzie returned five minutes later with a stone that was a little bigger than a pebble from Mrs. Madsen's flower garden. She gaped when she saw the door was wide open. "How'd you do that?" she hissed.

"The tip of my penknife. I just wiggled and jiggled. I'll close the door and hold my shirt up over the windows while you turn on the light."

Lizzie took a moment to admire Nathan's naked torso before she turned to look at Tom Madsen's black four-by-four. Her hands flew to her mouth when she saw how the car and windshield were riddled with bullets. "Aggie was in that car. She must have thought she was going to die that night. It's a miracle she didn't. The tires have been shot out, too. The Madsens must have had the car towed here. That means we can't take it out of here, Nathan."

"Dammit, Lizzie, you mean this was all for nothing? Let's just drive it on the rims. It's no good anyway. We need to get out of here. When you open that garage door, it's going to make noise. It might have an automatic light for all I know. Are you listening to me, Lizzie?"

"Shhh. I'm thinking. How far away does your friend live from here?"

"A couple of miles, and despite what I just said, I do not have a clue if the rims will hold up till we get there. If that's your game plan, you'd better give some thought to what will happen if that car conks out in the middle of the road. What are you going to do?"

"You will push it the rest of the way. I'm going to knock out the overhead fluorescent light with that shovel in the corner. I'll open the door a little at a time so it won't make noise. You push it down the driveway."

"Lizzieeeee! The Madsens' car is parked outside."

"On the other side, Nathan. The driveway is big enough for two cars across. You parked behind the Madsens. We can do this. Okay, I'm going to crack that overhead bulb. I know exactly where it is, so turn out the light."

Nathan clenched his teeth when he heard the long cylinder fall on top of the car. "I thought you said you knew where the bulb was."

"I guess it wasn't screwed in very tight. Stop worrying. Put your shirt on."

Nathan watched, holding his breath, as Lizzie inched the garage door up little by little until it was all the way up."

"Lizzie?"

"Now what?"

"How are you going to start up the car? You don't have a key."

"Oh. I'll hot-wire it. I used to work in a garage, remember. Trust me. Just push the car out, and it should roll down the driveway. Use those gorgeous muscles. Then follow me to the road and push me a little farther down the street. I don't want to start it up here. If you know this area, stick to the side streets. Stay close behind me."

Gorgeous muscles. Nathan felt his chest puff out. He pushed, using his gorgeous muscles. He didn't stop to wonder how Lizzie shifted the car into neutral.

Lizzie's gaze kept going to the passenger side of the car as she crawled along on the flat tires at ten miles an hour. Her sister had sat there that night, Gus in the backseat, while they waited for the action to start. How frightened she must have been. She felt herself shudder. "I'm going to make this right, Aggie. I'm mad now. Really mad."

Thirty-five minutes later, Lizzie looked at her watch. The time was 1:25 A.M. Several cars passed her two-car parade, then Nathan was ahead of her, signaling that he was going to turn into a driveway. Town houses. A yuppie haven. She sighed with relief. Yuppies were into themselves and not watching through windows. Unlike seniors, most yuppies had an aversion to the cops.

Lizzie coasted to a stop when Nathan parked his Intrepid at the opposite end of the driveway while she stopped at the curb. She crept out of the car, the engine running.

It was dark, the streetlights being situated at each end of the block. Artie Bennigan lived in the middle. A few lamppost lights glowed dimly toward the end of the street. The yuppies probably either forgot to turn them out, or they weren't home yet.

Lizzie's heart felt like it was going to explode out of her chest when Nathan opened the garage door. Moments later, the Beemer, Nathan at the wheel, slid backward until it was on the street. Like a crab, he scuttled over to where she waited and motioned for her to drive into the garage. She did, the rims grinding on the concrete driveway. Somewhere between the Madsens' house and here, all the tires had peeled away. She felt like she was sitting on the ground.

The minute she was inside the garage, the light out, Lizzie hopped out of the car. She was dizzy with relief. Nathan, what she could see of his expression, looked like he was going to black out at any second. She waved her hand in front of his face. "C'mon, Nathan, get with the program here. Let's close the door and get the hell out of here."

Nathan took a great gulp of air, just as headlights swung onto Artie's street at the corner. In seconds, he made a beeline for the Intrepid, and raced it up and into the garage. The door closed just as the approaching car was less than a building away. He grabbed Lizzie and smashed his lips against hers. She didn't protest. He mumbled against her lips, "I think it's a police cruiser on patrol. We live here, you and I, and I'm Artie Bennigan. Now let's break away and head for the front door. I have the key. Slow and easy, Lizzie. We belong here. Son of a bitch, he's stopping. Take the key and open the door. I'll follow. Go on, Lizzie. Do not turn on the outside light. Move, dammit. They might recognize you."

Lizzie played her part in a high, trilling voice. "Hurry up, honey, you promised to make my night."

Nathan stepped onto the small patch of grass on the side of the driveway to get out of the glare of the police lights. Even so, the light was illuminating. "I'm coming sweetie. Just hold on." He crossed his fingers that the cop in the cruiser was a rookie. Usually rookies got the midnight shift.

"Anything wrong, Officer?"

"Do you live here, sir?"

"Yep. Me and the missus. Is something wrong?"

"Is the Beemer yours, sir?"

"Sure is, and let me be the first to tell you, you don't want one. It's in the shop more than on the road. My license and registration are in the car. Name's Arthur Bennigan. I work for the *Journal-Constitution*. Hey, can I go in now? My wife is waiting for me?"

"Go ahead. Next time you come home this late, don't make so much noise."

"Okay, Officer. Sure. Have a nice night." Seconds later he was in Artie Bennigan's living room with Lizzie's arms around him. He felt faint. They held on to each other. "Turn on one of the lights," Nathan whispered.

Lizzie obliged. "I think I'm going to be sick, Nathan."

His eyes wild, Nathan said, "No, you are not going to be sick. Take deep breaths. We need to sit down right here on these steps and calm down."

"What . . . what made you put your car in the garage, Nathan?" Lizzie hated the way her voice was cracking with the stress she was feeling.

Nathan shook his head to clear it. "I don't know why. Something just said, park it in the garage. Some kind of instinct, I guess. Guess I'm going to have to borrow Artie's car for a little while. He won't mind unless we smash it up. If we do, you, being rich and all, will have to spring for a new one."

"Yeah, okay," Lizzie said agreeably. "What are the chances of your buddy Artie having some brandy? I could use a drink right now. I don't know when I've ever been this rattled."

Nathan turned on a lamp in the living room. "Hey, this is nice. I've never been here before."

Lizzie looked around approvingly. There was no

doubt that this was a man's pad, but it was comfortably and tastefully decorated. "I bet his mother did all the decorating. It has a woman's touch. Comfort first, good taste second. Why do men always think they have to be surrounded by dark colors like burgundy, hunter green, dark brown? Is it a cave-dwelling thing or what?" Nathan burst out laughing.

"Found some plum brandy," Nathan called from the dining room, where Lizzie could see him holding up a bottle. "Let's just swig from it and not dirty glasses, okay?"

"Okay with me. Oh, look, your friend smokes. Let's sit down for a minute, Nathan, and relax. We can smoke a cigarette and unwind. I don't mind telling you, I almost peed my pants out there when I saw that cop car. What do you think is in Tom's car?"

"God only knows, Lizzie."

They sat in silence, Lizzie staring at what she supposed was Artie Bennigan's family. Two sisters, younger, hamming it up for the camera, parents who looked like parents, Artie in his cap and gown at some graduation, and the family dog, a dalmatian.

She wondered if she would ever have a family picture on her mantel. Sadness engulfed her. She took another swig from the brandy bottle. Nathan, she noticed, wasn't drinking, other than the first sip. Once he'd told her he didn't drink and drive. She liked that about him, it made him a responsible person.

She thought about her own philosophy, which was, work like you don't need the money, love like you've never been hurt, and dance like no one is watching. She was jolted from her thoughts when Nathan poked her arm to get her attention.

"I lied to you, Lizzie."

Lizzie felt her shoulders sag. *Here it comes,* she thought. *Aggie said not to trust* anyone. *What do I do? I trust a reporter.* She felt like kicking herself.

"About what, Nathan."

"I lied to you when I said I thought I was falling in love with you."

Lizzie felt like her insides were crumbling. "Don't give it another thought. Stress . . . time . . ."

Nathan acted like he hadn't heard her. "I'm *not* falling in love with you. I'm *already* in love with you. You don't have to say anything or profess undying love. I just wanted you to know."

Tears rolled down Lizzie's cheeks. She moved closer, took his hands in hers. "I love you, too," she whispered. He squeezed her hands. She squeezed back. *For all the good it's going to do either one of us.*

It was Nathan who gently pushed her away. "It's getting late, Lizzie, we have to check Tom's car and still pick up yours. Maybe all your answers are in the garage. At least, let's hope so."

Thirty minutes later, Nathan looked at Lizzie in dismay. "Maybe that guy Zack was putting you on. There's nothing in this car but food wrappers, smelly tennis shoes, and dirty towels. There's nothing here. I looked underneath the car, under the fenders, under the hood, and there's nothing. Maybe it was the bullets he was referring to. There are enough of them embedded in this car to melt down for a doorstop. I even ripped off the felt on the ceiling. I did find thirty-seven cents under the seats, but that's it. There's nothing, Lizzie. Maybe he was trying to set you up or something."

Lizzie sighed. "Maybe we should rip the seats apart."

"To what end, Lizzie. They're just the way they came from the factory. I looked under them. I wanted to find something, too, but there's nothing to find. Come on, we have to get your car unless you don't want to do it."

"No, no. Zack was giving me a heads up. Wait a minute. Wait just a damn minute. Maybe they were going to plant something in the cars. That would be the setup. You're right, there's nothing to find because they haven't put *it*, whatever *it* is, in the cars yet. Come on, let's go."

Zack locked up, and they both climbed into the Beemer. "Jeez, I hope we don't run into that cop again."

At fifteen minutes past three, Nathan parked the Beemer on the opposite side of the street. Lizzie looked across at her sister's house. It was dark as pitch. "Show me where the bug is on the door and rip it off."

Like thieves in the night, Lizzie and Nathan crossed the street and ran up the driveway. Lizzie opened the car door. Nathan bent down, searched for the bug, and ripped it away from the bottom of the door. He pulled back his arm and tossed it across the lawn. They watched it land in a bed of daisies two doors away.

In less than ten minutes, they were back on the road and headed for Artie Bennigan's house for the second time in one night.

They used up another fifteen minutes opening the garage doors, pulling out the Intrepid, and driving Aggie's car into the garage. Nathan parked the Intrepid, the front end facing the street so the rear license plate couldn't be seen.

It was a few minutes before four when Nathan closed the door of Lizzie's car. "There's nothing in your car either. Let's get out of here. If we're lucky, we might get an hour or so of sleep."

Disgusted with the entire evening's events, Lizzie crawled into the Beemer. "Tell me again why we're leaving your vehicle here and taking this car that belongs to your friend."

"Lizzie, right this second, I don't remember. I'm sure it will come to me. I never get bad ideas. Whatever it was, you agreed. Can we just leave now?"

"Okay." Lizzie leaned back and was instantly asleep. Nathan had to wake her when he parked in his underground parking space.

In the chrome-and-glass condo, Lizzie headed straight for the couch. "Wake me up at six-thirty, Nathan."

At ten minutes past six, the squad room was rife with anger and testosterone. "What the hell do you mean both cars are gone?" Dutch Davis demanded.

"They're gone. As in they aren't there," a detective with flaming red hair said out of the corner of his mouth. "Neighbors reported a break-in at the Madsens' house during the night. The house wasn't broken into, just the garage, and the car is gone. There is no car at Jade's house. And, before you go ballistic, we checked Hawk's garage, and it isn't there either. Neither is his car."

"She's one step ahead of us," Joe Sonders said. He smacked his balled-up fist on a tabletop. "Now what?"

"Now what? Now what?" Dutch hissed. "I need to think. Can I just sit here and think for a minute. Is Aggie on duty today?"

"I looked at the schedule. She was on, then she was off. How the hell am I supposed to know. The space next to her name is blank." Joe banged the table again. He looked around. All he could see was fear on his fellow officers' faces. The same kind of fear he was feeling. "You better think quick, Dutch. The way I look at it, we have less than a day. You might also want to consider the fact that the chief is on high alert when you're doing all your thinking."

The room fell silent when the watch commander entered the room.

No one listened to a thing he said.

Chapter Thirteen

Chief of Detectives Erwin Shay knew something *big* was going on the minute he walked down the hall to his office. He could *smell* the secrecy. Whatever it was, it had been going on since Aggie Jade reported back to work.

He looked at his watch and felt pleased with himself that he was within a minute of his normal arrival. Six-thirty. He wasn't due in till seven, but he liked to be at his desk when the shift switched over in case one of his men from the night shift wanted to talk. It worked for him even though his wife grumbled and complained about having to get up at five o'clock to fix him breakfast. A special breakfast because among other medical problems, his diabetes was going haywire. She worried about him. He worried about himself, too, but he never let her know it.

He was more than worried now. He looked across the squad room at Sadie Wilkinson, who he secretly thought was older than God. She was already at her desk, because, as she put it, how did it look for her boss to be in and her still snoozing.

Sadie knew everything that went on and then some. She was mother, sister, aunt, confessor, and keeper of all kinds of secrets she never divulged. She was honest, loyal, and trustworthy. She was also personal friends with the commissioner's and mayor's wives. When you wanted to know the skinny on anything involving the department, all you had to do was ask Sadie. Asking didn't mean you'd get an answer. Sadie was also discreet.

Sadie always wore a smile, no matter what time of the day it was. She wasn't smiling this morning, and she also wasn't meeting the chief's penetrating gaze. Her thin lips were pursed tightly.

Erwin Shay's eyes narrowed. Whatever he was smelling was getting stronger. "In my office, Sadie. Now! Don't even think about telling me you're busy." He was barking at her. Later, he knew, he would have to apologize.

"Hold your horses, Erwin. I have to put my shoes on." Sadie wore platform shoes that were killers on her feet. She wore them so she could add height to her four-foot-eight frame. The minute she reached her desk, she kicked them off and put on her slippers. When she took her break or went to lunch or even made a trip down the hall, she put the platforms back on.

Sadie Wilkinson was a little bit of a woman. Chief Shay often said she was no bigger than a postage stamp. She weighed in at something close to eighty-eight pounds if she ate breakfast. If not, she weighed eighty-six pounds. Her hair was pearly white and tied in a knot at the top of her head. For added height, of course. Her face was weathered and lined, a road map of life. Her only concession to makeup was cherry red lipstick that bled into the wrinkles, and cherry red nail polish. She wore a strap watch fastened above her elbow because if she wore it on her wrist, even in the last hole, it would slide off her arm.

No one really knew Sadie's age because, among other things, she knew how to tap into the files, and constantly changed her birth date. The best guess was she was somewhere around seventy-five, give or take a few years, something she would never deny or confirm. All she would say was she was with the department from the day she graduated high school. She refused to divulge the name of the high school, and no amount of prodding could get it out of her. It was a mind-your-own-business kind of thing.

Today, Sadie wore a leopard print blouse with black slacks and a fanny pack around her waist. She constantly had to hitch it up because she had no hips to speak of, and it slid around. It was for her valuables.

"Today, Sadie!" Erwin barked again.

"I told you to hold your horses, Erwin. I'm coming," she barked back. "Furthermore, I am not hard of hearing."

"Close the door!"

Sadie obliged the chief.

"Sit!" he ordered.

"Sit! Sit! Sit! I'm not a dog, Erwin. What? All right,

I'm sitting." She perched on the edge of the hard wooden chair, her feet a long way from the floor. Her legs looked like skinny sticks with the bulky platforms at the ends.

Shay fixed her with a stare. "Watch my lips, Sadie. I want to know what's going on around here. Don't tell me you don't know. You know *everything*. You know more than I know, and I'm the chief of detectives. I'm not proud of that either. You are not moving out of that chair until you spill your guts. So, start spilling."

They were like two old warhorses, sniffing, snorting, and pawing the ground as each took the other's measure.

The red lips moved. "You give me too much credit, Erwin."

One of the chief's stubby fingers pointed at her chest. "Listen up, Sadie. Either you tell me what's going on, or I give this to the commissioner." He reached into his top drawer and pulled out an old yearbook. "See this, Sadie. It's your high school yearbook, and guess what. It has your age in it. You are ten years past retirement age. I'm personally going to plan your retirement party tomorrow night. Did you hear me, Sadie? Tomorrow night! The flip side to retirement is, I fire you on the spot. What's it gonna be, Sadie?"

"That's blackmail!" Sadie blustered. "Blackmail is against the law."

"So, sue me! I want it all, Sadie, every last tidbit."

The red lips moved again. "I want a lawyer."

"For what?" Shay bellowed.

Sadie reared back and turned her hearing aid down. It screeched, the sound like fingernails on a blackboard. Shay groaned.

"You're threatening me. Coercion. You don't even have a case to charge me with anything. If you do, will you Mirandize me?"

"I'll go you one better, Sadie. I'll call in IAD. I think you're withholding evidence or knowledge on Tom Madsen's murder. They'll chew you up and spit you out. How's that grab you, Sadie?"

The red lips puckered up. Sadie turned her hearing aid back up to the high position. It screeched again.

Shay watched as she literally shriveled in front of his eyes. She started to cry, something he thought she was incapable of doing. He was out of his depth, and he knew it.

"Maybe it is time for me to leave here. I always thought I'd, you know, keel over at my desk." She rubbed at her eyes with the back of her hand. "Erwin, you think I know everything. I don't. People say things in passing. I remember those things. Sometimes I put one thing together with another thing, and come up with what I think is going on. That doesn't mean it's right, or that something is going to happen. It's my version of events. If you want to sic Internal Affairs on me, go ahead. They deal in facts and not rumors." Sadie straightened her shoulders, and said, "If I leave, this place will fall apart, and we both know it. You don't even know where they keep the pencils, Erwin."

She was right, and Shay knew it. Sadie Wilkinson

was the glue that kept the department together. How it had happened, he didn't know. If she left, he wondered who would put up the Christmas tree and all the decorations.

Shay reached into his desk drawer and brought out a box of tissues. He handed them to the little woman. She sniffed, and waved them away.

"Sadie, I'm worried about Aggie Jade. Not just worried. I'm *really* worried."

"I'm worried about her, too, Erwin. She's one of your best." Sadie looked down at the floor. "They're trying to figure a way to get her. I don't know who *they* are, Erwin. It could be the whole department or it could be just a few. Like I said, I hear things. Believe it or not, I was going to talk to Aggie today. I have this creepy feeling something bad is going to happen."

Shay leaned back into the depths of his swivel chair. "Join the club, Sadie. The reason I let her come back was I thought she would be safe on site. At home, she's fair game. I'm losing sleep over this, Sadie. When I don't get enough sleep, I get real cranky. Ask my wife."

Sadie sighed. "What do you want me to do, Erwin?"

"Get me something I can sink my teeth into. I need something to go on. Aggie's playing it real close to her vest. I know she decked Dutch even though they both denied it. She had a run-in with him and Sonders at Zack's party. She looked like a million bucks, didn't she, Sadie?"

"Yes, she did, Erwin. It made me want a dress like

that. Every man in that bar was ogling her. Didn't think Aggie had it in her to wear something like that. She's different these days."

"I noticed that myself. I guess a near-death experience will do that to a person. I don't want anything happening to her, Sadie."

"I hear you, Chief. There's a meeting going on in the squad room," Sadie blurted. "I think it's about Aggie."

"You think!" Shay boomed.

"If you hadn't made me come in here, I might have found out more. Do not shout at me again, Erwin. I want that yearbook, too. Hand it over."

"No way. It's safe with me. Do I have to remind you that I am your superior?"

"God forbid."

Chief Shay grinned as Sadie clomped her way out of his office and down the hall in her platform shoes. He loved Sadie Wilkinson, he really did.

Lizzie marched down the hall, the smell of burned coffee teasing her nostrils. She flinched when she saw the chief's door opening.

"Good morning, Chief," Lizzie said.

"You're early today, Detective Jade."

Lizzie didn't want to tell him she hadn't been to bed yet. "Yeah, I had to take a cab. Car's in the shop. By the way, it was a nice party, Chief. I hope Zack and Millie enjoy their retirement. It was a really good turnout."

"Yes, it was. By the way, Holly Azure transferred back to the department. She's taking Zack's place."

Lizzie's mind raced. "That's nice. Gotta sign in, Chief."

Shay's mind raced, too. "What's wrong with your car, Aggie?"

"Don't know. Stalls out all the time. Could be all the rain we've been having. I might even trade it in. Depends what the problem is and how much they want to fix it."

"Car trouble, Aggie," Detective Jorgenson said, coming up behind her. "I saw you getting out of a cab a little while ago."

Aggie nodded as she wrote her name on the sign-in board.

"What's the problem. I'm pretty good with cars. I might be able to save you some money."

Aggie threw her hands in the air. "Where were you when I needed you, Jorgenson? You're too late. It's already in the shop."

"Where? I can go get it and work on it?"

"No, it's okay. A friend recommended a good garage."

"You gotta watch those guys. Half of them run chop shops, as you well know. They take great delight in screwing up a cop's car. Tell me where the shop is, and I'll pick it up on my lunch hour."

"Gee, I can't remember the name of the place. It's out there by the mall somewhere. Thanks for the offer, though. Next time, I'll be sure to call you first. I'm going, Chief. See ya, Jorgenson."

Chief Shay narrowed his eyes as he watched the vice cop's expression change from helpful to angry. His stomach started to grind in frustration. It was a sad state of affairs when the only person you could trust was a seventy-five-year-old woman. He wished, the way he'd wished a lot lately, that he'd gone into the plumbing business.

At eleven-fifteen, Aggie picked up the ringing phone. "Detective Jade, property room."

"Aggie, it's Mrs. Madsen. How are you, dear?"

"I'm just fine, Mrs. Madsen. How are you and your husband?"

"We're out in Seattle visiting our daughter and we were having a lovely time till one of our neighbors called this morning to tell us someone broke into our garage last night and stole our son's car. Gray wants to head home, but I don't want to. Can you look into it, Aggie?"

Aggie's stomach started to heave. "Of course I can. However, you should have your neighbor call in the report. They'll investigate right away. I don't get off duty till three o'clock. Do you know when it happened, Mrs. Madsen?" She felt like the scum of the earth for what she'd done. She hoped the end would justify the means.

"We don't know. Sometime this morning. Nothing else was taken although they did break the overhead light. The neighbors cleaned it up and locked up the garage. Why would someone want Tom's car?"

"I don't know, Mrs. Madsen. Why did you and your husband want it?"

"We were angry, Aggie. Actually, Gray was livid when they couldn't solve the murder. He just marched down to the lot one day and demanded the car and had it towed to the house. It broke my heart to see it so full of bullet holes. Do you think something was hidden in the car?"

"Mrs. Madsen, I just don't know. They have me working in the property room, so there's not much I can do on department time. I can check it out after I get off duty."

"Gray and I would appreciate it. Our neighbor told us the police did come around a quarter to five, but all they did was look in the garage. When they explained about the car, the officers got angry. That's all I know. Melba and Henry live directly across the street at 209. I'd like it if you'd talk to them. I just wish I knew what was going on."

"When are you coming back, Mrs. Madsen?"

"Our daughter wants us to stay till the end of June. I want to stay, too. Gray is all upset now. Maybe when I tell him you're going to look into things, he'll feel more comfortable about staying. I'm trying to convince him to move here."

"That would be nice for both of you, Mrs. Madsen. Give me your phone number, and I'll call you when I know something."

"Bless your heart, child."

Lizzie broke the connection and tried to call Nathan Hawk but was told he was out of the office and on assignment. She left her name and number.

Lizzie spent the rest of the morning watching the clock move slowly toward the noon hour, when she could take her lunch break. She needed to call Aggie and the girls, and she wanted to talk to Chief Shay.

Lizzie almost jumped out of her skin when she heard footsteps coming down the hall. Her relief was an older cop who refused to meet her gaze. He mumbled something that was unintelligible when Lizzie opened the door to admit him. She'd seen him at the party but didn't know his name. He wasn't in any of the pictures Aggie had given her. She made a big show of calling a rental car agency and ordering a car to be delivered to the precinct within minutes. Sometimes being a cop had its advantages. This was one of those times.

She didn't bother to say good-bye to the officer because she knew he wouldn't respond. Like she cared.

Lizzie made her way to the chief's office and knocked on the door. She entered when he told her to.

"Chief, I just need a minute. Tom Madsen's mother just called me. She said there was a break-in at her house last night and someone stole Tom's car. The Madsens are in Washington state. One of their neighbors called in the theft. Do you have anything on it?"

"Nobody saw or heard a thing. No damage was done other than a broken lightbulb. Either the door wasn't locked or it was picked. I saw that car, Jade. The tires were shot out and flat. I've been sitting here asking myself why someone would want that shot-up piece of metal so bad they would steal it. They had to drive it or tow it. I guess you don't know anything about that, huh, Jade?"

Lizzie shook her head. "Chief, I didn't even know the elder Madsens had Tom's car. When I visited them they didn't say a word about it. That's two break-ins for them. What do you suppose it means?"

"You tell me, Jade. What's it mean to you?"

"It means someone is looking for something they think Tom had. If he did have something, I don't know what it is. How could I know?"

"The department will handle it. I don't want you interfering with this investigation, Jade. Are we clear on that?"

"Crystal. Bye, Chief." The chief grunted something that sounded like good-bye.

Outside, a cream-colored Chrysler Le Baron waited for her. After doing the paperwork with the rental car agent, Lizzie climbed behind the wheel, aware of many sets of eyes following her. She admitted to herself that she felt jittery.

Lizzie drove slowly, her gaze going to the rearview mirror every few seconds as she tried to figure out if she had a tail or not. She did, an old, dark green Chevy Nova. She needed to call Aggie. She reached down for her cell phone and hit the speed dial. Aggie's voice came over the wire, a happy-sounding Aggie. *She got laid.* The thought brought a smile to Lizzie's face. She quickly related the past evening's events. "What should I do, Aggie?"

"God, Lizzie, I can't believe you gave Zack a heads up. What's going on right now may be the result of that heads up."

"No, you're wrong, Aggie. If it wasn't for Zack, the cars would be fair game. I think he was right and was just returning the favor. It was no skin off his nose to give me the high sign. You said he was a good cop at one time. I know as sure as I'm sitting here talking to you that they were planning on setting me up. I wish you could have seen Jorgenson's face this morning when he tried to find out which garage your car's at. There's nothing in the damn cars, Aggie, so it has to be a setup. They plan on putting something *in* the cars."

"Did you rip up the seats, Lizzie?"

"No. Nathan said they looked just the way they came from the factory. There was nothing behind or under them. I guess what you're saying is, we should have ripped them apart. Okay, I can get Nathan to do that before he goes home from work. Why aren't you complimenting me on the butterflies? That took some work, let me tell you that. It's all there, Aggie. Nathan said you were brilliant for coming up with that theory."

"Lizzie, you need to get out of there real quick. Bundle all that butterfly stuff up, give it to Nathan, and have him messenger it to Chief Shay. Make photocopies of every single page and mail them somewhere safe. Someplace only you know. I don't even want you to tell me. Swear on my life, Lizzie, that you will do it. Say the words."

"Aggie, I need another day or so. I'll do it then. I can't do it before tomorrow anyway since you want me to shred those seats. Two days, Aggie. Just two days. I can handle it."

"Okay, two days. Lizzie, you do realize, don't you, that if this all goes down the way we both think it will, Nathan will write a Pulitzer-winning story on it. It's what he lives for. I just want you to think about that."

Lizzie sighed. "Aggie, why do you always have to rain on my parade?"

"Because life is not all sunshine and roses, condos

and convertibles. Life is real. You've been living a fantasy life so long you don't know what real life is like. I don't want to see you get hurt."

Aggie was right, and Lizzie knew it. "Okay, sis. I'll call you when I can. You got your *stuff* . . . you know, for Plan B?"

"Yes."

Lizzie felt like there were twenty pounds of concrete on her shoulders when she pulled into the driveway of Aggie's house. She eyed the long black limo with a jaundiced eye. She stumbled and almost fell when she started up the walkway to the front porch where the girls were sitting entertaining a guest.

"Mr. Papadopolus!"

"Hello, sweet cheeks. Since Mohammed won't come to the mountain, the mountain has come to Mohammed. How are you?"

Lizzie allowed herself to be hugged. She met Noreen's eyes over Mr. P.'s shoulder. They looked worried and anxious.

"Let's go inside. This is lunch hour, and I have to get back to . . . I have to leave in"—she looked at her watch—"forty minutes."

"Where's your sister, sweet cheeks?"

For the first time in her life, Lizzie lied to the gambler. "In a rehab center." She opened the refrigerator door and took out a plate of fried chicken. "Want a piece?"

"No thank you."

Lizzie watched him as she gnawed on the chicken leg she didn't want. He looked exactly like what he was, a high roller with money to burn. A fatherly-looking high roller with money to burn. Custom-made suit, custom-made shoes, diamond pinkie ring, Rolex watch. The nails on his hands were buffed and polished, hands that had never done a lick of work other than to strip the cellophane off decks of cards. It hardly counted as worthwhile employment. It was almost beyond comprehension that he was one of the richest men in Las Vegas. Anthony Papadopolus, broker to high rollers.

He was tanned, his white teeth glistening when he spoke. "Cozy place."

"My sister is the frugal type. She's not one for a lot of show, if you know what I mean."

"The dining room is perfect. Tomorrow at eight. I arranged everything. I slipped the girls some bills, and they're going to sit on the porch all night. Great cover, Lizzie. This is so perfect it boggles my mind. You'll be eight in number. I took the liberty of ordering the wine and food. It will be delivered in the morning. I hope you have some fancy duds. You're lookin' kind of like a washerwoman."

A devil perched itself on Lizzie's shoulders. She hated it when people told her what to do and how to do it. She removed her jacket, the shoulder holster obscene-looking. Papadopolus stepped back, his eyes never leaving the holster or the butt of the gun. "What the hell . . ."

Lizzie put her finger to her lips. "Let's go outside so I can show you my flower garden. I know how much you like to putter in your greenhouse."

The gambler followed at a safe distance. His eyes were full of questions.

"I'm pretending to be a cop, Mr. P. My sister, who by the way, is my twin, was involved in a shoot-out and was almost killed. She is in a private rehab," Lizzie repeated the lie. "I'm taking her place. I'm trying to find out what happened that night. Yes, I know what I'm doing is illegal, but I have to do it. What's so important about this game anyway?"

"Two new players. Beaucoup bucks. One of them is a shipbuilder, new to Vegas. The other one is a big arms dealer. Don't panic. This is the last gig on your contract. Play it out, Lizzie, make me some money, and we're done. I sense you're losing your appetite for high living?"

Lizzie's mind raced. "Tell me what my percentage is again. This might be a good time to discuss a bonus. A *big* bonus. Just so you know, Mr. P. We could all end up in the slammer if we get caught."

"The boys will be around. Do this for me Lizzie, and you're set for life." He whispered in her ear. He laughed when her eyes grew round and her jaw dropped. "Do we have a deal?"

"Oh yeah. Tomorrow at eight." Lizzie bit down on the chicken leg in her hand. She smiled. "See ya," she called to his retreating back.

Alice, released from the laundry room, ran out to her along with the girls, who all jabbered at once. "We didn't know what to do, Lizzie. He drove up, got out, and we couldn't leave. We were just sitting on the porch drinking coffee. He gave us a rundown and handed us each a thousand dollars. We can pull it off, Lizzie. I know we can."

"God, I hope so."

"Where did you get that car, Lizzie?"

Lizzie told them just enough so they wouldn't worry about her. She knew they would still worry about her because they were her friends.

"Listen, I know this vacation has been a bummer. I'm going to make it up to you. I can't let Aggie down. She's depending on me. It's time I did something worthwhile in my life for a change. I actually want to do this for her and try to make it right. So, give me a rundown on *the guys* and how it's all going. I have five minutes."

They squealed and jabbered for a full five minutes. The bottom line was they would return to Vegas at the end of the week, and the guys would remain in Atlanta. Vacation romances were just that, vacation romances. Lizzie thought she saw tears in their eyes, but she could have been mistaken.

She dropped to her knees and hugged Alice, who lathered her with kisses. "Take care of my dog. I just need to get some more clothes. You'll see me when you see me. I will be here tomorrow evening. Take charge, okay?"

"You got it," Noreen said quietly. "Take care of yourself, Lizzie," she said, pointing to the shoulder holster.

"I will." She hugged each one of them before she got her clothes, grabbed her laptop from the dining room table, and raced out to the rental car.

She was literally running down the hall to the evidence room so she wouldn't be late when she ran into Luke Sims. Tom Madsen played poker one night a month with Luke and the other guys. Aggie had said the guys thought Luke was too dumb to cut him in on anything. She wondered if it was true. Luke was an honest country boy, round in shape and sincere in mind.

"Whoa, Aggie. Hold on. This is the first time I've had a chance to talk to you since you came back. It's good to see you again. Is everything okay? How's Gus?"

"Everything is fine, Luke. I'm running late. Gus is coming along. I'm going to retire him. The truth is, I'm thinking of retiring myself."

"That's understandable. I just wanted to tell you I'm getting married in September. Carol said yes over the weekend. We thought we'd do it right after Labor Day. I hope you can come to the wedding."

He was walking in step with her. She had no other choice but to reply. "I'd love to attend your wedding, Luke. Congratulations." He looked so young, baby-faced actually. Aggie said he wasn't the sharpest pencil in the box but he was dedicated to law enforcement.

"I heard this morning that someone stole Tom Madsen's car. I got so mad when I heard that. Can you *imagine* anyone doing something like that? It's evil."

"Yeah, I heard that, too. Well, gotta get to work. You on days now or what?"

"Yeah. They keep shifting me around. No one wants to partner with me. They think because I look young, criminals won't take me seriously. You and I are pariahs."

"Yeah. Look where they stuck me." Aggie waited for the cop to open the door to the evidence room. He didn't acknowledge her or Luke.

"See, that's what I mean," Luke said. "Everyone is buzzing about you, Aggie. You need to watch your back."

Concern? A warning from this baby-faced cop? What? "You know what else? Holly Azure is back. She's taking over Zack's spot. Oh, hey, wait till you hear this. Zack was supposed to call in when he hit the Keys this morning, but he didn't. They wanted to make sure he got there safe and sound with Millie. I heard he never got on the plane. What do you make of that?"

Lizzie felt her heart start to flutter. She shrugged. "Maybe Millie got sick, and they were delayed or something."

"Oh, no. He checked out of his motel last night after the party and left. He didn't go to Florida. They checked."

Lizzie busied herself opening her laptop. Was this guy for real or not? "Who is *they*, Luke?"

Luke pulled a face. "Joe Sonders for one. Sadie for another. Of course, she was more worried about Millie than she was about Zack. By the way, she was looking for you a little while ago. If you want my opinion, I think there's something fishy going on. You talked to Zack at the party. Did he say anything about changing his plans?"

Was the guy fishing for information? Lizzie couldn't decide. "Not to me, he didn't. He said he couldn't wait to get there to start fishing. He said

Millie had good days and bad days, and she was going to read and do crossword puzzles while he fished. He looked to me like a guy who couldn't wait for morning so he could begin his new life. Gee, I hope everything is okay."

"Me, too. He always treated me nice. Guess I'll leave you to your work. I have crossing guard duty all week. I'm real glad you're okay, Aggie. I missed talking to you while you were gone."

Lizzie looked him in the eyes and made an instant decision. "Luke, are the guys on the take? Do you know what they're up to?"

Luke actually looked relieved at the question. He didn't miss a beat when he said, "Yes, and no to your questions. No one talks around me. I pick up stuff here and there. Just be careful, okay? I'm not one of them, so you don't have to be afraid to talk to me."

"That's nice to know, Luke. Again, congratulations."

"Thanks, Aggie. See you around."

"Yeah, see you around."

When the door closed behind Luke, Lizzie yanked out her cell phone and hit her speed dial for the second time that day. She asked for Nathan and was told he was still out on assignment and no, he had not picked up his messages or called in.

Lizzie went back to her laptop and flexed her fingers. She watched a virtual blizzard of numbers bounce across the screen. She smiled. She'd just taken care of business. Business that would take care of her for the rest of her life.

Lizzie leaned back on the high-backed stool and

let her mind focus on Mr. P.'s game tomorrow night. Did she have a choice? No. Mr. P. was one man you didn't cross. Ever. She knew she was coming down to the wire when decisions would have to be made. She propped her chin on her elbows and stared off into space.

Just like at lunchtime, eyes bored into Lizzie when she climbed into the rental car. She sat quietly for a moment, not because she needed to meditate but to give her fellow officers something to worry about. She reached down and hit the speed dial again. She spoke slowly and carefully to the switchboard operator. "Please have Mr. Hawk call Detective Jade as soon as he gets this message."

Now what? She promised the Madsens she would check out their house. How ironic that she was checking her own burglary. Still, a promise was a promise. Chief Shay would fry her ass if he found out she was interfering. And what did Sadie want to talk to her about? She shrugged for the benefit of anyone watching before she turned the key in the ignition.

Lizzie didn't pick up her tail until she was halfway to the Madsen house. *Why am I even going there? I have their daughter's phone number. All I have to do is head for a pay phone and make the call there. Or, I can risk using my cell phone.* Without thinking, Lizzie turned at the corner, laughing when she sailed through just as the light changed. Her tail would have to wait for the next green light. She drove fast, making every right turn she hit until she was back out on the boulevard. She swerved into the parking lot of a Taco Bell, drove around to the back, got out, and walked into the fast-food joint, where she went immediately to the rest room. She picked up the pay phone, dropped in change, and dialed the number Mrs. Madsen had given her.

Lizzie was in luck. Mrs. Madsen answered the phone. She could hear conversation in the background and a baby wailing at the top of its lungs.

"Mrs. Madsen, it's Aggie. I want you to listen to me very carefully because I only have a minute. I need your promise that you won't say anything about what I'm going to tell you."

"Land sakes, dear, of course you have my word."

"I'm the one who broke into your garage. I'm really sorry about the light. A friend of mine and I drove the car away. I'm also afraid we ruined the rims. We thought someone hid something in Tom's car. Or mine. It's hidden, and it's safe. I'll make sure it's returned to you on a flatbed at some point in time. I'm just not sure when that will be, Mrs. Madsen. We didn't find a thing. We're going to go over it again. We're doing the same thing with my car. I'm not free to tell you anything right now because it is a police investigation. *Liar, liar, pants on fire.*

"Mrs. Madsen, I don't know if you planned to file an insurance claim or anything. If you were, don't. I have to go now."

"Gray and I will do just what you say, Aggie. Don't worry about us. Take care of yourself, dear."

"I will, Mrs. Madsen. I think you should move there so you can be close to your daughter. I think you'll be happier. Bye."

Damn, where is Nathan?

It was four o'clock when Lizzie let herself into Aggie's house. The girls were in jeans and tee shirts cleaning up a storm. The vacuum was whirring, dust rags were fluttering, and pails of water were everywhere. Tantalizing aromas wafted from the kitchen to vie with the scent of lemon furniture polish and the pungent odor of Pine-Sol.

Alice spotted her, ran to her to be petted before she ran from friend to friend to keep tabs on the cleaning system. The stereo blasted.

"What are you doing?" Lizzie shouted.

Noreen climbed down from the ladder, where she'd been cleaning the crystals on the dining room chandelier. "We're cleaning the house for tomorrow. All you have to do is worry about what you're going to wear. If you tell us the address where your bags are stored, we can go pick it up for you. You need to sparkle tomorrow night, Lizzie. Mr. P. is hoping for big things. We know you can deliver. It's the least we can do; the man did give us each a thousand bucks. We'll be done in an hour or so. The kitchen is done, so you can set the table. Have a drink and put your feet up."

Lizzie nodded as she made her way to the kitchen. She poured herself a large glass of wine and fired up one of the girls' cigarettes. It was all happening so fast. She really needed to talk to Nathan.

She realized suddenly that she didn't have a key to Nathan's condo. All the records were there. She also didn't have a key to Artie Bennigan's house, where they'd taken the cars. In addition she didn't even know the name of the person who was holding her baggage. Aggie's friend Alex had taken care of that. She could call Aggie and get the phone number and address. Maybe the man would deliver them personally. She should be so lucky.

Lizzie gulped at the wine, finished it, and poured another glass. *Where are you, Nathan?*

"Lizzie, will you please relax. Pacing isn't going to help the situation. Nathan is not going to screw you over. The man's in love with you. I'm sure there is a perfectly reasonable explanation for why he hasn't called you," Noreen said.

Lizzie plopped down on the top step of the front porch. It was a beautiful evening, not too cold and not too warm. A light sweater cloaked her shoulders. She could feel the heat from Alice's warm body against her leg. "I suppose so."

"Look on the bright side. At least that guy brought your luggage over. The house is clean, and tomorrow you are going to make a fortune. You have the world by the tail, honey."

"Noreen, Candy, Honey, would you take all the info to the chief if you were me?" Lizzie asked.

Three heads bobbed as one.

"Lizzie, we can look up that guy's address in the phone book. We could all go with you and help rip up those seats. It would, of course, be breaking and entering. If you want to do it, we're with you," Noreen said.

Lizzie sipped at the cold coffee in her cup. "Don't think I haven't thought about that. There's no point.

I'd have a tail on me as soon as we started out. The one thing I don't want to give away is the location of those two cars."

Noreen frowned. "Then let us do it. You stay here. We'll drive around, pretend we're out for some fun. They aren't going to tail us. We can do it, Lizzie. Please let us help you. Candy, go inside and see if you can find that guy's address in the phone book. You said you had a street map, didn't you, Lizzie?"

"It's on the front seat of the car. You know me, no sense of direction. It's not that far from here. Shouldn't be that much traffic at this time of night. The big question is, how are you going to open the garage?"

Noreen snorted. "Every woman's perfect tool. A nail file. A good nail file or a pair of tweezers can open anything. Trust me. I'll take my cell phone and call you if we find anything."

Lizzie agreed, but she was nervous. This whole thing wasn't the slam dunk she'd thought it was going to be. *Damn, where are you, Nathan?*

Chapter Fourteen

*L*izzie sat on the front steps of Aggie's house. She had watched as her friends trooped out to the rental car dressed seductively in spandex tube tops, short shorts to show off their long showgirl legs, and high heels. It was Noreen's idea to dress provocatively since they were going to a yuppie community. Just in case they were seen, she wanted them to fit into the neighborhood. The illusion of sex, she said, would open many doors that would otherwise be closed. Lizzie didn't even try to argue with her.

Where is Nathan? Why hasn't he called? Childishly, she crossed her fingers that she hadn't made a mistake by trusting him.

Alice wiggled closer. How comforting the dog was. She realized suddenly that she was chilly. When was it finally going to warm up? Probably after she was gone. The thought bothered her. "Come on, baby, let's go inside. I think I'll make some more coffee." Alice was on her feet instantly, waiting patiently for

Lizzie to stumble to her feet. Tears rolled down her cheeks. "We're in the tall grass, baby, I can feel it." Alice whimpered as she scooted through the door. She barked, a harsh sound, to remind Lizzie to lock the door. She obliged.

Less than four miles away, Noreen drove the car up Artie Bennigan's driveway, parked, cut the ignition, and climbed out, the girls right behind her. In her hand she had a long stainless-steel nail file and a pair of tweezers. Candy carried a canvas tool bag.

It was a dark night with excellent cloud cover. It would rain by morning. A low-lying fog was starting to roll down the road. Artie's neighbors, whoever they were, all appeared to be safely indoors. Candy and Honey shivered in the damp air in their skimpy attire as Noreen dropped to her knees to pick the lock. She had it open within seconds and was dusting her hands as the girls scampered inside. Noreen immediately lowered the door. She used her cigarette lighter to find the light switch.

Candy opened the tool bag Lizzie had shoved in her hands. Inside were pliers, a hammer, and four Ginsu knives sharp enough to cut down a tree. They set to work, quickly and quietly.

"Oh, God! Oh, God! Oh, God!" Noreen wailed. "Girls, come quick! Look at this!"

"Never mind that, come see what I found," Candy cried. "Quick, call Lizzie. Oh, God, what should we do? I thought it would be money. It's not money!"

Noreen climbed out of the car. She reached into the tool bag to pull out her cell phone. It took her three tries before she was able to successfully punch

in Lizzie's number. Her voice was squeaky but shrill.
"Lizzie, it's drugs in the car! Bags and bags of drugs
stuck down in the springs of the seats. All the seats in
the car! What should we do? My God, tell us what to
do?"

On the other end of the line, Lizzie's blood ran
cold. *Car.* That's what Will Fargo had been trying to
say with his last dying breath. "How . . . how many
bags, Noreen?"

Noreen looked at her friends. "Lizzie wants to
know how many bags there are."

"At least 150. They probably weigh two pounds
each, maybe three, we can't be sure," Noreen said,
balancing one of the plastic bags in her hand.
"Maybe there's more than 150. Lizzieeee!" she
wailed.

"I'm thinking. I'm thinking. Listen, this is what
you do. I saw a box of lawn bags on the shelf over the
laundry sink when Nathan and I were there. At least
I think I did. Pack it all up in the bags. Back your car
up to the door and stick it in the trunk. Wipe away all
your fingerprints. When you get here, we'll take it
somewhere. Maybe the chief's house. I'll have it figured out by the time you get here. Be careful. Don't
exceed the speed limit whatever you do. I just let
Alice out, and there's a low fog rolling in. Be sure to
use your fog lights. Hurry, Noreen."

Lizzie jumped to her feet and started to pace the
kitchen. Now she'd just involved her three best
friends in a drug deal. Damn. A hundred-plus bags
of cocaine. Possibly as many as two hundred. She

squeezed her eyes shut as she tried to calculate the street value. She gave up because her brain refused to comprehend what she was trying to figure out.

Aggie. She needed to call Aggie. She looked up at the clock. It wasn't too late to call. She looked down at the end of her index finger punching in the numbers. *When did I chew the nail off?* She wondered if she was on the verge of a nervous breakdown. "Come on, Aggie, pick up the damn phone," she muttered. A tinny voice came over the wire saying the party she was trying to reach was either out of range or had the phone turned off. "Double damn." Where were all these people who were supposed to help her through this mess?

Lizzie's eyes darted to the clock again. *The girls should be safely away from Artie Bennigan's by now.* She flipped open her cell phone again and dialed. Candy answered on the first ring. "It's me," Lizzie said. "How heavy are those bags, and how many do you have?"

"Five, and they are heavy. It takes two of us to lift one up," Candy responded.

"All right, listen to me. I want you to stop at a convenience store and buy a package of latex gloves and a box of trash bags. Buy some hair spray and candy or something so the clerk won't think anything of it later on if the police question him. Then I want you to go to the Winn-Dixie supermarket. The one closest to here. You shopped there. There's a Salvation Army bin in the far side of the parking lot. It looks like a Dumpster but there's a sign on it. Transfer the bags into the new bags, but be sure to wear the gloves. Put the stuff in the bin. I remember Aggie said they check it every day. I guess people in Atlanta are generous with their stuff. Whoever is in charge of the bin will call the police, and it's out of our hands. Or, we can make an anonymous call ourselves in the morning. Look, just do it, okay, and get back here as soon as you can. Bring the old bags, the new ones, and the gloves back here. Be careful, and stay alert. The cops cruise the parking lots at night because gangs like to hang out in parking lots to terrorize late-night shoppers."

Lizzie was angry now, angrier than she'd ever been in her entire life. If she ever got her hands on Nathan Hawk again, she would strangle him. As long as she had the phone in her hand, she might as well try him again. She did, but with the same results. She then tried his condo. His machine came on. She left a blistering message. She didn't feel one bit better. She tried Aggie again and was told the customer she was calling was either out of range or the phone was off.

"This stinks, Alice!" The shepherd raised her head, then lowered it to her paws when she realized Lizzie wasn't moving.

Five miles away in a suburban subdivision, Erwin Shay prowled his house, going from room to room. He muttered to himself until his wife of many years stood up, placed her hands on her hips, and said, "Erwin, either sit down or go outside. You are making me crazy with your pacing. Do you have gas or something? What are you muttering? My father used to mutter before he had his nervous breakdown. Are you having a nervous breakdown, Erwin? Will you please sit down."

"Something's bothering me, Ellie. When something bothers me, I pace. You know that."

"Most people talk, Erwin. I'm going to turn this television off even though my favorite program is on, and I am going to listen to your problem. It better be good, too. Now, talk. That's an order."

Erwin Shay knew that tone. He lowered himself to his favorite recliner, but he didn't recline. "I can't put my finger on it, Ellie. Something happened today that I missed. I didn't exactly miss it. I saw it, whatever it was, but I didn't act on it. I think it was important. So much is going on, and I'm stretched too thin. Maybe I'm slipping. I've been racking my brain since I got home. I know it's important. Don't ask me how I know it's important. I just know it is."

"For heaven's sake, Erwin, do what I do. Go back to your starting point and work forward. Re-create your day."

The chief groaned. "That means I have to go back to the office."

"I guess that's why you didn't change your clothes when you got home. Good-bye, Erwin. Don't wake me up when you get home."

Erwin leaned over and kissed his wife's plump cheek. She smelled like vanilla. "How'd you get so smart?"

"By hanging around you, that's how. Now, scat, and let me get back to my program that's almost over! I wish we'd had this little talk while the commercial was on."

Forty minutes later, Chief of Detectives Erwin Shay strode down the hall to his office. The look on his face bode ill to anyone brave enough to ask what he was doing in the office at this time of night. The second-shift detectives sitting at their desks looked at one another when the door to the chief's office slammed shut.

A pall settled over the office as cell phones were whipped out.

The chief paced the confines of his office. He muttered. Hell, he should have stayed home. There was more room. He talked to himself as he tried to remember the day in its entirety. He'd been early as always. He had his talk with Sadie. Then there was coffee and a bagel. He'd used the men's room. Phone calls, one after the other. Tom Madsen's car had been snatched. Aggie Jade's car was in the garage. Jorgenson had offered to fix it. He'd asked two or three times the name of the garage, but Aggie hadn't given up the name. Nothing important there.

More phone calls, paperwork. Sadie grumbled about so many faxes coming through one right after the other. He clearly remembered Sadie telling him he needed to look at something. He'd told her he would but later, because he had to go to a meeting. Sadie had scowled at him, saying he was going to be sorry. Sorry for what? A fax?

Erwin looked at the rat's nest of paperwork on his desk. He was not a tidy man, as his wife reminded him daily. Sometimes on her less charitable days she called him a slob. It was true, so he couldn't complain. He picked up the phone and barked into it.

"Get me Sadie on the phone. Be nice. She was real cranky today."

"Did I wake you, Sadie?"

"Oh, no, Erwin, me and my cat were just sitting here waiting for you to call. Why are you bothering me at home? I don't bother you at home, do I?"

"No, you don't. Look, I'm sorry. Take tomorrow off, sleep in."

"Why should I do that? Is that your way of telling me you're interviewing someone to take my place?"

"For God's sake, Sadie, no. I was trying to be nice. I need to ask you something."

"Talk louder, Chief?"

"I'm already screaming. Turn up your hearing aid and turn down the damn television. That cat of yours is going to go deaf. What was in the fax you wanted me to see and where is it?"

"It's somewhere on that pigsty of a desk of yours."

Shay clenched his teeth. "Just tell me what it said, Sadie."

"Anthony Papadopolus, Las Vegas's notorious gambler, arrived in Atlanta today with assorted friends. More friends are expected. That's what it said."

"The guy is here! Why? Where did it come from? Who sent it?"

"I'm not the police chief, Erwin, you are. I'm just an old lady you want to fire. Figure it out yourself. He certainly is brazen to come here on your turf. Your fine officers managed to follow him, and you'll never guess where he went, Chief. Then they lost him. That means he's loose, and there's a big game going on somewhere right under your nose. Can I hang up now?"

"No, you cannot hang up now. Where did he go, Sadie?

"You aren't going to like this, Chief. He went to Aggie Jade's house. In a big black limousine."

Son of a bitch! Sweat broke out on the chief's forehead. "Sadie, are you sure about that?"

"Of course I'm sure. That's all the department was talking about all day long. I thought someone told you, and you were just ignoring it the way you sometimes ignore things," Sadie sniped. "Can I hang up now?"

"Yes, you can hang up now."

Erwin pawed through the stacks of paper on his desk until he found what he was looking for. He scratched around until he found his reading glasses. He perched them on his nose and started to read. When he finished, he mopped at his bald head. He wished he was a kid again so he could cry. His stomach churning, he stomped his way to the door and bellowed, "Mooney, get in here! You, too, Carpenter!

"See this!" he said, wagging the fax under both detectives' noses. "Your sloppy fellow officers lost this guy and his guests this afternoon. I want you to find him. Don't come back until you know where he is. Move!"

The chief stomped his way to the door a second time. "Finley, Gerrity, in my office! I want Aggie Jade's house staked out, twenty-four/seven." He looked down at the oversize watch on his beefy wrist—10:15. "Starting immediately."

Finley smirked. Gerrity grinned. "Pleasure, Chief."

Alice threw back her head and howled. Lizzie raced to the door but not before she parted the sheer curtains on the front window. Her sigh was loud, even to her ears. The girls were home. She watched as they tripped out of the car, laughing and motioning with their hands for the benefit of any neighbors who might be watching. They barreled through the door the moment it opened and collapsed on the foyer floor. All three started to hyperventilate to Alice's distress. It was ten minutes past ten.

Lizzie dropped to her knees in light-headed relief. "Hey, it's okay. You're fine. You did it. You're back safe and sound. Sit up and take deep breaths. Did anyone follow you? Did you see anything suspicious?"

All three women shook their heads as they struggled to sit up. Noreen spoke first. "If this is what life is like in the suburbs, I'll take Vegas. Lizzie, you need to give some thought to your car being all torn up at that guy's house. We did our best to wipe off our fingerprints. I sure hope we got them all. You said you told that cop your car was in the garage. How are you going to explain that when it shows up in Artie Bennigan's garage?"

How indeed. "I'll think of something," Lizzie mumbled.

"Have you heard from Nathan?"

"No."

"Maybe they sent him out of town," Noreen said. "Or maybe the charge on his cell phone wore off. Don't panic, Lizzie."

"Easier said then done. Let's order a couple of pizzas."

"Sounds good to us. I want to take a shower and change my clothes. Here's the stuff," Noreen said, pointing to the box of latex gloves and the trash bags. "How are you going to get rid of it?"

"I'm going to cut it up in little pieces and feed it into the garbage disposal. God, I don't know how to thank you all. I don't know what I would have done without you."

As one, they hugged her. "That's what friends are for, baby," Noreen whispered. "Hey, a fire might be good. It's pretty raw and damp out there. Can you burn plastic?"

"I don't know. I never tried. Maybe a little bit. Go on, I'll order the pizza."

Lizzie ordered two pizzas with the works and two six-packs of Bud Lite. While she waited for the delivery, she went into the laundry room, where there were no windows, and proceeded to cut up the latex gloves, the box they were packed in, and the trash bags. She had a neat pile when she was finished. Outside on the small back porch, she raided the last of the wood from the woodbox. Within minutes, she had a nice blaze going. She hoped she would remember to open the trapdoor on the floor of the fireplace in the morning to dispose of the ashes. She fed the fire, a little at a time. She watched as the latex and the strips from the trash bags curled into a hot mass. She jabbed at it with the poker.

When the girls came down the steps, she pointed to the pile of plastic. "Feed it a little at a time in the disposal. Cut up some of the celery or maybe some potatoes to help it go down faster. If it doesn't work, bring the rest in here and we'll burn it. I hear a car. Keep poking at it. I gotta pay the pizza guy."

The delivery boy was the same one who had delivered to her before. He was wearing a wide grin when she opened the door. "Two pies, two six-packs. Fifty-five bucks. Lady, in case you don't know it, there are two guys, two houses down, who are watching your house. I can smell a cop a mile away. I saw one of them walking away from your house when I turned the corner. He got in the car. I circled the block pretending I was lost."

Lizzie's stomach started to churn. She struggled for nonchalance. "No kidding. Well, they'll be bored watching me." She paid him and tipped him twenty bucks. "Thanks for the info."

"Anytime."

"Hey girls, the cops are staking out the house. You made it back just in time. You didn't see a parked car out there when you got home, did you?"

"Nope. No cars were parked on the street."

"That's the last of it. It all went down the drain, Lizzie. How are you doing?" Noreen called from the kitchen.

"I'm done, too. I just want to wash my hands."

"Why are they staking you out, Lizzie?"

"I think they might be getting ready to arrest me

on some trumped-up charge. Cops have to be really careful when they arrest another cop. They stake you out for a few days, sometimes weeks, getting their ducks in a row, and then bam! If they don't already have a warrant, they're asking for one as we speak. With a warrant, they can bust in here anytime they feel like it. That's when they read you your rights and you get to call a lawyer. Come on, let's eat these pies before they get cold. By the way, I forgot to tell you, my day off is tomorrow. How lucky can one person be?"

When the girls trooped up the steps after midnight, Lizzie opened the back door to let Alice out one last time. Alice looked at the swirling fog in the yard and refused to budge. Lizzie shrugged as she closed and locked the door. "Guess it's papers by the back door for you tonight."

Lizzie knew she wasn't going to be able to sleep, so she turned the television low and curled up in Aggie's oversize chair, Alice half on and half off her lap.

If she had one wish right this moment, it would be to turn the clock back in time. Things were different now. Back in Vegas, she didn't have a care in the world. She lived high, partied hard, performed her job, and banked her money. And, it was all legal.

Everything she'd done since coming here was illegal. She didn't need a lawyer to tell her they could arrest her. There would be no bail for her because she'd pose a flight risk. She'd be old and gray when she got out of jail. Aggie, too. Add the fact that she'd fallen in love to the mix, and she was down for the count.

Well, by God, that isn't going to happen. Not if I can help it. She wiped at her wet eyes just as the doorbell rang. Alice sat up, her ears straighter than arrows. Lizzie put her finger to her lips to motion for silence on the shepherd's part. She slipped off the chair and went to the door where she slid the little door aside over the peephole. She fully expected to see one of the cops staking out the house. "Nathan!" She opened the door.

When she looked up at him she felt the same heart-stopping emotion she'd felt when Billy Summers gave her her first kiss behind the bleachers at the stadium at the age of sixteen. She was about to throw her arms around him until she looked in his eyes. She backed up a step, motioning him to enter the room. "Isn't it a little late for a visit?" was all she could think of to say. "Where were you all day, Nathan? I tried calling you at least twenty times."

"I work, Lizzie. I was on assignment. I did try calling you, but no one answers the phone in this house. I didn't want to call you at the station. Then the battery on my cell phone went out. Aren't you going to ask me what my assignment was? By the way, there are a couple of guys parked outside. They look like cops to me."

Lizzie blinked. Why was his voice so cold, so controlled? Why was he looking at her like she was a criminal? "It's kind of late for guessing games, Nathan. I assume you came here for a reason. Let's hear it."

"My assignment was going to the airport to meet Mr. Anthony Papadopolus of Las Vegas, Nevada. The paper wanted an interview. Mr. Papadopolus didn't want to give me an interview, so I had to dog him all day. He checked into the Ritz-Carlton in Buckhead with his entourage. Then guess where he went. Right here to this house, Lizzie, where he sat on the porch with your friends. Then you came home, he hugged you, and you went inside. I didn't get the interview. Is there anything you want to tell me, Lizzie?"

"Actually, Nathan, there are a few things I want to tell you. I'd like you to go home and bring back all the files we worked on. I've decided to turn it all over to the chief in the morning. In addition, I spoke to Aggie, and she said we screwed up. She said we should rip the seats apart in Tom's car, and hers as well, which we did. We found close to two hundred, yes, Nathan, two hundred, two-pound bags of either heroin or cocaine. We deposited it in the Salvation Army bin at the supermarket parking lot. Someone will turn it in to the police in the morning. At least I hope they will. You might want to think about getting those cars out of your friend's garage somehow. Like immediately."

Nathan looked like he'd been hit hard on the side of the head as he struggled to absorb everything Lizzie said to him. "What did he want, Lizzie? Why did he need to take over the whole eighteenth floor of the Ritz?"

"Get real, Nathan, how could I possibly know that? You must have a profile on him. He owns the Barb

Wire chain of restaurants. I think there are twenty-two of them, with two here in Atlanta. I would assume he's checking on them. He does that from time to time. He stopped by to say hello. I work for him, Nathan. He gives me health benefits and a 401k. I have a contract that says it's all legal and aboveboard."

"In Nevada. Not here."

"So? Stop beating around the bush, Nathan. If you have something to say, say it. I need those files tonight."

"Lizzie, listen to me. We have it on good authority that your pal, your employer, runs gambling dens everywhere he has those restaurants. My ass, the guy is checking on his steak houses. They're a front for his other activities. The feds are on to him. You set up a game with this guy, and you go down with him. It's just what they're waiting for. They're just waiting to pounce on him. If they pounce on him, they'll pounce on you. Why do you think those guys are staking out this house? Do you know what racketeering is, Lizzie?"

"Of course I know what it is. I live in Vegas, remember." They were closing in on her, and she knew it. Her heart started to race. "Did you drive here in the Beemer, Nathan?"

Nathan looked at her with such disgust, Lizzie cringed. "I dropped it off and picked up my own car earlier today. Tell me what you're going to do, Lizzie."

She didn't mean to snipe at him, but she did it anyway. "Are you worried about your Pulitzer?"

Nathan ignored the gibe. "I'm worried about *you*.

Us." She wanted to tell him there was no us. Instead she bit down on her tongue.

"Please, Nathan, trust me. Just go home and bring back the files. There's enough there for the chief to figure out the rest. I have to make copies. One set for you, one for the commissioner, one for me, and a set for my attorney. It's late, so I would appreciate it if you'd go get those files now. By tomorrow, it will be too late. Then you have to get those cars out of your friend's garage, and I can't help you. Wear gloves, okay?"

"Can we talk when I get back? Really talk."

"We'll see, Nathan. Please hurry."

"It's going to take me a while, Lizzie. The fog is pretty bad. It's like soup out there. At least an hour and a half. I can make the copies if you want." Lizzie nodded.

He looked like he wanted to kiss her. She wanted him to, but instead, he turned around and left, the door closing softly behind him. Lizzie ran to the window and looked out. He was right, it was like soup out there.

Lizzie debated all of five seconds before she changed from her slippers to her running shoes. "Stay, Alice."

Lizzie let herself out the back door, crossed the yard, and climbed the slippery fence. Climbing was easier than messing with the locked gate. She peered into the gloom as she tried to get her bearings. She was less than a mile, possibly a half mile from the Ritz-Carlton, which was on Peachtree Road N.E. Her eyes to the ground, she was able to tell where she was going. She huffed her way up the incline twenty

minutes later to the drive. A doorman held the door
for her. Inside, she waited till her breathing returned
to normal before she headed for the elevator. She
pressed 16 before she leaned back against the brass
railing. When the elevator came to a stop, she got out
to head for the EXIT sign and walked up two flights to
the eighteenth floor.

Lizzie stepped out into the hallway and was immediately surrounded by four men. They recognized
her. "I need to see Mr. P. right away. Tell him it's urgent." One of the men sprinted to the end of the hall.
He let himself into the suite. The door opened, and
he motioned with his hand for the men to escort her
back to the room.

Inside, Lizzie took a deep breath. "I need to talk to
you in private, Mr. P." She felt pleased to see the
alarm on the gambler's face. That meant he would
take whatever she said seriously. She wondered what
her own face looked like. Papadopolus led her to the
bedroom, where she started to talk. Her words ran
together in her anxiety but the man standing across
from her had no trouble understanding everything
she said. "Will you do it, Mr. P.?"

"For you, sweet cheeks, anything you ask. I appreciate your coming here. I'll make the calls now. I have
a coded mobile, so don't look so worried. I can take it
from here. You got enough money, kid?" Lizzie nodded. "What about your sister?" Lizzie nodded again.
"Okay. You ever need anything, you know who to
call."

Lizzie bit down on her lip as she nodded.

"Look at me, kid. When it comes to you, I'm all

talk. I never would have . . . if I ever had a daughter, I'd want her to be just like you. Go on, get out of here. You're wasting time."

Lizzie turned at the door and ran back to give the gambler a hug. "Thanks, Mr. P. Take care."

Forty-five minutes later, Lizzie was back in the house with no one the wiser. She spent the next half hour changing her clothes, packing her backpack, and writing notes to the girls. Her eyes kept going to her watch and then to the clock over the refrigerator. Every few seconds she swiped at the tears forming in her eyes. "Come on, Nathan, come on," she muttered over and over.

At five minutes to three, she hauled out her cell phone and dialed her sister's number. Aggie picked up on the third ring, her voice sleepy. "*Now*, Aggie. I'll call you in an hour. Take Gus with you."

Lizzie popped a bottle of Diet Pepsi. When she looked up, Nathan was standing in the doorway. "Everything's in the living room. I kept my copy. This one is for you. Since I'm such a neat freak, I bundled it all up for you. All you have to do is write a note and tape the box shut. I'm going to get rid of the cars, then I'm going home, Lizzie. I need some sleep. I'll be back in the morning, and you and I are going to talk. I want to leave you with something to think about. I'm going to want your answer when I get back. Will you marry me, Lizzie? I'm not going to kiss you, because if I do, I'll never leave."

Tears rolled down Lizzie's cheeks as she watched him walk away. "Bye, Nathan," she whispered. "Have a good life."

Lizzie sat down at the table, one eye on the clock, as she penned off two more notes. One for the box in the living room, a box she didn't even want to see. And another note to the girls, explaining what they should do. She propped them on the counter next to the coffeepot. She jammed her copy of the file into her backpack.

"Okay, Alice, time to go." She choked on a sob as she fastened the leash onto the shepherd's collar. She reached for the key to the backyard gate before she closed the door behind her. She quietly opened the gate, then closed it just as quietly. She led the dog through the neighbors' yards until she reached the corner. She walked two more blocks until she saw the car waiting for her. She opened the door and climbed in. She started to cry, gutwrenching sobs.

The driver spoke over his shoulder. "Don't cry, Lizzie, Mr. P. will make it all come out right. That was a nice thing you did for the boss, giving him a heads up like that. Too bad all those people out there don't know what a kind, generous man he is. He builds hospitals, schools, funds medical research all over the world. He builds parks for kids, makes sure kids with disabilities get what they need. He feeds the homeless and is one of the biggest contributors to battered women's causes. He's big on animal rights and sends money to churches and poor countries. No one knows about all that. They just want to haul his ass to jail because he's a lucky man. He does have legitimate businesses, as you know."

Lizzie continued to sob. "Why do you think I gave

him the heads up? He can't make this right for me, Manny. Will the Gulfstream be able to take off in this fog?"

"The fog is starting to lift. The answer is yes. Mr. P. said to tell you your sister will be three hours behind you. He had to get the other Gulfstream to Pittsburgh, and you said she had a two-hour drive to the airport. It's all taken care of, Lizzie."

Lizzie cried harder, Alice curled against her.

Her eyes red-rimmed, her voice hoarse from crying, Lizzie stepped out of the Lincoln Town Car when they reached Hartsdale International Airport. Her backpack was secure, her hold on Alice's leash fierce. Her throat started to burn all over again when Manny, Mr. P.'s personal bodyguard, gave her a bone-crushing hug. "You take care of yourself, Lizzie. You ever need anything, anything at all, you call. You know how to do that. Mr. P. said to give you this. It's a coded mobile phone. No one can ever trace this. He got it from some guy at Interpol. Your chariot awaits, my lady."

Lizzie looked across the airstrip at the sleek Gulfstream in the yellow light. The steps were down, the captain and crew waiting for her. A sob hooked itself in her throat as she led Alice across the tarmac.

Plan B was in effect.

Lizzie turned once and waved. Manny waved back. She knew he had his orders. Stay with her till she was safely airborne.

"Have a good life, Lizzie Jade!" Manny called.

Lizzie was crying so hard, the captain had to lead her up the steps. He helped her buckle in, made sure the seat belt next to her harnessed the dog. The pilot snapped off a salute, wondering who his important passenger was. Papadopolus said he would be informed of his final destination once he was airborne. For now, his flight plan said he was flying to Boston.

Gerald Sweeney taxied out to the runway, where he waited for clearance. Special clearance, to take off at this early hour. The Gulfstream was first in line for takeoff and was airborne in less than five minutes.

The stewardess informed him the dog was sleeping, and his important passenger was still crying.

Aggie Jade flipped on the windshield wipers, wondering why they weren't working. She needed them on her eyes, not the windshield. She swiped at her face with the sleeve of her shirt.

Plan B.

She cried harder. Gus stretched his long body across the console to put his head in her lap. "It's just you and me, big guy," she hiccupped.

Two hours and ten minutes later, Aggie drove as close to the tarmac as she could. She had her instructions. Get out of her car, keep the dog at her side, and she would be taken aboard an aircraft. She did as she was told. A man who could have passed for a Wall Street banker approached her. "Miss Jade?"

"Yes."

"Follow me, please."

"Okay, but wait a moment. Can you take this car back to the farm for my friend?"

"Absolutely."

"Do you need instructions?"

"No. We have it covered. Hurry."

Aggie swiped at her tear-stained face again. "I guess I should thank you."

"Not a problem, Miss Jade. Your sister will be waiting for you when you arrive. Don't worry about anything."

"Wait a minute. Just one second." Aggie fumbled in the pocket of her jeans and pulled out a wilted mass. "I want to give you this," she said, tears streaming down her cheeks. "It's an organic carrot. Well, it would have been an organic carrot if it had been allowed to grow. Please don't throw it away."

"No, ma'am. I'll put it in a glass of water. They're waiting, Miss Jade." Aggie ran up the steps to the Gulfstream, Gus at her side. She didn't look back.

"I'm sorry, Alex. I hope you have a good life," she whispered into the fur of Gus's neck. She cried so hard she fell asleep.

Chapter Fifteen

Noreen Farrell woke with a start. She sat up, then flopped back down. She must have had a bad dream. She could see that it was almost light out. She might as well get up and make some coffee.

Tying the sash of her robe as she went downstairs, she realized how quiet the house was. Exceptionally quiet for some reason. A chill washed over her. She wondered if she should wake the girls. Maybe after she had her first cup of coffee and the first cigarette of the day. It was time to go home, it really was. She sighed.

Noreen saw the box on the coffee table. It hadn't been there last night. She walked over to it, saw the note, and read it. She blinked, once, twice, as she absorbed the contents. Then she raced back upstairs, her voice shrill and incoherent.

The girls bounded out of bed. "Is the house on fire?" Candy asked hysterically.

"Worse. Quick, come downstairs. We have things to do. I'll make the coffee."

In the kitchen, Noreen picked up the two notes from the counter, looked at the key next to the coffeepot. She started to cry as she handed the notes to the girls, then filled the coffeepot. The women remained silent until Noreen poured the coffee.

"We have a busy day. First we pack. Then we go to the police station to drop off the box. We have to return Lizzie's rental car, close up this house. That means we turn off the water, the circuit breakers, clean out the fridge, take out the trash, close all the blinds, and walk away. We rent a car for ourselves and we drive to Vegas as soon we're done with everything. On the way out of town we stop at one of those storage places and take the stuff out of there and put it in the trunk. Lizzie said it's for us, whatever it is. That's the reason we have to drive back to Vegas. I guess she wants us to have some kind of memento of this trip. We don't know anything if anyone asks us questions. We were just guests. The card game is canceled, and we each get to keep the thousand bucks." Her voice was breathless with her monologue.

"Where do you think she went, Noreen?" Honey asked tearfully.

"I don't know, but wherever it is, I hope it's far away and safe."

"Do you think Nathan knows, or maybe he went with her," Honey said.

"No. Lizzie travels light. Remember, if anyone questions us, she's Aggie. We don't know a Lizzie Jade. Let's get all our crying done now before we put on our makeup." Noreen handed out paper napkins.

They blew gustily, then wiped at their eyes. "Okay, that's out of the way. Now, we take care of business."

It was eight o'clock, the girls showered and dressed. Their bags were packed and sitting by the front door, the box going to the police station piled on top. It took them another twenty minutes to turn off the breakers, the water, and empty the refrigerator. Candy took the trash out to the can and dragged it to the street.

Noreen pocketed the key to the self storage unit. "We aren't coming back here, so let's do a final check. Candy, you take the upstairs. Honey, do the front room."

They were just about to close the trunk of the rental car when Nathan Hawk pulled into the driveway. The fog was almost gone, giving all of them a clear view of the parked car two doors down."

"Where are you ladies going?" Nathan demanded.

"Home. Back to Vegas. We're driving." Noreen lowered her voice. "Lizzie isn't here, Nathan. We just closed up the house on her orders. If you want to check, here's the key." She handed over the brass key that opened all the locks on the doors.

"Where did she go? What do you mean you closed up the house on her orders?"

"We don't know where she went. When we woke up, she was gone. She left a note telling us what to do, and we're doing it. She isn't coming back, Nathan."

The reporter looked so devastated, the girls circled him with their arms. They could feel the shudders that racked his body. Noreen broke away first. "It was nice to meet you, Nathan. We enjoyed spending time with your friends. If you ever come to Vegas, give us a call, and we'll return the hospitality."

Nathan stepped aside, a blank look on his face.

He was still standing there staring at Aggie's house when the two officers in the unmarked car approached him. "What's up, Hawk?" an officer named Stevens asked. "Man, you look like you've been to hell and back. You okay?"

To hell and back summed it up pretty well. It had taken him three hours to move both cars to an old quarry on the Georgia border. He'd gambled that Madsen's car would make the trip riding on the rims, and it had. Before he'd pushed it over the edge into sixty feet of water, he'd removed his ten-speed bike, ridden it back to Bennigan's house, and done the same thing with Aggie's car. When he finally returned to his condo, it was all he could do to take a shower and drink a cup of coffee. Yep, to hell and back summed it up just perfectly. And now this.

Nathan cleared his throat. He sounded like a frog in distress when he said, "I'm fine. Why are you staking out Aggie's house? Don't tell me you aren't either. I'm a reporter, and I have a nose for stuff like this. She's gone. See for yourself," he said, tossing the cop the key Noreen had handed him.

"Where'd she go, Hawk?"

Nathan shook his head. "I don't know. I wish I did."

The second cop from the unmarked car appeared. "Don't I know you?"

Nathan looked at the young cop. He knew him

from somewhere. He was just too damn tired to try to figure out where. "I don't know. Do you?"

"Yeah, yeah, I know you. Your name is . . . damn, just give me a minute. Yeah, yeah, that restaurant, what's it called? Bennigan's. Your name is the same as the restaurant. I remember thinking that at the time. You're that guy who was making all the noise the other night. The one with the Beemer you said was always in the shop."

Nathan's insides started to roil. He wished he wasn't so tired. "I think you must have me mixed up with someone else. On what the paper pays me, there's no way I can afford a BMW. Your partner went into the house. Would you please tell him to hurry up, I need the key back. I have to get to work."

John Stevens loped down the front steps. "She's gone. Everything is locked up tight. The chief isn't going to like this. Not one little bit. Where you going, Hawk?"

"To work. I'd like the key back."

"It doesn't work that way. It's evidence now. I wouldn't leave town if I were you, Mr. Hawk."

"Kiss my ass, Stevens," Nathan said, walking away. Another time when he wasn't so physically and mentally beat, he would have stood his ground with the cop.

In his Intrepid, Nathan turned on the radio the moment the engine turned over. He tried to look into his future, but all he could see were lonely days, and there was no bright, vivacious, smart-alecky Lizzie in any of those days. The lump in his throat was so big he could barely swallow. Lizzie Jade, the love of his life, was lost to him.

Noreen parked the car in visitor parking at the precinct. She climbed out and reached into the backseat for the box Lizzie had left for Chief Shay. She carried it inside, where she walked up to the desk sergeant and waited to be recognized. "Officer, Detective Jade asked me to deliver this package to Chief Shay personally. She said there's a letter inside that will explain the contents to the chief. Will you see that he gets it?"

"I'll do that. And your name?"

"Courtney Love, Officer." Noreen watched as the sergeant wrote the name down without batting an eye. "Have a nice day, Officer."

Back in the car, Noreen said, "Okay, we're outta here. The car rental agency is four blocks east. I think it's called Enterprise Rentals. We pay for it in cash, and we rent another car."

An hour later they climbed out of their newly rented Lincoln Town Car to fit the key into storage bin number 11. Candy popped the trunk.

"I hope whatever we're supposed to take isn't too big. Our bags are taking up all the space as it is," Honey said, her voice worried.

"Get in here and close the door," Noreen hissed. "Take a look at what's in these bags. Look in both of them. Then do what I'm doing, sit down, put your head between your knees. We're all hyperventilating. I've never seen so much money, not even in Vegas," Noreen whispered. Her eyes were wide with shock.

"Lizzie said we were supposed to take it and have a good life. That's why she wanted us to drive back to Vegas. I'm going to cry. With everything going on in her life, with her sister, with Mr. P., with those shitty cops threatening her, she thought about us. She wants us to put it in the Caymans, and she'll manage it from wherever she is. I guess she knows how to do stuff like that. Lizzie said people died for this money, and she wants to know that it's going to good people who had nothing to do with what went on. She said if it was turned in, some crooked person would find a way to steal it. She said we shouldn't give it a second thought. There is one thing we have to do. Lizzie said we were to take a hundred thousand dollars and send a cashier's check to the Madsens. She wrote down the address." Her extended monologue finished, Noreen felt the air rush out of her lungs. She struggled to take a long, deep breath.

"That's good enough for me. If Lizzie said that's what we should do, then that's what we're going to do," Candy said smartly. "I say we just substitute our bags for these and get the hell out of here."

"I agree," Noreen and Honey said in unison.

The transfer of bags took less than ten minutes. They made one last stop before they headed for the interstate. They stopped at the office of the security unit and paid for the locker for three full years. They paid in cash. Noreen stuck the receipt in her wallet.

"All right, girls, we're going home!"

Chief Erwin Shay leaned back in his swivel chair. It was not going to be a good day. He could feel it in his bones. He buzzed Sadie and told her to get the commissioner and the mayor on the phone.

"I'll do that, but I think you should come out here right now, Erwin. Captain Ramos from the Salvation Army is here to see you. You better put rubber bands on your socks, Chief, because he's going to blow them off."

"Send him in, Sadie. Now! Cut the chitchat and get the commissioner and mayor on the phone. While you're at it, get that reporter, Nathan Hawk here, too."

The two men shook hands. The chief's eyes were full of questions. "I'm not here for a donation. Actually, Chief, I have something for you." Shay watched as the man opened a small grocery bag and took out a plastic bag filled with what looked like white powder. "There were 194 of these in one of our containers this morning. They weren't there yesterday, so someone put them in there during the night. One of my people has it all boxed up in our van. Who is going to take possession of it? I also want a receipt. And, I'd like the papers to know that we did bring it here. It will be good for our image and yours as well. I'd like it if you would say something, Chief Shay. Your silence is making me nervous."

"Where is your van now, Captain Ramos?" His voice sounded desperate. The chief took a deep breath and exhaled slowly.

"Right in front, in reserved parking. Three of my best people are guarding it. I want witnesses when we turn it over," Captain Ramos said.

"I understand." Shay wondered when his head

was going to pop off his neck. He reached into his desk drawer and pulled out a bottle of aspirin. He swallowed four with a gulp of cold coffee.

And then all hell broke loose.

Four officers, two from the night shift, and the two from the morning shift, were demanding an audience with the chief. They were all talking at once. Shay tried to listen but gave up. What he got out of the heated conversation was that Detective Agnes Jade had flown the coop. The day shift was blaming the night shift, who said no one but Nathan Hawk and the pizza deliveryman had been anywhere near Jade's house. Nor had Detective Jade left the premises.

"Then where the hell is she?" Shay thundered.

The silence was deafening.

"The commissioner is on line two, Chief," Sadie called.

"Tell him I'll call him back," the chief thundered.

"The mayor's on line one, Chief," Sadie shouted a second time.

"Tell him I'll call him back, too," the chief thundered a second time. "I want to see Nathan Hawk. Put out an all-points on him if he doesn't come in willingly," the chief thundered a third time. He stomped back into his office and slammed the door so hard the blinds rattled.

Erwin Shay sat down on his chair, pushed it away from the desk on its well-oiled rollers. He felt like he was twisting and turning in a wind that was approaching gale-force proportions. A timid knock on the door made him flinch. He didn't want to talk to anyone. He wanted to *think*. He watched as the handle of the door moved. No one but Sadie had the audacity to enter the chief's office uninvited. "A package just came for you, Chief. It's from Detective Jade." Sadie pointed to a clean corner of the chief's desk. The desk clerk set it down with a thump, then scuttled out of the room before the chief could bellow at him.

"What the hell is this, Sadie?"

Sadie kicked the door shut with one of her platform shoes. "I'm not a mind reader, Erwin. It's from Aggie. It doesn't have a red bow on it, so that leads me to believe it's not a gift. It's got at least two miles of tape on it, so that leads me to believe she didn't want anyone but you opening it or tampering with it. The message said it was to be hand-delivered to you personally. If you want to know what's in it, you're going to have to open it," Sadie snapped.

"You're supposed to sort through my mail, Sadie, and weed out the crap." Shay looked at the box, knowing he was going to hate the contents.

"It isn't mail, Erwin. It was a special delivery by some woman. For your eyes only. I'll watch when you open it. By the way, Captain Ramos is having breakfast in the cafeteria. I gave him a chit to use. What are you going to do about *that*, Erwin? You cannot blow off the commissioner and the mayor. Now you are going to have to make nice. Open the damn box, Erwin," Sadie ordered.

Chief of Detectives Shay rubbed at his temples. His voice was a bare whisper when he said, "I'm afraid to open it, Sadie. I think what's inside this box is my worst nightmare come to life. I don't give a damn what anyone says, Aggie Jade was a hell of a cop. The best."

"Why are you using the past tense, Erwin?"

"Because she's gone. You know why she's gone, Sadie? She's gone because she's smart. She knew . . . knows . . . oh, hell, here goes nothing." The chief pulled out his pocketknife and worked through the yards and yards of sticky tape. "Let's just hope there's a letter in here."

Sadie pulled back the flaps of the huge box. She blinked at the contents. "Butterfly books! Her gun and shield are in here, too. And the dog's shield. I feel like crying. There's your letter! Read it, Erwin!"

"I'm reading it, Sadie. Stop flapping your gums." Shay's hands started to shake when he sat down. Sadie snatched the letter out of his hands and read it. Her hands started to shake, too. She laid the letter on the desk.

"What do you want me to do, Erwin?" Her voice was soft and gentle, the kind of voice a doting grandmother would use when putting her favorite grandchild to bed.

"Christ, Sadie, I don't know. I've never had anything like this happen on my watch. Call the commissioner and the mayor. Tell them to come here as soon as they can. Tell them it's an emergency. If Hawk shows up, bring him right in. I'm going to put his ass in a sling the minute I get hold of him. Keep Ramos happy until the commissioner gets here. Not a word of this to anyone, Sadie."

Erwin Shay mopped at his bald head. He could

feel perspiration dripping down his arms. He sat down and reached for the letter. He wished he was a kid again so he could bawl his head off.

Dear Chief Shay,

I'm really sorry it's come to the point where I have to write this and you have to read it. Life sometimes just isn't fair.

Tom Madsen was not a dirty cop. Nor am I a dirty cop. I just want you to know that from the git-go. I can prove it, Chief. I know you told me not to get involved, but I had to. I did it on my own time. I knew in my gut Tom and I were set up that night. I was supposed to be killed, too, along with my dog. That is a hard thing to live with. It isn't something I'll soon get over. IAD cleared me, so you know I'm clean. Those guys don't miss a trick.

All the proof you need is inside this box. Just go page by page in each book and you'll see the proof. Unfortunately, I didn't have time to do each officer in the department. I'm sure you can find people who will finish the job. The code is simple once you know what you're looking for. Will Fargo kept records. I went to his brother's house in Washington after Will died. The brothers got scared, and they're long gone. They knew nothing, but they're scared just the way the Madsens are scared. I'm the one who broke into the Madsens' house and took Tom's car. Buried inside the seats were close to two hundred bags of cocaine. It was in my car, too. I took it all to the Salvation Army bin and dropped it off. I also got rid of both cars. I know how it works,

Chief. I'm a whistle-blower, and they'll come after me.

No one helped me, Chief. Everything I did, I did on my own. Consider this a confession for want of a better word.

As for Mr. Papadopolus, he's a friend. He stopped by my house to say hello. He was here in Atlanta checking on his restaurants. By the time you read this, I'm sure he'll be back in Vegas. End of story.

I want to thank you for the good years, Chief. I think I was a good cop. I almost died trying to be a good cop. I'm having a lot of trouble with that.

So now I'm on the run. I'll be looking over my shoulder for the rest of my life, just like that cop in New York. I'll handle it because my cop instincts are still intact. And, I have Gus.

I'm going to be watching the way this plays out. If I don't like what I'm seeing, I'll act on it. Everyone has a smoking gun, and I have mine.

My gun, minus the clips, my shield, and Gus's shield are in the box.

> *Agnes Jade*

Erwin Shay bit down on his lower lip. He suddenly felt like bawling. He reached inside the box and withdrew the gun and shields. He laid all three items on the desk. It was the dog's shield that brought the tears to his eyes. He started slamming things around then because he didn't know what else to do. He was like a scalded cat when the commissioner and mayor entered his office ten minutes later.

●　　●　　●

Nathan Hawk sat at his computer, his thoughts a million miles away. He knew he should be writing something, but his brain refused to function. All he could think about was Lizzie and Aggie. *Where are they? Are they okay? Will I ever see either one of them again?*

Nathan turned the computer off, opened his desk drawer, and took out his checkbook. He had enough money to tide him over for a while if he took a leave of absence. He had six weeks' vacation on the books. He could take it all now. And, do what? Find Lizzie of course.

Nathan shuffled his way into his boss's office. "Brad, I need to take my vacation, all six weeks of it. If you can't see your way clear to giving it to me, then I have to resign."

Brad Dewbury looked up at the tall reporter. "Are you okay, Nathan?"

"No. No, I'm not okay. This is . . . personal. I'm sorry I can't give you more notice."

"No, it's okay, Nathan. Summer is slow. Nothing ever happens. Will you stay in touch? If something comes up, will we be able to reach you?"

"I don't know, Brad. I want to say yes, but I just don't know."

Brad waved his hand to indicate he should leave. "Collect your vacation pay and get out of here. Call in once in a while, okay?"

"Yeah, sure. Thanks, Brad."

That was almost too easy. Nathan found his way to the payroll department, explained the situation, waited while the payroll clerk called Dewbury to confirm his vacation. Five minutes later he walked out of the building, the check in his hand. He walked across the street and deposited his check. Now he could go home to get some sleep. He whirled around when he felt a hand on his shoulder.

"Mr. Hawk?"

"Yeah."

"Chief Shay asked me to bring you down to headquarters. He said if you don't want to come willingly, I was to arrest you. What's it gonna be?"

Nathan shrugged. "I'll follow you." The young cop, who didn't look old enough to shave, nodded.

The ride to police headquarters took all of thirty-five minutes. Nathan parked beside the young cop and followed him into the smelly building. He was immediately taken to Chief Shay's office, where the commissioner and mayor stared at him with unblinking intensity.

"Sit down, Hawk," Shay ordered. Nathan sat and prayed he wouldn't fall asleep. "What do you know about this?" He handed over Lizzie's letter. Nathan read it, his eyes burning.

"Well?"

"Well what?" Nathan asked wearily. "I'm not a cop, I'm an investigative reporter. Is this supposed to mean something to me?" Lizzie hadn't implicated him. She was taking the rap for all of it. He felt like a deadly germ under a microscope.

"You two were a, what do you young people call it today, an item. You were seeing each other. What do you know about this letter?"

"Not a damn thing. I went by the house earlier,

and Aggie was already gone. The house was closed up. That's all I know. Yeah, I feel like hell. I thought the two of us had something going. I even asked her to marry me. She was supposed to give me her answer this morning. That's why I was there."

"You are one sorry-looking son of a bitch, son. I think I believe you. This stays in this office, understood?" Shay said through clenched teeth.

"Chief, I'm on vacation. Personally, I don't give a good rat's ass what you do with that letter. I'm going home to sleep. You know where to find me."

"You go when I say you go. I want to hear the words, Hawk. Do you know where Detective Jade went?"

"No. I wish I did."

"Do you know anything about any of this?" The chief tapped the letter, then the box.

"The only thing I know is Aggie said just about the whole department was dirty. She was afraid. You want a laugh, Chief? I can give you a laugh. I promised her I would take care of her. Guess she didn't think very much of that promise."

"What the hell kind of reporter are you, Hawk?" the commissioner asked. "You should be out there beating the bushes and bringing down the wrath of your paper all over the department."

"Let someone else do it. I'm on vacation. Can I go now?"

"Yeah, but don't make any plans to leave here."

Every bone in Nathan's body protested as he made his way through the building and out to his car. He was on Peachtree Road when he swerved at the last minute to roll up the driveway to the Ritz-Carlton. He parked, got out, and went into the hotel and over to the registration desk. "Anthony Papadopolus. Can you ring his room?"

"Mr. Papadopolus checked out last evening, sir."

"Figures," Nathan muttered as he made his way across the lobby to the concierge.

He identified himself, and asked, "Do you happen to know what time Mr. Papadopolus left last evening?"

"No, sir, I'm sorry. We were pretty busy all night. If he checked out, then I would assume he left immediately. They should be able to help you at the desk."

Nathan shook his head. *What the hell am I doing here?* He shook his head, trying to clear it.

He was back in his car within minutes. Knowing he was a hazard on the road, he stayed in the right lane and drove slowly. He was almost asleep on his feet when he walked from the garage to the elevator and rode it to his floor. Inside, he ripped at his jacket, threw it across the room, and fell onto the couch. The last thing he saw before he closed his eyes were the packets of money Lizzie had tossed onto the coffee table. For Aggie's snitch Pippy.

He closed his eyes and was asleep instantly.

Lizzie walked down the steps that would take her away from the Gulfstream. Her hold on Alice's leash was secure, her backpack was tight on her shoulders. She stopped at the bottom step and looked up at the pilot. She nodded her thanks. "Tell Mr. P. I said thanks." The pilot nodded and offered up a salute.

Lizzie adjusted her dark glasses and headed for the small terminal.

Portugal.

Her new home.

Alice walked as close to Lizzie as she could, stopping every few minutes to sniff the ground.

Lizzie tilted the dark glasses she was wearing to look about. What she saw was a beautiful blue sky, smiling people, laughing children, and helpful employees of the small airline. The breeze was warm, the sun warmer. It felt good after the air-conditioning of the Gulfstream. She stopped for a minute to pull a baseball cap out of her backpack. She plopped it on top of the blond wig. She looked up in time to see a young man wearing a blue uniform of some sort with a placard bearing the name Patricia Newfeld. She waved her hand at him before stopping at the immigration desk, where she presented her passport, bearing the Patricia Newfeld name.

When she saw the young man again he smiled, showing perfectly aligned white teeth. He handed over a sheaf of papers and pointed to the east. "An open-air Jeep, madam, just as you requested. If you will sign your name, you may take possession of the vehicle. I must, however, see a copy of your international driver's license. A mere formality."

Lizzie frowned. She had an international license but in her own name, not in the name of Patricia Newfeld, clearly an oversight. She waved her hands, a look of dismay on her face.

"It is of no importance," the young man said. He held out his hand.

A bribe. That she understood. Lizzie dug in her pocket and pulled out a fifty-dollar bill. "I'm sorry, I haven't changed my money to euros yet."

"It is of no importance, madam." The fifty-dollar bill disappeared so fast, Lizzie blinked. She signed the name Patricia Newfeld. The young man made a production out of staring at the documents before he finally ripped off a copy and handed her the rest, which she immediately stuck in her backpack.

Lizzie led Alice over to a bench outside the small airport. The game plan was to stay in St. Michael for a few days, then charter a small plane to the island of Fayal, where she and Aggie would take up residence.

For the rest of their lives.

Lizzie sat down on a hard wooden bench outside the small building. She stared off in the distance, across sparkling blue water. She blanched slightly when she noticed the short runway and the expanse of water beyond the end.

Six years ago she'd come to this very airport to vacation with friends. They'd stayed in Lisbon, though, because of the fine restaurants and night life. By day, they either took boats or the small puddle jumpers to explore the various islands. She'd fallen in love with the lazy lifestyle, the perpetual blue skies, the brilliant colorful flowers, and the warm, soothing sun. She and the others had visited a nude beach, and when she returned to Vegas, she had an overall tan even though she'd used a thirty-five sunblock.

Lizzie looked down at her watch. One o'clock in Atlanta, six o'clock here in Portugal. She changed her watch. She wished she knew what was going on back in the States. Noreen and the girls should be on the road. Chief Shay was probably tugging at the few hairs he had left on his head. *Nathan? Where is Nathan? What is he doing?*

The urge to cry was so great, Lizzie bit down on her lower lip. *Don't think about Nathan. Nathan belongs to the past. The past is gone.* "Tell that to my heart," she muttered.

Lizzie jumped up. Alice was on her feet in an instant. "Let's go for a walk, girl. I'll get you some water and a soda pop for me. We still have a couple of hours till Aggie arrives. Oh, it's going to be so good to see her again."

A small boy approached her, shouting something she didn't understand until he pointed to a cooler packed with ice. Water and soft drinks. She purchased two, pointed to a paper cup. Alice drank as greedily as she did. Money changed hands before Lizzie walked away.

She could, if she wanted to, get in the Jeep and drive around. The only problem was, she didn't want to. She didn't want to do anything.

They walked around the perimeter of the small airport until Alice nudged her leg, an indication that she'd had enough walking. Lizzie led her back to the small building. The sun had moved a little to the west, away from the bench she'd been sitting on. That was okay. It was still warm and a little breezy. She curled into the corner of the bench and dozed off.

Lizzie woke when Alice tugged at the leash grasped in her hand. She sat up, disoriented. She looked to her right when she heard the sharp bark of a dog. Gus! A heartbeat later she was on her feet, running to her sister. "Aggie!"

"Lizzie!"

They jiggled and wiggled, the dogs wrapping them in their leashes as the sisters hugged one another, crying, and laughing at the same time.

"I got us some wheels. No baggage, just our backpacks. I can't wait to take off this damn wig. It itches. We're dyeing our hair tomorrow. I'll go nuts if I have to keep wearing it. You okay with dyeing your hair, Aggie?"

"Yeah, I'm okay with it, Lizzie. Where are we staying?"

"I bought a little house off the Internet. I even have the key. It's a cottage, but it has indoor plumbing. We're going to stay in it for as long as we stay in the islands. I also bought a house in Lisbon. It's a little more palatial. It has two bathrooms. You aren't gonna love it, but you will like it. Trust me, this place will grow on you. Climb in and let's go. I think your dog likes my dog."

"I see that," Aggie said, settling herself in the passenger seat of the Jeep. "We need to talk, Lizzie. Really talk."

"I know, Aggie. We have the rest of our lives to talk."

Nathan slept deeply and soundly, around the clock. He might have slept longer, but the phone rang on the table next to the sofa where he was sleeping. Groggily, he reached for it and brought it to his ear.

He bolted upright at what he was hearing. "Nathan, this is Alex Rossiter. I'm down in the lobby. Can I come up?"

"Yeah. Yeah, sure, come right up."

Nathan sat up, knowing he'd slept the clock around. He should feel rested, full of spit and vinegar. Instead, he felt like hell. He staggered to the bathroom, where he brushed his teeth, groaning at his reflection in the mirror. From the bathroom, he shuffled his way to the kitchen, where he made a pot of coffee. He was pouring two cups when the doorbell rang."

Alex Rossiter held out his hand. Both men pumped vigorously. "Took me forever to get an elevator. Busy place you live in."

Nathan stared at the man standing across from him. He looked beaten and worn, stubble on his cheeks and chin, his eyes wary and sad, not to mention tired. "Everyone's getting ready to leave for work." He held out a cup of coffee.

Rossiter took the lead when Nathan led him back to the living room. "I know as much as you know, Hawk. So, let's not go there. Aggie's gone. I have to assume Lizzie is gone, too. Do you have *any* idea where they could be?"

"If I did, do you think I'd be sitting here? The short answer is no. Aggie's house is closed up tight. I guess they had a plan from the beginning if things ever got to this point. I'll tell you what I know, and you tell me what you know. Maybe one of them dropped a clue we didn't pick up on."

They talked steadily and earnestly for close to an

hour. The only thing they agreed on at the end of the hour was both women had to have had serious help in getting away.

Nathan looked down at his wrinkled clothing. He felt like a homeless person for some reason. "Ask yourself, Alex, who do either one of them know who could help them to that extent?"

Rossiter shrugged as he rubbed at the stubble on his cheeks. "Nobody that I know of. Lizzie had a wider circle of friends. Some of them are pretty influential, according to Aggie. I don't know names, though."

Nathan's face set in hard, grim lines. His voice was bitter when he said, "I know one name."

"What are we waiting for? Let's go talk to him."

Nathan sighed, his face full of pain. "Easier said than done. He's in Las Vegas. I know he isn't going to give up anything. If I'm right about him helping Lizzie, he isn't going to admit it, much less help us out. What did Aggie say when she left?"

Alex snorted, a sound of pure disgust. "I heard the phone ring. Aggie got out of bed and went downstairs. I just thought it was Lizzie calling early. Hell, I don't know what I thought. I rolled over and tried to go back to sleep. I could kick myself now. I must have had some kind of premonition because after about ten minutes, when she didn't come back upstairs, I got my sorry ass out of bed, but it was too late. She was gone. Her backpack was gone, too. She never told me this, but I kind of figured it out for myself. If she had to leave in a hurry, all she had to do was grab the backpack, Gus, and she was good to go.

She took my car, but somebody brought it back. Some guy drove it up the road, parked it, got out, and climbed into another car. Oh, there was one other thing. I didn't notice it right away. Aggie had all these nice neat rows of organic carrots. They were about three inches high. One was missing. I guess she took it as a memento.

"I turned everything off, packed, locked up, and here I am. We aren't going to find them, are we? Hell, I even toyed with the idea of going to the police and telling them what I know, which isn't much."

Nathan reached across for Alex's cup and carried it into the kitchen. He poured more coffee. "Save your breath. They hauled my ass in and grilled me. Lizzie wrote a letter taking all the blame for everything. Of course she signed Aggie's name. But, to answer your question, no, we probably are not going to find them on our own. I took my vacation time this morning. I have six weeks. I have enough money to tide me over until I have to return to work. How much time do you have off? Maybe we could partner up."

"I don't have to be back at school until the end of August. Maybe between the two of us we can come up with something."

"The chief warned me not to leave town. But I think the only place we'll get our answers, if there are answers, is in Las Vegas." Nathan dropped his head into his hands, his voice muffled when he said, "I asked Lizzie to marry me. I went by the house in the morning, and that's how I found out she was gone. She had a real head start on me. Christ, they could be halfway around the world by now."

Alex's voice sounded shaky when he said, "Aggie knows how to go to ground. She's a cop. You need to know what we're up against. If they don't want to be found, we aren't going to find them."

"You might be right, but I have to try. You with me or not?"

"I'm with you, Nathan. Listen, I'm going to go home, shower, and get some clean clothes. How about meeting up, say an hour from now at Becker's for some breakfast. It just occurred to me that I haven't had anything to eat since day before yesterday."

"Sounds good to me. I'll see you in an hour. Pack a bag, Alex."

Noreen Farrell opened the door, a look of stunned surprise on her face. "Nathan! How in the world did you find me?"

Nathan worked his facial muscles into something that resembled a smile. "I'm a reporter, remember. You're listed in the phone book under Noreen Farrell. This is Alex Rossiter, a friend of Aggie's. Can we come in?"

"Of course you can come in. I don't know anything, Nathan. Lizzie didn't tell me where she was going. She left me a note. She asked me to close up her sister's house and return her rental car. She also asked me to drop off a box at the police station, which I did. That's it."

"Can I see the note?"

"I didn't save it. Why would I?"

"I asked her to marry me, Noreen."

Noreen fiddled with the belt on her robe. "I'm sorry, Nathan. Please, sit down. Can I get you a drink or something?"

"No thanks."

Noreen perched on the arm of a La-Z-Boy. Nathan thought her eyes looked worried, or was it fear he was seeing?

"Lizzie needed help to get away on such short notice. Who do you know who has that kind of power?"

"Nobody. Lizzie always had what she called Plan B. I don't know what it was because she never told me, and I never asked. Whatever Plan B was, she was comfortable with it. I have to assume it was her getaway plan. That means she had it all planned out in advance if things went awry. That's just my own personal opinion."

"How can I get hold of Anthony Papadopolus?"

"Nathan, I don't know. I don't travel in those circles. He lives somewhere here in Vegas, but that's all I know. Your best bet would be to put the word out you're looking for him and let him find you. Again, that's just my personal opinion."

"Who do we put the word out to?" Alex said, speaking for the first time.

"The casinos. It's late, Nathan, we just got back, and I haven't eaten all day. I was going to have some cereal and go to bed."

"I thought you left yesterday," Nathan said, pouncing on Noreen's words.

"We did. We drove. The girls wanted to see the country. We took turns driving and drove straight through."

Nathan jumped to his feet. "Now, why does that sound like a lie to me?"

Noreen jumped to her feet and squared off with him. "I don't know why it sounds like a lie, Nathan. Furthermore, I don't care. Read my lips. I do not know where Lizzie is. I do not know how she got to wherever she was going. I'm sorry your heart is breaking, but I cannot help you. Please don't come here again."

"Can you at least tell me where Lizzie lived. Maybe she left a clue or something. What about all those cars and the yacht she owns? What happens to them?"

"I don't know. As to her address, that was part of Plan B. Besides, it was a comp. It wasn't hers. It's ready for the next temporary tenant. That's the way it works here. If you give me your number, I'll call you if I hear anything."

Nathan and Alex pulled out business cards and handed them over. Both men knew they'd never hear from Noreen Farrell.

Outside in their rental car, they looked at one another. "That was a bust. I didn't expect her to give up anything, but I hoped there might be something. I don't think she knows where Lizzie and Aggie went. Lizzie wouldn't want to involve her friends for just that reason."

"Let's hit the casinos. The night is still young," Alex said glumly. "Maybe we should split up. That way, we'll cover more territory in less time. Someone in this damn town must know where that guy lives."

"We can only hope."

Chapter Sixteen

*N*athan Hawk and Alex Rossiter were having lunch in the Mirage when Nathan felt a tap on his shoulder. He turned around and looked up at the tallest man he'd ever seen. His eyes were questioning.

"Mr. Hawk, Mr. Papadopolus will see you now. Follow me, please."

"Well, hot damn. Ten days later, and he's finally ready to see me. I'm glad it wasn't a matter of life or death," Nathan muttered as he slapped some bills on the table. The tall man offered up no response as the two men walked behind him out of the dining room.

The casino was jam-packed with people even though it was just a little before the noon hour. Busloads of senior citizens were descending in droves, forcing the men to walk faster to avoid a collision. Waitresses in skimpy outfits, trays held above their heads, also stepped aside. Free drinks to those playing the clanking slots and poker tables.

Nathan looked around. Where was this guy taking

them? He stopped short when the tall man stepped aside at one of the lounge areas. "Mr. Papadopolus is at the far end. He can give you ten minutes. Talk fast, Mr. Hawk."

Up close, Anthony Papadopolus looked like a benevolent Buddha. He was sitting in a comfortable swivel chair, his hands laced across his barrel chest. "Gentlemen, please sit down. I'm Anthony Papadopolus, and you are Nathan Hawk and Alex Rossiter. I was told you want to talk to me."

"Where are they? Don't pretend you don't know who I'm talking about either. Lizzie couldn't have gotten away so clean without some expert help. That goes for Aggie, too. I know Lizzie worked for you. She told me all about it."

"I'm sorry, gentlemen, I can't help you. Yes, Lizzie did work for me. But she canceled her contract. Normally, I don't allow such things, but she managed to convince me it was in both our best interests. I thought she was still in Atlanta."

"Lizzie is not back in Atlanta. If she were, I wouldn't be here, and neither would Alex," Nathan said, pointing to Alex Rossiter. "The house is closed up tight, and she's gone. G-O-N-E! If you're worried we might be with the police or the newspapers, we aren't. We're both here on vacation time. I asked Lizzie to marry me. She was supposed to give me her answer the day she disappeared. Alex here wanted to marry Aggie. We aren't wearing wires. If you want, we'll gladly strip down for you right here."

Papadopolus managed to look dismayed at Nathan's suggestion. "That won't be necessary. I'm sure, Mr. Hawk, Lizzie will be in touch with you at some point. She's a very compassionate, caring person. I'm sure her sister, because she is a twin, is the same sort of person. What you should be concerned with right now is the young women's safety, not your own personal desires. In other words, this is not about you, it's about them. I'm sorry, but I can't help you."

"Can't? You mean you won't. Okay, how about this? Get in touch with them and ask them if we can go to wherever they are. Will you do that?"

"No."

"Why the hell not?" Rossiter shouted.

"Because I don't know where they are."

"Don't give me any of that crap. I'd bet my pension that Gulfstream of yours took her to wherever she wanted to go. Somewhere along the way, Lizzie picked up Aggie. I know you were going to have a game at Aggie's house. I know it as sure as I'm standing here. I warned Lizzie they were going to pick you up. If not the locals, then the feds. She told you. That's why you're back here in Vegas. One hand washing the other, that kind of thing."

Papadopolus steepled his fingers. "I can see why you're a reporter; you have an active imagination. I wish I could help you, but I can't. If by some chance I hear from either one of the ladies, I'll call you if you leave me your business cards. I'm sorry, but I have to leave now. Good luck in your search, gentlemen."

Nathan's hands flapped in distress. Alex was shuffling from one foot to the other. "Doesn't it matter to you that we love them, want to marry, and raise families? How can you be so coldhearted?" Nathan demanded.

Papadopolus was on his feet. Standing, he didn't appear so round. He wasn't soft either. His eyes glittered now. "It's because I do care about both those women that I'm not helping you. If you love them as you say you do, that love will never vanish. They'll find you when and if the time is right. Be very careful, gentlemen, that you don't do something in your love quest that will jeopardize their safety. It was nice meeting both of you."

"Son of a bitch!" Alex sputtered. He flopped down on the chair Papadopolus had been sitting on. It smelled like his cologne. "Now what? Do we go home with our tails between our legs or what?"

"I don't know, Alex. We can try Noreen again. She was Aggie's best friend. She might crack if we put some pressure on her. Obviously, we need to fall back and regroup. Nothing's going on in Atlanta, and it's been ten days. I don't understand that either."

Alex flagged a waitress and ordered two bottles of Corona.

"Who the hell is that guy anyway. I know what you told me, but who the hell is he *really*?" Alex asked.

"I can only tell you what I've read and what Lizzie told me. If he isn't the richest man in Vegas, he's the next richest. He calls himself a broker. That means he puts people together to play poker. He gets a fee from each person playing. He has a stable of cardplayers like Lizzie, who are pros. They sit in on the game and play in his place. He pays them a percentage of whatever is taken in for the night. Here in Vegas, it's legal."

"He's got to be pretty damn rich to own his own Gulfstream. Those babies don't come cheap."

"Lizzie told me he pays very well and has no turnover as far as employees go. That's another way of saying they are all loyal and wouldn't rat on him if he does something on the shady side. Assuming he would even think about breaking the law.

"He's got all kinds of legitimate businesses, according to Lizzie. Now, you know as much as I know. I'm itching for some kind of confrontation. Let's take another shot at Noreen. If that doesn't work, we might as well go home. It's a given Papadopolus isn't going to part with anything. We'll just be spinning our wheels if we stay here."

"Okay, let's go," Rossiter said, getting up off the chair.

A light rain was falling an hour later when Nathan parked the rental car next to a Mercedes 560SL. The apartment complex looked just like any apartment complex. It was well maintained, with patches of close-cropped grass next to every door. Flower beds were colorful, and vibrant, and also well tended. He was surprised not to see bicycles and scooters or roller skates. Maybe this was an adult living complex, the kind Artie Bennigan lived in.

Noreen Farrell lived on the first floor. He rang the bell and waited. When there was no response he rang it again and again. The door next door opened and a matronly-looking woman poked her head out. "If you're looking for Noreen Farrell, she's gone. I saw her leaving a few days ago with two huge suitcases. I can take a message if you want to leave one with me, and I'll give it to her when she returns."

Nathan's eyes took on a desperate glaze. "Do you know where she went, ma'am?"

"No, I'm afraid I don't know. The only reason I know she's gone at all is, I was coming home from the dentist in the middle of the day. Root canal," she said by way of explanation as to why she was home during the day. "We aren't neighborly, if you know what I mean. Oh, we speak, say hello, that kind of thing. She works nights and sleeps days. I work days and sleep nights. I work in a bank, and our computers went down, so they sent everyone home. I guess that's more than you wanted to know, huh?"

It was, but Nathan didn't care. "Did she leave in a taxi?"

"No. One of her friends picked her up. I've seen them here a few times. They're both showgirls. Really pretty women. The one named Candy was driving. Honey was sitting in the backseat. Noreen got in the front. The reason I know their names is because Noreen introduced them to me when she invited me for dinner one Thanksgiving because my husband was away on business. Is something wrong? You look worried."

"No, nothing is wrong. We just need to talk to her about a friend of ours who turned up missing."

"Oh."

Alex fished in his pocket for one of his cards. He walked across the small patch of grass to hand it to the loquacious neighbor.

"Well, if I see her, I'll tell her you were looking for her. The bags were *huge*. I suspect they were going away for at least three weeks. I take bags like that when I go on vacation for three weeks. I always take the full three weeks. The bank hates it when you do that, but I don't care. *Big* bags. They didn't match. I don't know if that's important or not."

Nathan sucked in his breath. He struggled for a casual tone. "What color were they? Do you remember?"

Of course I remember. Hunter green. My husband calls it Dartmouth green. Is that important?"

"No. I guess it was a silly question. We appreciate your help. Thanks."

In the car, Alex turned to face Nathan. "What the hell was *that* all about?"

"The suitcases. Will Fargo's money. I bet you ten bucks, Lizzie told them to take the money. We packed the money up in two suitcases, and one of them was Hunter green, and took it to a storage facility. Lizzie kept the key. I think Noreen and her friends went to the Caymans. You up for a little trip?"

Alex nodded. "I'm your man."

Less than twenty-four hours later, Nathan and Alex stepped out of Brac Airport to head for the nearest car rental agency. They drove away in a Jeep, the islands' most popular rental.

"I've never been here before, have you, Nathan?"

"Nope. Heard about it, though. I read the brochure on the plane. It's 480 miles from Miami.

Supposedly it's peaceful. The Caymans are a self-governing British crown colony. There are three islands, Grand Cayman, Cayman Brac, and little Cayman. I have no clue about to which island the girls went to. I want to say Cayman Brac because that's where the airport is. I would assume they'd head for the nearest, nicest hotel, then do their banking thing." Nathan turned to his companion. "This could be a wild-goose chase."

Alex shrugged. "It's not like I have something better to do. Let's start with Cayman Brac since we're already here. According to this list that came with the rental car, the best places to stay are the Brac Airport Inn, the Brac Caribbean Beach Village, Brac Haven Villas, or Brac Reef Beach Resort. Where are we going to stay?"

"Whichever one is the closest. We can start making calls from there. I wish to hell I knew more about offshore banking. The truth is, I really don't know anything about it. I don't see how a showgirl could know either. This is going to be the blind following the blind unless you know something I don't know."

"Sorry, I know nothing about stuff like that. Never had enough money to worry about hiding it. I'm not exactly poor, but I'm not rich either. Hey, pull over, there's the Brac Airport Inn."

They parked, checked in, taking two rooms facing the ocean. The moment Nathan handed over his credit card, he said, "Can you tell me if my friend Noreen Farrell checked in yet? We were delayed in Miami."

"Let me check, sir," the honey-complexioned girl

said. "Yes, they checked in three days ago. Would you like me to ring their room for you?"

Nathan grimaced. "No, not till we look a little more presentable. We'll find them later." He decided to take a wild gamble. "Just out of curiosity, did they get room 711? We're all from Las Vegas, and it's a lucky number."

The young girl laughed. "No, I'm afraid not. They're in 802."

Nathan did his best to look impish. "Is 711 available?"

"No, sir, it was booked yesterday. Sign here."

Nathan and Alex obliged.

On the way up in the elevator, they clapped each other on the back. "It was pure dumb luck. Normally when you expect people to do the obvious, they fool you and do the direct opposite. I counted on Noreen and the girls wanting to do this deal as quickly as possibly with the least amount of effort. They're also probably scared out of their wits. Let's hit the shower, then visit room 802," Nathan said happily.

The first thing Nathan did when he hit the room was to turn on the television to CNN. He stared at the screen, his jaw dropping. He inched his way to the bed, where he sat down. The dark stuff had finally hit the fan. He didn't know if he should be happy or worried. CNN's headquarters were in Atlanta, so they would give full coverage to the police department. He waited through seven commercials. Since it was the top of the hour, he had to wait for the hourly rundown before the anchor got back to APD's corrupt police department. He listened to the excitement ringing in the anchor's voice. Three-quarters of the department had been suspended without pay pending an investigation. Whistle-blower, Detective Agnes Jade, who was also under suspicion, and missing, was given credit for turning the records over to Chief of Detectives Erwin Shay and the commissioner. Atlanta was working with a skeleton force until the National Guard arrived. It was unclear, the anchor said, whether Jade was in protective custody, hiding out for fear of retaliation, or had flown the proverbial coop.

The commissioner was quoted as saying this was a black day for the Atlanta Police Department. Chief of Detectives Erwin Shay agreed with the commissioner. The mayor, his expression fierce, said they would leave no stone unturned, and those guilty would be punished to the fullest extent of the law.

Nathan reared back when a full-screen picture of Aggie Jade appeared. The anchor went on to describe the shoot-out she'd been involved in, how she almost died, the extent of her injuries and the injuries of her canine partner. Another picture was substituted. This one was taken with the mayor, the commissioner, and the chief of detectives the day she'd been released from rehab.

The voice continued to drone on, rehashing what he'd said minutes ago as Nathan headed for the bathroom. He shaved and showered, dressing in khaki shorts and a white Izod tee. He slipped his feet into Docksiders before he headed for the minibar, where he popped a bottle of Beck's beer. His watch told him he had twenty minutes until it was time to head to Alex's room. He liked his beer icy cold. This was tepid. He drank it anyway.

A picture of Aggie's house flashed across the screen, followed by a picture of Tom Madsen's parents' house. Then a picture of Detective Madsen's bullet-riddled car appeared on the screen as the anchor explained that the car had been stolen from the detective's parents' garage. Detective Jade's car was also missing.

"And this man is Captain Darren Ramos of the Salvation Army. Captain Ramos is the one who brought the drugs to the police station twelve days ago. The same drugs that the police think Detective Jade put in the Salvation Army bin." Captain Ramos nodded at his introduction and spoke softly, smiling a lot, as he enjoyed his fifteen minutes of fame.

Nathan leaned back in his chair, propping his feet on the round table that came with every hotel room. He continued to sip the lukewarm beer. His phone rang just as he finished the beer. It was Alex.

"I hope you're seeing what I'm seeing. Let's go down to the bar. I'm sure they have a television set in there we can watch with better reception. The beer in the minibar is warm. By the way, I rang room 802, and there was no answer. Don't panic, I was going to hang up if someone answered. They're probably out taking care of business. We can watch the lobby from the outdoor bar. I'm kind of hungry, too."

In the bar, they ordered Philly steak sandwiches and cold Beck's, their eyes glued to the television over the bar.

Nathan looked around. Aside from three couples,

one of whom was fighting, the bar area was empty. It was pleasant, though, with island flowers on all the tables and bamboo blinds to ward off the hot sun. It was easy to see out through the thin slats but not easy to see in, which meant they would see Lizzie's friends before they spotted him and Alex.

Nathan leaned back in his chair to listen to the fight going on behind him. He wondered if he and Lizzie would ever fight like that. It sounded rather silly to him. Didn't they care? Didn't they have anything better to do at a vacation resort than fight? So what if the wife bought too many souvenirs. So what? Was the world going to come to an end? Couldn't the wife cut the husband a little slack because he didn't know how to swim and was afraid to go out on the catamaran? Such earth-shattering problems.

Nathan switched back to the television over the bar just as their sandwiches arrived.

His mouth full, Alex pointed to the television. Nathan grimaced when he saw Dutch Davis, his arm still in the blue canvas sling, take aim at the reporter interviewing him. Behind him, six deep, stood his fellow officers. He was using words like *scapegoat*, *witch-hunt*, and then he mentioned Aggie's and Tom Madsen's names. As a spokesperson, Dutch Davis left a lot to be desired.

Alex lost his appetite when Davis said, "Jade worked the evidence room when she returned to work. If there was sugar in the confiscated drug bags in the vault, she put it there. Then she must have gotten an attack of conscience and put the real drugs in the Salvation Army bin. It's just too damn bad poor Will Fargo is dead. He was the one who ran the evidence room. Ask the chief. Everything balanced out perfectly. If you want to believe a mentally ill detective whose proof is a bunch of butterfly books, then be our guest. That's all I have to say other than that all of us are going to fight this witch-hunt till hell freezes over." The cops behind him hooted their approval. Davis stomped the ground like a wild bull to show their solidarity.

"It's a slow day for news, Alex. No one is going to believe that creep. Hell, he even looks guilty," Nathan said.

"I'm confused. Which bags of drugs are they talking about?" Alex asked as he poked at his sandwich with his index finger. Nathan wondered what he was looking for.

Too much mustard, not enough mustard. What? Maybe there wasn't enough cheese or maybe it was the wrong kind of cheese. Another earth-shattering question without an answer.

"No, they are not one and the same. Lizzie told me there were lots and lots of bags of cocaine in the vault. I think she said there were two hundred. It stays in the vault until someone in authority gives the okay to burn it. It was Aggie's and her theory that Will Fargo replaced the bags, slowly, one at a time, with sugar. The bags the newspeople are talking about from the Salvation Army are another batch of drugs they confiscated before Aggie's shoot-out. Lizzie and the girls found it stuffed inside the seats of Tom Madsen's car and Aggie's car. There was a stakeout at Aggie's house so the girls, Noreen, Candy, and Honey dumped it all in the bin. On Lizzie's orders that I'm sure she got from Aggie. I'm the one who got rid of the cars. I drove them both to the Georgia border and ran them into a quarry that's at least sixty feet deep. No one will ever find them.

"As hard as it is for both of us to accept the results, it's something we're going to have to live with. Lizzie didn't involve the girls or me. You're in the clear, Rossiter. We're all accessories. That's jail time."

Alex leaned back in his chair and closed his eyes. "What do you think is going to happen, Nathan?"

"There's your answer. Take a look," Nathan said, pointing to a face on the television screen. "Atlanta's eight-hundred-pound gorilla. He's representing Dutch Davis and a few of the others. He's a seven-hundred-buck-an-hour attorney. We did a profile on him once for the paper. He never, that's as in never, lost a case. His name is Socrates Maris. His friends, colleagues, and judges call him Sox. The cops call him Magic Maris. The answer to your question is, they'll walk. Will they get back on the force? That, I don't know."

"Then that means they're on the loose. This is just like that damn movie, *Serpico*. I'd like to punch somebody right now. Here come your friends. Looks like they're coming into the bar."

All three women stopped in their tracks when they saw Nathan and Alex sitting in the bar. The trio looked poised to run but appeared to think better of the idea. "How did you . . . what are you doing here?"

Nathan looked around. The couple who had been fighting were now billing and cooing. The other two couples had left the bar by the side door. "Sit down, ladies. What can we offer you?" He made his voice friendly, chirpy-sounding. It wasn't working.

"White wine. Zinfandel for all of us," Noreen snapped.

Alex pointed to the television set. "Watch it and weep, ladies."

Nathan thought it was remarkable that Noreen's face could turn white under her makeup. Candy and Honey were twitching in their seats, their eyes going from the television to Noreen. It was obvious they considered her their leader and spokesperson.

"What are you doing here? How did you find us?" Noreen hissed.

"Your neighbor told us she saw you leaving with *my* suitcases. I know what's in those suitcases, and that's one of the reasons why we're here. We know why you're here, too. Look, I don't give a hoot about the money, it's yours. All I want to know is where Lizzie and her sister went. Either you tell me, or I'm going to blow the whistle on you. You don't get to wear high heels or makeup in jail."

"Don't threaten me, *Mister* Hawk. You're in this as deep as we are. Here," she said, opening her purse and pulling out Lizzie's notes. "Read them. I told you, we don't know where she went. If she had told me, I still wouldn't tell you. Lizzie is our friend. Friends help their friends. She didn't do anything wrong. Well, she did, but with honest intentions. No one is going to believe her, me, or you. As far as I'm concerned, she did the right thing by leaving. Did you talk to Mr. P.?"

"Yesterday, as a matter of fact. The strong, silent type. Like you, he knows nothing, but then he's a liar. I'm not sure about you yet." Nathan continued to read the notes Lizzie had left for the girls. He was convinced now that the women truly did not know where Lizzie and Aggie were. His last hope. Like Alex, he had the sudden urge to punch something.

Noreen started to cry. "This is like a nightmare." Candy and Honey started to blubber, too. Alex handed them wads of cocktail napkins from the bar.

The wine in Noreen's glass disappeared in one long gulp. She sat up straighter, her eyes watering. "Listen to me, you two. We aren't keeping the money, even though Lizzie wanted us to. We don't want dirty money. There were pounds of paperwork that had to be taken care of. Thank's to Mr. P. and his connections and sources the account is down as belonging to the Atlanta, Georgia, Police Department. We put the commissioner's, the mayor's, and the chief's names on everything. We did keep out enough to pay our airfare, our expenses here, to replace what we left behind when we left our suitcases at the storage facility, and that's it. We're staying on one extra day in case of any snafu, then we're going home. Just so you know we aren't lying, here are copies of the papers. Make it quick, Nathan."

Nathan's gut rumbled as he perused the papers. She'd told him the truth. The urge to punch something rose up in him again. He nodded. "Okay. If you hear from Lizzie, will you let me know?"

"No." The single word was so brusque, Nathan cringed.

Both men watched the women rush out of the bar like they couldn't wait to get away from their prying eyes and offensive questions.

"I guess we might as well go home, Nathan. We struck out all the way around. It's obvious neither one of us are big-league players. I think I'll spend the rest of the summer working on my house. Hell, maybe I'll actually finish it."

Nathan finished his beer. "Want some help? I'm pretty good with a hammer."

"Sure. You any good with a paintbrush?"

"Good but sloppy."

"You're hired."

Lizzie's hand made a shelf over her eyes as she stared down the beach. Her sister was running toward her, something clasped in her hand. Aggie was shouting, but she was too far away to hear what she was saying. As she got closer, Lizzie started to laugh.

"Look, Lizzie, it didn't die after all! It perked right up, and it's going to grow."

"Best-damn-looking organic carrot I've ever seen. Congratulations, Aggie!"

Aggie sat down and hugged her knees the way Lizzie was doing. "A penny for your thoughts, Lizzie."

Lizzie stared across the water. "I don't think they're worth that much. What did you think of the news this morning?"

"It's about what I expected. Already the *Journal-Constitution* has it on page seven. Not one byline by Nathan. I thought . . . expected him to take off running. He must really love you, Lizzie."

Lizzie stared down at the bright red polish on her toes. She'd been so bored the night before she'd given herself a pedicure. "He asked me to marry him, Aggie. He said he would be back in the morning for my answer. I wasn't there to give him my answer." A sob caught in the back of her throat.

Aggie draped her arm around her sister's shoulder. "What would you have said, Lizzie?"

"Yes. I would have said yes. He'll find someone else and forget all about me. Were you and Alex getting serious?"

"Yes. In a lot of ways, he's kind of old-fashioned. I like that. We've been here two weeks, Lizzie, and we haven't talked about either one of them until now. Why is that, do you suppose?"

"It's too painful. I don't want to talk about it now either. Did you talk to the people at the market?"

"Yes, and they said they'd buy all my vegetables. I'm starting with organic carrots like I did back in Pennsylvania. This is my prize, though," Aggie said, pointing to the carrot growing in the ceramic jar. I'm glad I had the brains that day to add a little water to the Ziploc bag when I pulled it out. I wasn't thinking too clearly that morning."

"All my equipment will be here by the middle of next week. It's coming from Lisbon by boat. I'll be setting up shop by next weekend. I bought three Jet Skis on a whim. If no one wants to rent them, you and I can use them. Hey, Aggie, do you want to go to that nude beach tomorrow?"

"Well, sure, Lizzie. I can hardly wait to show off my body." Sarcasm rang in Aggie's voice.

"Get real, Aggie. No one *looks* at you. People make a point of not looking at you. It's very liberating."

Aggie stared across the water. "What's going to happen to that yacht you won last year?"

"I signed the title to it and the cars over to the girls. You know what's ticking me off, Aggie? The stupid cops made fun of the butterfly code. That lawyer is shooting holes in it all over the place. The media are running with it."

"Lizzie, don't dwell on it. They're done for even if they get off. The department will not take a chance and hire them back. Where there's smoke, there's fire. That will be their attitude. They have their money stashed someplace. No one is going to rat on anyone else. It's the way it works. Eighteen months, two years till the trial. They're walking around free as the air. Too bad we didn't really have a smoking gun."

"Yeah, too bad. Do you like it here, Aggie?"

"It's quiet. It's peaceful. The people are nice and friendly, but I like Atlanta a lot better. Gus is happy. He romps all day with Alice. They even sleep next to each other. I think I'm just glad to be alive. Maybe someday we'll be able to go home." Aggie reached across to take her sister's hand in her own. She squeezed it tightly.

"Maybe."

Chapter Seventeen

The kitchen was a miniature room, barely big enough for both Lizzie and Aggie at the same time. Yet, they managed by sitting on high stools and keeping out of each other's way. Lizzie was sitting at the high table, her laptop open so that she could access the Internet and click onto the front page of the *Journal-Constitution*. She was glad Aggie wasn't around as she dreaded what she was about to see. All week, the headlines had dealt with the trial that was finally about to get under way.

It had taken the prosecution, and the defense, eight full days to select a jury. Opening arguments were scheduled for today and could well run into tomorrow, the spin meisters predicted. The blue spin was on, according to the papers. A reporter named Saul Baumgarten was doing the reporting for the *JC*.

The trial was being televised over the defense's objections. Unfortunately, if she and Aggie wanted to watch it, they would have to go to Lisbon since Fayal's television reception wouldn't bring in CNN.

Lizzie propped her chin in her hands. The trial had been a long time coming, but it had finally started. Both sides were talking the talk and walking the walk, but Aggie was convinced the officers on trial were going to walk away. "It's a gut feeling," she'd said. Lizzie couldn't argue because she felt the same way.

An hour didn't go by that she didn't think of Nathan. She knew it was the same with Aggie even though they didn't talk about it. For some strange reason, Nathan and Alex were taboo subjects. Probably because neither one of the twins wanted the other to see her pain.

Lizzie continued to read the front-page news, which aside from some disturbance in Pakistan, was all about the trial. Baumgarten hashed and rehashed what he'd been writing for weeks. There was very little news that was fresh and untold. She always hated the part about Aggie being a fugitive from justice and skimmed over it. She continued to read. Mr. and Mrs. Gray Madsen were going to be attending the trial but would not be called as witnesses. That was new. Seats in the courtroom were by a lottery system. Everyone, it seemed, wanted to see what was going to happen to Atlanta PD's finest. She couldn't help but wonder if Nathan and Alex would be at the trial. Alex would probably be off school for the upcoming holiday break. He would certainly have the time to attend, providing he could get a seat.

It was hard to believe Christmas was only three

weeks away. Lizzie and Aggie's second Christmas away from the States. The thought bothered her. She knew it bothered Aggie, too.

Lizzie reached for a cigarette. She'd started to smoke the day after arriving in Fayal. She had no idea why. Nervousness maybe. Something to do with her hands. She was going to quit, she really was, because it was a nasty, ugly habit. Aggie had taken up the bad habit right along with her. They'd also acquired another bad habit. They drank two bottles of wine at dinner every night. The wine was so they could sleep. Sometimes it worked, and sometimes it didn't.

Lizzie looked around the small kitchen. There was nothing modern about it at all. However, it served their needs. The stove was small, the kind found in efficiency apartments back in the States, and fired by propane gas. The sink was porcelain, with half the porcelain gone. It had one spigot. A flowered chintz skirt covered the opening underneath, where they stored dish detergent and other cleaning supplies. The refrigerator was just as old as the sink and stove, with half the enamel on the door missing. It was clean, though, and it worked.

Aggie had hung red-checkered curtains over the one window and back door. The curtains added some color and life to the tiny room.

Their home away from home.

The door opened, and both dogs rushed into the kitchen. Aggie followed. The kitchen was now filled to overflowing. "Let's have coffee outside," she said. "Anything new in the headlines?"

Lizzie slid off the stool and walked outside. "The Madsens are going to attend the trial. Opening arguments are today. The smart money is still saying your blue force is going to walk. There doesn't appear to be any smoking gun on the horizon. That's about it."

Aggie joined Lizzie at the little iron table on the small patio. She set her cup down so she could fix her hair, which was now shoulder length, into a ponytail. "Are we still going to Lisbon tomorrow?"

"Yes. I want to watch the trial. You're going with me, aren't you?"

"Yes. Lizzie, are we going because we're hoping to catch a look at Nathan and Alex, or are we going because we really want to watch the trial?"

"Both. No, that's not true. It's mostly to see Nathan and Alex. We know what the outcome is going to be. Nineteen months is a long time, Aggie. Sometimes I feel . . . it's like a lifetime. I wish we could go home."

Aggie bit down on her lower lip. She tilted her straw hat farther back on her head and looked at her sister. "You could go home, Lizzie. They don't know about you. It's me they want. All you have to do is call your friend Mr. P., and he could get you back the same way he got you here. You could slowly inch your way back into your old life."

Lizzie reached for Aggie's hand. "Oh, no. We're in this together. I'm the one who made all those cockamamie decisions. I let Zack go. I involved Nathan and the girls. They all broke the law on my behalf. No, I'm not going back. I broke the law myself when I impersonated you. If this place is getting to you,

Aggie, we could move on, but I think we're safer here. The village has accepted us. The townspeople buy your vegetables, and they use my services. Hey, we're actually making money. Look at us. You're fit and healthy again. We're pleasantly exhausted at the end of the day from being outside. We're safe, Aggie. That's the most important thing."

Aggie nodded as she picked at a string hanging off her tattered denim shorts. She leaned back on the steps, her back against a pillar, her brown legs extended in front of her. "Our biological clocks are ticking, Lizzie. I thought I'd be engaged or married by now, and thinking about starting a family. Damn it, it isn't fair."

"Who said life was fair, Aggie? Come on, let's start our day. Do you need my help getting your vegetables to market?"

"Nope, got it covered. Fernando is a real help. He picks the vegetables and loads the trucks. We did real well this week. The bell peppers and cucumbers are so plentiful, it boggles my mind. I made $480 so far this week. Even though I only hired him a little while ago, I feel confident leaving him to run things while we go to Lisbon. Are you shutting down or what?"

"Business was slow this week. I had one fishing party, two Swiss guys who wanted to snorkel, and four kids for the Jet Skis. I cleared $710. I wish there was someplace to spend the money. Let's treat ourselves to a makeover or something when we get to Lisbon. I feel the need to be pampered."

"Sounds good to me," Aggie said, jumping up to

take her cup into the kitchen. "I'll see you around five. Anything comes up, come and get me."

"You got it."

Nathan Hawk shivered on the courthouse steps as he waited for Alex Rossiter to join him. It was ten minutes to nine. He watched the gaggle of suspended police officers on trial make their way toward him and the huge double doors leading into the womb of the courthouse. He moved to the left to step out of their way. They were so cocky, so defiant, Nathan wanted to put his fist through their respective faces.

Suddenly, Alex Rossiter appeared out of nowhere. "Here comes the eight-hundred-pound gorilla. Look at him, Nathan. He's going to say a few words to one of the reporters. Don't expect anything profound, though. I think I hate that lawyer almost as much as I hate those cops. Tell me again why we're here, Nathan. Jeez, it's cold. People think Atlanta is warm. Ha!"

"We're here because the trial is being televised, and I know in my gut that wherever Aggie and Lizzie are, they're going to watch it. I want them to see us. Call me stupid, call me anything you want, but maybe seeing us will make them want to get in touch. Plus, Christmas is only three weeks away. A time of miracles and such.

"I woke up with an idea this morning, Alex. Want to hear it?"

"Sure." Alex held out his gloved hand. "Look, snow flurries."

"I'm going to see if I can wrangle an introduction

through Baumgarten to that CNN guy interviewing Maris. For both of us, Alex. You know how they always ask questions of the court spectators at the end of the day. If we talk fast, we might be able to say something meaningful in case Aggie and Lizzie are watching. What do you think?"

Alex clapped Nathan on the back. "I think you're a hell of a genius is what I think. That never would have occurred to me. Do you really think they're watching?"

"I really do. If you were in their position, wouldn't you be glued to the tube?"

Alex held the door for Nathan. "Yeah."

The courtroom wasn't overly large. Like all courtrooms, it was windowless, the bright fluorescent lights bouncing off the mahogany paneling. The judge was a big man, with snow-white hair, glasses, and a bulldog chin. He looked over the top of his glasses at the crowded room, banged his gavel, and called his courtroom to order.

"In the interests of expediency, the approaching holiday season, and my lack of patience, I'm allowing exactly two hours for each opening statement. I want this trial started as soon as the lunch break is over. Mr. Minelli, you have the floor," the judge said to the prosecutor.

Socrates Maris was on his feet in an instant. "Your Honor, I can't possibly keep my opening argument to two hours."

"Then you have a problem, Mr. Maris. Sit down!"

Minelli smirked. Chalk one up for the prosecution.

Nathan nudged Alex, and whispered, "Let's hope the judge's attitude is a harbinger of things to come."

• • •

The moment they arrived at the house in Lisbon that Lizzie had purchased, the women headed for the bathrooms, where they showered, washed their hair, and dressed in casual sundresses that showed off their beautiful tans. Aside from a slash of lipstick, they needed no other makeup.

The house nestled midway up a cliff and had every convenience possible plus a sparkling blue pool. A maid came in to clean and cook for them when the women notified her of their impending arrival. The property was as private as it was exclusive. Two motor scooters were in the garage, and that's how they got about town. Neither Lizzie nor Aggie was comfortable driving a big car up and down the steep, winding roads where more than one vehicle had gone over the cliffs. As Lizzie said, they were as safe here as they were in Fayal.

To Lizzie's delight, and Aggie's chagrin, there was even a nude beach a mile away.

Aggie poured them both a glass of local wine before she turned on the big-screen television set to CNN, where the trial was in its second day. Each time the cameraman panned the spectators, both Aggie and Lizzie leaned forward for a closer look.

Lizzie curled herself into the corner of a cream-colored sofa covered in a soft nubby material. She'd slept on the couch with Alice on many evenings when they came to Lisbon to get away from the sameness of the small island where they now lived. She looked over at Aggie, who was making a face at what she was seeing on the screen.

A botanist, and the author of one of Will Fargo's butterfly books, was on the stand. It only took minutes for both women to realize he was a poor witness. Aggie groaned.

"Is that prosecutor as stupid as he looks? He's not asking the right questions. I could do a better job. Hell, I did do a better job. I spelled it all out right on each one of those butterfly pages. Why aren't they getting it? Once you understand Will's code, it's a piece of cake. Maybe they didn't want to spend the time. You're right, Aggie, those guys are going to walk." In a fit of something she couldn't explain, Lizzie jumped up and turned off the television.

Aggie watched her sister out of the corner of her eye. She poured two more glasses of the fruity wine and held one out to Lizzie, who had begun pacing up and down the long living room.

Lizzie's voice was shrill when she asked, "Who else does the prosecution have to call as a witness? Nobody, that's who," she answered herself. "Sadie? The chief? Luke Sims. Maybe a few rookies. They aren't going to open their mouths, and we both know it. Why'd they even bother to take the damn case to court? They're going to hang this all on you, Aggie. A process of elimination."

"Lizzie, please, sit down. They can't hang it on me. Where's their hard proof?"

"They don't need hard proof. Circumstantial will do it. Your car is missing. Tom's car was stolen. Tom was your partner, and he's dead. D-E-A-D, Aggie. All those drugs conveniently showed up in the Salvation Army bin the day you disappear. They're going to say you got cold feet or something like that, and you bailed out. You worked in the evidence room. Not you literally, I did it for you. Conceivably, I could have switched sugar for drugs. All they were interested in was the weight, and it matched. They're going to say the night of your accident you and Tom were trying to peddle drugs and something went awry with the deal. Tom's dead, so he can't back you up, and you're left twisting in the wind. Add Dutch Davis's hatred of you, and that's the whole ball of wax. They'll try to pin that night on you, some way, somehow, too. Mark my words, Aggie, that's exactly how it's going to go down. Each one of those guys on trial is going to say the same thing. You and Tom were the bad guys. Maybe we should go back and tell the truth. When they see both of us, and understand what we were trying to do, it might sway the jury. I'll do it if you think it will work. It has to be your decision, Aggie."

"If it's my decision, then we're staying here. Maybe someday we'll be able to go back and make things right. Now isn't the right time. Chalk it up to cop instinct, okay."

It was the seventh day of the trial, with the defense calling witness after witness. To a man they said the same thing. To a man they said they were staunch defenders of the law. To a man they said there was something not quite right about Tom Madsen, Agnes Jade, and her killer dog. To a man they extolled each other's hardworking credo, sincerity, and dedication to making the city of Atlanta a safe place for its citizens. To a

man they said they would file suit against the Atlanta
PD if they weren't reinstated with back pay and benefits paid in full. To a man they said there was no such
thing as the blue wall of silence. It didn't matter that
they sounded rehearsed, defiant, and even cocky. The
words were loud and clear for the jury to hear.

Saul Baumgarten was rounder than a pumpkin.
He had sharp blue eyes and an even sharper tongue.
He sidled up to Nathan, and said, "Hawk, go out-
side, court's about to adjourn. The guy from CNN is
waiting to interview you. Take Dr. Rossiter with you.
Good luck, buddy."

"Thanks. I owe you one. By the way, can you be a
little less kind to those devils when you write your
column tonight? You know what they say about the
Devil. It's evil with a capital D."

Baumgarten grinned. "Nathan, I've been writing
blistering columns since this whole thing started.
The chief blue-pencils every single one. There's nothing else I can do."

"Keep doing it. I swear, if those bastards get reinstated, I'm moving out of Atlanta. If they're our
finest, we're in the tall grass. You need to put that in
your column, too."

"Consider it done, buddy. Beat it now before court
shuts down and they snag someone else for the interview."

Nathan and Alex walked down the steps to where
a young man holding a microphone waited. Make it
good, Baumgarten had said. Nathan felt tongue-tied
suddenly. It looked like Alex was faring no better
than he was.

They introduced themselves and looked straight into the camera.

"We'll start with you, Dr. Rossiter. How do you think the trial is going? Mr. Maris said he plans to wrap up the defense first thing in the morning. Any thoughts on that?"

"I have quite a few thoughts on the trial. Unfortunately, they are not fit for television news. I don't like what I've seen and heard inside that courtroom. If anyone has been set up, it's Detective Jade. I've known her for a good many years. She's a dedicated police officer. I see no good reason for those men on trial to malign her to save their own skins. They're trying to shift attention from themselves, and Detective Jade is their scapegoat."

"If what you say is true, Dr. Rossiter, why did Detective Jade cut and run?"

"Think about what you just asked me. Would you want that pack of jackals in there coming after you once you blew the whistle? There is a blue wall, and we both know it. She ran because she feared for her life."

The microphone was suddenly close to Nathan's face. He looked straight into the camera. "I'm Nathan Hawk, and I work for the *Journal-Constitution*. I agree totally with Dr. Rossiter. I'm going to take it one step further. If those police officers inside the courthouse, the ones on trial, walk away from this, I'm leaving Atlanta. I no longer feel safe living in this city."

"And that, ladies and gentlemen, are the views from two of Atlanta's upstanding citizens. What's this I'm hearing?" the interviewer said, moving quickly away from Nathan and Alex.

Nathan and Alex both turned at the excitement they heard in the reporter's voice.

They looked at each other expectantly, wondering what was up. They moved over to the side when the crush of spectators and reporters exited the courthouse. This time it was the prosecutor the newsmen headed toward, not Socrates Maris, who stood scowling on the side of the courthouse with his clients. For the first time since the start of the trial, he and his clients were not the center of the media attention. It was obvious that the lawyer and his clients didn't like the unexpected turn of events.

"Hey, the guy looks like he sprouted a set of brass balls all of a sudden," Alex whispered, pointing to the prosecutor. "He looks confident, too. Are you thinking what I'm thinking, Nathan?"

Nathan rubbed his hands together gleefully. "Maybe he found a smoking gun. What else could make him look like that. Shhh, what's he saying?"

"You'll have to wait till tomorrow. Mystery witnesses are the best witnesses, that's why they're called mystery witnesses. Smoking gun? I'll let you decide tomorrow. That's all I have to say, gentlemen. Perhaps Mr. Maris, who, of course, had to be informed of the new witness's identity, will answer your questions. Have a nice evening," the prosecutor said, tripping lightly down the steps to the sidewalk.

"Well, well, well," Nathan said happily. "Maybe we are going to get a smoking gun after all. I'm not going to be able to sleep tonight. How about you, Alex? Before I forget, don't you think it's a little strange that no mention was made of those two packets of money I sent back to the police? We were going to use the money to pay off Aggie's snitch, Pippy, but then things started happening so fast, we never did get to talk to him."

Alex shrugged. "Aggie said the whole department was on the take. Maybe that means the money never got to where it was supposed to go. But you sent it back, so it isn't your problem."

"No, I am not going to be able to sleep either. Want to help me wallpaper the upstairs bathroom? Free beer, and I'll even spring for a pizza."

They were good friends these days, meeting up once or twice a week to have dinner or just to pound a few beers and talk about their lost loves. In the beginning, it was a way to talk about Aggie and Lizzie, but as Nathan started helping Alex with his renovations, the two developed a real bond of mutual respect and friendship.

"I'm your man. I have to go back to the office first, though. I'm going to see if any of the troops have an in with the prosecutor. Maybe we can get some kind of a heads up. Maris isn't talking. Seven okay?"

"Seven's fine."

"Good, I'll see you then. Don't start without me. Believe it or not, I know how to wallpaper. I used to help my dad. I even know how to match seams. Whatever you do, don't start cutting the paper till I get there. By the way, if Aggie saw you, I can guarantee you she's in tears."

"Yeah. For all the good it's going to do me. You did okay yourself, Nathan."

Nathan waved as he walked off. The officers on trial and Socrates Maris watched him, speculative expressions on their faces. He turned around once, a wicked grin on his face. His middle finger shot upward in a single-digit salute. "Every dog gets his day, you assholes," he muttered.

"Lizzie, Lizzie! Wake up! Lizzieeee!"

Lizzie bolted upright. "What? Her sleep-filled gaze went to the television set. Her heart pounding in her chest, she slipped off the couch and crawled over to where Aggie was sitting in front of the set. "It's *them!* It's really them." Lizzie's voice cracked with emotion. "Oh, he lost weight. Look how tired he looks. Look! Look! He's looking right at me."

"Shut up, Lizzie. I'm trying to hear what Alex is saying. Oh, God, he looks so good. I could just cry. He lost weight, too. He looks just as tired as Nathan. How sweet. Listen to the way he's defending me. That's love. That's really love." Aggie's voice was ecstatic.

Lizzie hugged her knees, tears rolling down her cheeks. How dear he looked. How wonderful. She moved closer to her sister. They huddled together, crying unashamedly.

"Shhh, listen," Aggie said. When the camera moved closer to the prosecutor, they could still see Nathan and Alex on the fringe of people clustered around the television reporter. "It's snowing there."

"Did you hear that? A mystery witness! Who,

Aggie? My God, who? Think! Think hard, Aggie. Who would cut a deal and turn state's evidence?"

"None of them. The fix was in. You've heard the same thing I've been hearing. There would be no need for one of them to squeal. It's got to be someone else. I don't have a clue, Lizzie. Whoever he or she is, they better be damn good because Maris will chew them up and spit them out all in one breath. On the flip side of that, maybe it was just something the DA said to get a rise out of Maris. Oh, God, Lizzie, I am so homesick."

They clung to one another, sobbing their hearts out. For the would haves, the could haves, the should haves.

"What I have here, Alex, is better than gold. Better than the new sled you got Christmas morning when you were a kid. Better even than your first kiss. You, Dr. Alex Rossiter, are going to be in my debt forever."

"I had thirty minutes of sleep, and you want to play guessing games. Hell, I haven't even had my coffee yet. What, Nathan?"

"The crown jewels! Two passes to court this morning! Bum came through and weaseled them somehow. I didn't ask questions. No seats, standing room only, but who cares."

"Not me, that's for sure! Make some coffee, Nathan. I still have to shower and shave. In my newly wallpapered bathroom. I can be in and out in fifteen minutes. There are some English muffins in the fridge if you're hungry. We have time. Man, I am psyched."

"Okay."

Nathan rolled his neck to loosen the tension in his shoulders. He was wearing a suit, white dress shirt, and a tie. He wasn't sure why. He was stunned fifteen minutes later when Alex appeared, also wearing a suit, shirt, and tie.

"I took my cue from you. Figured we were getting dressed up for a reason. My mother always said look your best when you're preparing to go to battle. I feel like this is my own personal battle."

"Drink that coffee fast, Alex. There's going to be a lot of traffic this morning. By the way, in case you didn't look outside, it's snowing, and it's sticking on the ground."

"No kidding. Damn, maybe it will wash everything clean. A new day. Justice is served. The good guys win. That kind of thing." Alex gulped at the coffee in his cup. He was finished in seconds. "Okay, I'm ready."

Nathan turned the coffeepot off, then took a last swig from his cup. "This could all be one giant letdown. I've always been an optimist, but this whole thing has turned me into a pessimist. My fingers are crossed. I don't know what either one of us is going to do if this goes awry. I am personally not prepared for defeat. What about you?"

"Never heard the word before," Alex said, locking the door behind him. "It really is snowing." Nathan just rolled his eyes.

They reached the courthouse, parked, and made it through the metal detectors with three minutes to spare. Both men were breathing hard when they took their places against the back wall.

The courtroom was packed. Nathan flinched when he heard the locks snap into place. Two deputies took up their positions on either side of the door. If Lizzie were there, she would have said she could smell the testosterone.

"All rise! The Honorable Stanley Eberhart presiding," the clerk of the court said loudly.

The shuffling, the throat clearing, the chairs scraping back sounded like thunder in Nathan's ears.

The judge banged his gavel. He looked down at the laptop sitting on his desk. His fingers moved, then he looked out at the crowded room. "The defense informed this court yesterday that they were going to rest their case this morning. Is that still your intention, Counselor? If so, the prosecution has one last witness. I'll allow two hours for cross-examination, then another three hours for closing arguments. Don't even think about using up any more of the court's time. Are you resting, Mr. Maris?"

"Yes, Your Honor, the defense rests."

"Mr. Minelli, call your last witness."

Nathan looked around the crowded courtroom. The officers on trial looked fearful. Maris looked *beaten*. It was almost as if he knew his platinum record was about to be broken. A giant *swooshing* sound echoed around the room, everyone sucking in their breath in anticipation of the mystery witness about to take the stand.

The prosecutor looked at the deputies at the back of the room. He nodded. He turned to the judge, and said, "I call to the stand,"—he turned to look at Maris and the defendants—"Detective Zachary Miller!"

Nathan thought he was going to pass out. Alex gripped his arm so tight he knew he was going to have bruises for a week. In his life he'd never heard such silence. He craned his neck to stare at the defendants' expressions. They weren't pretty.

Two federal marshals escorted Detective Miller to the stand and moved off to the side, their hands placed loosely on their sidearms.

The court clerk stepped forward, the Bible in her hand. "Do you swear to tell the truth, the whole truth, and nothing but the truth, so help you God?"

"I do."

"State your name for the record."

"Zachary John Miller. I'm a retired detective on the Atlanta Police Department."

"Please be seated."

"Detective Miller, did you come forward voluntarily?"

"Yes, sir, I did. I called your offices yesterday and asked if I could testify for the prosecution."

"I'm not going to ask you any questions, Mr. Miller. Just tell your story to the court. Mr. Maris can ask the questions when you're finished."

Zack Miller looked out across the room, his gaze finally coming to rest on Dutch Davis.

"I came here today for three reasons. My wife died six months ago. She made me promise to do the right thing. I spent those six months grieving and trying to figure out how to go about doing the right thing. I was diagnosed with pancreatic cancer two months ago. That diagnosis alone made it imperative that I come here. The third reason is, I will not allow my fellow officers to ruin the life and career of Detective Jade."

"Easy, big guy," Nathan said to Alex, who looked like he was going to pass out. "Easy does it. That tall grass is flattening out right in front of us."

"It all started ten years ago. It was small stuff in the beginning. Most of us just looked the other way. As the operation got bigger and bigger, the temptation to take money for looking the other way became greater. Speaking strictly for myself, what turned me was my wife's medical bills. I was drowning in debt. I'd lost two children, my wife needed constant medical help, round-the-clock nurses. I never used a penny of the money they paid me except for the medical bills. I turned over the rest to the district attorney yesterday, along with the dates, the amounts of money, and who those amounts were paid to, mainly doctors, nurses, and hospitals.

"They are the officers in my old outfit. Dutch Davis and Joe Sonders were the leaders. If an officer made noises like he didn't want to go along with it, he had an accident, or his family was threatened. Detective Tom Madsen had a blowup with Dutch in the squad room one morning. Tom knew what was going on, but, he kept quiet and looked the other way. Then a big bust went down, only all the drugs disappeared. There were 210 three-pound bags of pure, uncut cocaine.

"That's when I put in for early retirement. Tom started acting strange. The guys said he was a wild card and couldn't be trusted. No one knew if he confided in Detective Jade or not.

"That night, the night Tom was killed, he and Detective Jade were on their own time. Tom scheduled a meeting with one of the guys who was supposed to buy those 210 bags of cocaine. Tom was flying blind. I know that because Dutch Davis was howling about how they couldn't let that happen, prior to that night. Tom and Jade's snitch, a guy named Pippy, turned them on to the deal, and how it was going to go down. Davis, Sonders, and some of their cronies ambushed them. Detective Jade and the dog were supposed to die, too. As you know, they were hit with automatic weapons' fire. Thank God Jade and the dog didn't die. I didn't find out about it till the next day. I had been called out of work earlier in the day because my wife was taken to the hospital. The gang had hidden the drugs inside the seats of Madsen's and Jade's cars. Then after that night, when the cars were taken to the impound lot, they couldn't afford to take the drugs out."

The judge leaned forward to stare at the witness. "Detective, would you like to have me call a recess? Would you like a glass of water?"

"No, Your Honor, I'm fine. I just want to get this over with."

"Take your time, Detective. As much as you need."

Zack nodded, struggling to take long deep breaths. Some of the color returned to his face. He nodded to show he was ready to continue.

"They all thought when I retired to the Florida Keys, they were going to continue their operation. They had big plans to use me and my fishing boat. I didn't go to the Keys, though. Instead, I went out of the country and moved around a lot until my wife couldn't take it anymore. She became too ill. She knew something was wrong. I finally told her what I'd been doing. She told me I had to make it right. She made me promise. I knew I had to make it right, and had plans to go to the DA as soon as . . . when it was time. I just didn't expect it to be so soon. I had to grieve for my wife and figure out how I was going to make it all come out right. Then I found out I was terminally ill. The decision was made for me, and here I am."

Zack did his best to straighten up in the witness chair. He looked straight at the jury when he said, "Those men sitting there, the defendants on trial today, that's only the tip of the iceberg. Contrary to what you might have heard and read, there *is* a blue wall.

"Yes, Detective Jade ran. She's probably going to be running for the rest of her life because what you have here is just the tip of the iceberg like I said. She's an honest cop. One of the good guys. The kind of cop I used to be."

The entire courtroom watched as retired Detective Zack Miller slumped forward. The prosecutor ran to him. "Pills, right pocket." The prosecutor fumbled in Zack's pocket for a brown vial. "Two," Zack said. A deputy appeared with a glass of water. Zack swallowed the pills, leaned back, and waited for them to kick in.

"This court will take a ten-minute recess. Mr. Minelli, bring your witness to my chambers. Mr. Maris, you are free to join us."

"Let's go get a cup of coffee, Alex. "The engineer looked so dazed, Nathan had to lead him out of the room.

"I think I'll just go on home, Nathan. Maybe I'll stop and pick up a Christmas tree. I didn't do any shopping yet, either. You're supposed to pick out a tree when it's cold and snowy. It really is sticking even though the roads are slushy. I hope they don't freeze. The roads, I mean."

"Alex, shut up! This could all turn on a dime. It does not mean we'll never see them again. You are not going home, and you are not going to pick out a Christmas tree without me. We're going to see this through to the end. You and me, together. Now, let's get that coffee."

Two thousand miles away, Anthony Papadopolus looked away from the television set he was staring at. He pressed a button on a console next to his chair. The door opened silently. "Do it!"

"Yes, sir. Right away, sir."

"Aggie! It's Zack! Zack Miller. Zack is the mystery witness. Are you listening to me, Aggie? Oh my God, he looks . . . he looks *sick.*"

Both girls scooted closer to the television set. They held on to each other as the retired detective took the oath, then walked slowly to his seat behind the railing.

They listened, hardly daring to breathe, as Zack started to speak. Aggie kept wiping her eyes with the hem of her tee shirt. Lizzie sniffed, blowing her nose every few seconds.

A long time later, Lizzie nudged her sister. "It's over, right?"

Aggie shook her head. "Didn't you hear what he said, Lizzie? Dutch and Joe and a few of the others are just the tip of the iceberg. The others will go to ground." She swiped at her eyes again before she turned back to the television. Lizzie cried harder.

It was twenty minutes to three when the judge again called a short recess. Again, Zack Miller was taken to the judge's chambers.

The detective was tiring, but he had refused to give in, even to Maris's ruthless cross-examination.

Alex led the way down the hall to the elevator. "I need some fresh air. And, I'm going to bum a cigarette off someone."

"You won't have to. I have a pack in my coat."

Outside, the wind seemed to be whipping from all directions. Nathan held his arm up to ward off the wind so Alex could light his cigarette. A plume of smoke fought with the swirling wind and snow-flakes. Nathan shook his head to show he didn't want a cigarette.

"The steps are icing up," Alex said flatly. "Some surprise, huh?"

"Maris isn't getting anywhere, and he knows it. For as sick as he is, Miller is unflappable. So he cut a deal, so what. The man is dying. There's no reason for him to lie. He did clear Aggie, though. That's what I care about."

Nathan felt the presence, whirling around to see a tall man who looked familiar.

"Mr. Hawk?"

"Yes, I'm Nathan Hawk."

"Dr. Rossiter?"

"I'm Dr. Rossiter."

"Will you follow me please."

Alex and Nathan looked at one another. Like robots, they followed the tall, impeccably dressed man down the steps to a long, black stretch limousine.

In an instant, a chauffeur in uniform was holding the door open. Nathan bent down to peer inside. He straightened up, and said, "Are you a cop?"

The man laughed. "Hardly. Get in, gentlemen. You're safer with us than you would be with your mother at your side. And take these, please. You will need them where you are going."

"What the hell. Okay."

The door closed the moment they were settled inside. The glass partition dividing the front from the back slid upward.

"This is a pretty stupid move on our part, Hawk. Who the hell is that guy?"

"I don't know. I do know I've seen him or else met him somewhere. I got a nose for stuff like this. Remember what I do for a living."

"How can I remember when your body parts wash up off the Atlantic somewhere."

Even with the slushy roads and the swirling snow, the driver was making excellent time.

"Where the hell are we going, Nathan?"

"I have no clue, Alex. But I think we're about to find out. This road takes us to the airport. It's kind of hard to see out these black windows. I don't know why I say this, but I think this vehicle is bulletproof."

"What!" Alex sputtered.

The limo stopped. The chauffeur and the man in the front seat both got out at the same time. The door opened. Nathan and Alex both got out. They looked around, their eyes full of questions.

The tall man pointed to the right. "They're waiting for you."

The sleek, impressive Gulfstream was indeed waiting. The steps were being lowered as they watched.

"The pilot's cleared for takeoff. Hurry," the tall man said.

"Wait just a minute," Alex blustered.

Nathan reached for the tall man's arm and squeezed it. "I remember where I saw you. You're . . ."

"Mr. Papadopolus said to tell you, Godspeed. Sometimes he gets overly dramatic. Jet fuel is expensive. Go!"

Nathan and Alex both sprinted to the Gulfstream and barreled up the steps. The steps were taken away, the door closed, and the aircraft was taxiing down the runway before they were buckled into their seats.

"This is just a guess on my part, partner, but I think we're on our way to see those two women who are in our bloodstreams."

"Hot damn!"

Epilogue

It was midafternoon, Portuguese time, when Nathan and Alex stepped off the rickety plane that had been chartered for them, onto hard ground. After clearing immigration using the passports they had been given, they made their way to the car rental agency, carrying their jackets and overcoats. They were told there were no cars available, but there were two scooters. They signed off on them and stuffed their winter clothing into the wire baskets attached to the back fenders. With a map, they headed down the main road that would take them to the little village on Fayal they had been instructed to go to.

They stopped once at a local shop to show the proprietor a picture of Aggie that Alex had taken back in Pennsylvania. She was standing next to her organic carrot patch, Gus at her side. She was smiling into the camera.

"Sim." A chubby woman pointed down the road. "Veg-a-ta-bals," she said. She held up one finger.

"I think she means one kilometer," Nathan said. The woman pointed to Gus and pretended to cower in fear. Then she laughed. They laughed with her.

Ten minutes later, both scooters came to a screeching halt. The marketplace was almost empty. A few late stragglers were picking up vegetables and fruit on their way home from work.

Aggie, newly arrived back on Fayal after an urgent summons that she and Lizzie still had not made any sense of, looked up when Gus stood, his tail swishing. He barked, a bone-chilling sound, until he saw two figures running toward them. Aggie's hand went to her heart and then to her mouth. "Alex! Oh, my God, is it really you! What? How? Nathan! I'm not dreaming, am I?"

"You better not be dreaming because I'm going to kiss you until your teeth rattle."

"I don't know what to say. Ohhhhh."

Nathan dropped to his haunches as he tussled with Gus. "How's it going, big guy? I wish you could talk. I think they're going to be at that for a while," he said, looking at the liplock going on between Aggie and Alex.

"If you tell me where Lizzie is, I'll get out of your way."

Aggie disengaged herself for a second. "She's at a nude beach a mile or so from here. Go slow, and Gus will show you the way. You gotta strip down, or they won't let you on the beach. Don't worry, no one *looks*. Take Nathan to Lizzie, Gus." The dog barked, prancing alongside the motor scooter. Nathan climbed on, revved the engine, and crawled forward. Gus looked back once as if to say, can't you go a little faster. He did.

Gus came to a halt at a thatched hut on the roadside. A high wooden fence separated what he assumed was the beach from the main road. There were a number of signs in different languages. The one in English said NO CLOTHING ALLOWED.

When in Rome.

Nathan stripped down to the buff, paid his admission, and walked through the gate. *No one looks* was what Aggie said. Everyone on the damn beach was looking at him. His hands immediately went downward. A woman walking past said, "First time, huh?" Nathan's head bobbed up and down.

Gus raced ahead, to where a woman was reclining in a canvas chair. He barked at the dog lying beside her. Alice reared up, and the two of them raced down the beach.

"Hey, Lizzie, guess who?" Nathan called, his voice cracking with all the attention he was getting from the other nude sunbirds.

"Nathan! Nathan Hawk! My God, I must have had a sunstroke. Nathan, is it really you!"

"In the *flesh!*" He ran then, not caring if the whole world saw his wobbly ass. She was in his arms in a heartbeat. She smelled of seawater, sand, and soap. He hugged her so tight she squealed. Then he kissed her. And she kissed him back. They only broke apart when all the sun worshipers clapped their hands.

"Oh, Nathan, kiss me again. Don't worry about them, no one *looks.*"

• • •

They were on their third bottle of wine outside Lizzie's little house. Aggie had cooked dinner, and now they were sitting on the grass, making plans to go to Lisbon on the morning boat.

"The pilot gave me this thick envelope and said it was from your friend, Mr. P. I forgot all about it until now. I guess we should read it before we make any more plans."

Their heads bent together so they could read the papers by the lanternlight.

Nathan looked at the three of them, his voice suddenly serious. "You realize, you can't go back, right?" The sisters nodded. "That's the bad news. The good news is, Alex and I are staying here. It seems Mr. P. bought Fayal's newspaper for me. I will be running it. He also secured a position for Alex teaching at the school. He's taking care of all our business for us, and it will be forthcoming. Whatever that means. He said he will be visiting us for a friendly game of cards sometime in the spring, when he comes here on his honeymoon. He said he's sailing here in *your* yacht."

Nathan looked over at Lizzie. "He and Noreen are getting married. Noreen wants to know where she should register in Fayal for wedding gifts."

Lizzie and Aggie broke into peals of laughter.

They stopped laughing long enough to ask, "Is that all?"

"Nope. There's one more thing. He said, 'Merry Christmas, kiddo.' "

"Come on," Lizzie said, jumping to her feet. She reached down for his hand. "Let's go for a walk on the beach." She stood on her toes, and whispered, "I never made love on a sandy beach before."

"I'm your man, lady. Let's go."

"Wait for us, we're going, too," Aggie said, yanking Alex to his feet. The dogs ran ahead.

"And they said you were a wild card, Lizzie Jade. They don't know the half of it. Did you miss me?"

"With every breath I took."

"Me, too."

"Oh, life is so good," they heard Aggie squeal happily.

"Better than good, it's perfect," Alex said.